Four Weddings and a Puppy

"Shane has created a friends-to-lovers trope simmering with emotional depth, snappy banter, and swoony romance."
—*The Romance Dish*

"A wintery treat! Dog lovers will lap up this romance—as will Shane's many fans."
—*Publishers Weekly*

Pride & Puppies

"Entertaining subplots add zest to this sweet tale. Thoroughly saturated with Austen allusions, this cute contemporary is sure to charm."
—*Publishers Weekly*

To All the Dogs I've Loved Before

"Adorable second-chance romance."
—*Publishers Weekly*

Once Upon a Puppy

"The endearing characters will capture readers' hearts from the first page...It's hard not to fall in love with this spirited tale."
—*Publishers Weekly*

"Could not put it down...Beautifully written."
—Harlequin Junkie

The Twelve Dogs of Christmas

"Just right for animal lovers seeking a seasonal happily ever after." —*Publishers Weekly*

"Shane's heart-warming plot, perfect mix of small-town charm and buoyant wit, perfectly imperfect human characters, and adorable canines truly capture the thrill of love and the magic of the dogs-and-people connection." —*Booklist*

LIKE
CATS
&
DOGS

LIKE CATS & DOGS

LIZZIE SHANE

FOREVER

NEW YORK   BOSTON

Copyright © 2024 by Lizzie Shane

Cover design and illustration by Sarah Congdon. Cover copyright © 2024 by Hachette Book Group, Inc.

Hachette Book Group supports the right to free expression and the value of copyright. The purpose of copyright is to encourage writers and artists to produce the creative works that enrich our culture.

The scanning, uploading, and distribution of this book without permission is a theft of the author's intellectual property. If you would like permission to use material from the book (other than for review purposes), please contact permissions@hbgusa.com. Thank you for your support of the author's rights.

Forever
Hachette Book Group
1290 Avenue of the Americas, New York, NY 10104
read-forever.com

First Edition: November 2024

Forever is an imprint of Grand Central Publishing. The Forever name and logo are trademarks of Hachette Book Group, Inc.

The publisher is not responsible for websites (or their content) that are not owned by the publisher.

The Hachette Speakers Bureau provides a wide range of authors for speaking events. To find out more, go to hachettespeakersbureau.com or email Hachette Speakers@hbgusa.com.

Forever books may be purchased in bulk for business, educational, or promotional use. For information, please contact your local bookseller or the Hachette Book Group Special Markets Department at special.markets@hbgusa.com.

Print book interior design by Marie Mundaca

Library of Congress Cataloging-in-Publication Data
    Names: Shane, Lizzie, author.
    Title: Like cats & dogs / Lizzie Shane.
    Other titles: Like cats and dogs
    Description: First edition. | New York : Forever, 2024.
    Identifiers: LCCN 2024022644 | ISBN 9781538710371 (trade paperback) |
       ISBN 9781538710395 (ebook)
    Subjects: LCGFT: Romance fiction. | Novels.
    Classification: LCC PS3619.H35457 L55 2024 | DDC 813/.6—dc23/eng/
       20240524
    LC record available at https://lccn.loc.gov/2024022644

ISBNs: 978-1-5387-1037-1 (trade paperback), 978-1-5387-1039-5 (ebook)

Printed in the United States of America

LSC-C

Printing 2, 2025

For all the readers who fell in love with Pine Hollow.
This one's for you.

Chapter One

His cat was in her apartment again.

Alerted by the sound of Cupcake's piteous whimpering, Magda emerged from the bedroom, where she had been repacking her bag for the fifth time, and found Satan's tabby lounging smugly in the middle of an oversized dog bed while the pit bull looked on with soulful puppy-dog eyes.

Cupcake was approximately five times the size of the devil's cat, but the giant sweetie of a pittie didn't have an alpha bone in her body. Whenever the tabby snuck in through the window, she would cower in the corner while he swanned around as if he owned the place, seeming to take particular enjoyment in terrorizing Magda's helpless seventy-pound baby.

Magda glared at the furry orange interloper. "That isn't your bed. Get out of here!" She flapped the apron in her hands at the cat—which gave her a bored look and began to clean his undercarriage.

The animal hated Cupcake, but couldn't seem to stay away from her—which made sense in a perverse way, considering his owner. If she didn't know any better, Magda would think he'd somehow trained the cat to come here and harass her dog.

She didn't have time for this today.

"Go on!" Magda tried again. "Get!"

The cat paused, as if considering her command—and then deliberately went back to his personal grooming.

Cupcake whined softly, and Magda comforted her with a rub on her silky head.

She knew better than to try to pick up Satan's tabby—the thing had scratched the hell out of her on multiple occasions, and she had no desire to appear on national television for the first time with welts on her face and arms.

She was going to have to call his owner.

Calling Satan himself was high on her list of Things to Be Avoided at All Costs on any given day, but today especially she had no desire to see her nemesis. Magda eyed the cat, trying to think of another option. *Any* other option. But nothing was springing to mind, and she really didn't have time to waste.

In two hours, her best friends were scheduled to arrive to drive her down to Boston to compete in the upcoming season of *The Great American Cake-Off.* She'd been working toward this day for the better part of three years, and it was finally here.

She was actually going to live her dream. And she was freaking *terrified*.

She needed to be focusing. Preparing. Packing and repacking and mentally going over her recipes, as she'd been doing nonstop for the last two weeks. She'd barely been able to sleep she'd been so excited.

Or petrified.

It was hard to tell the difference sometimes.

She was normally an early riser—with the bakery she pretty much had to be—but this last week she'd been waking up at three in the morning every day. She'd manically worked during the predawn hours, filling her freezer with every variety of dough she could think of so the bakery wouldn't completely shut down in her absence. She'd even planned to whip up one more batch of dough to freeze this morning—just as soon as she finished repacking one last time. Magda always had a plan.

And the absolute last thing she needed was to be spending any mental energy whatsoever thinking about *him.*

"Please leave," she begged the cat—anything to avoid giving That Man even one inch of her brain space today. But the cat ignored her. Because of course he did. It was *his.* Why would the cat ever do anything that wasn't designed to aggravate her?

Magda had never thought of herself as the kind of person who would have an archnemesis—she was *nice.* To a fault. Everyone said so. Too nice. Too sweet. Too yielding.

But Mackenzie Newton brought out the worst in her.

Mac to his friends. Bane of her existence. And owner of Satan's tabby.

Magda picked up her cellphone. She had his personal number, thanks to a group chat they were both on since her best friends had an unfortunate habit of marrying his best friends—but everyone in Pine Hollow knew where Mac would be at the crack of dawn on a Sunday morning. She called his diner.

"We don't open till eight," his voice came down the line, brusque and impatient.

"That's how you talk to your customers?"

There was a slight pause as he recognized her voice. "Since when are you a customer?"

"Fair point," Magda acknowledged. "I try to only support local businesses that aren't run by thieves."

"I didn't—" A growl in his voice. "Are you just calling to insult me? Because I'm a little busy. Some of us have breakfast rushes to prepare for. Though I'm sure your cute little bakery never has to worry about things like that. A rush is when there's more than one person who wants to buy your product."

Cupcake whined again, and Magda resisted the urge to snark back at Mac. "Your cat is in my apartment again."

"And?"

"And someone should come get the feral thing before I call animal control."

"We don't have animal control. And you would never call Levi this early on a Sunday."

Magda gritted her teeth—equal parts annoyed that he'd called her bluff and mad at herself for giving him the opening. Mac was in a poker group with the sheriff, who handled all the pest complaints. "You could just come get your cat," she snapped.

"And you could learn to shut your windows. Who keeps their windows open when it's forty degrees out anyway?"

Magda ground her molars. April in Vermont wasn't exactly known for its sweltering heat waves, but Magda's apartment was cozy (microscopic) and historic (the radiator was several hundred years old and stuck in the "on" position), and it had a tendency to absorb all the heat from the ovens in her bakery downstairs. Keeping a window open was the only way to get any semblance of airflow. "I shouldn't have to bolt my windows just so that creature doesn't break in and terrorize my dog."

"It weighs fourteen pounds. The terror."

"Just get your cat, Mackenzie."

"You know, cupcake, if you want to see me, you don't have to invent—"

Magda ended the call in the middle of his sentence. She flung her phone on the couch with a barely human-sounding growl of aggravation—and it rang before it even had time to bounce.

She snatched up the phone, accepting the call and snarling, "Just get the damn cat!"

"I'm sorry?" a very confused—and very familiar—female voice asked.

Magda groaned internally, sinking down on the couch. "Mom. Hi. Sorry. I thought you were someone else."

"Are you getting a cat?" her mother asked, still audibly puzzled.

"No, it's just, uh...inside joke. What's up? Did you need something?"

Her mother never called unless she needed something. Magda tried not to take it personally. As the matriarch of the Miller family, with seven children, sixteen grandchildren, and the family dairy to run, essentially by herself since Magda's dad's heart problems had made it necessary for him to retire, she had a lot on her plate. Family updates were done by group text or at the semiweekly family dinners—which Magda had a tendency to skip. Evelyn Miller would always pick up the phone when one of her kids or grandkids called, but Magda could count on one hand the number of times her mother had actually been the one to call her in the last two years.

"I was just calling to wish you safe travels," her mother said.

The words were normal enough, but there was a note in her voice like there was more to it, and Magda felt a sudden flash of guilt.

She knows.

Why had she thought she could hide it?

"Thanks," Magda replied, keeping her tone as innocent as possible.

She hadn't told her mother about the show, but she should

have known she would find out. There were no secrets in Pine Hollow, Vermont. Even if the only people Magda had told were her two best friends. Charlotte and Kendall had undoubtedly told their husbands. Charlotte might have told her sisters... who would have told their spouses, and by then the entire town might as well have known. She was lucky it hadn't been published in the *Pine Hollow Newsletter*.

"I also wanted to say carpe diem."

"Oh?" Crap. Her mother definitely knew.

Magda was allowed to tell people about *Cake-Off.* She'd been a little surprised that the show people hadn't demanded secrecy—though they'd told her so little about what to expect that it wasn't like she could have spoiled anything. She was barred from putting the show's name in marketing materials to promote her business—she didn't even try to understand all the legalese about infringement—but other than that it was pretty much fair game.

She hadn't *had* to lie to her family and tell them she was going on a three-week European cruise instead. She'd just been so scared to tell them the truth.

They would make a big deal of it—with a family as large as hers, nothing that happened was ever a small thing. Even non-events got blown out of proportion, and something like this? Her family would lose their minds. It would be huge. There would be fanfare. Celebrations. A send-off party with at least sixty guests—all of them looking at her and feeding the smothering sense of pressure she already felt.

They would all say they were sure she was going to win—as everyone she'd actually told had said. And she would drown under the weight of their good wishes. The need to live up to their expectations. The pressure to make the town proud.

It had sounded like a nightmare.

So Magda had invented a story about an old pastry school friend and a cruise in countries where she didn't have cell reception to explain why no one would be able to reach her for a month.

If she was gone that long. She might not even make it a week.

Nerves twisted like acid snakes in her stomach, and she latched on to the distraction of her mother's voice.

"I just think this could be a really great opportunity for you," her mother said, her tone so gentle and encouraging that Magda felt like the worst daughter in the world for keeping things from her.

"Look, Mom, I meant to tell you—"

"No, let me just say this," her mother insisted, her voice somehow both firm and gentle. "I know you haven't had much luck, here in town, romantically speaking."

"What?" Now Magda was the confused one.

"You're always so focused on your bakery, and your father and I are very proud of what you've managed to build there, all by yourself, but I think sometimes you use it as an excuse not to put yourself out there, and I just think this could be an incredible opportunity to meet someone, if you let yourself."

"Mom." Magda frowned. "That's not why I'm going." She wanted to *win*. To make a name for herself. She certainly wasn't going to be trawling for a husband in between baking challenges.

"Oh, I know, I know. Just don't close yourself off to it. You could meet the man of your dreams at sea. Maybe even get engaged in Paris!" her mother gushed—and Magda realized with a jolt that her mom did not, in fact, have a clue where she was really going. That none of this had anything to do with the competition—and everything to do with her mother's desperate attempt to marry off her last unmarried child.

Now that Magda knew this was actually about her love life, the guilt receded on a tide of irritation and she felt a familiar defensiveness knotting her shoulders. "Mom, I *like* being single."

"I know. You're happy as you are. I hear you," her mother insisted, then ruined it by adding, "I just don't want you to die alone."

"You do realize being unmarried isn't actually fatal."

"You say that, but I was reading an article the other day that said ninety percent of breast cancer cases are first detected by romantic partners."

Magda pinched the bridge of her nose. "You literally just made that statistic up."

"Okay, maybe it wasn't ninety percent—I couldn't remember the actual number, but it was a lot. And the article was real. This could save your life, baby."

"I'll get a mammogram, okay?" she snapped, louder than she'd planned, but lately this topic had become a sore spot.

Magda had six siblings and eighteen cousins, *all* of whom were now married. Her best friends had both tied the knot in the last few years, and it was starting to feel like she was drowning in a sea of happy couples. And yet she had never seemed to be able to find her person.

A few years ago, after a bad breakup, her friend Charlotte had drunkenly declared that they must all swear off men and get dogs. And the Puppy Pact was born. And something had finally clicked for Magda.

It wasn't just adopting Cupcake. She adored the pittie. The dog was her angel. Her whole heart.

No, it was being single. *Voluntarily* single. Charlotte and

Kendall had both since gotten married, but Magda hadn't even dated since that day.

It wasn't that she hated marriage. She liked the idea. In theory. She sometimes daydreamed about the whole thing—spouse, kids, domestic bliss. She'd always done what was expected of her, a born rule follower, and it had felt like there was so much pressure to do the normal thing and settle down with a nice guy—but she had a nasty tendency of falling for guys who either didn't want the same things she wanted out of life or didn't want her back, and there had been something incredibly freeing about swearing off men.

Suddenly her singleness hadn't felt like a failure, but a choice. And she had *loved* that feeling.

She'd taken a hard look at her goals then, refocusing on the ones that *didn't* rely on magically meeting the man of her dreams in a small town where she was related to over half of the single population. And on that man of her dreams actually wanting her too.

She'd admitted to herself for the first time that she'd always dreamed of going on *Cake-Off*, and she'd started training and auditioning for the show immediately. It had taken three seasons of auditioning, but she'd finally made it.

She loved not looking for love. And the last thing she wanted was to miss this moment because she was crushing on some guy.

A heavy knock sounded at her door before she could say another word, let alone explain any of that to her mother.

"Mom, I've gotta go. Love you. I'll call when I can."

She hung up the phone to her mom yelling, "Just be open to it!"

Magda opened the door, already tense from the conversation

with her mother, and there was another source of frustration, standing on the landing.

The ginger Lucifer himself. Mackenzie Newton.

He was tall—but then, Magda had to stretch to reach five foot one, so she thought everyone was tall. He wore his usual uniform—a T-shirt from some Broadway show she'd vaguely heard of that was too tight on his stupidly muscular arms and a baseball cap mashing down his dark auburn curls. His deep brown eyes usually watched her with an arrogantly knowing expression that always made her want to thwack him with a wooden spoon—but at the moment he was looking at her strangely.

So strangely that her oh-so-polite greeting was to snap *"What?"*

His eyebrows arched, disappearing beneath the brim of his hat. "Everything okay? I heard yelling about mammograms as I was coming up the stairs."

Embarrassment flashed, quick and hot—and because this was Mac, it was quickly followed by an aggravation chaser.

Magda was the nice one. Everyone said so. *Too* nice, Kendall was fond of pointing out. The pushover. Too quick to rearrange her life to help others. Too willing to let things slide. Too eager to forgive.

With everyone except Mac.

Magda didn't know what it was, but there was something about him that brought out the worst in her. Ever since she was eighteen years old, he would speak and she would see red. Her usual filters would fall, and things she would normally *never* say out loud came out of her mouth.

Which was the only possible explanation for why she snapped, "My mother thinks I'm going to drop dead because

I don't have a husband regularly mashing my boobs for me. Because God knows modern medical technology is no match for a *man*."

Mac's mouth fell open, and she almost thought she saw a tinge of red on his cheeks before his gaze dropped to her chest.

"Don't," she snarled.

His gaze pinged back up to hers. "Sorry?"

"If you offer to check for lumps, I will chop you up and serve you in a pie."

"Thought never even crossed my mind," he promised. And of course it hadn't. The man had made it vividly clear how repulsive he found her. "Though I appreciate the Sweeney Todd–ness of the threat. Very nice."

Magda set her teeth. Today was going to be a good day, damn it. And she wasn't going to let her mother, or Mac, or anyone else get in the way of that.

"Can you please just get your cat?"

Chapter Two

Mac ambled into the apartment, trailing along in the wake of Magda's anger—pointedly *not* thinking about her... attributes. Which, with all the talk about breast exams, was like trying not to think of pink elephants. They were very nice... *attributes*. But she'd always fallen very firmly in the oh-*hell*-no category when it came to dating. She'd hated him for ages because he was a dick to her when she was eighteen—and no one could hold a grudge like Magda Miller.

He certainly didn't *want* to find her attractive, but he'd always been excruciatingly aware of her. There was no denying she was hot when she was mad—her cornflower-blue eyes flashing and her all-too-angelic face flushed. It would have been easier if she wasn't. If she could just be invisible.

So he tried to pretend she was and focused on getting the cat and getting out as fast as possible.

The oversized tabby lolled arrogantly in the middle of the much-too-big dog bed. "You proud of yourself?" he asked the cat as he approached.

The cat stretched, looking even smugger, if possible. Mac had thought for months now that the thing understood English—and had a definite tendency toward sadism. Or at least took entirely too much pleasure in being contrary. His obsession with Magda's place was a prime example.

For the last decade, Mac had avoided ever needing to go to Magda's bakery or—worse—her apartment. But in the six months since the cat had wandered into his life, claiming him as his personal slave and making himself at home in his house, Mac had been summoned to Magda's to fetch the cat more times than he could count.

It was like the cat *knew* how much they rubbed each other the wrong way and took particular delight in it.

Though it might have been the dog that he loved torturing the most.

The pit bull whimpered pathetically in a corner, ceding all territory to the cat. "She does know she's bigger than he is, right?"

"She's a gentle soul," Magda said—with something distinctly *un*gentle in her tone. "A lover, not a fighter. And your asshole cat takes swipes at her whenever she gets close. And at me. Can you please just get him out of here?"

"I came, didn't I? C'mon, Cat." He scooped up the animal, who thankfully decided he was willing to be relocated. Mac had more than a few half-healed scratches on his arms from times when the cat had decided he did *not* want to be picked up. This time, however, the tabby snuggled into his arms, glaring balefully over Mac's biceps at the dog.

He turned back toward the door—get in, get out, get back to the Cup and focus on what needed to be done, that was the plan. But then he saw the bag sitting next to the door and his steps faltered.

He shouldn't say anything. He really shouldn't say anything.

"Going somewhere?"

"What?" Magda asked a little too sharply, before following the direction of his gaze. "Oh. Right. Yeah, that's Cupcake's stuff. She's going to be staying with Charlotte and George while I'm—" She broke off, her face flushing. "I'm going on a cruise. Europe. Pastry school friend."

Mac blinked, nodding slowly. "Right."

And the urge rose up to tell her he knew exactly where she was going. Because he was going, too.

He'd signed a million NDAs. If he told Magda the truth, he'd get sued into his next lifetime—his friend Connor doubled as his lawyer and had been *very* clear about that point. *Cake-Off* didn't want anyone to know about their exciting new twist until they could reveal it on camera.

But still he found himself strangely tempted to tell her. Why? To get a reaction out of her? To piss her off? To warn her? He'd never been very good at deciphering his emotions when it came to Magda. Sometimes it was almost fun, sparring with her. And other times...

He'd never met anyone he couldn't get along with. Until her.

But Mac would be the first to admit the feud had gotten out of hand.

It had started so long ago—a little misunderstanding on his part when she was eighteen, a small backstabbing on hers a few years later—and then it had just snowballed for the last decade. What had started as a harmless grudge, some slight bristling animosity, had somehow become a feud that involved the whole town.

They both owned businesses in Pine Hollow, Vermont— his espresso-shop-turned-cozy-local-eatery, and her frou-frou French bakery on the town square. The locals had chosen sides. He'd even seen a few #TeamMac T-shirts at a parade a few weeks back.

The competitiveness was only natural, and the edge beneath it might have been fun . . . if he'd been feuding with anyone else.

But Magda . . .

Magda got under his skin. Like a splinter. A festering infected splinter. And she seemed to feel the same way about him.

Lately it had been harder and harder to just avoid each other. All of his friends were her friends, and it definitely felt sometimes like Pine Hollow wasn't big enough for the both of them.

They drove each other nuts—but Mac was mature now. He could bury the hatchet. Be the bigger person and extend a peace offering.

Hence, the *Cake-Off*.

When the producers had approached him after learning about their feud on social media, Mac had been wary.

He was a decent enough baker—he loved trying out dessert specials at the Cup and baking his own bread whenever he had the time—but reality television had never been his dream. That was Magda's thing, and she'd made no secret of it.

But apparently this next season was going to have a gimmick— and only bakers with some sort of nemesis would be invited. Which meant Magda would only be able to compete if Mac went.

Peace offerings didn't get any better than that.

Not to mention, the $250,000 first prize wouldn't be terrible to win. And the free publicity for the Cup was nothing to scoff at. Mac wanted to expand, move into a bigger, better space, and if a month of being filmed smiling over a mixer could make that happen, he was game.

It was the definition of a win-win.

But a little whisper of misgiving in his gut told him she didn't know what she would be walking into...that she deserved to know...

"You know, don't you?"

At her words, Mac realized he'd been standing there staring at Cupcake's puppy suitcase for far too long. "Know?"

"Did George tell you?" She shook her head. "Never mind. It doesn't matter. Just don't say anything, okay? I know I'm representing Pine Hollow, but I'd just as soon not have the entire town making a huge thing of it."

Mac met her eyes, weighing whether he dared tell her, studying her face. Always so sweet—to everyone but him. She had one of those open, angelic faces that hid nothing. "Are you a good actress?"

"What?" Her pale blue eyes, such a startling contrast against her pitch-black curls, flared angrily. "This isn't about acting. I don't have to pretend to be a good baker."

"I just mean, can you control your reactions? Like if you had to pretend to be shocked by some twist..."

"They don't want me because I'm fake. They want me because I'm *good*," Magda snapped. "I don't have to pretend to be someone else to—" She broke off, midsentence, her blue eyes firing. "Look, I know you auditioned, too. Kendall told me. And I'm sorry you didn't get it," she said without an ounce of regret. "I know they never take two people from the same town, and that sucks, but I have been working my butt off for this for the last three years, so maybe, just maybe, I deserve it. Did you think of that?"

Mac snapped his mouth shut. Now was *definitely* not the time to tell her that he'd helped her get in. "Okay. Good luck."

It was a sign of how barbed every word between them always

was that Magda's eyes narrowed dangerously. "What's that sup-posed to mean?"

"Can't I wish you luck?" He truly hadn't meant it sarcasti-cally.

"Oh, so you think I need it? Keep it. I am going to dominate that competition."

"You don't know who you're competing against, cupcake."

"It doesn't matter. I can take anything they can dish out. Just watch."

"I plan to," Mac promised.

By the time Mac made it back to the Cup after dropping the cat back at the converted carriage house where he'd moved last year to be closer to his gran, he was regretting every word he'd said after he'd spotted the suitcase. He should have kept his eff-ing mouth shut.

He was positive Magda hadn't figured out the twist—so his danger of being sued into his next lifetime was nil—but he was also positive she was going to go after him with a flambé torch when she saw him at the competition. Which would probably make the producers deliriously happy.

But the show was tomorrow's problem. Right now he needed to get through the Sunday rush and finish getting the Cup ready for his absence.

He had a great staff, but Mac always handled the specials himself, and he hadn't done nearly enough in the last few weeks to prepare for being gone. He didn't have to be in Bur-lington until tonight, so he had a few more hours to get his life in order and throw some clothes into a suitcase. The producers had warned him not to react if Magda said she was heading to Boston—apparently the surprise nemesis group was flying into a separate airport so their paths wouldn't accidentally cross. The producers were leaving nothing to chance.

The *Cake-Off* never filmed in the same city twice, bouncing around the country with each new season, but they'd never filmed in Boston or Burlington, as far as he knew, so either site could be the one. Mac was secretly hoping it was Burlington—the home audience always loved the "local" chefs.

He slipped in the back door of the Cup—which creaked ominously on its hinges. The building was "historic"—which meant falling down around his ears, and keeping up with all the repairs often felt like trying to plug holes in a dam with his fingers. But that was a problem for another day.

He heard his staff moving around in the front of house, getting ready to open, and he headed back to the kitchen to finish the prep he was now even more behind on. He popped in his AirPods, pulled up his Broadway playlist on Spotify, and got into the zone.

He normally loved this part of the morning, when his breakfast crew was trickling in, but they all knew better than to bother him. When it was just him and the music and whatever random culinary creation his hands felt like making today.

He was whisking up a hollandaise when the music suddenly cut off, replaced by the sound of his phone ringing. He glanced down at the caller ID and grimaced—but he never declined this call.

"Hey, Gran."

"Mackenzie." Her voice was as curt and authoritative as ever. "Are you eloping with Magda Miller?"

Mac nearly choked on his own spit. *"What?"*

"You were seen leaving her apartment this morning, and apparently both of you have mysterious out-of-town trips planned.

For a *month*. I just want you to know that I do not approve of eloping."

"I promise I am not eloping with anyone, least of all Magda. I'm going to New York to catch some shows. Like I do every year," he said, hating the lie. He *never* lied to his grandmother. Evade, sure, but outright lying made his chest feel tight.

"So you two are just, what's the phrase now? Fuck buddies?"

"Jesus." Mac nearly choked again, this time on air. Breathing and swallowing were suddenly incredibly challenging with his grandmother's prim voice saying those words. "I am not now, nor have I ever, nor *will* I ever, sleep with Magda Miller."

"Hm."

"What?"

"That's just a lot of protesting."

"Gran. Magda and I hate each other. You know this."

"Well, yes, but there's a lot of passion there. I just want you to know that if you were to have some hate sex, as it were, you could tell me."

"Gran. I love you. But there is no world in which I'm going to call you to talk about hate sex. Or any kind of sex."

"I just want you to know you can. I'm not a stodgy old lady. Your generation didn't invent bad decisions—"

"I'm hanging up now."

"Call me when you get there," she said hurriedly before he could disconnect the call. "I hate when you drive to the city."

"I will. Love you."

"Hm," she said—which was her version of "I love you too."

His grandmother had raised him, and he hated lying to her. Magda might want to keep things quiet about *Cake-Off*, but Mac *wanted* to share it with the entire town. Maybe because he didn't have that one special person to share it with.

The *Cake-Off* people had told him that he could tell his significant other and his lawyer, and only them. But Mac didn't have a significant other. He never really had. He liked women. He liked relationships and sex and intimacy and all that. But whenever things started to get serious, something would happen, and he'd find himself single again.

He'd never really minded it. He had great friends. A great life. Until recently, he'd had a friend-with-benefits he visited whenever he was in New York. And his grandmother was the only high-maintenance woman he needed in his life. But these last few years, it was like everyone in his life had started getting married and having kids. Even his former hook-up in New York.

Things had shifted so slowly that it had taken him a while to realize what was happening. He still had his poker nights and a regular gig singing with his band, but these days it was rare for everyone to make it, and the conversations were often about spouses and kids. Mac didn't mind it—he loved hearing about his honorary nieces and nephews—but all those assurances at bachelor parties over the years that nothing was going to change had been total bullshit. Everything had changed. Except him.

He loved his life. He loved his town, and his friends and his family. But when he'd had to fill out the forms for *Cake-Off*, he'd felt a little sad that his emergency contact was still his grandmother, and he hadn't had anyone special to share the news with when they asked him to be on the show. It was funny how lonely good news could make you feel.

But the Cup was opening and he didn't have time to dwell on it. Not today.

He briefed his staff on the specials and ran through last checks before he flipped the sign on the front door, and the first rush began. There was invariably a line out the door when they opened—the Cup's too-small seating area always filled up fast, and those who didn't make the first seating always queued up at the to-go counter. When it got warm enough in the summer, the sidewalk out front would double the number of tables, but there still wouldn't be an empty chair in the house for the first three hours they were open.

He needed a bigger space, but opening another location was expensive, and finding the right spot had proved challenging— and doing it all while still keeping the Cup afloat sounded like a Jenga tower about to fall.

But if he won *Cake-Off*...

That money could mean a new location. A bigger staff. Maybe even some of that work-life balance that Mac had been hearing such good things about.

They were slammed all day, and Mac flowed between the kitchen and the front of house as needed, cooking, chatting with the locals as he bussed tables, and quietly worrying about how the place would fare in his absence.

Not that he never took time off. Unlike Magda, who he didn't think had taken more than two days off in a row in the last five years, Mac made a point of going down to New York to catch a few Broadway shows and unwind every year. And last year he'd gone on a ski trip to Alaska. He wasn't all work and no play, but the Cup was his baby, and he always worried about it when he was gone.

Though he wouldn't miss the gossip.

All morning the locals asked him where he was going, making not-so-subtle references to Magda and early morning visits. And all morning, Mac lied.

He kept a smile on his face the whole time, playing his part, but when Connor arrived to pick up a takeout order, Mac dragged him to the back office as soon as he walked through the door.

"I'm not cut out for this shit," he grumbled when the door closed between them and the din of the restaurant.

Connor had a sleeping toddler in a neon tutu draped over one shoulder as if it was the most natural thing in the world—a sight that would have been alarmingly out of place for the rigid lawyer only a few years ago. "You mean reality television?" he asked, unfazed.

"The lying. Telling everyone I'm going to New York."

"It's just until the first press release," Connor reminded him. "Which is while you're filming, right? So by the time you get back, everyone will know."

"Yeah. They'll know I lied."

"For good reason. Just focus on why you're doing this."

Except he couldn't even remember right now why he'd thought this was a good idea. The money, obviously. And the exposure.

But the Cup didn't really need extra exposure. They were always packed. No, the problem was that it was falling down. And too small. But either a major renovation or moving to a different location while staying open so he could *afford* a move or a renovation was a logistical nightmare he'd never had the time or mental space to tackle. He knew the problem. He just didn't have a solution. But if he won...

Money solved a lot of problems.

"You all ready to go?" Connor asked. "When do you leave?"

"A few hours," Mac said dismissively. "I'll throw some stuff in a bag."

"Throw some...? Mac. You gotta go pack."

"We're busy. And it's not like I have much to pack. They have all these rules about what I'm supposed to wear on camera. No logos—I'm not sure I *own* five shirts that don't have logos on them."

Connor stood there staring at him for a moment, swaying slightly to soothe his sleeping daughter, and then a slow smile spread across his face. "You're nervous."

"What? Shut up."

"No, I'm relieved. You've been so blasé about all this, I wondered sometimes if you knew you were about to go on national television."

"With Magda."

Connor's eyebrow arched. "Is that what's bugging you? She always did get under your skin."

"It's fine."

"You can beat her. You know that, don't you?"

Mac looked at one of his oldest friends. "Do I?" He'd started to wonder what the hell he'd been thinking. He wasn't a baker. Not really. Not with the fancy French training that Magda had. He was creative and resourceful—but with the exception of a few classes at the King Arthur Baking School back in the day, he was mostly self-taught. Was he about to make a fool of himself?

"Trust me," Connor said. "You can win the whole damn thing. You've got this." Then he grinned. "Now can I pick up my wife's breakfast before she sends a search party after me?"

Chapter Three

Magda was still in the kitchen with flour up to her elbows when Charlotte and Kendall arrived to pick her up.

"Your driver has arrived, Ms. Miller," Charlotte called out as she walked in the door, pulling up short when she spotted Magda. "Whoa. I can't tell. Is this panic baking or regular baking?"

"That *man*." Magda kneaded the bread dough harder.

"Ah," Charlotte nodded. "Rage baking."

"Let's get this show on the—" Kendall came in behind Charlotte, breaking off when she saw Magda. "You're not ready? I thought you'd be waiting for us on the sidewalk." She rubbed absently at her lower back, a habit she'd picked up now that she was approaching her third trimester.

"I'm almost done." Magda thwacked the dough she was kneading with cathartic force—and knocked her knuckles on the counter hard enough to bruise. "Ow, *biscuits*!"

"Mac," Charlotte stage-whispered.

Magda shook out her stinging hand. "Someone told him."

"It wasn't George," Charlotte said quickly. "He promised not to tell a soul."

"It's fine," Magda said, giving her hand one last shake before returning to taking out her aggression on the rye. "It doesn't matter. Everyone's going to know soon anyway."

Kendall leaned against the counter. "So why are we rage baking?"

Because Mac had implied she'd need to be a good actress on the show and all of her deep, dark fears had come out to play. Because it was easier to be angry at him than it was to face her anxiety that she wasn't good enough. That they'd made a mistake in casting her.

Magda wasn't the special one. She wasn't the smartest or the funniest. Kendall had been a world-class athlete. Charlotte had skipped grades and become a doctor by the time she was twenty-five. They were the stars, not her. Even in her family, Magda always had a tendency to disappear. She was the quiet one.

The boring one.

Hence the reason she'd been rejected for *Cake-Off* twice. And her current anxiety was in no way eased by the fact that they'd picked her this time.

Just don't be yourself.

The words had been a joke. Kendall had been giving Magda a pep talk before her last interview. Magda *knew* Kendall had meant them sarcastically—but she *hadn't* been herself that day.

It had been a freaking out-of-body experience, that interview. After years of working toward getting on the show, after two dull-as-dirt, boring-old-Magda interviews that had resulted in "not quite right for this season" rejections, she had been determined that this time was going to be different. She would be dazzling. She would wow them.

Then, five minutes before she was supposed to go in for her interview, Kendall had let slip that Mac had *also* scored an interview, and that his had apparently gone brilliantly.

Magda had seen red.

Something inside her had unlocked. Something wild and a

little feral. From one second to the next she'd gone from desperate hope that this time she would get it to blazing anger that he would dare to try to take this from her.

She barely remembered what she said in the interview—she just knew she'd been energized. Her blood had felt like it was rushing in her veins—and not from nerves. She hadn't stumbled over her words; she hadn't had to be reminded to speak up so the cameras could hear her. She'd been vibrant and witty and bold—all the things Magda usually wasn't.

And she'd gotten a call two days later that they wanted her on the show.

But that wasn't *her*.

They wanted personalities. They wanted vivacity. And Magda desperately wanted to be what they wanted. But she wasn't a good actress.

She was going to let everyone down—the producers who had finally cast her after years of auditions, the friends who believed in her and expected her to win the whole thing, and the town that would be rooting for her when the show aired. It wasn't even the baking that terrified her. It was that feeling that it was *her*, that *she* wasn't enough.

And Mac had somehow known exactly what to say to trigger an entire tidal wave of insecurity.

But she couldn't say that to her friends, so Magda just shook her head and kneaded harder.

"Mags?" Charlotte prompted gently.

"I don't want to talk about Mac. I don't want to think about Mac," Magda said, throwing the dough into a bowl and shoving it into a proving drawer. "The best thing about the next four weeks is that I don't have to think about Mackenzie Newton at all." She cleaned up her working space with brutal efficiency, slapping a sticky note on the proving drawer with instructions for what her bakery assistant needed to do with the dough. "Though it might not be four weeks. It might not even be one." She turned vulnerable eyes on her two best friends. "What if I'm eliminated first?"

"Then at least you did it. You were on *Cake-Off*. That is bad-ass, even if you totally crash and burn," Kendall insisted.

Magda cringed. "Please don't say burn. I've had recurring nightmares about burning pies for the last two weeks. What if I panic?"

"Don't borrow trouble—isn't that what you're always saying?" Charlotte reminded her. "Just take it one bake at a time."

Don't borrow trouble. It had been her Aunt Lena's mantra. Her aunt who had first taught her to bake and paid for her to go to the fancy pastry academy in France when she was eighteen. Who had given Magda the money to open the bakery.

Lena had always believed Mags was special, even when she didn't believe it herself. She'd always known Magda would do big things. And now she had the chance to do them.

"I'm just so scared of letting everyone down. And that I'm going to show up and they're going to tell me they made a mistake and accidentally cast fourteen bakers and I'm out." It was a well-known fact that the *Cake-Off* always started with thirteen bakers. The famous Baker's Dozen. "I didn't know it was possible to be this scared of going—and making a complete fool of myself on national television—while also being totally petrified of *not* getting to go—when they realize they never wanted me and the whole thing was a huge mistake."

"You think anyone fills out that much paperwork as a mistake?" Kendall asked skeptically, still absently rubbing her back.

"You're in, Mags," Charlotte confirmed. "And you're going to be amazing."

"Mac doesn't think I can do it."

"Since when have you ever cared what Mac thinks?"

"I don't." Except she'd always cared what he thought—no matter how much she wished that weren't true. That was why he'd always been able to get under her skin.

Kendall and Charlotte exchanged a look. "Apron?" Charlotte asked.

"Apron," Kendall confirmed—reaching into her bag.

"We got you a little something," Charlotte explained as Kendall withdrew a small tissue-wrapped parcel. "We were going to give it to you in Boston, but I think you need it now."

Magda wiped her hands on her apron and pulled back the wrapping. "You didn't need to do this."

"Yes, we did," Kendall said.

The last of the paper came away and Magda released a startled burst of laughter at the sight. The hot-pink apron was bedazzled—which was very Charlotte—and the sparkly writing spelled out "Not Here to Make Friends"—which was all Kendall.

"Remember that," Charlotte said, pointing to the words. "You're a baking badass. Be mercenary. No playing nice."

Because Magda was always nice. *Too* nice.

Don't be yourself.

"Thanks, guys."

"You're going to win the whole damn thing," Kendall said with absolute confidence. "Don't worry about Mac or the town or anything else. Just go wild. Enjoy this. Though I don't know how this town is going to survive without you for a month."

Nerves did a conga through her stomach. "It might not be a month..."

"It *will*," Kendall insisted.

"Pine Hollow will just have to miss you. You have a competition to win," Charlotte said. "Though it will be weird with both you and Mac gone."

A whisper of alarm rose at the back of her thoughts. "Mac's going somewhere?"

"George is feeding his cat for him," Charlotte explained.

"I'm planning to start a rumor that you two ran away together," Kendall said, wicked laughter glinting in her eyes.

"Too late," Charlotte said. "I heard that one this morning. Along with something about Mac being seen leaving your house at dawn?"

"His cat broke in again." Magda hesitated, uneasiness teasing at the back of her neck, raising the hairs there. "You don't think..."

"What?" Charlotte prompted.

"He did audition... but the *Cake-Off* never takes two people from the same small town. They wouldn't."

Would they?

God, that was the last thing she needed. This was supposed to be *her* thing. And it had nothing to do with him.

"I'm sure they wouldn't," Kendall assured her. "And if he was going, someone would have heard. No one in this town can keep a secret."

"You two did," Magda reminded them.

"He's just doing one of his Broadway binges," Charlotte said. "*You* are the star. And we should get going. We still need to drop Cupcake off with George before the drive."

"Right," Magda agreed, squashing that last frisson of doubt.

She wouldn't even *think* about Mac for the next four weeks. This was *her* moment.

Just don't be yourself...

Chapter Four

Magda stepped out of the Doubletree elevator at five fifty the next morning and reminded herself to breathe. Breathing was important.

She'd already been awake for nearly two hours, due in part to the habit of the early schedule she kept for her bakery, and in part to the crippling nerves that had made sleep impossible— and were now making her hands sweaty on the handle of her roller bag.

The producers had told her to be in the lobby at six with her hair done, but no makeup. The driver would pick her up. She was to check out and bring all of her things with her, but have a separate go-bag with two changes of clothes and anything she would need for the day. No patterns that would make the cameras dizzy. No logos for her business or other brands.

That was all she knew. That and "expect a long day."

She was literally about to get into a strange van and go God knows where. All the contestants were responsible for getting themselves to Boston, but then they entered the "show bubble," not to emerge again until they were eliminated.

Please don't let me be first.

Magda rolled her bag across the shiny lobby floor toward the exit—and immediately spotted four other very nervous humans clutching suitcases and go-bags, standing in a little cluster just outside the revolving door.

There was no van in sight, but these had to be other members of the famous *Cake-Off* Baker's Dozen. The show always started with thirteen contestants with varied backgrounds from all over the country.

Charlotte and Kendall had given her tons of pep talks about being mercenary and "in it to win it." There was a quarter million dollars at stake, after all—but she still smiled tentatively as she stepped out into the predawn light outside.

It was hard to think of these people as her adversaries when they all had the same expressions of excited terror on their faces as she knew must be on hers. "Hey," she said as she approached. *"Cake-Off?"*

A tall, angular Black woman with gorgeous box braids smiled. "That's us." She gave a little wave. "Leah. California." Then she pointed in turn to the other three. "That's Josh, Texas. Abby, Minnesota. And Eunice, Seattle."

Eunice was petite, Asian, and incredibly young, with a bubbly smile. Abby had more of an Italian mom vibe, and Josh was wiry and Latino, with a soft, shy smile.

"Magda," she said with an answering half-wave of her own. "Vermont."

After everyone had exchanged tentative smiles and nods, Magda asked, "Does anyone know what happens next? Are we even baking today?"

A collective laugh rippled through the others, and then Leah, who seemed the least tongue-tied by nerves admitted, "We were hoping you knew."

Magda shook her head. "Not much with the info, are they?"

An older man with a dapper grandpa aesthetic emerged from the hotel then—and the introductions started all over again. Walter. Florida.

By the time the van arrived, precisely at six o'clock, Caroline, North Carolina, had joined them and there were seven of them waiting there. Anxiously commiserating about how completely in the dark they were.

The driver wasn't much help. He quickly checked them each off his list, confiscated their cellphones, and loaded all the bags into the back of the van, saying only that they had a long drive ahead and they might as well make themselves comfortable— try to get some sleep since it would be such a long day.

Though what that day would consist of remained to be seen.

The idea of sleeping seemed patently ridiculous—how could anyone sleep at a moment like this?—though four of her fellow-passengers immediately leaned against the windows and did just that. Magda, instead, caught Leah watching her and gave her a timid smile.

Leah leaned across the aisle separating them. "I don't know how they can sleep," she whispered. "I've wanted to be on this show for *years*. I auditioned five times." She mouthed the last two words—as if they were shameful, and Magda felt a swift kick of camaraderie.

She held up three fingers. "Third time's the charm."

Leah's relief was palpable. "Thank God. I thought I was going to be the only one who didn't get in first try. I feel like the pity contestant. The one who badgered them until they couldn't say no any longer, but who gets eliminated in the first episode."

"Hey. No talking about elimination," Eunice said, twisting around in her seat in front of them. "We're gonna be the final three."

"At which point I will show you both no mercy," Leah said, grinning.

Magda grinned back. "I would expect nothing less."

Leah scooted over to sit in the seat beside Magda, and Eunice faced them over the back of her seat. "So which week are you most scared about?" Eunice asked. "I am terrified of improperly tempered chocolate."

Magda groaned sympathetically. "Bread. I have nightmares about faulty proving drawers."

"Oh God! Me too!" Leah grabbed her arm, groaning. "Like poor Alan from the British version! Did you see that episode? I cried."

Eunice reached back to grab her hand. "Me too!"

Two hours later, after talking and laughing through a hundred miles of highway, Magda had two new best friends. Or several. About an hour into the drive, the other bakers started waking up, and joining their conversation.

Kendall and Charlotte would always be her ride-or-die, but there was something so incredibly *comforting* about meeting someone who geeked out about the same things she geeked out about. Who got excited about flan and could share the absolute agony of a failed soufflé.

She'd never been able to just sit around and talk about baking without boring her friends to tears, but these were her people. Even if she did get eliminated in the first episode, this feeling of connection might just be worth it.

By the time the driver picked up his walkie and told someone on the other end that they were ten minutes out, the group in van B had bonded and were determined that none of them would go home first. There were always thirteen, so there had to be at least one more van—and sadly one of those folks was going to have to go, because Magda and her new soulmates were in the competition to stay.

She was a little surprised there hadn't been cameras positioned to catch their conversation—but this at least explained how the bakers always seemed to have such strong connections going into the first episode, with people they'd never met before that day.

As the van began to slow, Magda looked around for the first time in hours. She'd been so caught up in talking that she hadn't really noticed where they were going. It was just countryside—similar to the landscape where she'd grown up in Vermont.

Incredibly similar.

And then she realized why.

"Are we at King Arthur?" she asked, suddenly—and all of the bakers *oooh*ed.

Every baker worth their sugar knew about the King Arthur Flour Company. The Vermont institution had started out just selling flour but had become a baking academy and tourist attraction.

It was also where Magda had taken her first baking class when she was eighteen.

The van stopped and Magda and her new best friends piled out into the very familiar parking lot of King Arthur, where signs announced the building was "Closed for a Private Event."

Her heart lifted. It was a sign. She'd been meant to come on this season. And yes, maybe she'd only been picked because they wanted a local girl for the Vermont season of *Cake-Off*, but it didn't matter why she was here. She was *here*. And she was going to make the most of it.

The producer who had conducted Magda's most recent pre-taping interview was standing outside waiting for them, a tablet in hand and a smile on her face. As soon as they'd all unloaded from the bus and collected their go-bags—who knew what was happening to their other suitcases—the producer's smile broadened as she looked at each of them in turn.

"Welcome to *The Great American Cake-Off*."

Magda couldn't help it. She whooped—and all of her new friends laughed, as they cheered as well.

It was happening. She was here.

"Are you excited to be in the *Cake-Off* kitchen?"

"Very," Magda gushed, and then flushed, stammering, "Sorry. Full sentences. Repeat the question. I remember."

Julia, the producer who had conducted her last audition interview and was now assigned to help her capture her confessional footage, gave a reassuring smile. "You're fine. Just relax. Editing can work wonders. Just keep going until you get in the flow."

"Right," Magda said, squirming in the director's chair.

She'd been separated from her cohorts from van B shortly after they arrived. They'd each taken turns getting their makeup done and their hair touched up, signing even more paperwork, and being whisked away for their introductory confessional interviews. It was now after ten in the morning and she still hadn't laid eyes on the kitchen—or gotten any sense of whether they would be baking today.

And no matter what Julia said, Magda was pretty sure even the magic of editing wasn't going to be able to disguise her awkwardness. She was just so *nervous*. She'd already answered questions about her background and why she'd wanted to be on the show, but each response had felt more stilted and stumbling than the last.

"Go ahead whenever you're ready," Julia coaxed.

"I forgot the question," Magda admitted.

"Are you excited to finally be in the *Cake-Off* kitchen?"

She knew what she was supposed to say. *Dream come true. Been waiting my entire life to get into that kitchen. Can't wait. So excited. Chance of a lifetime.*

But all that came out was "Are we baking today?"

Julia's smile stayed reassuring but added a note of compassion. "I know it's torture not to know what's going on, but I'm not allowed to give you any hints. They're very big on making sure everyone learns the competition details at the same time so there's no appearance of favoritism. But I will say that you will be told more about the competition soon—and you should take the chance to grab a snack when we get back to the green room."

Magda's brain went into overdrive. Did that mean they were going to bake right away and she'd need her energy? Or that they wouldn't be baking for hours and she shouldn't make herself so crazy with nerves that she forgot to eat all day? Either way, she knew she should take the advice, but how did you eat when your stomach was busy twisting itself in knots?

"Magda?" Julia prompted gently. "Are you excited to finally be in the *Cake-Off* kitchen?"

"I feel like I've been waiting my entire life to get into that kitchen." Even though the words could not have been more true, they still came out robotic and stilted. How did people do this? How had *she* done it? She'd been good during her audition. She knew she had.

But she'd also been pissed. She'd been angry at Mac—the only time she was ever rash and impulsive. It had felt like he was trying to steal her dream and she'd been electrified. And now she was the one here and he wasn't. She'd won.

And she didn't know what to do with herself.

Just don't be yourself.

She could be Charlotte. Or Kendall. Or one of her many sisters. She could play the part—anyone but boring, quiet, invisible, too-nice, too-accommodating Magda.

But before she could channel any of those so-much-more-interesting humans, Julia lifted a hand to her earpiece, indicating she was listening to something, and flashed Magda a quick smile. "Here we go," she said, rising from her own director's chair.

"Go?" Magda echoed. "Are we done?"

"We'll do more later," Julia promised. "Don't worry. You're going to have so many hours in that chair you'll start dreaming of confessionals. But right now we need to get you to the Proving Room—time for some of that information you were waiting for."

Magda's heart skipped a beat at the words *Proving Room*.

She'd seen that room on so many episodes of *Cake-Off*. She'd seen the confessionals too, but strangely this was the moment it started to feel real. The Proving Room was where the bakers would gather and wait and chat before and after the challenges. Where the best bakers would "rise" to the occasion—and others would fail to.

Julia ushered her into the room, where Magda was reunited with her van B cronies. She sent them nervous smiles and finger waves as the producer pointed her toward her mark and scooted behind the cameras. Julia flashed her double thumbs-up as Magda took her spot beside Leah—until one of the producers frowned and shuffled them all for a more aesthetic clustering.

Magda was in front of Leah now, next to Eunice—but there were still only seven of them. Where was van A? Where was the rest of the famous Baker's Dozen?

She glanced around, as if searching the room for the missing bakers, but then the head producer—Stephen, a man with a huge presence and an even bigger voice—called everyone to order.

The *Cake-Off* was all sugar and smiles, but Stephen had an impatient, businesslike air, and there was something cynical about his eyes that made her uncomfortable—though that might have been her standard-issue crippling nerves.

"All right, folks, let's get through this fast so we can get to the baking!" he bellowed. "To my left you see our lawyer." The woman in the gray suit waved. "She's here to make sure we're adhering to the standards and practices designed to ensure this is a fair show. None of you have been given advance information about the competition tasks, is that correct?"

There were vague affirmative mutterings, but Stephen went on as if the idea of anyone being tipped off was impossible. "In a few minutes, you will be let into the *Cake-Off* kitchen for the first time, and meet our host and judges. This *will* be filmed. From here on out, assume that anything in the kitchen, the Proving Room, or the confessionals is being filmed. There will then be a challenge—"

Excitement rippled through the van B group, and Stephen paused to give it time to die down.

"The judges will lay out the show structure and announce the details of the challenge. If you have any questions, you can ask them *after* the hosts have introduced the parameters of the challenge for the cameras. If you forget to ask or freak out and draw a blank, there are a list of challenge requirements taped inside the top drawer of each station for you to refer to. Do *not* try to take them out or open the drawer to look at them before the judges introduce the challenge."

Magda tried to focus on the words that were coming at them rapid-fire, but part of her brain kept spinning.

Were there really only seven of them this season?

"There will be cameras roving around the kitchen—just pretend they aren't there unless a producer, host, or judge asks you a question. If a producer asks you a question, remember that they will *not* be seen by the home audience and you are to always answer as if you're just spontaneously talking to the home viewer. Don't give me any 'yes' or 'no' bullshit. And don't ruin my audio by swearing. If we have to bleep you, I will personally fine you double the cost of covering up your language. This is a fucking family show, people. Be classy."

Magda heard Leah snort behind her, but her heart was starting to beat so fast she couldn't remember how to be amused. This was happening. This was really happening.

"Those of you who are still in the competition at the end of the day will be taken to the *Cake-Off* house. There is no Wi-Fi. You will have noticed that you do not have your cellphones. No, you will not be getting them back—unless we want to film you telling your wife or your adorable child that you won a challenge."

It was hard to focus on anything that came after "those of you who are still in the competition at the end of the day."

Someone was going home.

Please don't let me be first out.

"The schedule will be grueling," Stephen powered on relentlessly. "You will be exhausted. In addition to the challenges, you will have interviews and promotional spots and anything else we want you to film. The hours will be long. You may break down on camera—even if you're certain right now that's something you would never do. Don't worry. The viewers will love you if you let yourself be real. That's all you've gotta do. Be real. And bake fucking amazing food."

A nervous chuckle rippled through the bakers, but Stephen didn't pause for it. "We want you all to have a good time, but anyone found to be in violation of the rules—which you all signed this morning—will be eliminated from the competition."

Magda's stomach churned. What if she forgot a rule?

"Be personable. Be charming. Be *energetic*, but most of all have fun. And good luck, everyone!"

And with that blisteringly fast monologue, Stephen disappeared through the door.

"Where are the rest of us?" Leah asked, but the producers didn't answer, ushering the bakers toward the door Stephen had just gone through.

Were there really only seven of them?

Magda swallowed hard, her stomach doing a series of backflips. She definitely should have taken the chance to eat a Power-Bar in the green room when she had the chance. She was going to pass out—or run in the other direction. Which was *not* how she wanted to start her *Cake-Off* career.

Everything was happening too fast.

Yes, she'd been waiting for this moment since four in the morning—or, more accurately, for three years—but all of a sudden everything was rushing forward at warp speed and she just wanted to scream *Wait! I'm not ready! Just give me five minutes to process all this!*

But there was no time to process. Eunice was squeezing her arm excitedly. "It's happening!" she whispered.

Magda wondered if they would stop the show if she puked all over another contestant. Was that why they'd all been told to bring two changes of clothes? Did that sort of thing happen a lot on day one?

Her body was moving—but she was having an out-of-body experience, floating above herself as the group half-walked, half-trotted into the kitchen for the first time.

Only it wasn't her first time.

The King Arthur Baking Company teaching kitchen had been refitted with *Cake-Off* logos to look like the famous *Cake-Off* kitchen, but she knew this space. She'd been here before. She knew those rows of workstations. Those neatly lined-up ovens.

Suddenly she was back in her body, a sense of calm washing over her.

At the front of the room, the host, ultra-suave Jeffrey Flanders, stood lined up with the familiar judges. Sweet, grandmotherly Joanie. And, of course, impossible-to-please Alexander Clay.

Magda's heart began hammering, but this time with eagerness. It was really happening. She was here. She was going to be on *Cake-Off*.

The bakers, each in their crisp scarlet *Cake-Off* aprons, reached the front of the room and stood on the marks the producers pointed them toward. Eunice grabbed Magda's hand and she squeezed it hard, excitement glittering brightly in her chest.

Then another door opened.

And another group of bakers—these each in bright *blue Cake-Off* aprons—began to file eagerly into the room, rushing toward their own marks—a dozen feet to the left of the red-apron cluster.

Behind her, Magda heard Leah gasp—and her stomach, already touchy, sank down to her toes at the sight of those blue aprons. Why had they been separated into two groups? Were they going to be competing against the Blue Team? *Cake-Off* had never done that before.

She was busy panicking, so it took her far longer than it should have to see him—his auburn curls wild without his usual baseball cap pinning them down. She almost never saw him without a T-shirt from some Broadway musical, but today he was wearing a simple gray Henley, pushed up to display his muscular forearms. And a blue apron.

Mac.

He was here.

Dread swallowed Magda, even before she heard the smooth, smarmy host voice of Jeffrey Flanders.

"Welcome! To the first-ever Archrivals Edition of *The Great American Cake-Off!*"

Behind her, Leah whispered a word the producers would have to bleep.

Magda's sentiments exactly.

Chapter Five

Magda wasn't looking at him, but Mac had the distinct feeling that she was silently considering how many pies she would get if she chopped him up and served him to the judges.

Music from *Sweeney Todd* began running a macabre theme track through his head.

Mac knew he was supposed to be paying attention to the host as he introduced the concept—each baker in a red apron had a nemesis of some kind on the blue team, most *dramatic* season of *Cake-Off* ever, blah blah blah, this time it's personal, blah blah blah—but he couldn't stop sneaking glances across the *Cake-Off* kitchen to where Magda stood.

Her black curls were piled on top of her head, adding an extra couple of inches, but she was still in the front row, partially blocked by the petite Asian girl, who didn't look much older than a teenager and was clinging to Magda's arm. Magda stared fixedly at the host, but her face was flushed, and he knew her. He knew she wasn't seeing the host and judges at all—and that he'd never seen her so angry.

And he'd seen her *very* angry over the years.

All the other members of the red team looked varying degrees of shaken and pissed. The showrunner was whispering excitedly into his headset, directing the handheld camera operators to make sure they got every reaction—and looking entirely too pleased with himself.

Around Mac, some of the blue team seemed shocked or angry—and he had to wonder if they'd been coached to pretend, because they'd all known exactly what was coming. The producers had explained to Mac that all of the rivals had been recruited and sworn to secrecy—since they'd learned over the years that contestants were terrible at keeping their participation a secret and if they hadn't expressly told the Blue Team not to tell their rivals, *everyone* would have known about the gimmick before they arrived and there would have been no big reactions on camera.

Beside him, Tim, an arrogant five-star hotel pastry chef from California, was making a show of being horrified, but Mac had no interest in playing the actor.

His gaze kept returning to Magda—and the one time he caught her looking back at him...well. It was definitely a *Sweeney Todd* moment.

And yes. Okay. He could see where this looked deceptive, but he would explain. The producers had wanted to get her genuine reaction on camera, but as soon as there was a pause in filming, he would go over there. He'd apologize for not giving her a heads-up and explain that as far as he was concerned there was no vendetta. Not here. He would compete with her the same way he would with any other baker on the show—so she could stop looking at him like she was planning his imminent disembowelment with a cake knife.

She wouldn't even be here if he hadn't come, too. Once she understood that, she'd be grateful.

Someone shouted "Cut!" and Mac started to take a step toward Magda—but a crew member was suddenly in front of him, blocking his path, and another voice was shouting, "Hold places! Going again!"

Mac was ushered back into place, makeup people patted noses that had gotten too shiny, and crew members moved with brisk efficiency to reset the cameras and get the entire thing from another angle. It was kinda cool—seeing behind the curtain as the host repeated his lines as if saying them for the first time. Mac would have been fascinated by the entire process, if he wasn't also itching to clear things up with Magda.

When she wasn't shooting him death glares, she was gnawing nervously at her full lower lip, looking like she was about to chew through it from nerves—and forcing the makeup people to rush over to touch her up every time the director paused to adjust lighting or have the host repeat a certain line.

Jeffrey Flanders continued with his spiel, introducing the familiar judges. Mac had made a point of watching several episodes of the show over the last few weeks, so he had the strange, disconnected sense that he knew these people.

Flanders. Joanie. And the terrifying Alexander Clay.

It was surreal, but somehow familiar—but Mac didn't have time to dwell on the thought because Jeffrey Flanders's next words wiped every other thought from his mind.

"Now some of you may have noticed we have fourteen bakers in the *Cake-Off* kitchen, and as you all know, *Cake-Off* always starts with our famous Baker's Dozen—so I hope you're ready, because before we can truly begin the season, we have to determine which thirteen of you will be continuing with us—and which one will be going home. That's right, bakers, our first Elimination Challenge starts right now."

A ripple of shock worked through the group around him, and Mac stood up a little straighter. In all the episodes of

Cake-Off he'd seen, they'd *always* started off with a low-stakes Skills Challenge that provided some advantage for the winner in the later Elimination Challenge.

Apparently the archrivals theme wasn't the only thing different this season. Mac's heart began to pound harder on a rush of adrenaline. When Flanders said *right now*, did he really mean *now*? Or after three more setups and repetitions?

"Each of you has a rival on the opposing team, and for your first Elimination you'll go head-to-head against your nemesis in a Mystery Ingredient Challenge. The winners will be safe. The losers will have one last chance to impress the judges in a Speed Bake, after which one of you will be eliminated."

Shit. Head-to-head. He had to beat *Magda*.

Mac's pulse thundered in his ears as he looked toward Magda, who was pointedly not looking at him.

One of them would be in the bottom.

Shit.

This wasn't how this was supposed to go.

"Take your positions!" Jeffrey called out—and Mac realized he'd missed something.

Fortunately, there was a producer there, pointing him toward his station.

And then he was standing next to Magda. Their stations were side by side, even sharing a long stretch of countertop. Each with a box with a big white X on it.

"Hey," he said, under his breath.

She stared straight ahead, all of her attention focused on the judges at the front of the room. He should be focused on them, too—one of them was saying something about time limits and judging criteria—something about a signature dessert, you on a plate—but he'd noticed Magda's hands were shaking, and he couldn't look away.

It was funny how that jogged his memory. Those shaking hands.

They'd been here before. In this very room. Did she remember that? She'd been nervous then too. And so effing *young.*

"Magda," he tried again, to no response. "Mags."

She gave the slightest shake of her head, like brushing away a fly, still not looking in his direction. A curl fell down, drawing his gaze to the line of her throat.

"Magda."

A crew member caught his eye, making a slashing noise across his throat and pointing imperiously toward the front of the room where Flanders was speaking. Apparently this wasn't a talking time. Not that Magda was interested in talking.

But he needed to say something—that he was sorry, that everything would be okay, that she could do this. He felt the most ridiculous urge to calm those shaking hands, to take them between his and look deeply into her eyes, convincing her that she belonged here—but she wouldn't believe him even if the crew would have let him get the words out. He was her competitor.

He'd known they would be competing against each other, but he hadn't really thought this through, if he was honest. It had been impulse to say yes to the audition in the first place when the producers had approached him after learning about their feud online, impulse to come on the show at all. He'd told himself he was doing it for Magda—altruistic, noble, a peace offering—but it had also been exciting.

Reality television! Once-in-a-lifetime experience! Sure, it was kind of terrifying, since Magda had forgotten more about baking than he'd ever learned, and he was probably going to make a fool of himself, but he didn't want to say no to something just because it scared the crap out of him. When life threw an opportunity like this in your path, you took it. At least Mac did.

He liked the show. Liked the idea of being on it. He hadn't planned on this, but it felt like he was meant to be here—and he meant to win.

But if he was going to win, he would first have to knock Magda down to the loser bracket.

He should have known they would be pitted against each other from the start. He should have expected this. But he'd been too busy getting the Cup ready for his absence and trying to remember all the things he'd learned back when he'd first taken lessons at King Arthur to anticipate the production team's machinations.

"And...*reveal!*"

All around the room, bakers were lifting their mystery ingredient boxes, and Mac jerked to attention. He wasn't going to win a damn thing if he didn't get his head in the game. He didn't usually bother to medicate for his ADHD, but now he was wishing he'd brought some Adderall—or at least a shot of caffeine to help him focus.

Mac belatedly lifted his own box, frowning at the bowl of brown powder in front of him. Some kind of spice? Powdered cocoa? Around the room, other bakers were sniffing and tasting the powder, so he dipped a finger into the bowl and brought it to his mouth.

Cardamom.

The spice immediately burst on his palate, and he smiled as everything clicked into focus. He could do this.

"You have ninety minutes to prepare your signature dessert featuring this mystery ingredient."

A giant digital timer dominated the wall beside the judges, and now it lit up: 90:00 in bright blue digits.

"Your time starts…*now*!" Judge Joanie called out—and the entire kitchen seemed to lunge into action.

Holy shit. *Now?*

Mac had been woolgathering, but the challenge instructions were always taped into the top drawer with the measuring spoons—just in case a competitor suddenly blanked. It had happened before, and the audience never liked to see a favorite baker eliminated on a technicality because they hadn't heard some detail of the instructions.

Mac jerked open the drawer, but the instructions weren't much more than he already knew: 90 minutes. Signature dessert. Anything you want as long as it's you on a plate. Feature the mystery ingredient.

Right. Okay.

Him on a plate. What the hell was him on a plate?

Magda was already in motion. Flour and sugar and butter already arrayed on her station. She'd make a cake. She was known for her cakes. She would go with familiar. And it would be amazing.

If he wanted to beat her, he would have to do something unexpected. Something so much more difficult than a delicious cake so he would win for the sheer balls of it. With cardamom.

Spiced panna cotta.

It was a risk. If it didn't set in time—which it probably wouldn't—he'd be royally screwed. But Mac hadn't come here to play it safe. If this blew up in his face, he would save himself in the Speed Bake. Always bet on yourself. That was his motto.

Suddenly all the distractions faded into the background and everything was calm, that perfect focus of the kitchen settling around him. Mac reached for the ingredients he needed, humming "A Little Priest" from *Sweeney Todd*.

He had this.

As long as he didn't get distracted by the woman at his side with the shaking hands and the black curls that had always smelled of vanilla and cinnamon.

As long as he didn't think about the last time they'd been in this room.

Chapter Six

Fourteen years earlier...

"Hey. It's Magda, right?"

"I...yeah...yeah, that's me. I'm..." Magda flushed as she stammered.

Mac grinned, his smile seeming to shine right on her as he took the stool next to hers. "Didn't expect to run into anyone else from Pine Hollow."

"Yeah, no, me neither," Magda managed, glancing around the kitchen at King Arthur while a single thought kept ringing loud in her head.

Mackenzie Newton noticed me.

No one noticed Magda. Sometimes it felt like her single most remarkable trait was how singularly unremarkable she was. To most people in Pine Hollow, she was "one of those Miller girls"—not the oldest, not the youngest, not the prettiest or the smartest. Just an average sort of Miller offspring.

Her unremarkableness might not have been quite so glaring if her two best friends hadn't also been so distinctly remarkable. Charlotte had skipped two grades and was already finishing up her sophomore year at Dartmouth, and Kendall was well on her way to being a freaking Olympian—and then there was Magda, with no particular skills or ambitions, just an average sort of girl who graduated at the normal time and was going to go to a perfectly average state school in the fall.

"You taken one of these before?" Mac asked, tying on an apron as he surveyed the room, his muscular arms flexing with the motion.

Magda managed to stammer out that she hadn't.

She liked to bake—she used to try out new recipes with her aunt Lena—the only one of her aunts who didn't have kids of her own, and who had decided for some reason that Magda was her favorite. It had felt so special, those afternoons making cakes and pies and cookies—*she* had felt so special. And when her aunt had offered to pay for her to take a real professional baking course at King Arthur as a graduation present, Magda had jumped at the chance.

But she'd been wondering what she was doing here, among the *real* bakers, her hands shaking with nerves, long before Mackenzie Newton had swanned in and tossed himself onto the stool beside hers.

She knew Mac—sort of. He was six years older, and friends with her best friend's older sister, so really she knew *of* him, in the sort of vaguely familiar way she knew everyone in Pine Hollow. She was pretty sure they'd never spoken more than two words to each other, and if anyone had asked her fifteen minutes ago, she would have sworn he didn't know her name. But here he was, sitting beside her, chatting up a storm.

"Yeah, me neither," he said, exuding confidence in a way that was frankly a little daunting.

Where were his nerves? Why wasn't he worried he was going to mess up and burn the entire place down?

"I'm thinking of adding a few muffins or something to the

menu at the Cup," he continued, mentioning the little espresso shop he'd opened up a couple of years earlier.

"I heard you make good coffee," Magda offered hesitantly.

Mac's eyebrows bounced up merrily as his smile widened. "Not good enough to get you to check it out?"

Magda flushed hotter. "I'm not much of a coffee drinker," she mumbled. Which was a spectacular understatement. Coffee was one of the most singularly disgusting beverages ever invented as far as she was concerned. People kept telling her she was going to develop a taste for it, but it still tasted positively foul to her.

"That's why I'm expanding into muffins," he said, his smile still shining on her like a spotlight. "After this course, I expect to have the best muffins in Vermont."

Maybe it was the way he was smiling at her, but Magda suddenly found playful words tripping off her lips. "Why stop at muffins? Be really daring. Go for apple turnovers."

Mac laughed—and the sound felt like it streaked right down to her stomach and bounced around there. "One step at a time."

Then the instructor called the class to order, before Magda could figure out the answer to the question that was suddenly pinging through her brain.

Was Mackenzie Newton flirting with her?

He had auburn curls and incredibly dark brown eyes in a combination she'd never realized was incredibly sexy—but then Mackenzie Newton had never smiled at her like that before. Like he couldn't imagine anything more fascinating than sitting there chatting with boring old Magda Miller.

All through the class, as they learned about different kinds of cake sponges, Magda kept stealing glances at Mac—and more than once he'd looked back at her, winking or smiling or making an exaggerated woe face at his own less-than-fluffy cake.

It was an eight-week intensive. All summer long. With two two-hour weeknight classes each week and a four-hour block on Saturdays for the longer bakes.

Magda had been overwhelmed before the class began—eager to learn but also convinced she was completely out of her depth, and considering running out the back door before anyone saw what a pathetic amateur she was.

But now she was looking forward to every single session over the next few weeks, wondering if she would have many more chances to chat with Mackenzie Newton.

And that was before he turned toward her as they were walking to the parking lot at the end of the night and said, "You know, since we're both coming from Pine Hollow, we should carpool. For the environment."

Her heart had exploded into sugar sprinkles and she'd agreed—for the environment, of course.

By the following week, she was looking forward to the drives to and from King Arthur almost as much as the courses. She loved baking—she was *good* at it too, she was realizing. Good in a way that made the instructor's eyebrows go up as he tried her pastries and had him mentioning scholarship programs to fancy French academies.

She was so *happy*—and a big part of that was Mac.

He was so easy to talk to, and such a good listener. He shared with her his plans for the Cup, and she encouraged him to think bigger—why not add even more desserts? And why stop at desserts when he made the best fresh bread in class? People would come from all over for his baguette sandwiches.

He was addicted to coffee and kept trying to convince her

that she actually liked it; she just hadn't found her perfect drink yet. Every time she hopped into his car to drive to King Arthur, he would hand her a new to-go cup with a new fancy coffee drink that was going to convert her—and every time she made exaggerated gagging noises after the first sip.

Until one day he handed her a chai latte—and she realized she was completely in love. And not just with the chai.

Magda had never dated before. She was what her sisters patronizingly called a "late bloomer" and what her friends called "too shy for her own good"—which meant she faded into the wallpaper at every high school party. Aunt Lena assured her that her time was coming—that she was the kind of girl who would thrive in college—but now Magda realized it was only that she hadn't met the right person yet. Maybe it was a symptom of too many rom-coms, but she'd always had this sense that she would *know*. When it was right.

And then she had. With Mac.

They were so perfect for each other. She'd never felt so perfectly in sync with another person—even though they couldn't have been more different. He was always so confident, and he never took his mistakes to heart. He messed up constantly in the kitchen at King Arthur, but he would just laugh and say he learned "by trial and error, with an emphasis on the error." But he had good instincts for daring flavor combinations, encouraging her to expand beyond her tried-and-true chocolates and vanillas.

They *balanced* each other. And for the first time in her life, Magda finally had someone she wanted to make her grandmother's legendary "man-catching" maple cake for.

He made everything seem possible. He didn't even laugh when she told him she might actually apply for that fancy

French pastry academy after week three—though by week six, she was pretty sure she didn't want to go. It would be too far away from Mac.

And they had plans. One time when she'd been talking about marketing partnerships with other businesses in town for the Cup, he'd said, "You know what we should do..." and her heart had beat so loud in her ears she hadn't even heard the rest of the sentence.

We.

Her future was so clearly with him. At the Cup.

He was her soulmate. And nothing was going to happen to change that.

Nothing.

Chapter Seven

Fourteen years later...

Magda had made a mistake. A terrible, stupid, *thoughtless* mistake.

The *Cake-Off* timer ticked mercilessly down as she stared at her soggy cake in mounting horror.

She'd put the glaze on too soon. She'd known it would melt into the cake and turn it into a soggy mess if she didn't wait for it to cool all the way, but she'd gotten so nervous with that giant clock ticking down on her.

She'd wanted this first bake to be perfect. To "announce her position among the front runners" as Charlotte had encouraged her on their drive to Boston. She'd made this cake a thousand times. She knew everything that could go wrong—and she'd never made such an obvious mistake before. Not even when she was a rookie taking her first class at King Arthur over a decade ago.

It would be okay, she tried to tell herself. All she had to do was beat Mac.

She'd resisted the urge to look over at him for the last eighty-six minutes. She refused to let him tarnish this experience for her—this was *her* moment, damn it. But Mac had always gotten under her skin and made her do rash, impulsive things just by existing near her. Ever since that first awful summer.

Normally, her anger at him brought out her competitive side, but today her focus had been fractured by his presence. Her self-doubt had been waiting to pounce, and his confidence, his *ease* had given it the opening it needed. She'd found herself rushing—trying to ignore the sound of his voice as he chatted oh-so-comfortably with the cameras, telling them all about the spiced panna cotta he was making.

Panna cotta! As if there was half a prayer of it setting in time. His dessert was bound to be a gooey blob of almost-flan—but right now her sodden cake wasn't looking much better.

A camera was suddenly in her face, the producer she'd thought she liked before this moment standing just behind it and gently asking, "How are you feeling about your bake right now, Magda?"

She was *feeling* like she was going to burst into tears if she had to say a single word about the glaze mistake. She'd ruined it. She'd been rushing and nervous and she *knew* not to put it on too soon, and yet she'd done it anyway. There was no unglazing the cake. Now all she could do was try not to ugly cry on national television.

"Magda?" Julia prompted softly, her eyes all compassionate understanding.

"I...I just hope I've done enough..." She trailed off on a shaky breath.

How quickly she'd gone from wanting to dominate the first challenge to simply hoping Mac screwed up even more spectacularly than she had.

She dared a quick glance in his direction as she decorated her cake with delicate edible flowers—as if the professional judges wouldn't notice the mushy consistency of her sponge if it was just pretty enough.

Mac was still schmoozing the cameras. His freaking charming smile was flashing everywhere, doubtless making the producers swoon—though Magda had learned long ago not to trust that smile.

He looked like he hadn't a care in the world. As if he couldn't care less whether the panna cotta that was currently waiting in the blast chiller had set or not.

She should have chucked her cake in the freezer. She hadn't wanted it to get too cold and dry out. She'd wanted it to be *perfect*. But she'd failed to take into account the heat of the high-powered lights they'd added for the cameras. With all the ovens blasting, the air conditioners had been struggling to begin with, and the kitchen had just gotten hotter and hotter as the ninety minutes ticked on.

She knew the usual temperature of this room and how long her cake usually took to cool—but the kitchen was currently closer to the surface-of-the-sun temps she'd heard other bakers bemoaning on the show as their cakes failed to cool and their chocolate work melted before their eyes.

But the panna cotta would melt too. That was her only hope. And her cake was still delicious. Even if it was moist to the point of mushiness. Her flavors were solid.

She should probably feel bad that Mac was going to be at risk of going home—maybe she'd even feel some sympathy later when they had her record her confessional footage to be intercut with the final few dramatic seconds of the clock ticking down, but right now she was just praying that panna cotta was goo as Mac jogged over to the blast chiller and hauled it open.

She didn't bear him ill will—well, not a *lot* of ill will, anyway.

She'd never intended to start a feud. Certainly not a decade-long one. Though it could be argued that Mac had started it. And she would definitely argue that, given the chance.

But she didn't want him to fail. She just wanted him far away from her and her dreams.

Once he was gone, she'd be able to think. She'd be able to focus. And she could work her way back to the top of the leaderboard.

Charlotte would probably say it was a good thing she wasn't going to dominate from the beginning. Everyone liked an underdog. She'd come from behind.

She just had to beat Mac.

The buzzer echoed through the room. Everyone—including Magda—threw their hands in the air to show that they weren't doing any last-minute adjustments. And Magda looked over at Mac's station—

At the flawless, glistening panna cotta.

She'd barely been able to talk during the bake, her throat closing off every time a camera appeared in front of her—but when she saw that luscious, tempting dessert sitting on his station she involuntarily gave them a soundbite.

"Oh, *sugar.*"

It wasn't close.

All of the bakers were ushered out of the kitchen within moments of the buzzer going off. They were hustled into fresh outfits and fresh aprons, the sweat dabbed off their faces and their makeup touched up before they were herded into the Proving Room for the cast photos.

Magda was shoved next to Mac—whom she did her best to

ignore, which was actually easier than it might have been, since all she could think about was mushy cake.

While the contestants forced smiles for the cameras, the kitchen was tidied by an army of production assistants and each of the desserts put on pedestals for glamour shots before the judges could defile them with forks and knives.

And all Magda could think was that her cake was just getting soggier the longer it sat.

She was so doomed.

The cast photos would have normally been taken before the first challenge, when all the bakers were shiny and eager, rather than bracing for the executioner's ax in the first round of judging—but the producers hadn't wanted to spoil the "surprise" arrival of the rivals.

When they filed back into the kitchen and lined up behind their perfectly spotless workstations, Magda's cake at least *looked* presentable on its little pedestal. The home viewers wouldn't know it was a disaster on sight.

And maybe Mac's panna cotta would be horrible. Too bland. Too rubbery. *Something.*

The judges tried to build a sense of suspense. They gushed about Magda's flavors and sympathized with the heat of the room, but it was obvious the second they each took a bite of Mac's panna cotta which way the verdict was going to go.

"That panna cotta was unbeatable."

Back in the director's chair, facing the confessional camera again, Magda grimaced ruefully—or at least she hoped her expression looked like some suitable combination of disappointment and chagrin. The last thing she needed was the entire world seeing what she was really feeling at this moment.

She wasn't even sure she could put into words the wretched combination of anxiety, exhaustion, and anger—at herself and at Mac.

The Speed Bake had been hell. Cupcakes she should have been able to make in her sleep had been underbaked thanks to an idiotic mistake with the oven temperature. She was just grateful she'd managed not to cry on camera when she'd been called down front as one of the bottom three out of the seven bakers who'd been forced to compete in the forty-minute challenge.

She'd had to stand there as the judges enumerated all the mistakes that had landed her in the bottom, and wonder if she was going to be the first eliminated. Wonder if this was it. If her entire *Cake-Off* experience was going to be defined by Mac and his damn panna cotta. Too mentally drained to do anything but nod numbly as the judges commented on her obvious skill, her impressive technique—and the thoughtless mistakes that had derailed both of her first bakes. The melting glaze. The undercooked cupcake.

The numbness spread, her thoughts fuzzy and jumbled, as the judging seemed to last forever.

And then they said Caroline's name.

She'd survived by the skin of her teeth. And she'd almost cried all over again, something inside her collapsing in intense relief.

All while Mac had watched from the safety of the sidelines, making the experience that much more excruciating.

"Do you have any idea why today didn't go as planned?" Julia asked, her tone so gentle and curious she might have been talking about a minor misstep and not the pair of massive brain freezes that had nearly sent Magda home.

Magda had already walked Julia through both bakes,

step-by-step, reliving every detail and talking about it all as if it was happening in real time, so they could edit this footage in with the bake as they cut the episode together. But now apparently they needed to dig deeper.

This was part of being on the show, Magda knew that, but she was *exhausted*—not just physically but emotionally after coming so close to screwing up her dream, and she just wanted to go back to the *Cake-Off* house and curl up in bed for as many hours as she could manage before it all started over again tomorrow.

"I don't know," she hedged. "I planned for this. I practiced for months, but I was always in my own kitchen, with my own ovens. I think I underestimated how much the heat in the *Cake-Off* kitchen—both the literal heat and the pressure—would get to me. I timed everything out perfectly for the glaze—but the cake wasn't cooling as quickly as it usually did. And then with the cupcakes—I haven't underbaked a cupcake since I was nine years old, but by the time I noticed I'd set the oven to the wrong temperature, there was no time—and no coming back."

"And Mac?" Julia prompted, still in that gentle tone. Not a judgment in sight. Just curiosity. "Did seeing him in the kitchen rattle you?"

"I was definitely rattled by seeing Mac standing there." Magda obediently repeated the question in her answer. "I'd heard that he had auditioned too, but *Cake-Off* never takes two people from the same town, so to have him walk into the kitchen—and then to have to compete against him head-to-head in order to stay in the competition...it was a nightmare. An actual nightmare I've had before."

"I understand you and Mac have known each other a long time?"

"Pine Hollow's a small town."

"Right." Julia nodded. "And I understand there's something of a long-standing feud between you two?"

"Yep," Magda said curtly, suddenly not nearly so interested in being the good little interviewee and repeating the question in her answer. She was *tired*. "Look, can we do this tomorrow? Mac and I have been feuding for over a decade. I don't think one more day is going to change anything."

"Of course," Julia agreed quickly, glancing at her Apple Watch. "You'll want to get some rest. Another big day tomorrow. We'll go over the rest of this then."

Magda didn't want to go over the rest—because she was pretty sure the rest was all Mac, and the last thing she wanted was for this experience to be about him. This was supposed to be her dream, her moment, and none of it had felt right since the second he walked into the *Cake-Off* kitchen in that damn blue apron.

She stood, statue-still as the sound guy, Richie, unhooked her from the wires snaking underneath her clothing. Then she turned to Julia, too tired to remember her own name at this point. "Where do I go?"

"One of the vans will shuttle you over to the house. Remember, no attempting to contact anyone outside the bubble. Just try to get some sleep. We'll see you back here tomorrow, bright and early."

Magda nodded obediently—even if she'd wanted to, she was too tired to try to funnel spoilers to the outside world. The *Cake-Off* people ran a surprisingly tight ship—no devices of any kind that could connect to the internet, either to give the bakers an unfair advantage or leak hints about what was happening on the show.

She wasn't going to publish spoilers, but she did desperately wish she could call Charlotte and Kendall. If only to tell them that Mac was here. And so she could get her equilibrium back.

It had almost ended today.

Because of Mac.

Okay, perhaps not entirely because of him, but it *felt* like it was his fault. She'd been off her game from the second he walked through the door. She never would have made those mistakes if she hadn't been so rattled. And he'd *known*. He'd stood there in her apartment when she was telling him about the show and let her make a fool of herself. Probably laughing at her the whole time.

Who did that?

A production assistant walked her through the darkened halls of King Arthur. Magda had long since lost any sense of time she had. She only knew that it was fully dark outside as the PA opened the exterior door, chattering into her headset about "5B rolling to transpo." She herded Magda toward the waiting black van, and Magda hesitated, feeling like she was forgetting something.

"My stuff…?" she asked.

"Already at the house," the PA assured her, yanking open the van door—

And suddenly Magda's vague sense of unease vanished, along with her exhaustion, replaced by a rush of angry adrenaline.

There was one other passenger already waiting in the van.

Mackenzie freaking Newton.

Chapter Eight

They'd been set up.

That was Mac's first thought when the door to the van he'd been waiting in for ten minutes opened and Magda was ushered inside.

The producers were no fools. Magda had been playing nice in the kitchen, in front of the cameras and other contestants— quiet, contained—but now her eyes flared with the fire he was used to seeing in them and she snarled *"You."*

"Hey, Mags."

He was pretty positive the vans were all wired for audio and video. Connor was a contract lawyer and he'd gone over everything Mac had signed with a fine-tooth comb. He'd told Mac that according to the contracts, only bathrooms and their designated rooms at the house were considered off-limits. Everywhere else—vans, green rooms—they should assume was fair game.

Mac had never seen them include any footage when the contestants didn't seem to know they were being recorded—but this was the Archrivals Edition, and he wasn't sure the same rules applied. The entire day had been different from what he had expected. *Cake-Off* was a cuddly teddy bear of a show, but this . . . this was something different.

He had a feeling Magda was relying on the way things had always been done when she flung herself onto the seat beside his.

"I hope you're proud of yourself," she snapped.

"Well. It was a pretty great panna cotta."

Shit. Why did he say that? What was it about her that always made him want to goad her when he knew he shouldn't? This was his chance to clear the air between them, and here he was making her eyes flare with anger and her face flush scarlet.

Which always made his own heart beat faster. There was just something about her when she was all fired up.

"You let me make a fool of myself. You let me stand there and tell you I was going on the show." She buckled herself in almost savagely, only a narrow empty seat separating them.

"I mean, technically you assumed I already knew—"

"Which you did. But it wasn't George at all, was it?" Blue eyes bored into his in the low light of the van, the darkness making it feel like they were the only two people in the world.

Mac lowered his voice. "Look, Magda, I wanted to tell you, but they had me sign all these nondisclosure agreements. It's shitty that they blindsided you—"

"And you helped them do it."

"What was I supposed to do?" he snapped, guilt sharpening the words. "They recruited me."

Her eyes flared again. "Are you serious? I auditioned for three years and *they* came to *you*?"

"One of the producers saw something about our feud on social media—"

"You barely bake! What are you even doing here?"

And because it was Magda, and he couldn't help himself, he heard himself quipping "Winning?"

He half expected her to lunge across the empty seat and strangle him, but her next words were icy cold. "Is this revenge?"

"What?" The insult rippled through him, stirring his own temper. "You really think I'm that petty?"

"You knew how much I wanted this—"

"I'm not the one who has a history of taking something just because the other one wants it, cupcake," he growled.

"It was ten years ago! And do you honestly think I started a business just to piss you off? Do we need another van just to fit your ego?"

"You could have started the bakery anywhere. You didn't have to take my location—"

"If it was your location, I wouldn't have been able to sign the lease, would I? It's not my fault you were too slow."

"You only knew it was coming available because of me!" he growled.

"And you only wanted to move the Cup because *I* wrote up a business plan for you. I was the one who talked you into expanding the menu! You'd still be an espresso stand if not for me."

"Don't give yourself so much credit, cupcake. I wanted to expand long before I started that baking class."

"Will you stop calling me cupcake! Cupcake is my *dog*."

"You're the boss, sugarplum." Her glare could have melted metal, those blue eyes searing hot. "Look, I'm doing you a *favor* by being here." There. That was back on message. Though he had thrown the words at her a little more aggressively than he'd intended.

His best intentions had a tendency to go up in flames where Magda was concerned. He'd been wanting to talk to her all day, but the second they were alone—nuclear meltdown. No survivors. There was something about them, some chemical reaction, that made his brain shut off.

"A *favor*?" she yelped. "Oh, thank you so much for nearly getting me eliminated from the competition on day one."

"You think you would have gotten into the Archrivals Edition without an archrival? *Think*, Magda."

"If the only reason you're here is to do me such a favor, then why try so hard to beat me?"

"I didn't have to beat you, sugar. You beat yourself today."

Her eyes widened—but this time there was hurt blended in with the anger, making him feel like absolute shit. She leaned away from him, only then making him realize how much they'd been leaning toward each other, the air between them charged with an angry magnetism.

"You're a real asshole, you know that?" she whispered, her face suddenly illuminated as the van pulled into a brightly lit parking lot.

"So you've said."

The van stopped and in the front seat the driver spoke into a walkie, "5A and 5B arriving at the house."

But Magda didn't move to get out. She was too busy looking at him like he'd poisoned her dog. "You knew I was about to be blindsided on national television, and you didn't say a thing."

"The contract—"

"Bullshit. You wanted the advantage. You wanted to knock me out, and you knew you couldn't beat me unless I was rattled."

He hadn't been *consciously* thinking that. But he'd seen some of the things she could do. Exquisite pastries and magnificently decorated cakes that must have taken hours of precision work. Stuff he genuinely couldn't have accomplished in any amount of time. She'd been off her game today, and he'd definitely bene-fited from that, but that wasn't the only reason he'd won.

This show would eat Magda alive.

"Maybe I was doing you a favor," he said. "Shows like this aren't for everyone. The person who wins *Cake-Off* isn't going to be rattled by a few surprises. You're right—you're a better baker than I am. You're probably better than all of us. But you almost got eliminated tonight—and I killed it. And it wasn't because I knew you were going to be there. It's because I thrive on this. I love a challenge. And some people are better at home, safe in their own kitchen where everything is under their control and no one ever rocks their narrow little world."

"I despise you," she whispered.

"Yeah, I know, honey," he said—his own anger retreating enough to let the feeling-like-shit portion of his interactions with Magda begin. Mac didn't have a temper—except with Magda. And he almost never said things he regretted—except to her.

He'd actually thought about what he wanted to tell her—that they didn't have to feud here. That just because she'd had an off day didn't mean she wasn't the best damn baker here. He'd meant it when he said she was better than him. By far. He'd meant to console her. To tell her that the show wasn't everything, that it didn't determine whether she was great or not. There were so many factors—the heat, the time constraints—these shows weren't the real world. Losing on here didn't mean anything.

And he'd said a lot of that. In the most dickish way possible.

Why were his emotions always turned up to eleven whenever she was in the room? He was *nice*, damn it. He liked that about himself. But he always ended up hating himself with her.

His eyes caught on that escaped curl, lying against the curve of her neck. The rapid pulse there.

"Look, you should be flattered. They wanted you badly enough to recruit me," he said. "It's the Archrivals Edition. Just think of me as the price of admission. You wanted to be on the show, didn't you?"

"Not like this." The look in her eyes killed him. "It wasn't supposed to be like this. This isn't *Cake-Off.* This is... I don't even know what this is." She swallowed thickly. "Maybe I should just leave..."

"Magda..." He reached out a hand on the unfamiliar urge to comfort her—there was something so uncertain about her in that moment, so vulnerable, and he just wanted to hold her—but the van door was suddenly whisked open by a production assistant.

"Hi." Her gaze flicked back and forth between them, as if sensing something uncomfortable in the air, and then she spoke into her headset. "Eyes on 5A and 5B."

Magda climbed quickly out of the van, but she paused to throw a final poisoned glance over her shoulder. "Do me a favor, Mac. Stop doing me favors."

"Good idea," he muttered to himself after she'd stalked into the building with the PA scrambling at her side. A glorious baking goddess on the rampage.

He followed more slowly, giving her a chance to put some distance between them.

The "house" wasn't actually a house at all. The production had taken over an inn for the week. Mac had overheard two of the producers discussing the impossibility of finding the kind of house they usually used that could accommodate all of the bakers within range of King Arthur. Apparently filming in smaller towns rather than a city was a giant pain in the ass logistically, and the *Cake-Off* crew veterans were annoyed.

It was fascinating, seeing the way the sausage was made. There were so many people—dozens of them—behind the scenes of the hit show. It always seemed so quaint and cute. The American version was more cutthroat than the British one, but it still had an air of wholesome warmth.

A wholesome warmth Mac had yet to experience during filming. Though it was early days. And maybe they were skipping the wholesome warmth on the "rivals" season. Going edgier. More table flipping. Less hugging.

Magda didn't seem terribly pleased with the changes. But would she actually leave?

Mac didn't mind a little fabricated drama—he actually found it all kind of fascinating. Like a Broadway production. But Magda was so sensitive. Too sensitive for this. And she wanted it too badly.

He wanted to win, but he had the distinct impression that it meant something different to her. Like it wasn't just about money and the chance to build her business, but like winning and losing actually said something about her.

And he hadn't helped with his diatribe in the van.

He would apologize, but he'd long since learned that attempts to apologize only turned into worse fights. There were times when he liked bickering with her—when it made him feel alive and awake and *present* in a way that was downright electric—but then he'd see a flash of hurt in her eyes and feeling like shit would take over. Better just to avoid her.

Thankfully, she was already out of the reception area by the time he made his way in there. The production assistant was waiting there with his room key and instructions on when to be ready in the morning.

"You aren't allergic to pets, are you?" the PA asked anxiously as Mac accepted the key. "The inn has a cat and a dog we didn't know about, and we already had to move Javier—"

"No allergies," Mac confirmed, cutting off the panic. He glanced around, telling himself he wasn't looking for Magda. "Are there cameras around here?"

The PA blinked in shock. "At the house? This isn't *Big Brother*. We don't care what you're doing when you're not baking. As long as you aren't cheating. You know about the anticollusion rules, right?"

"Right. Yeah." At least they wouldn't be on camera here.

He made his way up the stairs. The inn was similar to several in Pine Hollow—converted from a historic building and therefore full of creaking stairs and narrow, zigzagging hallways. A gray cat twined around his legs, and he knelt to greet the true master of the house, offering pets in tribute. After the cat swaggered away, Mac straightened and walked past several doors before finding his own—wondering which one was Magda's. Not that it mattered. He needed to avoid her. Pretend they were strangers.

As if that would work. As if he hadn't always been aware of her the second she walked into a room, everything in him going sharp and alert before he even saw her.

They were gasoline and an open flame—and they somehow needed to avoid exploding for the next four weeks. Or until one of them got eliminated.

Four weeks. Barely any time at all.

All they had to do was avoid fourteen years of bad habits.

No problem.

Chapter Nine

"Jules, we have a problem with 5B."

Julia looked up from the footage she'd been marking and frowned as she squinted blearily at the clock. It was nearly midnight, and she had a six a.m. call time. "What kind of problem? Is she sick?"

Greg—another producer who'd worked with Stephen before—shook his head. "A PA was reviewing the van footage—Stephen had her ride to the house with 5A—and apparently there was some kind of indication that she didn't like it here or might not want to stay. I don't know. The PA's probably freaking over nothing, but Stephen wants you on it."

Julia hissed out a curse under her breath and got to her feet, snatching up her tablet. "Can you send the audio to my tablet?" she asked, already moving toward the exit.

Freaking Stephen.

It was too early to put Mac and Magda in a car together. She'd *told* him that, but he was so convinced he was right about everything. Right about the show's new concept. Right about blindsiding half the contestants. Right about pitting them against each other right off the bat.

This was Julia's fourth season of *Cake-Off*. She'd started out as a PA, but she'd had good instincts, and the show's previous showrunner had noticed her rapport with the bakers from the

74

start. Deanna had believed in mentorship—and she'd quickly moved Julia from being a general PA to her personal on-set assistant. She'd taught Julia a metric ton about how reality television—good, *positive* reality television—was made. Julia had been promoted to producer and started nurturing her very own bakers through the process last season.

But then Deanna—kind, wonderful Deanna who had grown the American version of *Cake-Off* into the success that it was—had a stroke. Her doctors told her to stop working such insane hours. To go home and spend more time with her grandkids. So Deanna—who *was Cake-Off* to so many of the crew—had abruptly retired. And the network executives had panicked.

They needed a seasoned showrunner to take over their precious ratings-winner baby. And there was Stephen. Fresh off the most successful season ever of the most cutthroat competition series on television. He knew how to make audiences tune in week after week—even Julia had to admit that the man knew how to craft a compelling hour of television. The tension crackled on his shows, and something dramatic was always right on the verge of happening.

But that wasn't *Cake-Off*. At least it wasn't supposed to be.

In the past, the most significant difference between the British version of the show and the American one was that all of the Americans were professionals who made their living from baking in some form, while all of the Brits were hobbyists with other jobs. But both were warm and fuzzy.

Until now.

Stephen had easily sold the network execs on the Archrivals Edition—the man was persuasive. When he wasn't being a dictatorial ass, like he was to most of his crew.

Julia had voiced her dissent, along with most of the other

long-term *Cake-Off* producers, but they'd been overruled—and told to get with the program or get out. So Julia had gotten with the program. She'd wanted Magda on the show for years—ever since she first saw her in casting—and the feud with some guy in her hometown seemed ideal.

Until today. When Julia had seen that raw, hurt look on Magda's face when he'd walked into the *Cake-Off* kitchen. That didn't look like a harmless small-town feud. It looked personal.

And now Magda was considering leaving?

Julia cursed under her breath as she drove the two miles between King Arthur and the inn they'd taken over. At least Stephen had stuck with Deanna's original plan to film this season at King Arthur—even if accommodating the needs of the baking school had been a logistical nightmare.

As soon as her tablet pinged with the incoming audio, she listened to it—and then cursed some more. She took the stairs up to the room Magda had been assigned and knocked gently at the door, holding her breath as she waited.

She didn't know what she was going to say to convince Magda to stay. She never planned this stuff out. She was good at her job because she *listened*, because she made the bakers feel comfortable and let them guide the conversation. She never tried to manipulate. She coached. She encouraged.

But for her to do that, Magda actually had to open the door.

Julia started to knock again—then caught sight of the time on her tablet and silently kicked herself instead. Of course Magda wasn't answering. She was *sleeping*. That conversation had been recorded nearly an hour ago, and Magda's call time tomorrow was almost as early as Julia's.

Okay, this is fine. I'll just catch her first thing in the morning. Julia gave herself a silent pep talk. It wasn't like Magda could go anywhere. The contestants had no transportation of their own and there were PAs on all the entrances 24/7 to make sure no reality show vloggers tried to sneak onto the property and get information about the upcoming season or its contestants. Which also meant none of the contestants could leave without being spotted.

Magda was sleeping. And everything was going to be fine. Julia would talk her into staying—and do her best to protect her bakers from Stephen's machinations. He was not going to ruin Deanna's legacy if there was anything Julia could do about it.

Now she just had to get some sleep herself. They were filming a marathon Skills Challenge tomorrow, with one of Stephen's special twists thrown in. Julia needed to be on her game almost as much as the contestants did. It was going to be a *very* long day.

"Can't sleep?"

Magda froze when she stepped into the inn's common room and was greeted by that question. The last thing she wanted was to have to be "on" for one of the crew people. Well. The second to last thing, after running into Mac again.

She didn't want to play the perfect little contestant, but what she saw when she squinted into the shadows was actually a cluster of van B—now Red Team—bakers, huddled together around one of the small tables in the breakfast area, illuminated only by the glow of the pendant light over the coffee station.

"Not a wink," Magda admitted, resuming her progress into the room.

Leah and Josh were in pajamas, while Eunice had almost completely disappeared inside one of the inn's fuzzy bathrobes. The inn's resident dog—a scruffy little terrier Magda had fallen instantly in love with—was curled up on a small dog bed in the corner, paws twitching and making little noises in his sleep.

Magda nodded to the mug in Leah's hands. "I thought some tea might help."

"Might I suggest something stronger?" Leah held up a flask, tilting it invitingly.

"Sold." Magda was a lightweight, and she rarely drank, but right now she needed *something* to unknot the fist of tension that had kept her from being able to sleep. Her brain wouldn't stop spinning, but she *needed* rest, or she was going to fail as spectacularly tomorrow as she had today.

Magda got a mug, filling it with chamomile tea, and sat across from Leah, nodding her thanks when Leah tipped some amber liquid into the tea.

"Scotch," Leah explained. "The good stuff. My father got it for me to celebrate my wins." She eyed her own cup. "Somehow today doesn't really feel like a win."

Leah had been one of only two Red Team bakers to make it through to the winner's bracket with an exquisite cardamom and vanilla bean cheesecake. But Magda knew what she meant. All of Leah's enthusiasm and vivacity was dimmed now, their shared excitement for the show tainted.

"Did you know about the twist?" Eunice asked softly.

"Not a clue," Magda admitted.

"It's so unfair," Josh complained, matching Magda's internal indignation. "How can they tell some of us and not others? After all that business about no one getting information about the competitions early."

"I'm learning fair doesn't really play into reality television," Leah said with a grimace.

"But *Cake-Off* is supposed to be different," Magda said. "It's not about feuds and backstabbing. The Baker's Dozen always support one another. They become friends. It isn't supposed to be like this."

"I guess they wanted more drama," Leah said.

Josh tipped his head, studying Magda. "Your nemesis is the hot ginger with the arms?"

"Josh," Leah scolded.

"I'm sorry. Am I not supposed to notice that he's hot?"

"No, he's hot," Magda confirmed. "You're not wrong."

"You're hot, too," Josh assured her.

Which was a very sweet lie. Magda wasn't hot. She was the prototype for cute. Sweet and pleasant. So unbelievably *pleasant*. But sex appeal? Yeah. No. That was more Leah with her crystalline confidence. And Mac, who always made everything look so easy.

"He your ex?" Josh asked. "My station was behind yours, and I thought I picked up on some tension."

"Oh, no, nothing like that," Magda rushed to explain. "He's just from my town—competition for my bakery—and we've never been able to stand each other."

"Really? It seemed personal."

Because it absolutely is.

"We just..." Magda shook her head, diverting the conversation away from her. She looked to Leah. "What about yours?"

"Lying, cheating, scumbag ex-husband." Leah lifted her mug in a mocking toast.

Magda winced. "Ouch."

"Yeah. Tim. And he's a good baker too, the bastard. We were all lined up to have our own show on the Food Network—until I caught him sleeping with a twenty-two-year-old makeup artist. This was supposed to be my fresh start, and now I get to spend the next month talking about him. Seeing him every day. Being reminded why I needed a fresh start in the first place—and, God, if he wins..." She shuddered.

"May his bottoms be soggy and his dough underproved," Josh said, raising his glass.

They all clinked their mugs against his.

"I talked to the others," Leah went on. "Abby's is her estranged little sister. Walter said something about his business partner cheating him. And Taylor was Caroline's best friend for fifteen years before she slept with Caroline's husband."

"Damn," Josh marveled. "No wonder Caroline was so pissed when she got eliminated."

The first baker to go had definitely seemed more angry than sad.

"They're lucky no one got punched in the face during the first bake," Leah said. "Though they probably would have loved that."

Magda looked to Eunice and Josh. "Who are your rivals?"

Eunice made a face. "Mine's not that bad. Just the guy from culinary school who always made me feel like I was worthless and wasting my time."

"Mine's my dad," Josh said into his mug. "Whom I haven't spoken to since he told me that *he* doesn't have a problem with my sexuality, but couldn't I just break up with my fiancé and try dating women so my mother could save face with her church group?"

"Josh," Magda whispered, horrified as she put her hand over his. "I'm so sorry. It's so horrible of the producers to do this to you."

"Yeah, well, they did it to all of us."

"I think Stephen might be Satan," Leah speculated, her tone managing to lighten the mood.

Mac made Magda feel unhinged—and like she was still that desperate eighteen-year-old girl, but things could have been a *lot* worse. "I think I got off the easiest."

"I don't know," Leah said. "I suspect Walter and Roy might be pretending to hate each other for the show."

"The adorable bowtie grandpa and Idris Elba's sexy uncle?" Josh asked. "Say it isn't so."

Magda took a sip of her whiskey tea. "It's so unfair that some people knew in advance. It obviously affected how we baked— *five* out of seven Red Team bakers lost. You and Abby were the only ones who weren't thrown."

"Oh, I was thrown," Leah corrected. "But I bake when I'm angry, so I've had years of practice."

Magda shook her head. "We weren't supposed to *have* to bake angry. It wasn't supposed to be like this. I was ready for the challenges. Nervous, but ready. I wanted to test myself. To push myself to my limits and see if I'm really as good as I think I am. It wasn't supposed to be about them."

"Forget them. Don't let them ruin this for you."

Leah made it sound so easy.

"I actually considered leaving earlier," Magda admitted— and raised a hand in surrender when they all chorused their objections. "Just for a second. I performed so badly today, but it wasn't even that. I felt *cheated*. This was supposed to be our *Cake-Off*. I just wish we could have a regular season. Only us. No more Blue Team."

"So let's do it," Leah said. "Let's knock them all out of the competition, and then finish as just us."

"Like it's that easy?" Eunice asked softly.

"All those people who say 'don't get mad, get even' have it wrong," Leah said. "Your anger is your superpower. Get mad.

And then get even. Use the anger as fuel. Let it focus you. And then destroy the other side. Forget Tim. Forget—" She glanced at Magda.

"Mac."

"Forget Mac and Josh's dad and—"

"Zain."

"And Zain. This *is* our *Cake-Off*. And we're not going to let the bastards take that from us. To winning."

Leah lifted her mug and they all clinked theirs against it.

"Do you really think we can knock them out?" Eunice asked, as uncertain as Magda felt.

"Don't you? You had to know you were awesome to get this far. So own it. Use it."

Magda smiled—she'd never been good at knowing she was awesome, but when Leah said it, she could almost believe it. "You give really good pep talks, you know that?"

"My dad's a basketball coach. It's in the blood."

They all went upstairs not long after that—the morning was going to come whether they were ready for it or not. They split up to head back to their rooms, and Magda lay down on her bed feeling...well, if not better, at least less alone.

She'd been off-balance even before she arrived, doubting herself, wondering why they'd picked her, terrified of not being good enough. But Leah was right. This was *their Cake-Off*.

Magda wasn't going to be thrown again. She shouldn't have let herself be thrown in the first place. It was just Mac. She'd been competing against him for years. She knew him—which meant she knew his weaknesses. He'd never survive sugar working. She could beat him. As long as she stayed focused and stayed in the competition.

Mac may not think she belonged here. He didn't think she

was cut out for the pressure of the *Cake-Off* kitchen? Fine. She'd just have to prove him wrong. Just as she had when she'd started her own business.

She had a plan. And Magda was always amazing at executing a plan.

She wasn't that eighteen-year-old girl anymore. She didn't need Mac's approval.

And she was going to destroy him.

Chapter Ten

The next morning, Magda put on her bedazzled "Not Here to Make Friends" apron—even though she wouldn't be allowed to wear it on camera since it wasn't the official *Cake-Off* apron—and faced herself in the bathroom mirror.

"You're a killer," she told her reflection—which still looked like her usual too-nice-for-her-own-good reflection. "No more playing nice."

An hour later, after hair and makeup touch-ups, she sat down in her confessional chair.

Julia's face flashed with vivid relief. "Oh, good. You're here."

"Am I late?" Magda asked.

"No, no. You're perfect. How are you feeling?"

She could have said nervous or excited or played the part, but she went for honesty instead. "Angry."

Julia nodded. "That's fair."

And Magda realized it wasn't just Mac she was angry at. "You lied to us. We've all wanted this so long, and you made it about shock value."

"I know," Julia said immediately. "I'm sorry."

"All that stuff about fairness, about no advantages in the competition—did you really think half of us being blindsided on national television wasn't a disadvantage?"

"The standards and practices department ensures fairness,

but they deem the producers withholding or revealing information not pertaining directly to the challenges as legally valid—" Julia broke off, as if sensing Magda wasn't buying the legal mumbo-jumbo. "Look, this wasn't how I would've...There's a new showrunner. I'll do whatever I can to protect you, but he's going to be throwing things at you—both on and off camera. It's his MO. So you need to be ready."

Magda nodded, an eerie peace that was somehow both enraged and utterly calm settling over her. "Okay."

"So." Julia shifted in her director's chair, settling back into friendly producer mode. "Are you excited about Pastry Week?"

Mac was so screwed.

They'd started the day with a classic Skills Challenge, back in the standard *Cake-Off* format. The winner of that first challenge always had an advantage in the big Elimination Challenge that decided the winner and loser of the episode. Or in this case, a disadvantage to give to another player...

"And the winner of the Skills Challenge, who will have the power to sabotage a player of their choice in the upcoming Elimination Challenge, is..." Jeffrey Flanders paused for dramatic effect—as if they didn't all already know who had won.

Magda had been a different person today. Utterly confident. Calm and poised. And absolutely *dominating*. That kind of blatant display of skill would have been sexy as hell if it hadn't also meant Mac was probably about to be sabotaged.

One of the judges had actually *moaned* after tasting her croissant. Another had used the word *flawless*. It was just a croissant. It should not have induced moaning, but apparently it was hard to argue with perfection.

The challenge had been two dozen identical croissants and

fresh jam to go with them—and croissants, Mac had learned today, were an absolute bitch to make. Involving chilling and laminating and *hours* of preparation. They'd actually taken a lunch break in the middle of the challenge, it was so long.

Mac's croissants hadn't been terrible—solidly middle of the pack, which had felt like a minor miracle. But that wasn't going to save him if Jeffrey Flanders said...

"Magda!"

Yep. Totally screwed.

Mac fought to keep his face blank as Magda was invited up to receive handshakes and stand next to the judges for this next part. Her face was flushed with pleasure, and he actually felt a little lurch of happiness for her. Just a small one though, since she was about to screw him over.

"Now, Magda, as winner of the Skills Challenge," Flanders said, repeating himself in a way that made Mac think they were planning to put a commercial break in there, "have you thought about who you might want to sabotage in the upcoming Elimination Challenge, after which another baker will be going home?"

Sabotage had never been part of *Cake-Off* before, but welcome to the Archrivals Edition, boys and girls. And Mac was about to be the first to experience this delightful little twist. He'd be ice-skating in hell before Magda passed up the chance to take him down.

"I have." Magda, to Mac's surprise, wasn't looking at him. Instead, she gazed right back at Flanders—as if her mind was made up, perhaps? She didn't even need to look to know what she was going to do?

Right now, Mac was just wondering how bad the disadvantage he was going to have to deal with was.

"This is your chance to take out your biggest competition . . . or anyone else you might want to see leave the competition."

There was a camera getting a close-up of Mac's face right now. He was sure of it. They were really milking the drama, but he wasn't sure how this was supposed to be suspenseful. Everyone in the room knew what was about to happen.

He hadn't had a chance to speak with Magda since that disastrous van ride yesterday, when he'd practically *invited* her to sabotage him.

"So who would you like to sabotage in the upcoming Elimination Challenge?"

Magda looked around the room and Mac was already practicing his resigned determination face when she took a deep breath and said—

"Tim."

Wait. What?

"What?" Tim himself yelped.

"And what brought you to that decision?" Flanders asked. The host looked vaguely nonplussed by the choice—like he'd been hoping she would pick Mac.

"He's a tough competitor," she said, her expression incredibly neutral.

"So all strategic."

"Mm-hmm." She nodded.

It could have been strategic. Tim was good—but he hadn't been in the top three in the Skills Challenge. Neither had Mac, though. He'd been off his game today. He hadn't slept well, replaying the conversation with Magda, feeling guilty for his part in deceiving her, and wondering if this was only going to make things worse between them, rather than bury the hatchet as he'd originally planned.

But maybe she wasn't mad at him after all. Maybe she'd seen that he was doing this at least in part for her.

He still wasn't sure why she'd picked Tim—until he realized she wasn't looking at Tim, but at Tim's rival, Leah. Were they forming alliances? It had never happened before on *Cake-Off*, but the producers would probably love it.

"All right, Tim. If you'd like to move to the side."

Tim moved to his mark, glaring daggers at Magda—she'd definitely made an enemy there.

Jeffrey Flanders turned back to Magda. "And now, please pick one more player you'd like to sabotage."

A gasp rippled through the room.

"Um..." Magda's gaze flicked around the room, before she finally landed on the dad of the father-son rivalry. "Javi."

He'd been near the bottom consistently, so it couldn't be about strategy—was it about her friend Josh? She'd had two chances, and she'd spared Mac both times. That had to mean something...

Javi moved to stand beside Tim.

"And now," Flanders intoned, looking unimpressed by her choices, "please pick one *final* player to sabotage."

This time Magda's gaze went straight to him. Their eyes met and his stomach dropped.

Shit.

So much for burying the hatchet.

Magda told herself she shouldn't feel guilty as she stood in the inn's practice kitchen that night and tried to focus on her choux pastry.

That was the penalty for those who'd been sabotaged—no advance notice of what the Elimination Challenge was (an éclair tower at least thirty inches high) and no practice time in the kitchen tonight. Though Magda had a feeling that might have been as much about the fact that there was limited time and space to fit in the practice bakes tonight as it was about messing with their minds. As it was, Magda was practically bumping elbows with Leah and Abby as they all worked feverishly.

No recipes allowed, but they could all make éclairs in their sleep—and if Mac couldn't... Well, that was how the game was played.

He would have done the same to her.

They were even now. He'd put her at a disadvantage on the first day, and she'd returned the favor on the second.

And she felt like crap.

She *should* be feeling amazing. She'd come in first!

Her croissants had been *flawless*, thank you very much. And Alexander Clay had shaken her hand. She should feel incredible!

Today had been the first day that *Cake-Off* had actually felt like *Cake-Off*. They'd had their first blind-judged Skills Challenge. Typically the *Cake-Off* staple opened every episode, but apparently the producers had felt that pitting the rivals against one another on the first episode was more important than keeping to their usual structure. But today, with thirteen bakers left, there hadn't been any rivalry nonsense. Just baking.

Until the sabotage bit.

She really shouldn't feel guilty. It wasn't like she could have chosen *not* to sabotage someone. Or three someones, as it turned out. The competition had rules. She had just been playing the game.

So why did she feel so wretched? When they'd called her name she had felt a brief flash of triumph—but it had only lasted a fraction of a second before it had been tainted by the realization that she had to do something ugly to another baker. That was who she had to be on national television.

A Skills Challenge win wasn't as big as being named the winner of an entire episode, but it should have been an incredible moment—something she'd dreamed of, proving she belonged in this competition—and instead she felt sick when she thought back on it.

She wanted to call Kendall and Charlotte. To tell them about the Archrivals Edition and beg for their advice—but the producers still had her cellphone under lock and key.

Which also meant she couldn't text Mac.

Even if she wanted to apologize, she had no idea which room was his, and the second she asked a PA, there would be a camera crew wanting to record the moment. The thought of it made her skin crawl.

Baking in front of the cameras was one thing. All this emotional exposure was something else entirely. She liked Julia, but it was hard to trust the producer—especially when she kept prodding Magda to talk about the feud.

Even the people of Pine Hollow didn't really know what had started it all, and the absolute last thing Magda wanted to do was talk to Mac about it in front of the entire television world. But it also didn't feel quite right, targeting him.

He would have done the same to her. She kept telling herself that. But when she thought about her parents watching the show, her friends and all of Pine Hollow watching, the glory of her perfect croissant got lost in worrying that they were all going to be disappointed in her.

Yes, they'd been feuding for years. And yes, the townspeople got a kick out of choosing sides. Some industrious local had even started selling Team Mac and Team Magda T-shirts. But this felt like it was bigger than that. They both had a chance to compete on a national level, and it felt a little wrong to be sabotaging one of her neighbors—even if it was one she hated.

Except it had never been as simple as just hating him.

If part of her hadn't wanted his respect so badly, she never would have been so ugly to him. It was the stupid hurt she could never get over that fueled her anger. But it had never felt so wrong as it did now. And it was memories, as much as regret, clogging up her thoughts as she burned her second batch of éclairs.

Chapter Eleven

Fourteen years ago . . .

Mac snuck an impatient look at his watch as he hurried through his closing routine at the Cup. The CLOSED UNTIL MONDAY sign had already been taped to the door. The people of Pine Hollow would just have to get their coffee somewhere else this weekend. He had a hot date with some Broadway shows and some no-strings sex. Which, after this summer, he needed more than ever.

He needed to get away—and get a certain someone out of his head.

Mac liked to think of himself as a good guy—and if he wanted to be able to keep thinking of himself that way, he needed to stop having age-inappropriate thoughts about a certain jailbait brunette with big blue eyes. She was a teenager, for Christ's sake. Barely out of high school. And he knew when to keep his damn hands off.

But that hadn't stopped his thoughts from going a little haywire these last few weeks. She was fun to talk to. Fun to flirt with. Fun to watch blush over the most unexpected things— like when he complimented her soufflé.

But she was also the same age as Elinor's baby sister, which put her firmly in the *hell no* zone.

Which was why he needed this weekend.

A few days of total distraction and evicting Magda Miller from his thoughts.

The shows wouldn't start until tomorrow—Mac had all the rushes and lotteries and standing-room-only procedures copied down so he could hopefully see four shows for less than forty dollars each. But the sex could start tonight, if he made it down to the city before Cleo fell asleep.

They'd met in college—the two years he'd gone before his grandfather had gotten sick and he'd dropped out. They'd hit it off back then, but never dated. Cleo had been adamant that she had *not* come to college to get an MRS. degree. She was going to be a big-city lawyer, thank you very much, and did not want her identity to be defined by who she was dating. So she didn't date.

She'd been a good friend, but they actually got closer after he left school—exchanging long but sporadic emails over the years. When she moved to New York for law school, Mac had come down to visit her for the first time. He hadn't expected anything to happen—Cleo was still as anti-relationship as ever—but one night after winning lottery tickets to *Wicked*, they'd hooked up. It was fun, it was no-strings—which suited them both—and so their routine had been born.

Two or three times a year, he'd go down to the city for some great shows, good food, and casual sex. It was his vacation from the responsibilities of his regular life. He loved Pine Hollow, and he wouldn't have chosen to be anywhere else, but when he went to New York, he was completely taken out of himself and put back again refreshed.

And he *needed* that. This summer had been especially busy. The Cup was doing better than ever. His grandmother seemed to be doing a little better, too—for a while there he'd worried he was going to lose her, too, after his grandfather passed away, but she seemed to have finally rallied and started to get interested in life again.

The classes at King Arthur had eaten up his weekends for the last couple of months, making a New York trip impossible, but the class series had ended last night. Cleo wanted to see *In the Heights* again. Mac just wanted to feel the energy of the city pulsing around him, smell that trash-on-the-sidewalk-in-the-hot-sun smell of summer, and just forget about everything else. Every*one* else.

He was sweeping up—a necessity if he didn't want to get bugs or vermin, and his last task before he could get out of here—when a thumping knock came on the front door.

"We're closed!" Mac shouted before he even looked.

A thud came—as if someone had stumbled into the door—and he looked then.

Magda was standing on the sidewalk, both of her arms wrapped around a large bakery box and what looked like a school binder. She'd knocked with her foot, he realized, his brain identifying the odd sound even as something in his chest shifted at the sight of her.

Mac set aside the broom at the earnest, pleading expression on her face and went to unlock the door.

"Hey." He leaned a shoulder against the doorjamb, torn between inviting her in and getting on the road. His conversations with Magda had a tendency to stretch into hours. "What's up?"

She glanced past him, her expression a mixture of anxiety and hope. "Can I, um, can I talk to you for sec? Inside? I promise it's good."

"Ah…" Something in her expression made the hairs on the back of his neck rise, but he pushed open the door all the way. "Yeah, of course. Come on in."

He stood back and Magda stepped across the threshold, looking around as if seeing the place for the first time, as if she hadn't gotten in the habit of meeting him here when they drove out to King Arthur together. She was almost always early, and he was almost always running late, so she'd been here a fair amount, waiting on him, but now she looked around as if everything was new. And perhaps it did look different with the lights off.

The kitchen light was still on, and it shone golden through the pass-through, keeping it from being pitch-black.

"So, what's up?" Mac asked as Magda set her armful on one of the café tables. He didn't usually rush her, but he was suddenly entirely too aware of the fact that they were alone in the dark.

"I, um, well, you, uh…Would you like some cake?" The last words came out in a rush after the stammering, and Magda turned suddenly to the bakery box. Opening it to reveal a gorgeous brown cake drizzled in some kind of white drip icing. "It's my grandmother's famous maple cake," she was saying, not looking at him as she immediately started cutting a slice.

She'd brought him a cake? "Mags, you know I'd never turn down your cake, but I really don't have time tonight—"

"Just try it," she urged, shoving a slice at him on a paper plate—she'd even brought plastic forks. "Please?"

There was an urgency in her eyes, and Mac had the distinct feeling he was missing something—or a lot of somethings—but he accepted the cake and took a big bite.

Damn. His eyes closed involuntarily as he chewed. Light and moist—she'd called it a maple cake, but there was a spice to the glaze that accented the sweetness, balancing it. "That might be the best cake I've ever had in my life."

"I'm in love with you."

"Whoa." That opened his eyes—and he found her staring at him. "Uh…Mags…" His brain was stuttering, *ohshitohshitohshit* repeating on a loop.

"Sorry," she flushed. "I meant to say that part later. I just… after this summer, and getting to know you, and sharing all our plans for the Cup…"

"Our plans?" He had the distinct feeling of this conversation spiraling out of control.

"I wrote up a business plan." She snatched up the binder— which looked like a little kids' Trapper Keeper. "A schedule for rolling out the new menu items and eventually moving to a better location. I would work for a share of the profits—you wouldn't even have to pay me until we were successful, but I know we're going to be—"

Panic crawled up his spine. *Shitshitshit.* "Magda…"

He'd done this. He'd let it go too far. He should've put distance between them weeks ago, when he started feeling…

She stepped closer, putting a hand on his arm where he'd frozen, still holding that slice of cake. "Mac, this has been the best summer of my life. Getting to know you and this thing that's been happening between us—"

Alarm bells jangling in his head finally jolted him into motion. "Magda, there's nothing happening between us." There couldn't be. She was a *baby.*

A flicker of uncertainty flashed over her face. "What?"

"I'm not...we're not..." He set the cake on the table, look-ing down, all the way down, at her hopeful *young*—God, she was so young—face. She was beautiful and sparkling and fun, and maybe if she were five years older this would be a different conversation, but she'd *just* turned eighteen. And the look in her eyes... "Look. You're a really sweet kid—" He tried to ignore her flinch. "But I think you've got the wrong idea."

She shook her head, confusion and hurt flickering in her cornflower-blue eyes. "But we've been planning this. For months."

"I mean *I've* been making plans," he agreed. "For the Cup. And you've been great, I mean, a really good listener. Our drives have been really helpful, and I've enjoyed getting to know you. A lot. Just not...like that." He raked a hand through his hair, scrambling for words to make her understand. "I shouldn't've... I mean, seriously. You're practically jailbait."

Her throat worked as horror moved across her face, and he felt like absolute shit. "I'm eighteen," she whispered.

"Which is when you should be screwing up and trying new things." He tried a smile, hoping it didn't look as strained as it felt. "In a few years you'll come back from college, and we'll laugh about this."

And maybe something could happen then. When she was more than three months away from prom dresses and senior skip days. When her eyes didn't gleam with a wholesome sort of hero worship when she looked at him that made him feel like he could never live up to who she thought he was. When there wasn't so much pressure and he didn't have to be quite so terri-fied of breaking her perfect, innocent heart.

Hurt worked across her face—and Mac tried to think of

something to stem it. "Trust me. When you're older this will be funny."

"He practically laughed at me. He said it was *funny*."

"Can I kill him?"

Magda paused, mid-pace, startled out of her agitation by Kendall's casual offer of violence. "Would you?" Then she shook her head almost immediately. "Except I don't want him dead. I just want—"

"For him to realize he's madly in love with you and come stand in front of your window with a boom box?" Charlotte suggested.

Magda's best friends had come over as soon as she'd called them both in a panic. They hadn't known about her plan to profess her feelings to Mac and propose both a personal and business partnership. She hadn't told anyone. Perhaps someone else would have been able to tell her what a train wreck this was going to be, but she'd been so blinded by her own feelings, so blinded by certainty, that she hadn't even thought to consult with anyone else.

"He isn't going to show up with a boom box." He had made his feelings—or lack thereof—brutally clear. "Who even has a boom box? I just want him to be sorry." She pivoted and started pacing again. "I just want him to look at me and realize I'm *not* a child and he's made a huge mistake and—" Okay, yes, she also wanted him to realize he was madly in love with her. But she'd take the huge mistake part to start.

She was just so *angry* at him.

Sure, she'd been hurt to start—when he'd called her a kid and dismissed all of her contributions as her being a 'good listener,' all with that expression that was somewhere between patronizing indulgence and horror—but after running out of the Cup so fast she'd left her grandmother's supposedly man-catching cake behind, anger had kicked in.

Magda had always been petite, but she wasn't a *child*. And she may not have dated much, but she knew what flirting was.

She wasn't wrong, damn it. There had been something there. But he was so busy judging her for her age that he refused to see it. And even if she was wrong, even if this thing between them wasn't a thing, she had good ideas.

She was the one who'd come up with half of the promotional ideas—more than half! She was the one who'd mapped out a plan for expansion. When he'd just had vague ideas and big dreams, she'd broken them into realistic steps. Action plans. She'd contributed, damn it!

It felt like he'd just invalidated everything she thought she knew about the last two months. All that confidence that had been building. All that certainty.

"You could always pull a Sabrina," Charlotte suggested, plucking a thin envelope from L'Ecole Lenôtre off her desk and waving it. "Run away to Paris, hone your awesomeness, and then rub his nose in your goddessness when you return."

Magda dismissed the suggestion with a wave of her hand. "I haven't even opened it. It's probably a rejection."

The slim letter had arrived two days ago. When she'd first seen it, a sharp, excited sort of terror had jabbed into her gut. Only Charlotte, Kendall, and her aunt Lena even knew that she had applied to the notoriously cutthroat French pastry academy.

Two days ago, she hadn't wanted to know whether she'd gotten in or not—because she hadn't wanted to leave Mac. She'd been so certain that all the pieces of her life had already fallen into place. She'd known exactly what she wanted.

And she'd somehow completely missed that he didn't want it too.

How could she have been so *wrong*? How had she so completely misread the signals?

She'd seen her entire life stretched out in front of her—happily-ever-after in Pine Hollow, with cakes and coffee and a guy who had a propensity to sing show tunes as he drove. Now she couldn't imagine staying here. She'd gotten into college, but that didn't seem far enough away. She wanted to *show him* that she wasn't a child—not do exactly what he thought a girl her age should be doing.

"Open it," she suddenly declared, whirling toward Charlotte.

"What?"

She didn't speak French. She'd never been out of the country. She'd taken only *one* proper baking class, and this was a freaking *world-famous* pastry academy. She hadn't really planned to go when she applied. She'd mostly done it to please her teacher at King Arthur, who had written her a glowing recommendation, gushing about her talent. It had been so nice to have someone gushing about her talent. To have someone *see* something in her. But the idea of enrolling in a notoriously grueling program where bakers regularly had nervous breakdowns didn't sound like the kind of environment where Magda would excel. She'd never really considered it.

Mac would think she couldn't do it. He thought she was a child.

Magda strode over to Charlotte. "If I got in, I'm going." She wouldn't let anything stop her.

Charlotte's eyes widened. "Seriously?"

"Open it."

Kendall was smiling—but then Kendall loved risk and adventure. Magda was the one who always played it safe. Maybe a little too safe. The invisible Miller girl. Maybe it was time for her to be more.

Charlotte opened the letter. "Oh, thank God, it's in English," she muttered—and then her eyes widened, a huge grin slowly spreading across her face. "Holy shit. Magda."

Magda didn't need to ask what it said.

She was going to France.

Chapter Twelve

"Can we talk about your feud with Magda? How did it start?" Julia's tone was mild and inquiring, but Mac felt that internal screw tightening, the way it always did when someone asked that question. He hated that question. But he disguised the tightness with a lazy, unbothered smile. "Oh, you know how it is. She's a dog person; I'm a cat person. We were doomed from the start."

If Julia was annoyed by his evasion, it didn't show as she studied him with a slight smile, her stylus tapping idly against her ever-present tablet. "All right. What's your cat's name?"

Mac blinked, thrown by her easy acceptance. Wasn't she supposed to dig into all his emotional baggage? Wasn't that what these confessional sessions were for? In addition to recapping exactly what he'd felt at every single moment of the last bake, of course.

But they'd already done that bit.

It was day four—or week three, as the producers kept reminding him to call it when he was being interviewed, since this would be the third episode. After the marathon croissant challenge on Tuesday when Magda had sabotaged him, Mac had barely survived the Elimination Challenge yesterday with his chip-a-tooth éclairs—though one of the older gents from

Florida hadn't been as lucky. Roy had gone home with admirable dignity—which was really all Mac had to say about him since he'd barely met the man.

Today was a light day. There'd been only the one bake—a Skills Challenge making some crazy German cake called baumkuchen, which Mac would definitely have flubbed if he hadn't been at a station behind Magda's. He'd shamelessly copied her—and managed to come out solidly in the middle of the pack.

The winners and losers of the third episode would be chosen after tomorrow's Mystery Challenge—which meant more time for interviews today. Lucky him.

"You really want to know my cat's name?" he challenged. "That's what the home viewer is dying to know about me?"

Julia shrugged. "You never know what's going to be useful in the edit."

It was a perfectly reasonable answer, but it bugged him and he shifted in the uncomfortable director's chair. "It's all about getting that soundbite, huh?"

"Sometimes," she admitted. "Sometimes a question is just about starting a conversation. Putting a subject at ease with a comfortable topic. Though that hasn't really been a problem with you. You've been comfortable in front of the cameras since day one. Very sure of who you are."

"Don't know how to be anyone else."

Julia nodded with a slight smile. "Makes my job easier."

"Oh yeah? How's that?"

"It's my job to introduce you to America. To make them fall in love with you and root for you—or against you, if they fall in love with Magda first. You'd be amazed how much of that depends on the edit. What we keep in, what we leave out. The audience loves conflict—but also honesty. Emotional truth. Vulnerability. The best way to win them over is to be real. So if you're sitting here bullshitting me about your feud, there's no point pursuing that. At least if you're talking about your cat, you're being real."

He could do vulnerable. He was emotionally evolved. He'd been to therapy. Though he'd never talked about Magda with his therapist. And opening up about their past just felt *wrong* somehow. Especially on camera.

He folded his arms. "You're so sure it was bullshit?"

"Did her dog eat your cat?"

"No." He was pretty sure Cupcake didn't realize she was bigger than the tabby. "She's scared of him."

"Then I somehow doubt Magda being a dog person is the origin of your feud. Unless you hate all dogs."

He lifted both hands in surrender. "Hey, I don't hate dogs. I'm not a monster."

Julia nodded. "But you're a cat person. Why's that?"

All of a sudden it felt like a weirdly personal question. "I don't know. Cats are...independent. They know who they are. My cat lives his life, and I live mine. Dogs are needy. Desperate."

"And you don't like needy."

"Needy is too much responsibility."

Julia's eyebrows arched. "And yet you own your own business. That's a lot of responsibility."

He shrugged. "That's different."

"How so?"

"I don't know. I just sort of fell into it." The Cup had always felt more like an evolution than a choice. He'd opened it when he'd moved home after his grandfather got sick and then the rest had just sort of... happened. Like most of his life. Mac searched his thoughts, trying to put into words something that always felt so self-evident he'd never needed to explain it. "I'm not letting anyone else down. If I succeed or fail, it's all on me. And that's how I like it."

"Is that why you're single?"

"What?" That had come out of left field. "Of course not." *Shit. Was it?* "No."

Julia's question had been casual, not at all confrontational, but he still felt defensive as she clarified, "But you don't like being needed."

"I—" He broke off, frowning. "I didn't mean it like that. I'm not an asshole. I'm there for my friends. For my family. I have good relationships." But it was always on his terms. And he heard the defensive note in his voice.

"Didn't mean to imply otherwise," Julia assured him. "So, what's this cat's name?"

"I just call him Cat."

Julia smiled suddenly. "You have a cat named Cat."

"Far as I know. He didn't tell me otherwise."

"Like *Breakfast at Tiffany's*?"

He shrugged. "It's a good movie. But it wasn't because of Audrey Hepburn or anything. He just wandered in one day and made himself at home. I started calling him that, and it stuck."

Julia nodded. "So you're a cat person—aloof, craves independence—and Magda is a dog person—needy, craves connection—"

His vague sense of unease suddenly sharpened. "I didn't say that. I never said she was needy."

"Is she?"

The question was innocuous. Mild. And Mac glowered. "I'm not going to talk shit about her. You're never going to get that soundbite."

This feud between them... it was complicated. But he wasn't going to let *anyone* insult Magda.

If Julia was taken aback by his vehemence, it didn't show. "Right." She studied him, her head cocked, a slight smile on her face. As if she saw more than he wanted her to see.

"She's a great baker," Mac said firmly. "A great person. We're just oil and water. We don't mix. We never have."

Julia's eyebrows slid upward skeptically. "Never?"

That single word was so heavily loaded, Mac felt that screw in his chest twisting uncomfortably tight again. "Why? What did she tell you?"

"Let's talk about you and Mac."

Magda groaned. "Do we have to? I'm trying my hardest to pretend he isn't here."

He'd survived yesterday—so she told herself she didn't have to feel guilty anymore. It had been a near thing—his éclairs had been overcooked to granite hardness, and he'd landed in the bottom three, but a complete disaster from Roy had saved him.

Today, Mac had been behind her, so it had been easy to pretend he wasn't there—she could even convince herself she couldn't hear his voice, charming the camera with his self-deprecating mispronunciation of baumkuchen. She'd put her head down, let her old habits take over, and her baumkuchen had been beautiful.

It had been a good bake, and she'd very easily avoided Mac when they broke for lunch while the crew took glamour shots of their baumkuchen all lined up in a row.

She could have apologized to him then. If she'd really wanted to, there had been plenty of chances, but her apologies so often turned into new fights that she'd decided avoidance was the better part of valor.

Avoid and ignore, that was her new motto.

After lunch, the judging had been meticulous, but the judges had raved about the "obvious technique" evident in her cake and she'd landed in the top two—second only to Tim, who had barely edged her out. Mac had actually placed fourth, between Abby and Leah—which had shocked her because she didn't think he'd ever made the challenging German cake before.

Then it was interview time, and she'd hoped they could just talk about the good run she was on, about finding her stride, but Julia had hit her with a different question as soon as she sat down. It was always about Mac.

"Is that why you sabotaged him?" Julia asked, the question surprisingly gentle.

Magda really wished they could stop talking about that. "I'm not proud of that."

Julia cocked her head—a gesture Magda was coming to recognize as her *tell me more* encouragement. "Then why did you pick him? Really."

They'd already been over this, and Julia hadn't asked her to rephrase her answer in a camera friendly *I'm not proud of sabotaging Mac during the second challenge*, so there was an illusion that they were just talking. An illusion she had no intention of being drawn in by. "He's a great baker. Maybe I was just going after my biggest competition."

"He hasn't come in first," Julia pointed out.

"Wait until we get to breads."

"You could have gone after Leah. Or Abby. They've both been steadily in the top."

Magda scoffed. "I'm not going to go after my friends." She knew she was supposed to be mercenary and "not there to make friends," but she *liked* the red team.

"So Mac isn't a friend."

No. Mac was a lot of things. But a friend definitely wasn't one of them.

"What's the feud about, Magda?" Julia pressed. "We had our researchers dig into it, asking around Pine Hollow, and they couldn't find a thing. Just that you two have been at each other's throats for over a decade, and no one knows why. It's impressive, actually. I'd almost think it was fake—I'm pretty sure a couple of our rivals have exaggerated their animosity for the show, but not you two. So what is it? Love gone sour? Family thing? Business dispute?"

All of the above.

But Magda didn't admit that out loud. "What's he told you?"

Julia smiled. "No more than you have. Yet. But one of you is going to get to control the narrative. Don't you want it to be you?"

"Any luck?"

Julia collapsed onto the couch beside Greg, groaning. A bunch of the producers were all housed in a rental property a short walk from the inn, and Greg had been calmly reviewing footage on his tablet, flagging the most promising snippets to be used in the preliminary edit, when Julia flung herself down next to him.

"Total fail," she said morosely.

The interviews today had been less than fruitful—and then

she'd had the delight of being chewed out personally by Stephen because her pairs weren't talking to her. She'd been informed—in no uncertain terms—that her *job* was to make them talk and someone else could certainly do her job if she couldn't. She'd already pushed them more than she normally would today, saying things to see if she could get a reaction, which was never her style. And even that hadn't worked.

"Magda implied it was about a recipe. Mac said she snagged a prime location on the town square that she knew he'd had his eye on. There's obviously more there, but neither of them is talking."

"I almost envy you. I can't get Tim and Leah to *stop* talking about all their grievances. I can barely get them to talk about the bakes."

"Any advice?" This wasn't her wheelhouse. Being encouraging and coaxing out their honest reactions about their bakes was her thing.

Greg shrugged. "Keep at it. Be patient. Be their friend."

"How am I supposed to get Magda to open up to me when we broke her trust by lying to her on day one? And Mac—he seems like he's this easygoing I'll-tell-anyone-anything kind of guy, but then the second you mention her he clams up."

"Definitely something there."

"I *know*," Julia snapped. And she was sure she could have gotten them to talk about it with time, but with Stephen threatening her job, she felt like she was being bullied into pushing them too fast. Which was only making them defensive. "I don't think I'm going to get there with trust, so I made it about control. I told both of them that someone is going to get to control the narrative and they should want it to be them, but that only got me the he-stole-my-recipe, she-stole-my-spot stuff.

Neither of them wants to be vulnerable in front of me or tell me anything real."

"Or it might not be you," Greg suggested. "It might be the cameras. The home viewer. All their friends and family. Have you tried off camera? Just talking to them?"

Julia shook her head. "Not about the feud. Stephen would murder me if they started opening up and I didn't have it on film."

Greg shrugged. "Maybe see if you can get them talking when it's not in the confessionals. Or better yet—put them in a room together when they think they aren't being filmed."

Julia didn't move, but she felt her insides shifting away from Greg at the words. "Isn't that sort of dishonest?" *And morally gross...*

"They signed the contracts."

"Yeah, but... I don't want to trick them."

"It's not a trick. It's just part of the job."

"Yeah, but *Cake-Off* is fluffy. It's as sweet as the treats they make. It's not supposed to be about digging into people's pasts and making them talk about things they don't want to talk about." It was why she'd wanted this job. This show. Because it was lovely and positive. A force for good in the world of reality television—where those things could be very hit or miss.

"That was before. Stephen's *Cake-Off* is about drama. And if you won't get it, someone else will."

"Right," Julia whispered, something inside her deflating.

"We have those promo shoots tomorrow," Greg said, referencing the photo shoot that would take up the morning before the Elimination Challenge.

The publicity team had declared the cast photos from day one virtually unusable. Shockingly, taking photos of the bakers when they were traumatized by their first bake hadn't been as good as their hopeful eager smiles beforehand typically were. The publicity team was getting ready to do a big press release announcing the show's new twist, and they wanted shots of pairs of rivals glaring at each other over mixers and threatening each other with whisks.

"You could have a PA wandering around getting behind-the-scenes footage and see if you can get them to talk," Greg suggested.

"Yeah, I guess," Julia mumbled. It was a good idea, but she didn't feel good about it.

She'd always loved her job before this season. She'd felt good about what they were making and what she was doing to make it happen. Yes, there were times when people fell apart, when an ice cream cake melted or a soufflé collapsed, but when the contestants broke down, it wasn't because the producers were trying to drive them to the brink. It was just because they cared so much, because this experience meant so much to them, and it *was* stressful to bake to a timer on national television. The show didn't *need* all this. It hadn't been failing—and yet here they were, being told to fix something that wasn't broken, and cross their contestants' emotional boundaries to do it.

And the difference showed on the bakers' faces.

Magda, in particular, seemed different. More guarded than she had been before the rivals arrived. Not that she'd ever been as open or comfortable as Mac. She'd always been reserved, a little shy and awkward in all of her early audition tapes. Julia had figured Magda would need a little coaching to bring her out of her shell, but she'd always been so sweet and smiling.

Now she just looked miserable. Which made Julia feel like absolute garbage.

Everyone was tense now. Defensive. And Julia was caught between needing to keep her job so she could at least attempt to protect her bakers and needing to get her bakers to talk about things they clearly didn't want to talk about in order to keep that job.

She didn't know what to do. But tomorrow was the photo shoot. She'd have Mac and Magda in a room together. Maybe a miracle would occur.

Chapter Thirteen

Magda's plan to avoid and ignore Mac had hit a bit of a snag.

"Great, that's great, now threaten him with the spatula."

Magda obediently raised the spatula, but since she'd never threatened anyone with a spatula and she was still trying her hardest to pretend Mac wasn't there, she wasn't sure it had the desired effect.

And sure enough, the next words from one of the publicity folks running the photo shoot were, "Magda, darling, do you think you could look more, er, menacing?"

"How's she supposed to do that?" another random PR person muttered. "She's half his size."

The photographer then called for someone to get an apple box, and there was a great deal of shuffling before someone appeared with a crate that Magda was apparently supposed to stand on in order to menace Mac more effectively with a silicone spatula.

There were probably only a dozen people in the room, but it felt like hundreds of eyes were focused on her. The photographer; his handful of assistants; the publicity people; her usual producer, Julia—who was hanging back and observing—and an intern who was rushing around with a cellphone catching behind-the-scenes content for the show's social media pages.

"Maybe a knife?" someone suggested, and Magda had to resist the sudden and inappropriate urge to laugh.

"Mac!" the publicist shouted. "No smiling! Look angry!"

Magda's eyes flicked up to his face then, just in time to see him suppressing a smile. Her breath hitched inappropriately. Damn the man and his too-charming smile. He looked entirely too good in his *Cake-Off* apron with his ridiculously muscular arms crossed over his chest, his dark brown eyes glinting in the lights.

"Sorry," he said, "but if she gets a knife, I want one too."

It was obviously a joke, but two minutes later they were both holding butcher knives.

"Let's try back-to-back," the publicist coached. "And remember you despise each other!"

Magda did her best to look pissed off—but her stomach was churning with a welter of confusing emotions, and she'd always been a terrible actress. And judging by the expressions on the faces of everyone watching, she still was.

She felt Mac's shoulder blades pressing against hers while they were positioned in front of a *Cake-Off* Archrivals Edition logo—her standing on a crate to bring her within three inches of his height—but she could almost pretend he was a stranger. Almost pretend she wasn't excruciatingly aware of his every muscle. He was just another *Cake-Off* baker doing just another promotional shoot.

Until he spoke.

"I'm sorry," he said, so low that only she could hear him, as the photo crew were all frowning over the shots they'd already gotten and debating how to salvage them. "About not telling you they were going to ambush you."

Her neck muscles tightened as her heart shifted strangely in her chest. "I'm sorry, too," she whispered. "For sabotaging you."

"Are we even now?" he asked softly.

"Even," she confirmed, just as soft. And her breath went short again as she held herself perfectly still. As if by moving too much she would shatter this fragile peace.

After a moment, while the publicists mumbled among themselves, his voice came again, "Do you think we could have a truce while we're here?"

Before she could answer, the head publicist raised her voice. "Okay, let's try facing each other again. We're going to have you on opposite sides of a counter, leaning toward each other like you want to jump across the counter and throttle each other. Okay? Lots of energy! Lots of anger!"

Magda avoided looking directly at Mac, but she was keenly aware of him as she was hustled to a new mark. Once they were suitably posed—and the publicist was fussing about exactly how *much* baking paraphernalia should be on the counter between them—Magda met Mac's eyes and replied sotto voce, "I just want to focus on the competition. That's all I've ever wanted."

His relief covered his face—but he didn't get yelled at because the mixer was apparently a problem, and the publicists were all distracted. "Great. So truce? I won't target you; you don't target me?"

"Yeah," Magda agreed softly, as the PR folks were finally satisfied and bellowed, "Show me the feud!"

Magda leaned across the counter, glowering her best fake glower as Mac fake-glowered right back.

His rich brown eyes held hers, something almost warm in them. "Sometimes I don't even know why we're feuding anymore."

Wait. What? Suddenly Magda's glare got a lot less fake. "You're kidding."

"That's it, Magda!" the publicist cheered.

"You know what I mean," he said. "It's been a long time."

"So I'm just supposed to forgive you? Is that it? The statute of limitations on my anger has run out?"

His eyes darkened. "I wasn't aware *I* was the one who needed to be forgiven. At least not the only one."

Familiar frustration surged through her. "You didn't have the deposit for the spot on the square, and I did—if I hadn't taken it, someone else would have."

A muscle ticked in his jaw.

"Good, Mac!" the publicist encouraged. "Get angry!"

"You did it to get back at me," he snapped.

"My bakery isn't about you!"

"You so sure about that?"

Magda fumed. "It's not like it's the only storefront in Pine Hollow. Pick another one!"

"I plan to. Right after I win the *Cake-Off*, I'm going to buy a big place right next to yours. See how you like that."

"Do we need them to stop talking?" A tentative voice.

"No, it looks like they're yelling. It's perfect."

"You'd have to win *Cake-Off* first," Magda reminded him. "And I don't think your wing-it method is going to fool them for long."

Something entirely too smug entered his eyes. "It worked yesterday."

Yesterday. The Skills Challenge. The baumkuchen and his fourth place...

Magda studied his face. He'd been right behind her station... and suddenly she just *knew*. She wasn't sure how, but a jolt of clarity had her eyes flaring. "You cheated! You copied me."

He shrugged. "Nothing in the rules says I can't look at you."

His eyes held hers, and she realized they were both leaning so far across the table that only inches separated them. The apple box had brought her up to his height, and it was heady stuff. She could feel her heart beating hard, the way it always did when he provoked her.

"It's a *skills* challenge. *Your* skills."

"I maintain there's skill in knowing who to watch. You should be flattered."

"And you should be eliminated," she snapped. God, it was so unfair. "I studied for this. I trained for this. And you just waltz in here and think you can take whatever you want. Without a second to think about who you're taking it from." He'd beaten Leah. There was no way he could have done that on his own. "That is so like you. It's my grandmother's cake all over again. I guess once a thief..."

Anger flared in his eyes. "I didn't steal anything—"

"So you just *magically* knew the secret ingredient?"

"You actually mad because I took something, cupcake? Or because I didn't take what you were *really* offering?"

Her hand was flying before she could even process what she was doing.

She didn't even realize she *wanted* to hit him until after her hand had flown halfway across the space between them. She stopped herself, inches from his face—but he caught her wrist before she could retract it, leaving them frozen in a tableau that must have looked like...

Oh God. It looked like she'd tried to slap him and he'd grabbed her wrist to stop her.

Magda heard the gasps from everyone in the room and couldn't move as horror flashed through her, along with the confusing tangle of *everything* that only Mac inspired.

She'd never struck another human being in her life. She hadn't believed she had it in her. She was a pacifist. Violence was *never* the answer.

And yes, she hadn't actually hit him, but it had been a near thing. And it must look…God, it must look so bad. The cameras…

"I'm sorry," she said immediately—but Mac just stared. She wasn't sure which one of them was more surprised by what she'd nearly done.

Her heart galloping, she could feel the imprint of each of his fingers on her wrist. His hand was so much bigger than hers, wrapping all the way around her arm, his thumb shifting softly against her pulse point. Magda's breath hitched.

"Did you get it?" the publicist asked, almost wetting herself with joy—though Magda was hoping they wouldn't be able to use her near-assault on another contestant in the promotional shots.

Oh God, what had she done?

Still holding his gaze, she tugged on her wrist, and Mac released her as if he'd burned his hand on her skin. Magda leaned back abruptly, no longer wanting to play at their feud for the cameras—and suddenly Julia was there.

"You guys okay?"

They had a zero tolerance policy for violence. She'd almost hit another contestant. From most angles it must have looked like she didn't stop herself—like Mac did. If he wanted her gone…

Was she about to be ejected from the show? "Julia, I—"

"Did it look real?"

She and Julia both turned to Mac. "What?" Julia asked.

"We knew you wanted big feud energy. We agreed to a little

tussle. How'd it look?" Mac said—lying for her. Why was he lying for her? It would be so easy for him to send her home.

"Looked great," Julia said immediately, playing along—though Magda had a feeling she hadn't been fooled for a second. "Very realistic." Her gaze tracked back and forth between Mac and Magda. "You guys good to keep going?"

"Golden," Mac said.

Julia turned to Magda.

"Yeah. Good," she stammered, still feeling like she wasn't quite inhabiting her body as Julia moved away and the shoot resumed.

What the hell had just happened?

Magda didn't break rules. She didn't make waves. And she *certainly* didn't hit people. Or even *consider* it.

She'd lost her mind. He'd referenced that idiotic time when she was eighteen and she'd felt so horribly exposed. All those eyes watching them. All those people knowing her great shame. That she had once stupidly thrown herself at Mackenzie Newton and he had laughed in her face.

A sick, curdling thought moved through her. "Have you told them?" she whispered. "About that summer?"

He shook his head, small enough that she only noticed it because she was staring at him fixedly. "I shouldn't have said that."

"I shouldn't have . . ." She didn't even know what to call it.

"You didn't."

She met his eyes. "That isn't me. I don't . . ."

"I know. We bring out the worst in each other," he said. There was something tight about his expression. Cautious. "We still good with a truce?"

Magda agreed with a nod, and then decided perhaps it was

best they didn't talk. They followed directions from the publicists for a few more minutes, then the shoot was finally over. Magda gathered up her things quickly, she and Mac heading out opposite doors. There was still a bake this afternoon, and they needed to focus.

And she needed to get her heart to stop beating so fast. What had she been thinking?

She was almost out of the room when she overheard two of the production assistants.

"I didn't know if she was going to kiss him or hit him—but if you'd asked me, I would have put money on it going the other way."

"They've definitely banged. Or, if they haven't, they absolutely need to."

Magda flushed, ducking out of the room. At least if they were speculating on that they must not have heard Mac. But she still felt like she'd just been stripped naked in front of a room full of people.

And now she had to go bake.

Chapter Fourteen

"Four your Cake Week Elimination Challenge, we have a little twist," Jeffrey Flanders announced as they all stood obediently at their stations, waiting to see what the producers were going to throw at them next.

Mac knew he should be focusing on the words coming out of Flanders's mouth, but he was distracted.

Between the interview last night—which had left him feeling weirdly introspective about whether he'd been subconsciously avoiding serious relationships for the last decade in some kind of self-defense mechanism to keep from letting people down—and then the minefield of a photo shoot he'd just been through with Magda—where they'd managed to trigger several of the mines—his head was in a weird place as he stood waiting for the next challenge.

This was supposed to be a baking show, not an unearth-all-your-baggage show.

Alexander Clay picked up the spiel. "For today's challenge, you'll be baking us a wedding cake—which I realize sounds simple, but we are expecting three tiers of absolute *perfection*—and you won't be doing it alone. You'll be paired off, and each team will present a single three-tiered masterpiece for judging. Which means, yes, you will be judged together. And yes," he paused dramatically, "this is a double elimination."

A gasp rippled through the room, and Mac's distraction evaporated as his heart started to beat harder.

They wouldn't.

They couldn't make them work with their rivals, because not everyone had a rival left. Walter's and Taylor's had gone home. It wouldn't be fair.

Not that the producers seemed to care much about fair this season.

But still.

It would be random, he assured himself. They would draw spatulas or something. Whenever the *Cake-Off* paired contestants off, it was always the hand of fate—and fate would not be so cruel. It wouldn't be Magda. Not immediately after that nightmare of a photo shoot.

Judge Joanie spoke next. "Tim, as the winner of the Skills Challenge—though you did just edge Magda out by a hair— you have won an advantage in this round. Which means not only do you get to choose who you will be partnered with, you will actually have the privilege of choosing *all* the teams."

A glimmer of hope.

Mac and Tim had met up for beers in the inn's common area the other night, bonding over both being sabotaged. The high-end hotel pastry chef from California was *extremely* confident he was going to win, but Mac couldn't really blame him for that confidence based on how he'd been baking so far. Mac was just hoping that his own bond with Tim was enough to get him a good partner.

Mac saw Magda and Leah exchanging looks of dread. The two of them were definitely the most likely to be sabotaged by being paired with the struggling bakers—Leah as his ex and Magda because she'd sabotaged him during week two.

Mac felt a little bad for Magda as Tim was ushered to the front of the room to stand beside the judges to announce his picks. He didn't want her to go home. She'd looked even more rattled by the almost-slap at the photo shoot than he'd been.

Though he didn't know why he cared so much.

Guilt, probably. It had been a low blow, throwing her old crush back in her face like that. They'd both been so careful never to reference it in all the years they'd been feuding, and then today it had just fallen out of his mouth.

What was it about Magda that made him the worst version of himself?

It probably hadn't helped that he'd gotten about two hours of sleep total last night. He'd had the weirdest series of dreams about all of the women he'd dated shaking him awake and demanding he make them cake to show that he cared, but he didn't have any flour.

Not exactly subtle with the symbolism there, his subconscious.

He'd never really worried about his relationship status. He liked dating—when he made the time for it, which wasn't often. He worked too much—not because he felt he had to, but because he loved the Cup. He loved his life. He spent time with his grandmother—the lovable martinet—and had regular poker nights with his friends. He'd been recruited into a band a couple of years ago, with a couple of retired rockers from the local senior community, and they performed a couple of times a month.

His life was good, and when he'd wanted female companionship, he had been able to pop down to New York to see Cleo. No muss, no fuss.

Except Cleo was married now. And the poker nights could

be irregular—with all of his friends starting to have little kids. And his grandmother had started hinting that he needed to settle down—which he always reacted to by telling her lots of people were perfectly happy without being tied down.

But Julia's perfectly innocuous question about why he stayed single had kept him awake last night, distracting him when he should have been charging up for the competition.

He knew he had weird hang-ups about responsibility. He'd been raised by his grandparents because his parents hadn't wanted to take responsibility for him. They'd been teenagers—but his mom had made the choice to hand him off to his grandparents, and his biological father had never been in the picture, even though the whole town had known who he was.

Mac made a point never to let anyone see how much that bothered him. He cultivated a carefree attitude that made him a town favorite even before he opened the Cup. Easygoing Mac. Fun Mac.

He'd done the therapy thing when he was younger. He knew how to process his feelings. How to talk about them. How to control the things he could and let the rest go.

Don't want things you can't have—like a normal relationship with your biological parents or the college degree you left behind when your grandfather got sick. Be flexible. Be adaptable. Don't dwell on regrets. When something ends, it isn't your fault; it just wasn't meant to be. No harm, no foul.

But it had become a pattern.

He hadn't set out to avoid commitments, but he did like being on his own. He'd gotten spoiled by his freedom. He could do whatever he wanted—like be there for his friends and family when they needed him. Because he wasn't obligated to anyone. He didn't owe them anything.

What he hadn't realized was why he was doing it, pulling back whenever they started to get too serious. Applying too much pressure. Starting to become someone who expected something of him. Someone he might let down. Or who might let him down...

Shit. He needed to focus. Tim was speaking now. He'd already picked Abby—who had won week one and come in third on yesterday's Skills Challenge—to be his own partner. It made sense. She was one of the strongest bakers in the kitchen.

He announced Leah would be paired with Walter. The older man with his multitude of bowties had definitely been struggling, barely making it through Pastry Week.

Mac felt a flicker of relief when he recognized Tim's strategy. He was matching the best bakers with the worst bakers, to give himself the best chance of winning. Smart.

But Mac could work with anyone—and as someone who had been generally in the middle, he'd probably be paired with another generally middle baker, which with all the best bakers other than Tim and Abby at a disadvantage, might actually give him a chance of placing near the top.

Then Tim gave a smug little smile, his gaze landing on Magda. "For the next pair, I've chosen Magda to be partnered..."

Tim really was good at the dramatic pauses. He might be an arrogant sonofabitch, but he knew how to work the cameras.

"With Mac."

Aw, *hell.*

Of course he picked Mac.

Magda had walked into the kitchen determined to put the morning behind her. To forget that she'd *lost her freaking mind* and nearly slapped Mac in a room full of people. She was here to bake. After that first day's catastrophe, she'd actually found something of a comfort level in the kitchen. Pastry Week had settled her nerves, and she'd very nearly won yesterday's baumkuchen challenge.

She could do this. She was braced for any catastrophe.

Or so she thought.

Until the producers threw yet another twist at her.

She should have known this was coming. She'd certainly suspected how this would play out as soon as Tim had been called up to pick the teams, looking entirely too smugly pleased with himself. Especially since the producers looked particularly smug, too—and Julia looked like she might be sick.

Mac seemed surprised as he came to stand beside her—maybe he'd thought Tim was his friend, but Tim was the prototype for "not here to make friends." He'd paired up all the remaining rivals who seemed the most rattled by their nemeses—Eunice and Zain, Josh and his dad, Mac and Magda.

It was good strategy. Some detached part of Magda's brain could acknowledge that.

Actually, all of her felt strangely detached at the moment. Maybe this was how it ended. A double elimination. Both she and Mac going out in a blaze of ignominy. Maybe that was for the best. Maybe she wasn't cut out for this show. It certainly wasn't helping her grow as a person—as all the former contestants always raved. Part of her was almost relieved. She just wanted out of this mess.

Tim finished picking the teams and joined Abby, so they were all paired off. Six stations. Twelve bakers. Set dressers rushed around making sure the excess stations that had been set up to fake them out were cleared.

And then Jeffrey Flanders was speaking at the front of the

room, an unnerving gleam in his eyes. "Now. You will have ten minutes to plan and three hours to complete your exquisite three-tiered wedding cakes, but we have one last surprise."

He held up what looked like strips of dangling black cloth. Magda frowned, trying to figure out what the heck the surprise was. Were they going to be blindfolded? Have their hands tied behind their backs? *What?*

Then Jeffrey beamed—not in a nice way—and she realized it was some kind of Velcro harness as he announced, "You and your partner will be quite literally *attached at the hip.*"

Magda closed her eyes. Of course they would. "Shoot me now."

Chapter Fifteen

She and Mac didn't speak as the PAs strapped them into their
Velcro harness thingies.

Technically they were barred from speaking because they
weren't supposed to plan their bake until the official planning
time began, but Magda wouldn't have known what to say even if
they could have spoken.

The harnesses were less involved than they'd looked dangling from Jeffrey Flanders's hands. It was a padded belt around
her waist, attached to one around Mac's by a *very* short bungee,
and a padded cuff around her left wrist and his right attached by
another, thinner bungee. They could move about two feet away
from each other before one of those bungees yanked them back.

"Well, this'll be fun," Magda muttered darkly—and one of
the PAs shushed her before scurrying out of the shot. On the
plus side, she'd gotten over her brief this-is-where-it-ends mood.
She would *not* let this beat her. But that meant working with
Mac—and they had definitely proven this morning that this
was a bad idea.

"All right, bakers, now that you're all suited up...your
ten minutes of planning time starts...*now!*" Jeffrey Flanders
announced.

Magda turned to face the man she'd been handcuffed to.
She'd made a million cakes, and several dozen of those had been

128

wedding cakes. She was *amazing* at cakes—when she didn't glaze them too soon. This was her chance to redeem herself. All she had to do was convince him to hand her ingredients and stay out of her way.

"So..."

"Obvious choice, right?" Mac said before she could suggest he be her personal assistant for the afternoon. "The maple cake."

Her jaw dropped incredulously. "Did you seriously just suggest that we make the secret family recipe *you stole from me*?"

He groaned, casting a glance up at the ceiling as if asking for divine intervention. "I didn't steal it, Magda. I just make a similar cake. But it's one we both know, it's unique, and it's delicious."

"We both know it because *you stole it*."

"I've never even seen the recipe. How am I supposed to have stolen it?"

She planted her hands on her hips. "I don't know. I just know that I made it for you, and when I got back from France three years later, it was a freaking *staple* on your menu at the Cup. People were raving about it, and it tasted *exactly like mine*."

"I thought it was a good idea to have *a* maple cake—"

"My maple cake! And *my* idea! I was the one who suggested—"

"Is this still about that goddamn business plan?"

"You took all my ideas!"

"You gave them to me!"

"And you laughed me out of the building—only to turn around and use every idea in that binder."

"It was a Trapper Keeper. You were a *kid*."

"And that makes it okay to steal my ideas?"

"I didn't steal—" He broke off on a growl of frustration. "I'm *sorry*, okay? I didn't take you seriously, and maybe after you left I looked through the binder, and there was some good stuff in there, but it was all stuff we'd talked about *together*. You're making it sound like it was all you. Like I needed to beg your forgiveness for growing my business. It was *why* I enrolled in that baking class. Because I *wanted* to add cakes and muffins—"

"But I was a part of it, we planned it together and you just dismissed me—"

"What do you want me to do? It was almost fourteen years ago. You left, and when you came back you barely *spoke* to me for ten years. I just said I was sorry. I don't even know what I'm supposed to apologize for anymore."

"You don't *know*?"

"You were just a kid—"

"This isn't about that!"

A buzzer went off at the front of the room—reminding them both where they were, and that there was a camera crew eagerly catching every word.

"All right, bakers! That's the end of your planning time! Your three hours of baking time starts...*now*!"

Magda stared at Mac, her heart pumping hard and her brain still fizzing uselessly. They had a bake to complete. "Maple cake?"

Mac nodded, suddenly all business. "Maple cake."

The bake could have gone very, *very* badly. They could have been bickering and yanking each other off-balance and shouting recriminations at each other—there was certainly plenty of that going on around the kitchen. Eunice's partner berated her to the point of tears. Josh and his father spent more time arguing than baking. The camera crews were actually struggling to keep up with all the drama.

But somehow, miraculously, as soon as the timer started and they both kicked into competition mode, Mac and Magda worked together like a well-oiled machine.

Magda had trained at her fancy high-pressure French pastry academy, and Mac had worked countless rushes in his kitchen at the Cup, so they both knew how to buckle down and get the work done—and how to be aware of other chefs in their space. It was a little different, being physically tied together, but being handcuffed to Magda actually wasn't as limiting as he'd worried it might be. He was excruciatingly aware of her every move, but they were both very careful not to brush against each other.

After the timer started, the only conversation they shared was about the cake. When she corrected his technique, he listened, because he would never have her level of expertise. When he suggested adding a touch of bourbon to the icing—since it could sometimes be too sweet-on-sweet-on-sweet—she studied him for a long moment, and then nodded, ceding to his touch with flavors.

When the layers had cooled and it was time to ice and decorate, he knew the best thing he could do was make sure she had whatever she needed and stay out of her way. He'd seen the wedding cakes she'd made, and he knew he couldn't compete with her for decoration. Or for speed. He watched her deftly spin the cakes, smoothing the icing with a long, flat palette knife, and then take up the buttercream bag and begin creating a waterfall of flowers—all while he soaked candied orange peel in bourbon maple syrup.

Magda used tweezers to place the candied peel as the clock

ticked down and Flanders called out the numbers like it was New Year's Eve.

Magda and Mac threw up their hands when Flanders called, "Time!"

Their wrists were still held together by the short bungee—and Mac felt a surge of relief that they'd managed it, they'd actually worked together and created something that looked pretty damn close to perfection, while around the room other bakers were swearing.

The surge of end-of-challenge endorphins must have clouded his brain, because he didn't even realize he'd pulled Magda into a relieved hug until he felt her soft body stiffen slightly.

"Good job," he said gruffly, dropping his arms.

"You too." Magda didn't meet his eyes as she pulled away, her face flushed. She turned to face their cake instead.

Three tiers. Maple cake with bourbon buttercream, exquisite buttercream roses, and candied orange peel accents. He already knew it would be heaven. He didn't even need to look around the room to know they had a definite shot at winning this one.

Which was surreal.

That had actually felt...*good*. They'd been good together. He hadn't hummed show tunes or made jokes to the camera—they'd both been totally, brutally focused. And intensely aware of each other's every move. He knew her every breath. Her rhythms. Unbidden, the analogy popped into his head that working together like this was like sex. Really good sex, where they were both fully focused on each other's movements, so in sync and working, straining, toward the shared goal of pleasure.

Fuuuck.

This was Magda. They brought out the worst in each other. Didn't they?

Mac looked over at Magda, his mood feeling off-kilter and his heart beating strangely. Was it possible they actually made a good team? What might happen if they just let go of the past and stopped trying to hate each other so hard?

He'd come here hoping that a side effect of the competition might be burying the hatchet between them, but this felt... different.

The feud was complicated. It had always been this strange, living thing that felt like it was more than the sum of its parts. It hadn't been just about them for years. The whole town had gotten involved. But now he realized it was also something else. A kind of connection. An unbreakable link.

Then the PAs were there, literally unlinking them from each other, and Magda was moving away from him as quickly as possible, her face flushed. They were ushered toward the Proving Room so the cameras could get shots of all the bakes, and Magda went straight to Leah, Eunice, and Josh, making sure her friends were okay. Asking how their bakes had gone. She didn't look back at him.

Mac trailed behind, pausing at the Proving Room door to look back at all the workstations. At their three-tiered maple cake.

He hadn't stolen it. But maybe they could finally settle this. And then...

Then who knew what would happen?

"Hey. Can I talk to you for a second?"

Magda had been in a huddle with her friends in the Proving Room, but she looked up when she saw Mac standing over her. Though she'd known he was there. The last three hours seemed to have attuned her senses to every move he made.

It had been...strange. Working with him. Not horrible. Just odd. For three hours they'd actually communicated without snarling at each other, and now...She didn't know what was different about his expression, but for once it didn't make her want to snarl.

"Yeah, okay," she murmured.

She stood and followed him to the other side of the Proving Room, perfectly aware that the cameras around the room would catch their entire conversation—and hopefully that would keep her from going off the rails. She was tired of fighting with him.

"What's up?" she asked when they were as alone as they were going to get.

"I have a proposition for you," he said, blushing slightly when she raised her eyebrows. "Not like that. Think of it as a side bet. A way to finally put the past behind us."

Magda studied his face, but she saw no sign of trickery. "I'm listening."

"We wipe the slate clean. I stop giving you shit about taking my location. You stop accusing me of stealing your recipe. And whoever gets the farthest in the competition gets to keep the maple cake on their menu."

Magda didn't bother to hide her skepticism. "You want me to stop making *my* family's recipe?"

"You think you can't beat me?" he challenged. "Don't get me wrong. I want to win. But we both know you're better than I am when you aren't panicking and sabotaging yourself."

She frowned, looking for the catch. "Why would you offer this if you didn't think you were going to win?"

"Maybe I'm sick of the feud."

"I thought we had a truce."

"We still wouldn't sabotage each other," he clarified. "This would just be between us. Anyone who doesn't fight fair forfeits the cake."

"You would actually stop making the maple cake?"

"I would," he promised. "Look, Mags, I really didn't steal it. I adapted a recipe my grandmother had. But I am offering this as an olive branch. Olive cake. Whatever."

She looked to their left, eyeing the cameras in the corner, designed to catch all the Proving Room conversations. "We're being recorded right now. I have proof."

"You don't trust me?"

"Should I?"

If she didn't know any better, she'd think he was hurt by that. But she'd long ago learned she didn't have the power to hurt Mackenzie Newton.

"Deal?" he asked, holding out his hand.

It was *her* cake, and one of her most popular items at the bakery. She was risking never being able to make it again if he outlasted her. But the truth was, she was tired of the feud, too. She was tired of clinging to her anger where he was concerned.

"Yeah, okay. Deal." She slid her hand into his, shoving down the strange feeling of rightness as his larger fingers wrapped around hers. This was still Mac. He still didn't want her like that. But maybe, just maybe, they didn't have to hate each other anymore.

Chapter Sixteen

The judges adored the maple cake.

Magda stood at the front of the kitchen beside Mac as they presented it, and Joanie raved about the flavor and texture. The bourbon had been a "stroke of genius" and the bake was "just perfection." Alexander Clay narrowed his eyes and declared that the decoration might perhaps be a bit *too* simple, but even he seemed to be stretching to find fault, and he acknowledged it was elegant.

Magda and Mac nodded and thanked the judges before carrying their cake back to their station, their shoulders brushing as they stood and waited through the rest of the judging. That was one thing that felt the most different about being in the show versus watching it at home—how *long* the judging took.

The timed bakes took exactly as long as the judges laid out on camera. It was all the rest of it that meant long days and late nights.

She'd learned in the last week about "turnaround"—a rule mandating rest for the cast and crew. If she was dropped at the house at eight p.m., they weren't allowed to pick her up the next day until eight a.m.—and since there were sometimes sixteen-hour days, that meant the call times slid later as they moved later in the week—and this was why some episodes could be filmed all in one day while others needed to be broken up over two.

It was strange how quickly she'd acclimated to the routine. This was normal now. Waking up. Being shuttled from hair and makeup to the Proving Room—only to be plucked out of there for interviews and dropped back in when it was time for challenges.

After a challenge the bakers would be herded back into the Proving Room, where the waiting would begin. Crew members would be frantically cleaning the disastrous workstations—Mac's always seemed to be the most disastrous—and taking glamour shots of the bakes, while the bakers were pulled aside to postmortem the bake in confessionals. That process could easily take over an hour. Then it was back into the kitchen for judging.

On the show, it always looked like judging was just a matter of seconds—quick bites, quick quips, and a quick retreat to their workstations—but each tasting lasted at least ten minutes, often longer—which meant hours of sampling and critiquing. Then back to the Proving Room again as the judges deliberated—and the bakers were pulled aside to talk about how they felt judging had gone. That could take another hour. Then back into the kitchen for the results. Another hour as the best bakes were praised and the worst bakes reminded of their flaws—all while the bakers stood lined up in a row.

No wonder former contestants had all recommended good shoes and a cardio regimen as the best way to prep for the show. It was exhausting. And Julia had been right. Magda did feel like she spent more time in that director's chair talking about the challenges than she did actually baking in them. Though that may have had something to do with the strange way time seemed to move in the kitchen. She would blink and an hour would have passed, so focused was she on what she was doing.

It had been that way in the challenge with Mac. They'd

clicked into a kind of zone that she'd never shared with another person before. That flow, when everything just *worked*.

It was especially surreal that she'd shared it with *Mac*.

As they waited for the results, Julia tried to get them to talk about what it was like, working together, and this time Magda wasn't being evasive. She just didn't have the words to describe it.

Mac sat beside her, in a director's chair of his own, and seemed equally at a loss. "It just...worked," he said.

"Yeah, we, um..."

"Made a good team?" Julia prompted when Magda trailed off.

But neither Mac nor Magda obediently repeated the phrase for the cameras. It was still too strange.

"It came out well," Magda said finally.

Julia nodded, changing tacks. "So this maple cake—where did that recipe come from?"

Magda felt Mac stiffen where their shoulders touched. "It's a modified version of my grandmother's secret recipe, which I made for Mac once, years ago, and he liked it so well he put his own version of it on his menu." That was the sanitized version of the story. The one she was willing to tell America.

Mac cleared his throat. "So we both have practice baking something similar."

Julia nodded, glancing briefly down at her tablet. "Shall we talk about the altercation during your photo shoot?"

"That's not going to be in the show, is it?" Magda asked in a rush.

"Like we said, it was totally staged," Mac added.

"Of course," Julia agreed. "But we did get footage of it on the behind-the-scenes camera, and it seems like the kind of thing Stephen might want to include in the edit, so I'll need footage of you two talking about it. Telling us the motivation behind it as if it's totally real. We can do it now or later one-on-one."

"Now's fine," Mac said, as Magda simultaneously said, "Later."

Magda flushed, stammering, "Or now."

"Okay." But before Julia could ask anything, she put a hand to her ear and frowned. "But unfortunately we need you back in the kitchen for results."

Mac and Magda stood, shuffling awkwardly in the tight space until they were back in the Proving Room—and then quickly ushered into the kitchen and lined up behind their station.

"Why did you say now?" Magda whispered as they waited for the other teams to take their marks.

"Easier to keep our stories straight if we're together," Mac mumbled back.

"Right." Except Magda was a terrible liar. It was going to show on her face. She needed time to prepare, mentally. To psych herself up. "So what do we say? Do you think they heard what we were talking about?"

"We weren't wired then," Mac reminded her—but he touched the lavalier mic tucked beneath his apron as he said it—reminding her that they were definitely wired now.

"Right." She snapped her mouth shut, her brain still circling the almost-slap and wondering what explanation she could possibly give for it, as the judges came in and lined up at the front.

That was one of the things that had surprised her about the show too—how little contact they had with the host and judges. They literally never appeared until they were ready to film. In order to avoid favoritism, the contestants were forbidden from speaking to them unless it was about the bakes—and caught on camera. They still seemed like intimidating strangers. Though perhaps that was on purpose. Everything about this show seemed designed to put her on edge. Frankly, it was exhausting.

Thankfully they were about to have two whole days to catch up on sleep, since crew regulations and the contract with King Arthur meant they couldn't film on weekends.

Joanie was speaking.

Crap. They must be rolling already. Magda was so exhausted after the emotional roller coaster of the day, she just hoped her face looked some semblance of engaged and not as wiped out as she felt.

"...winners this week gave us elegance and refinement, with a luscious rich flavor. They bickered so much we weren't sure they were going to have a cake to present, but then worked so seamlessly together as a team, that we actually wondered whether they were rivals at all. I'm delighted to announce that the winners this week..." Dramatic pause. "Are..." Yet another dramatic pause. "Mac and Magda!"

Magda's jaw fell as Mac let out a whoop.

Okay, yes, their feedback had been good and she loved that cake, but she hadn't actually considered that she might *win* an episode of *Cake-Off*. Winning the Skills Challenge was one thing, but to *win* an entire episode...

With Mac.

She'd won with Mac.

That might be the most surreal part of all.

He was jostling her in a side-hug, his arms around her shoulders. And she numbly raised her hand to pat his biceps—the movement so awkward the cameras must be catching it, but her brain was still stuttering over *winning* a freaking episode of *Cake-Off*.

Mac was laughing—and a camera was right there, catching every nuance of shock on her face.

What the *hell* had happened today? They'd started the morning with a truce. Then she'd nearly hit him. Then he'd covered for her. Then they'd been literally *tied* to each other and fought about the maple cake on camera—which she'd sort of forgotten until this moment—and then the bake, when she'd been maddeningly aware of his body beside hers, but the cake...it had been poetry. Everything had just *clicked*. And ever since she'd felt dazed and off and now they'd *won*?

But would they have won without his bourbon suggestion? It had made the bake better, adding a depth of flavor while perfectly cutting the sweetness.

She'd only won because of him.

Mac kept one arm slung around her shoulders as they faced front again—and Magda just stood there woodenly.

This was what she'd been afraid of, before she came—that she would freeze up and be the boring contestant that no one rooted for—but she'd almost forgotten her *don't be yourself* mantra. The second Mac had walked into the *Cake-Off* kitchen, all of that had fallen to the side.

People were going to love him. He was gregarious and effusive. And hot. Anyone looking for eye candy would go wild for his freaking dark eyes and auburn curls. Not to mention the wicked Lucifer dimples. And the *arms*—which she was sure the cameras were going to *love* during bread week. But he was also the kind of guy that dudes could see themselves grabbing a beer with.

The home audience was going to side with him, she realized numbly. Take his side in the feud. She didn't know why she hadn't seen it before.

But she couldn't do what Julia wanted. She couldn't confide all and get the home viewer on her side—because the whole truth was embarrassing and pathetic. That she'd fallen for him at eighteen and he'd treated her like she was nothing and she'd been fighting to prove she wasn't nothing ever since.

She'd just *won* a freaking episode of *Cake-Off*. This wasn't how that was supposed to feel. It was supposed to be validation. It was supposed to be victory.

And she felt like nothing again.

Just don't be yourself.

Too late for that now.

Chapter Seventeen

"Did you really punch Mac in the face on camera?"

Magda groaned as Leah sat down across from her with those words. "Where did you hear that?"

"From two different PAs. It's the hot rumor on set," Leah explained as she opened a bottle of wine.

"I heard it too," Eunice added—and Magda cringed.

"I didn't punch him," she clarified. "I might have *almost* slapped him, but it was all for the show. We staged it for the photo shoot."

Leah snorted her disbelief, and even sweet, bubbly Eunice looked skeptical.

The remaining Red Team cohort had congregated in the inn's breakfast room with a couple of bottles of wine that Leah had somehow managed to procure—though it was a smaller group since Walter had declared himself too exhausted to grab a drink, and Abby was off trying to get the *Cake-Off* producers to let her call her family again. She'd been able to wrangle supervised calls a few times already, but being separated from her kids was proving harder on her than she'd anticipated.

Beyond them, Magda, Eunice, and Leah were all that was left of the Red Team, after Josh's tearful exit this evening when he and his dad fell victim to the double elimination, but Leah had insisted they had to celebrate Magda's win and the three of them making it through the first week of filming—or week three, as it was becoming bizarrely natural to think of it.

Before they'd been released for the day, Jeffrey Flanders had announced the week four theme in the most vague and confusing way possible—calling it a "World Series of Pies"—but other than their designated practice times in the inn's kitchen, the weekend was their own.

Though the same rules applied. No phones. No internet. No recipe books. No leaving the inn.

It did limit what they were able to do quite a bit—but it didn't stop them from celebrating, small though their celebration may be. They could have invited the Blue Team bakers to join them, but there was still too much animosity between the two groups.

It was a strange season. They would forever be linked to those Blue Team bakers, sharing this bizarre experience, but Magda felt like a line had been drawn between the two teams that couldn't be crossed.

The Blue Team didn't seem to have bonded the same way the Red Team had. They were much more "every man for himself." But Magda was incredibly grateful for Eunice and Leah. Having someone to go through this crazy experience with was invaluable.

Even when they were watching her with expressions that screamed they didn't believe a word she'd just said.

"I believe you almost hit him," Leah said. "I just don't believe it was all for show. Even if you did plan it."

"Are people really talking about it?" Magda wanted to crawl under the table. As if sensing her distress, the inn's terrier, Ethan Allen, padded over to her and hopped onto her lap. She immediately sank her fingers into his wiry fur for some puppy therapy.

"If it makes you feel any better, you weren't the only ones who lost it," Leah said. "Apparently Abby and Cherise got in a screaming fight at their photo shoot, during which Abby called Cherise a spoiled brat who'd always had everything handed to her, and Cherise called Abby a judgmental bitch who couldn't stand anyone who had made different life choices than she did." She lifted her wine glass in a mock toast. "Good times."

Magda grimaced. That did not, in fact, make her feel any better. "How were your rival shoots?"

"I didn't cry," Eunice said, as if that was an achievement in itself.

"And I didn't stab Tim in the throat with a paring knife. We're all winners here."

"I can't picture you with Tim." Magda took a sip of her wine, still feeling far from celebratory.

"Can you believe I used to find his confidence sexy? He was always a dick, but he was so good at what he did, and he never doubted himself or whether he belonged in the best kitchens. Somehow, being with him felt like that extended to me. Like I belonged more, too." Leah grimaced. "Welcome to my emotional baggage."

"He'll go home soon," Magda promised—though it was more hope than confidence. Tim and Abby had been the other team in the top today.

"I'm just glad Walter and I squeaked through. Poor Josh."

"Poor Josh," Eunice and Magda echoed, all of them raising their glasses and taking a sip.

"Stephen really is a gargantuan asshat. And Tim—but we knew that already."

"Were you okay today?" Magda asked Eunice. "Your bake looked pretty contentious."

Eunice groaned. "I wish it didn't bother me. I tell myself his opinion doesn't matter, but it's like I can't do anything right, and then I hear my parents saying I should go back to school for accounting and do something practical. That this is a nice hobby, but it's time to be responsible because there's no way I can win."

Magda took Eunice's hand. "And here I thought I was going to be the shy one who needed to believe in herself."

"Shy?" Leah asked incredulously. "With the way you and Mac glare lasers at each other? No one was going to believe that."

"What's the deal with you two?" Eunice asked.

"No deal," Magda evaded. "We've just never gotten along."

Leah arched an eyebrow. "Is that what you're trying to sell the cameras? Because it isn't very convincing."

"She's right," Eunice agreed.

"We've told you ours," Leah coaxed.

She wasn't wrong. Her friends had been so open with her. Magda didn't want to lie to them, but...

"It's embarrassing."

"The reason you hit him?"

"*Almost* hit him." Magda blushed, but took a fortifying sip of white wine and forced herself to admit. "A million years ago, we both took a baking class at King Arthur."

Leah *oooh*ed eagerly, settling in for the story.

"I had a huge crush on him—and I got it in my head that it was reciprocated, even though I was barely eighteen and he was twenty-four and owned his own business. I actually thought he wanted me as his business partner—in addition to his romantic partner."

Both of her friends winced sympathetically. She hadn't told this story in a long time—not since it happened. And then only

Kendall and Charlotte had known. But she forced herself to keep going.

"At the end of the summer, I wrote up this whole business plan and made him a special cake that all the women in my family make for the man they love—"

"Uh-oh."

"Yeah. He laughed me out of the building." He'd been so repulsed by her. Horrified by the very idea. "So I ran away to Paris and enrolled in a pastry academy. Best thing I ever did. I learned everything I could, staying in Europe and taking more courses. It was three years before I came back—and I'd probably seen *Sabrina* too many times, but I really thought he would take one look at my posh Parisian-trained self and beg me to be his pastry chef—after which he would naturally realize what a fool he'd been and fall madly in love with me while we were making pain au chocolat. And I would reject him, of course," she insisted, because she *wanted* this next part to be true. "I didn't want him anymore. I simply wanted him to fall at my feet, showering me with apologies until I ultimately decided whether he was good enough for me."

"Of course," Leah agreed. "But?"

"But instead, I came home to find that Mac had used my business plan to expand his business—to the letter. And he was selling my grandmother's famous maple cake in his café."

Leah winced. "Damn."

"He kept insisting he had no idea what I was talking about, but he'd obviously stolen my family recipe on the same night he rejected me."

"Dick move."

"Total dick move," Magda agreed. "I'm standing there with my resume like an idiot—and he tells me he can't afford to hire anyone because he's getting ready to move to a prime location that's opening up on the square. He just needed to get his deposit together."

Leah nodded, already seeing where this was going. "And you snagged it."

"Oh no," Eunice moaned. "I wanted you to open a place there together—"

"Yeah. This is not that story. I may have wanted him to beg me to be his pastry chef, but my aunt and I had been talking about opening a little French bakery in Pine Hollow for years—and it really was a prime location. It's not my fault he didn't have the deposit and I did." She shrugged. "The feud sort of snowballed from there. He refused to be on a town committee because I was on it, and the word got out that we hated each other. It became a whole thing. People in town took sides—for a while, it was almost a game."

"But then why did you try to smack him today?" Eunice asked.

Magda flushed, embarrassed all over again. "We never talk about why we're feuding—people in town make a game of guessing, but no one really knows, except my best friends. I didn't think it even meant enough to Mac for him to talk about it, you know? But now the producers keep asking us how it started and telling us one of us is going to get to control the narrative, and I keep saying he stole a family recipe—and I think he's been telling them I stole his spot on the square—but then today, when we were at that photo shoot, he referenced the night he rejected me. In front of twenty people and cameras and . . . all of a sudden I was eighteen and begging him to want me, and he was laughing at me again. I've never even *thought* about slapping someone before. I don't know what came over me. And then I panicked.

Even though I didn't actually hit him, do you know how easy it would be for them to make it look like I did? Or for him to say the only reason I didn't was because he stopped me? He could have gotten me kicked off the show. But instead he said it was planned. It was staged. And I don't know why. I don't know… Do I owe him now? Is that what this is?"

"Maybe he wants to make amends," Eunice suggested softly.

"He did suggest a truce, but how do I trust that? We've been at each other's throats for fourteen years. How do I trust that this isn't some tactic?"

"You don't," Leah said firmly. "This show is not about amends. Not this season."

"But it could be," Eunice argued.

"People don't change," Leah insisted. "They just reveal who they are."

"Yeah, but it was a long time ago. What if he regrets it, but he doesn't know how to change the pattern you've fallen into?" Eunice said. "You guys obviously worked well together today. We all tasted that cake. It was insane—" Her eyes flared. "Wait, was that *the* cake?"

At Magda's nod, Eunice groaned. "I should hate him for that, shouldn't I? For stealing your cake? But I just want everyone to live happily ever after."

"Again, sweetie, this is not that season," Leah said.

"Why not?" Eunice demanded. "I would love to change the way I am with Zain. I don't think he's actually a bad person. And I thought maybe since he *knew* I was coming on this show, he had to want that pattern to change, too. At least on some level?"

"You're too nice," Leah said. "Tim came on this show to prove he's better than me and fuck with my head."

"So why did Mac come?" Eunice asked.

"I don't know," Magda admitted. A week ago she would have said it was some kind of revenge, but if he'd wanted to take her dream away, he'd had the perfect chance this afternoon. So why *was* he here?

Was it just to win? To beat her? To claim ownership of the maple cake?

Or could it be something else?

And did she want it to be?

She couldn't open herself up to being hurt by him again. When it came to Mackenzie Newton, her walls were sky-high and fortified. But was there something else there?

Today had been good. At least when they were baking together. Those three hours had felt...

No. He'd said they brought out the worst in each other, and he wasn't wrong. That wasn't going to change. She just needed to ignore him and maintain the truce and focus on the show. This surreal reality they were all trapped in now.

"Forget about them," she said, raising her glass. "To the top ten."

Eunice and Leah clinked their glasses against hers. "To the top *three*," Leah corrected.

Magda smiled, trying to absorb some of her confidence.

She would reset her equilibrium. She would focus on her bakes. And hopefully Mac would be knocked out soon.

But somehow that thought wasn't as comforting as she'd hoped it would be.

Chapter Eighteen

The weekend was strange. They'd all been corralled into the inn, and there were a handful of production assistants and lower-level producers watching them to make sure none of them broke the rules or made a run for it, but after the nonstop rush of the week, it felt odd to suddenly have nothing but time. Too much time to think. Too much time to dwell on all the twisted-up emotional shit the last week had dislodged.

Mac was relieved when it was time for his designated practice time in the kitchen—finally something to *do*.

He heard pans clattering inside before he opened the door, the inn's cat slinking in around his ankles.

"Almost done! Sorry!" a voice called out from around the corner near the ovens—and of course it would be her. Of course the producers would have scheduled them back-to-back.

"It's fine. No rush," he called back—and there was a sudden eerie silence from the back.

Magda appeared a moment later. "Hey." After a long pause, she frowned. "I don't know what to say to you when we aren't fighting."

He released a startled laugh. "Yeah. Me neither." He nodded to the clean countertop—Magda was a clean-as-you-go baker and her workstation was always eerily spotless. "If I get set up over there, will I be in your way?"

"No. And I'm almost finished. Two more minutes."

"You're fine," he assured her, turning to start his own pie prep as she retreated to the ovens.

It smelled downright amazing in here—all apples and cinnamon—but he wasn't sure whether he was supposed to say that or pretend he didn't know what she was baking. He finally settled for "Smells good."

She glanced over her shoulder, frowning as if she wasn't sure whether she should believe him, and mumbled, "Thanks."

He turned to his prep.

They hadn't been given many hints—all they knew was that pie week was next and they each got three hours in the kitchen to prepare. He'd decided to practice a few savory and a few sweet versions, just so he'd have options on the day.

Mac quickly inventoried the ingredients he'd requested, marveling, not for the first time, at the grocery bill this show must have. The cat continued to explore the kitchen as Magda opened the oven, checking on her pies.

Another waft of decadent smells hit him, and Mac closed his eyes as he inhaled deeply. So he never saw the first domino fall.

His first hint that anything was wrong was a startled canine yelp, followed by a feline hiss.

Mac hadn't realized the inn's dog was also in the kitchen, curled up on a small dog bed near Magda's feet. He'd never seen the two inn pets in the same room at the same time, but he'd assumed they must get along if they both lived there.

How wrong he was.

The terrier let loose a stream of snarling barks and the cat hissed again before bolting—straight through Magda's legs, pursued by the barking dog.

It probably would have been fine—if Magda hadn't been standing in front of an open oven with both hands full of piping-hot pie.

"Magda!" He'd never moved so fast in his life.

Mac crossed the distance as she yelped and pitched toward the oven. He caught her around the waist and yanked her back against his chest. The pie went flying from her hands, but all he cared about was that neither of them got burned as it splatted dramatically onto the floor.

For a long moment, he just stood there, his heart banging like a drum and hands still braced on her stomach. She was breathing quickly, too, leaning slightly back against him—and suddenly he wasn't sure if he wanted to push her away or pull her closer. Vanilla and cinnamon. It wasn't just the pie. Her hair curled below his nose, and he inhaled.

Her breath caught.

"You okay?" he rumbled, his voice like gravel.

"Yeah." Magda shifted away from him, avoiding looking at him as he released her and she shut the oven door. "Thanks," she murmured.

She knelt next to the pie debris, and he crouched beside her to help. They both reached for the pie tin, their hands brushing and she glanced at him quickly.

"You don't have to," she said, still not meeting his eyes. "I don't want to eat into your practice time."

"I have plenty of time," he assured her. Awkwardness crackled in the air between them, but he didn't want to walk away. He didn't know where the cat and dog had gotten to—they must have managed to swing the door open.

"Mac. I've got it."

He pulled his hands back but didn't stand, eyeing the pie goo on the floor. "You didn't get to test it properly. If you want to stay and make another—"

"No, I'll be out of your hair in a second. Please."

He stood then, forcing himself to turn back to the counter because she wanted him to. He began to throw together a crust, trying to ignore the sound of her behind him. At some point, the dog came back into the kitchen and began licking the apples off the floor.

He wished he knew what to say to her, but all he had was this insane *awareness* of her. When he finally glanced over at her, she was gathering up her things. "Good luck," she said softly before disappearing through the door.

Look at them.

That had almost been civil.

The rest of the weekend was murderously dull. Mac spent far too much time in the inn's tiny gym, just to tire himself out enough to be able to sleep—and to quiet his brain. He'd started thinking about his grandfather. About Magda. About regrets and responsibilities. Thoughts he was usually good at avoiding.

He was intensely relieved when Monday morning rolled around and the craziness resumed at the crack of dawn.

He hadn't seen Magda again for the rest of the weekend, and he glanced around for her automatically as he was ushered into the Proving Room.

Tim and Leah were bickering. Eunice was sitting close to Cherise and murmuring something encouraging. Mac kept to himself as he took a seat, which wasn't his habit outside of the competition—he was sociable by nature, but there was always a tension between the bakers, and he didn't want to get in the middle of anyone else's feuds. Discretion definitely seemed to be the better part of valor.

He was aware of Magda in the space with him, but kept his eyes and his thoughts to himself until they were all ushered en masse into the kitchen for the first challenge.

The producers must have decided there wasn't enough animosity between the two teams, because they'd decided to pit them against one another. Red Team versus Blue Team, with Mac and Magda as captains since they'd won the previous challenge.

The front of the kitchen had been decorated like a baseball diamond—and Mac realized this episode must be airing in October. The *Cake-Off* loved a tie-in.

Apparently in the World Series of Pies, the bakers would compete head-to-head again. In each round, each team would put forward one baker who would present their pie. The judges would hold up either a red paddle or a blue paddle to indicate which baker won the match-up, and that team would take that "game" in a best-of-seven series.

The losing team would be pitted against one another in a speed bake, and one baker would be going home.

Mac and Magda, as team captains, decided who went in which round. And since there might be seven rounds, two bakers might have to compete twice.

It was all about strategy. Did you have your best bakers compete twice, or did you let them focus entirely on a single dish so there was more of a chance that they would win their round? Did you pit best against best? Or concede the point for their best player and try to take all the others?

Abby, Leah, and Magda were all strong, with Eunice and Walter being more erratic, while on the blue side, Mac was confident that he and Tim could score points, but less certain about the others. Did he and Tim each go twice? They only needed to win four rounds to win.

Always bet on yourself. That had always been his motto—and when he looked at Tim, he knew the pastry chef would have just as soon done every single round himself, so confident he could win them all.

Mac nodded to him. They had this.

Magda hated the pressure of being team leader, but Abby volunteered to bake two, and Magda actually had two recipes she'd been debating between, so she offered to do two as well—which Walter, Leah, and Eunice seemed relieved by.

Abby took the first round easily with her chocolate cream masterpiece, defeating her sister Cherise. Then it was Magda's turn with her caramel apple crumble—and she thought for sure Mac would pit himself against her, but he sent up Tim instead with a black currant and pepper pie. The judges praised both—but then unanimously voted for Tim's pie, telling Magda she was staying in her comfort zone too much. She retreated to her station with a queasy feeling in her stomach. And it just got worse.

Mac beat Leah in the next round. And Walter lost his to Eunice's culinary school rival, Zain, who gloated smugly. Three to one.

The Red Team couldn't afford another loss—and Magda found herself thinking ahead to the speed bake.

But then Eunice surprised everyone by beating Tim. Abby destroyed Taylor in round six, and it was tied.

Mac versus Magda. Because it always came down to that, didn't it?

Her silky chess pie might be in her comfort zone, but she'd been making it for years. Her family loved it. Surely the judges would, too.

Except they didn't.

"It just feels so derivative," Alexander Clay drawled. "Where are *you* in your bakes?"

"It's delicious, but a bit expected," Joanie agreed, with a pitying look—and Magda was suddenly certain she was going to lose.

Until Mac's judging.

His pastry was undercooked. The bottom was soggy. It had absorbed all the juice from his blueberry compote.

She didn't win. He lost.

Magda's team cheered, but she couldn't find much joy in their victory. Her stomach kept twisting as they all stood watching while Taylor was eliminated. "Expected" and "derivative" didn't win *Cake-Off.* It got voted off in week six, when the competition got serious.

Mac might have lost to her with the soggy pastry, but he'd redeemed himself in the Speed Bake and had the judges gushing about his flavors and creativity again. She could already see the arc they would give him. Most improved. Most creative.

While she was going to be the Skills Challenge winner who had no soul.

And she had the sudden, horrible feeling that she was going to lose their bet.

Chapter Nineteen

On Wednesday, *everything* went wrong.

Week five on the show was Tribute Week—which meant each bake was in honor of someone. Filming the episode started on Tuesday with a cherries jubilee Skills Challenge. Magda had performed well enough, but so did everyone else. Mac was actually ranked above her, and her nerves were shot going into the week five Elimination Challenge on Wednesday.

Cupcakes. The judges announced the challenge before they left the kitchen Tuesday night. A cupcake in honor of someone who had impacted their baking journey.

After the disaster of her underbaked cupcakes on week one, Magda *needed* to redeem herself, but all night she'd had nightmares about presenting underbaked goo, while the judges stood over her and called her flavors "expected" and "unoriginal." Alexander Clay's voice sneering, "derivative—where are *you* in your bakes" had haunted her.

She woke up Wednesday morning feeling off—and things had gone downhill from there.

Her lucky hair-tie had snapped when she was putting her hair up. A glittery stone had fallen off of her lucky "Not Here to Make Friends" apron when she put it on for her morning pep talk in the mirror. And then the van bringing her to set had gotten a flat tire—forcing them to send another van for her and making her late for hair and makeup.

They'd rushed her through, but the entire morning had been harried, and she was frazzled and anxious before she even walked into the *Cake-Off* kitchen to face the judges and their serious frowns.

The judges ran through the same instructions they'd been given the previous afternoon. A dozen perfect, identical cupcakes. Filled and iced. Unique. Perfectly baked. With something special to honor someone who had helped them on their baking journey.

"Wow us," Alexander Clay demanded.

Then they were off. And Magda felt a low buzz of panic, like a bee inside her mind.

Every contestant had a story—not just who their rival was, but who *they* were in the competition. Tim was the hotshot from the fancy hotel kitchen. Mac was the "unique flavors but slapdash technique" guy. Eunice was brilliant but inconsistent and insecure. Abby was the frontrunner. Walter was all flash, no flavor.

And Magda? Magda was "great technique but no personality."

The judges had started saying her flavors were "expected," and though her technique was always flawless, they just wanted *more* from her. They wanted her to *surprise* them. Which felt less like an indictment of her cooking and more like a criticism of her.

She wasn't creative enough. She wasn't *fun* enough.

Boring, invisible Magda. With her flawless, forgettable food.

Another anxiety bee joined the first that was already buzzing around her head.

After the cupcake debacle during week one, she was especially desperate to redeem herself. She'd planned to wow them with her technical expertise and classic flavors—she'd practiced a light-as-air angel food cupcake to honor her "angel" investor aunt—but now she was second-guessing everything.

Should she do something more exotic? Mac would make something surprising—but she couldn't compete with him for inventiveness. She needed to do what she did best—only she no longer knew what that was.

People raved about her vanilla cupcakes, but she couldn't do vanilla. Maybe pineapple? Was that unexpected enough? Mango?

She made up the batter, slower than normal, staring into it and wondering if she needed to add another flavor profile. Ginger? Turmeric? Something surprising? She had always focused on being deeply excellent at the classics—in Pine Hollow, her vanilla cake was *legendary*, but the judges weren't going to be satisfied with vanilla. They'd made that clear.

She filled the cupcake cups with mango batter and popped the cupcakes into the oven, setting the timer—and checking the temperature twice. A blast of heat had hit her when she opened it, so she knew it was on, and the numbers read 325. Perfect.

Then she started on her icings. Maybe she could go a little wild there. Passion fruit? Coconut? Or citrus was always good, right? Maybe yuzu?

There were still three minutes left on her timer when she smelled burning.

Magda glanced around. Was someone burning caramel? It was easy to do if you didn't pay attention to it. But no...she didn't see any blackened pots nearby.

She sniffed again, frowning.

And then she saw the smoke coming out of her oven.

"No! *No-no-no-no-no!*"

The camera crews zoomed in on her like distress-seeking missiles as she frantically grabbed for a hot pad and yanked open the oven.

A billow of smoke belched out, making her cough—and making a PA run over with a fire extinguisher.

"No!" Magda yelled, throwing out a hand to stop the over-zealous PA before they could lay down a layer of foam and make the oven unusable for the rest of the challenge. She lunged forward and grabbed her cupcake tin—nearly burning herself even through the hot pad.

She hissed, flinging the cupcake briquettes into the sink and turning the faucet on full blast—and when her back was turned, the PA went to town on the oven with the fire extinguisher.

"No!" Magda wailed.

A producer rushed over and powered down the oven—and Magda could only stand and stare.

"I don't know what happened. The oven said 325. I checked. It shouldn't have..."

"It's okay," Julia said, appearing at her side. "You can use another station."

But it wouldn't be preheated. It would take precious time to preheat, and the clock was ticking down. The cupcakes had to cool. They had to be filled. Iced. If they were too hot the icing would melt—a total repeat of her glaze debacle.

"It'll take too long to warm up," Magda said, feeling a hollow emptiness as it all began to slip away. This was an Elimination Challenge. Everyone had been close after the Skills Challenge. If she didn't have cupcakes to serve, she was going home.

On a challenge that was supposed to be honoring Aunt Lena. She had failed. She had let everyone down—

"Use mine."

Mac's voice seemed to echo in the sudden quiet that had taken over the kitchen as everyone stared at Magda's station with horror.

Magda turned to him, her eyes wide. "What?"

"My cupcakes come out in two minutes. Then it's all yours. Already preheated to 325."

Which meant her cupcakes could go in as soon as she could get the batter ready. Relief surged through her so fast she was almost dizzy.

"Thank you."

Magda had never made batter so fast in her life. She didn't think. She didn't worry about impressing the judges. All that mattered was having something to serve them.

So she went for angel food.

Classic. Boring.

And she flew.

The cupcakes went into Mac's oven and she whispered "Thank you" again as she rushed back to her own station to set the timer and salvage her neglected icings and fillings.

She'd never paired guava curd with an angel food cupcake before, but what the hell?

When her timer went off, she raced back to Mac's station and there they were—pale and perfect. Magda whispered a silent prayer of thanks to the cake gods, and then grabbed the muffin tin and rushed back to her station to frantically cool, fill, and ice them.

The clock was ticking down. Two minutes. Not enough time.

A serving plate landed on her station.

Mac. He'd gotten her one from the pantry.

She said thank you without looking up—and quickly plated her cupcakes, finishing them in place.

"Ten...Nine...Eight..." Jeffrey Flanders's voice rang over the room as Magda's hands flew over the piping bag.

"Five...Four...Three..."

Oh God. Her heartbeat felt like thunder. Her hands were shaking so damn hard and the icing was starting to waver.

"Two...One...TIME!"

Magda threw up her hands.

And burst into tears.

They weren't delicate tears. They were gulping, hyperventilating sobs, and she couldn't make herself stop.

She'd held on to herself until time was called, but then everything she hadn't let herself truly feel for the last half hour had come crashing down on top of her all at once and she completely freaking lost it.

Arms closed around her, warm and comforting—she didn't even know whose. She couldn't breathe.

She knew there were cameras on her. She knew she was falling apart on national television right now over a freaking *cupcake* and there was *no way* this wasn't making it into the final edit. But she still couldn't get herself under control. Magda never lost control. Mac was the only person who ever made her lose her cool—but this wasn't Mac. This was everything else.

This was how badly she'd wanted this experience to be something *other* than what it was. This was all the frustration and aggravation of the last ten days. This was all the pressure of trying to make her town and her family and her friends proud. This was how badly she wanted to be seen and admired. How badly she wanted to be *special*. And how much she felt like she was just being told over and over again by different people and in different ways that she wasn't. That she never would be. That no matter what she did, she would never be able to escape the basic boring invisible thing that was *her*.

That her loneliness, her not-enoughness was her fault. All the freaking fear. All the longing. All the *hope* she had put into this experience. That it would change things. That it would change her.

All that shattered hope.

And *she* had shattered.

The stakes felt ridiculously high—and even *knowing* they weren't didn't help her breathe.

"It's okay. We've got you," a deep voice murmured—and Magda latched on to that voice.

It was Mac. She was tucked against his chest. Sheltered. Safe. She could fall apart here, and his arms would hold the pieces together. Mac had her.

One of his large hands rubbed a circle on the small of her back. *You're all right*, that hand said. *I'm here.*

But then she felt other hands on her shoulders, and the "we" managed to penetrate the panic. She lifted her cheek from where it had pressed against his shirt.

"We" wasn't just Mac. It was Leah. And Walter. And Abby. And even Eunice—who was even shorter than Magda. All of them forming a human shield around her, protecting her from the cameras, and holding her at the center of their huddle.

And suddenly she wanted to cry for a whole new reason.

God, she loved these people.

Yes, she'd only known most of them for less than two weeks, but they were her freaking soulmates. They were her rocks. And she didn't know how she would have done this without them.

"Thank you," she whispered brokenly, when she could form

words, touching their hands gratefully and using her apron to wipe away her tears.

Mac was the first to drop his arms—as if he knew that she had a hard time managing her emotions when he was touching her. Leah lingered the longest, keeping her arm around Magda until the producers realized they weren't going to force her to move away and let them walk to the Proving Room arm-in-arm.

The cameras continued to circle Magda in the Proving Room, moths to the flame of her emotional collapse.

She kept waiting for Julia to appear, to drag her away for a confessional where she would probably burst into tears again, but when Julia finally did appear, she didn't pull Magda away, instead crouching in front of her.

She put her hand over Magda's, as if trying to ground her—and Magda had the strange sense that Julia really was on her side. Then she spoke.

"It was Celsius."

"What?"

"Your oven was set to Celsius. We don't know how it happened. The judges have been made aware of the situation and they will take that into account during judging."

Magda shook her head, uncomprehending. "How could that happen?"

"We aren't sure. It might have been a malfunction. We'll know to check all the ovens for that in the future—"

"325 Celsius...what is that? Six hundred degrees? Do the ovens even go that high?"

"Six hundred and seventeen. We're not sure it got that hot—"

"But it was enough to turn my cupcakes to charcoal."

"It was." Julia confirmed.

And Magda would have been eliminated. If not for Mac.

Again.

Her gaze went to him, across the room.

Why had he done that?

She couldn't make him out. He competed with her. He made her crazy. And he helped her, without hesitation. And then his arms, that feeling of protection. Of safety...

She'd worked so hard at hating him for the last decade, but now they were here, yanked out of their usual routine, and everything was different. *He* was different.

She didn't know who he was anymore. But she had the strongest feeling he was the man he'd always been. And she had no idea how to feel about him anymore.

Chapter Twenty

Mac was in the bottom three.

Helping Magda had distracted him and the judges had scolded him for his broken buttercream, but if he'd had to do it over again, he still would have offered up his oven without hesitation.

In the end, his flavors saved him. Walter went home, and Magda survived. She'd even been in the top three, her face still red during judging from the torrential tears.

He'd never seen her break like that. But who could blame her? This place. The pressure. He knew it was just cupcakes, but it felt like so much more, and he knew how badly she wanted to do well.

He hadn't been thinking—during the challenge or the immediate aftermath. He'd just been acting on instinct, but now his brain wouldn't settle. He was agitated when he got back to the inn. He ordered a room service burger, as had become his habit, and then took a shower to wind down and wash off the stress sweat of the day.

The Red Team had gotten into the habit of eating together in the inn's dining area, but Mac steered clear because the truce with Magda was a tentative one. The PAs often ordered from local restaurants and brought in food for all of them. He was well fed, but he missed cooking. He missed his kitchen.

He'd never baked so much in his life—and he did enjoy the test of the various challenges—but he missed those quiet mornings before his staff came in when it was just him in the Cup, figuring out what he wanted to do for specials, prepping sauces, trying out new combinations when no one was timing him or judging him, and no one even knew if a new recipe crashed and burned.

Those mornings centered him, and he was distinctly off-balance now.

He'd just stepped out of the shower when a knock came at the door—the PA with his burger, no doubt.

"Just a second!" he called out, yanking on pajama pants and a T-shirt so he wouldn't scandalize the poor kid, and padded barefoot to the door, rubbing at his wet hair with a towel draped around his neck.

He yanked open the door—

But it wasn't a PA.

Magda stood in the hallway in soft yoga pants and a long-sleeved T-shirt—one of those ones with thumb holes that she'd tugged down over her hands. Her black curls were wet and piled up on top of her head in a messy knot secured with a pencil. There was something determined, almost confrontational about her expression—but also something else that he couldn't quite identify.

"Hey," he said brilliantly. "Uh...did you want to come in?"

"I can't. Production rules." She frowned up at him, her bright blue eyes narrowed. "Why did you do it?"

"What?"

"You know what. You didn't have to help me."

"I know." She seemed almost angry, and he frowned. "You don't owe me anything, okay? It just wouldn't have been fair for you to go out like that."

"You would have done it for anyone," she said, something almost accusing in the words. Or insistent. As if she was forcing them to be true.

"Sure. Yeah."

She shook her head, glaring at him. "You almost got eliminated."

"Yeah, well. Horseshoes and reality television. Almost doesn't count."

"Was it so people would like you?" she demanded. "The guy who almost got eliminated because he's such a noble guy he gave up his oven to help another contestant no matter the cost."

He arched a brow. "I almost got eliminated because my buttercream was crap."

"And you're saying it would have been crap even if you weren't distracted helping me?" she challenged. "I don't think you're supposed to help other contestants outside of team challenges. It's a rule. You could have been eliminated—"

"They weren't going to eliminate me for sharing an oven—"

She went on as if he hadn't spoken. "You could have gotten rid of me. Taken ownership of the maple cake. Won the feud. Pride of Pine Hollow."

"That's not how I want to win." He met her pale, angry, confused eyes. "You would have done the same."

She shook her head—more baffled than disagreeing. "I can't figure you out. You hate me, but you won't act like it."

"I don't hate you, Magda. I never hated you. You just drive me crazy."

"I hate owing you. I hate feeling like you're—" She broke off, struggling for words. "Is it just for the cameras? You're playing the good guy so America will love you instead of me? So they'll side with you? You always were better at the people stuff."

Irritation flashed through him. "Are you seriously accusing me of helping you just to make myself look good after I saved your ass today?"

"Well, is that why you did it?"

"Maybe I didn't want you to go home!"

"That's not how this works," she snapped back. "We're competitors. We're supposed to be cutthroat. You're not supposed to be nice to me. The only thing that makes sense is that you're doing it to mess with my head or to make yourself look good—"

"Or because I'm not a complete asshole?"

"Then why have you been an asshole to me for the last fourteen years?" she shouted.

"I don't know!" he shouted back.

He was vaguely aware that they were yelling at each other in a hallway that was very far from private, but right now Magda had driven all logic and reality television self-preservation instincts from his brain.

"I don't know, Magda," he repeated. "I don't know why you make me insane and I lose all rational thought when I'm with you. I'm sorry about the cake, okay?" He hadn't stolen the damn thing, but he would apologize for anything right now just to *end this*.

"It wasn't about the cake!" she shouted—and he roared back.

"*Thank you!* Finally!" Finally she was admitting he hadn't stolen it.

"I was never mad because you stole from me," she said— ruining his moment of victory. "I was mad because you dismissed me. You treated me like I was nothing—"

"You were a child!"

"*Stop saying that!*" she yelled, taking a step forward, almost as if she wanted to take a swing at him again. "I had feelings. I had ideas. Yes, I was younger than you, but you treated me like I was a joke, and you *still* have not admitted that I helped you. All those car rides, talking about the Cup, how to expand it—so what if you didn't want me? So what if I embarrassed myself by throwing myself at you? You could have at least acknowledged that we were *friends*. Real friends. But instead you treated me like I was so far beneath you that the very *idea* of me contributing anything was laughable. I have always been invisible, but I thought you saw me—"

"Invisible?" he barked incredulously. "You are impossible to ignore. I wish I could. I wish I didn't notice you whenever you walk into a room. I wish you didn't suck up all my attention and focus and make me feel so goddamn irrational. I can't *think* when you're here!"

"Then why didn't you let me get eliminated?" Magda yelled.

"Because I don't want to be here without you!"

He shouted the words, and for a moment they hung in the air as they stared at each other, breathing hard, air crackling—

Then his hands were cupping her head, and he was kissing her like he needed her to keep breathing.

And she kissed him back.

After a startled beat, she softened with a groan and her hands gripped his T-shirt, dragging him closer. She'd gone on her tiptoes, but he still hunched over her to compensate for their height difference, his mouth devouring hers. His brain was gone. Evaporated. A flash of heat like a kitchen fire, and it had vaporized. All that was left was instinct and need, and *fuck* did he need her right now.

She made a small sound in her throat, and he chased that sound, backing her across the narrow hallway until she bumped into the wall and he pressed against her front. Her hands were in his hair now, her nails lightly scoring the back of his neck, and he released her lips at the sharp-sweet sensation, moving along her jaw to the curve of her neck, sucking the soft pale skin.

"Mac." His name was a sigh.

He ran his hands down her sides, cupping her hips in those insanely soft pants, and it was the most natural thing in the world for her to raise one leg, hooking it around his waist, and he stroked his hand down, catching her behind her knee, his brain completely consumed with the necessary calculations of lifting her up and pinning her against the wall with his body so they aligned just right—

A throat cleared.

Magda's soft body went suddenly rigid in his arms before the tentative voice spoke.

"I, uh, your burger, Mr. Newton?"

Fuck fucking room service.

Mac hissed out a curse under his breath and went motionless, his still cloudy brain now working on the complex calculation of how exactly to get out of this position in the least incriminating way possible.

He had just pinned Magda to a freaking *wall* in a hallway that was possibly bugged and most definitely public.

Shiiiit.

He released her knee, and she dropped her foot to the floor. He looked down at her, his body still curled protectively over hers, but she was staring at the floor, her face incandescently red in the low light of the hallway.

Mac turned, still using his body to block Magda from the PA's view as much as possible—as if they didn't all know exactly who she was and exactly how much the young man had seen.

"Thanks," Mac said, as casually as if he was caught groping a fellow competitor in the hallway all the time. He reached for the burger tray, accepting it, and then giving the twenty-something PA a very pointed look that meant his work here was done.

But the PA didn't take the hint. Instead he fidgeted, looking incredibly uncomfortable, but as if he absolutely had to say something. "Um...so...fraternizing is..."

"I was just leaving."

Magda slipped out from behind him before he could put out a hand to stop her—not that he would have, but his entire body was protesting the sudden absence of her warmth behind him.

"Good night," she said, either to the PA or him, it was hard to tell since she was pointedly looking at neither of them as she started down the hall, head held high. Nothing to see here. The most regal walk of shame he'd ever seen.

Not that either of them had anything to be ashamed of.

"I'm sorry, Mr. Newton," the young PA offered when she was out of earshot. "But you know the rules..."

"I know," Mac acknowledged, moving toward the open door to his room. It wasn't the kid's fault he'd interrupted one of the most insane and perfect and unexpected and incendiary moments of Mac's entire life.

Madness. That had been pure madness.

And he'd never wanted anything as badly as he wanted to do it again.

Mac closed the door between him and the PA, and swore again, this time in a sort of prayer of thanks for whatever the fuck had just happened. He'd had good chemistry with women before, but that had felt like he'd been plugged into an electrical socket. He'd lost his fucking *mind*. And he wanted to do it again as soon as possible.

But this was Magda. And they were in a competition where

they weren't allowed to be alone in a room together—and even if they were home in Pine Hollow there was no world in which this wasn't going to get complicated.

He didn't know what had just happened. He didn't know if this thing between them had grown out of the feud, or if they'd been feuding all along because both of them had sensed this thing between them under the surface—and he didn't care.

Their past was a shitshow, but the future? The future was suddenly very, *very* interesting.

Chapter Twenty-One

Magda slammed into her room at the inn, feeling like she'd just narrowly escaped...*something*. But something terrible or something incredible was anyone's guess.

What the *hell* had just happened?

Well. She knew what had happened. Mac had kissed her. And she'd *definitely* kissed him back. Her brain hadn't even registered the shock of it until after the fact because she was so busy participating with every fiber of her being.

Until they'd been interrupted—and thank goodness they'd been interrupted. Or maybe not? Obviously nothing could happen here and now. They were still competitors. There were rules. So yes, definitely thank goodness.

Except her heart was still beating in triple time. And she couldn't even call Charlotte and Kendall to tell them about it and ask them what the hell she was supposed to do next. She couldn't talk to Leah and Eunice about it because that was *absolutely* not supposed to have happened.

And the PA had seen them. So the production knew. Would they be kicked out? Magda had signed dozens of policies about sexual harassment and not colluding with other bakers—though at the time she'd been snickering at the idea of how one even colluded at a baking competition and hadn't really paid attention to the finer details. She'd never expected it to be a problem.

Could they be kicked out for that? Surely not. Right?

Because I don't want to be here without you.

Magda pressed a hand to her chest, feeling her heart thudding against her palm. Did he mean that? She wanted to beat him. She wanted to outlast him. But she'd felt so horrible today when he was in the bottom three. She'd told herself that it was just guilt—he'd helped her and the idea that he might be punished for it was excruciating.

She had wanted so desperately for him to survive elimination. She'd nearly cried out in relief when they'd said Walter's name. Which had made her feel like a horrible friend to the older man, but there it was. Her relief had been so acute, so sharp, but then as soon as Mac was safe, her brain had begun to spin.

Why had he done that? Why would he risk it?

Magda paced over to her bed, then back to the door, wondering if she needed to reach out to Julia. Apprise her of the situation. Julia had seemed to be somewhat on her side. At least more so than anyone else in the production. She'd even felt bad enough about the Celsius mistake—though it hadn't been her fault—that she hadn't asked questions when Magda asked for Mac's room number at the inn, on the pretext of needing to thank him.

But really Magda had needed to know *why*.

Because I don't want to be here without you.

Had he really meant that?

And the kiss—that insane firestorm of a kiss—what that meant? Did he want her now? Had he wanted her before?

Why now?

A whisper of uncertainty crept into her spiraling thoughts. Mac was smart. He was tactical. He'd helped her when the cameras were watching, when it would make him look like a hero and make America fall in love with him. And then he'd kissed her in a darkened hallway—which was, quite possibly, the one thing he could have done that would have had her retreating to her room even more confused than when she'd arrived.

She didn't think there was any possibility he was playing her... but if he'd wanted her off her game, he'd succeeded. And if she went home because she was distracted by never-ending questions about what it all *meant*, she'd only have herself to blame.

He would win—not just the competition but the contest for the viewing audience's hearts and minds. He'd be a fan favorite. They'd give him his own baking show. He'd walk away with her dream.

And she would never forgive herself.

But what if—perhaps even more terrifyingly—it wasn't a ploy? What if this—whatever this was—was real?

Her heart tried to lurch up happily at the thought, and she smacked it down. It was impossible to know the truth as long as they were both in the competition. How could she let herself trust him completely in this insane environment?

She thought she knew Mac, but $250,000 was a lot of money. People would do a lot worse than mislead a girl who'd had a crush on them since she was eighteen for that kind of money. Not that she still had a crush on him. At least she didn't want to. She'd never wanted those feelings that lingered beneath the surface, but they might still be there nonetheless. Making her susceptible to him. Gullible. She wanted too badly to believe that kiss. Her body and her stupid heart had leapt into it without looking back.

Yes, *absolutely* thank goodness they'd been interrupted.

As long as they were both in the competition, she needed to keep her wits about her.

Which meant absolutely no more kissing Mac.

"A PA just caught Mac and Magda making out in a hallway at the inn."

Julia looked up from her tablet and swore under her breath.

She wasn't surprised. There had been plenty of signs that those two had some very hot unresolved feelings for each other—and she'd heard the audio of Magda telling her friends about their history in the common room last weekend. So she'd definitely suspected things were moving in this direction.

The problem was Stephen.

Julia had done a good job of keeping Stephen from learning the whole truth behind their feud—there had been plenty of other drama with the almost-slap and them being forced to work together to keep him happy—but this was the kind of thing he would *definitely* want included in the edit.

"Is there footage?" Julia asked Greg, who had appeared with the news. The man seemed to know everything that happened anywhere on the production.

"Just an eyewitness," Greg said—and Julia breathed a small sigh of relief. Only the kitchen and the common area at the inn were bugged, since the tiny hidden cameras were expensive and hadn't been deemed a necessary production expense by the higher-ups.

"But apparently it was pretty hot," Greg went on. "He had her up against a wall, and it appeared to be extremely consensual."

"Right. Thanks." Julia nodded, her brain already working on how to get in front of this so Stephen didn't find some way to use it against them.

Should she go talk to him? Or try to hide it from him like she had the previous audio? Though this was much juicier than a few contestants shooting the breeze over drinks. And Greg already knew. Which meant the PA was obviously blabbing, and there was no realistic way to keep Stephen from finding out.

Okay. So how to work with this? How to turn it in their favor?

Maybe play up the showmance? Convince Stephen that audiences loved shipping the contestants, and if they leaned into that it would go better than using this to somehow throw the bakers off? But keep it vague to keep the audience interested? Don't let on that they've already kissed?

It wasn't great, but it might actually be the best way to maintain any privacy for Mac and Magda. By partially invading that privacy.

She could talk to them both in the morning, get a sense of whether they would go along with a little flirtation subplot, but first she needed to talk to Stephen—to make sure he hadn't already heard about the kiss and to get a sense of where he stood on all the different contestants, just so she knew what she was working with.

Julia rose, tucking her tablet under her arm, and made her way through the darkened hallways of King Arthur toward the space that Stephen had set up as his lair.

Julia heard raised voices when she was still several feet down the hall. Multiple raised voices, but Stephen's was definitely the loudest, per usual.

But then a phrase jumped out from the mish-mash of voices and Julia stopped in her tracks.

The lawyers. Stephen had definitely just said *the lawyers.*

Something was very wrong.

Chapter Twenty-Two

On Thursday, Magda and Mac were both off their game.

Mac had half expected the producers to pull him aside when he arrived at King Arthur that morning and read him the riot act about fraternizing with other contestants, but if news of the kiss had spread, there was no sign of it. In fact, all of the producers seemed sort of tense and distracted—and he just hoped that had nothing to do with him or Magda.

Magda was the last one into the Proving Room, and he tried to catch her eye, but she was very focused on Leah and Eunice—and very much *not* looking at him. Something uneasy twisted in his stomach, but they were called into the kitchen before he could make his way across the room to talk to her.

He tried to get close to her in the cluster of bakers as they made their way to the front of the room, but when he murmured, "Mags," she just shook her head and walked faster.

Crap. Was she mad at him? He'd thought she was with him all the way last night, that the kiss had been mutual and consensual. Could he have read that wrong?

Had he freaking assaulted her?

The Skills Challenge was French macarons. He'd practiced them because they seemed to pop up on *Cake-Off* nearly every season. The judges exited the kitchen, Flanders called for their ninety minutes to begin, and Mac fought to stay focused.

He heard Magda's voice at the station two behind his, talking about beating the egg whites, and he hummed to himself to drown out the sound of her voice. *Focus.* He was here for a reason.

Even if sometimes he couldn't quite figure out what that was.

At the end of the ninety minutes, he had something passably resembling macarons. He glanced back after he carried his tray up to the judging table and saw Magda frowning at her own tray. Apparently her bake hadn't gone well, either. He tried to position himself near her as they were ushered out of the room, but she was sticking close to Leah and Eunice again.

"Magda." He approached her when they were back in the Proving Room. "Can we talk?"

She flushed, shaking her head. "Not now," she mumbled.

Okay, yes, they were both wired for sound, and there were cameras everywhere, but still. "I just wanted to make sure you're okay. That we're okay."

She flicked a glance up at him as Leah and Eunice looked between them and subtly moved away to give them space.

"We're fine. We're good," Magda said as soon as they had the completely inaccurate illusion of privacy. Then she met his eyes, something meaningful in her gaze. "I just want to focus on the competition. I don't want any distractions."

Well, that was clear enough. "Right. Message received." But something prompted him to add, "But you're not, uh..." How was he supposed to say this in a coded way. "I didn't...want to make you uncomfortable..."

"You didn't do anything," she said firmly. "We're fine."

"Right."

The conversation still felt unfinished—but of course this was the one time that the kitchen clean-up and glamour shots took no time at all, and they were suddenly being called back in for judging. There were still PAs rushing frantically to wipe down counters as they were lined up at the front of the kitchen and the judges entered.

Normally, judging took ages, but there was a strange sense of urgency today, and it almost felt like they were rushing through it.

Magda was in the middle of the pack—which was clearly a disappointment for her—while Mac was second from the bottom. Not exactly a great position moving into the next challenge. Which they were informed would be starting right away.

A ripple of surprise went through the remaining eight bakers—they never went straight into another challenge without doing a round of interviews.

"For your Elimination Challenge today, you have been tasked with constructing a cookie tower—it must be at least eighteen inches high, self-supporting..."

Mac knew he should be listening, but he barely heard the judges' instructions—though thankfully they'd been told about today's Elimination Challenge before they left last night. He'd been supposed to plan his cookie tower—but he'd been distracted by thoughts of Magda.

Magda.

Who didn't want a distraction. And okay, yes, he could get that. They were in the middle of a competition, and the last thing either one of them needed was to be off their game. He'd actually had the same thought last night—that this wasn't the best time to be starting something.

But was that just until the competition was over? Or was that a nicer way of saying *this was a mistake and we should never do it again*?

Did she regret it? He was still having flashbacks—that little sound she'd made echoing in his ears.

"Your time starts...*now!*"

Shit. Jeffrey Flanders's host voice rang over the room.

Okay. Cookies. He could do this in his sleep.

Mac immediately started measuring ingredients, his hands moving smoothly through the familiar recipe—until he heard Magda's voice across the kitchen.

His body felt like it had been tuned to the sound. He could easily pick out her voice in a room full of chatter—and he found himself focusing on it. Did she sound a little wooden? Was there a waver in her voice?

"Mac! What are you making for us today?"

The judges were suddenly standing in front of him with a camera crew, all of them smiling expectantly.

"Uh..." Shit. What was he making?

The bakers had all been given the instructions last night so they could plan their towers—Mac had roughed out an idea this morning, but now as he looked around, he saw Tim to his left working from a little notebook open to a detailed diagram.

"I'm making, uh..." He looked down at his hands. "Ginger snaps. And snickerdoodles. And raspberry sandwich cookies, and lemon curd sandwich cookies, and..." Shit. He'd definitely had a fifth kind, but maybe the judges weren't counting. "And it's going to be on a Rice Krispies Treat structure in the shape of—" Why was his mind so blank? What was tall? "The Eiffel Tower."

The judges all *oooh*ed as if he'd said something shocking.

"It's going to be the battle of the Eiffel Towers," Flanders said melodramatically.

"Magda is making an Eiffel Tower of French cookies,

drawing on her experience living in France," Joanie explained. "What drew you to that structure?"

Oh no. No, that was bad. Crap, he'd probably heard her voice say *Eiffel Tower* and his brain had latched on to it. "Sorry! Sorry, did I say Eiffel Tower? Wrong thing. Empire State Building. New York. I go there to see shows all the time. Broadway. And these, uh, these cookies are all the star of the show."

Bullshit. It was such bullshit. But the judges were nodding along as if he'd said something meaningful.

"Just remember," Alexander Clay cautioned ominously, "it's all about the flavors and the bake. Don't get too caught up in the structure and lose that."

"Absolutely," Mac agreed—breathing a sigh of relief when the judges and their cameras finally moved away.

Usually he loved chatting with the camera crews—he pretended he was on his own baking show and hammed it up—but today he was having a hard enough time remembering what he was supposed to be doing.

He needed to be focusing on his baking. The clock was ticking.

He reached for the salt—and his hand froze. Crap. Had he already put in the salt? He couldn't remember. His hands had been moving on autopilot, and if he didn't get his shit together, he was going home.

Mac slammed a lid on his thoughts about Magda. He was making an Empire State Building out of cookies, and he needed to get his act in gear.

Her Eiffel Tower was going to collapse.

Magda stood in front of the judges with her cookie Eiffel Tower on the table between them and silently willed the caramel to hold. She'd taken a chance, making her tower out of cookies as well. Around the room, towers made of Rice Krispies Treats or nougatine stood firm, while her cookies glued together with caramel were seconds away from crumbling.

They hadn't had a chance to practice, and Magda had failed to account for the weight of the cookies that were piled on her Eiffel Tower. The first floor was slowly buckling under the weight as Alexander Clay muttered about a "lack of refinement" in her construction.

Joanie staunchly pointed out that her design goal was clearly identifiable—which could not be said of all the cookie towers in the room—and then they began sampling the cookies. Perhaps time was moving strangely again, but it felt like this part was moving faster than normal.

They tasted all her cookies in quick succession. Joanie commended her baking skill—and then she and Alexander began their usual tag-team routine. Joanie with her gently disappointed "Oh, but we were hoping for so much more from you." And Alexander with his "delicious, but uninspired as always" condemnation.

Magda forced a smile to her face and thanked the judges for their feedback, before picking up the Eiffel Tower—which promptly collapsed under its own weight and cascaded toward the floor in a waterfall of cookies.

Everyone froze. Magda stared in horror at the mess, wondering if this was going to affect the judging. Did it have to stay upright all afternoon? Or just long enough for the judges to see it? Had she somehow jostled it or knocked it in a way that had caused this? Would this be what America watched over and over and over again on the commercials for week six? Was she going to go out as the contestant with the collapsed cookie tower? Oh

God, she was going to be Collapsed Cookie Tower Lady for the rest of her life, wasn't she?

"Well, that's the way the cookie crumbles!" Jeffrey Flanders declared, in what he clearly thought was an incredibly pithy joke—which just made her want to fling the remaining lower levels of the tower at his face.

As if that was a signal everyone had been waiting for, the director bellowed for Flanders to help her get the crumbled remainder of her tower back to her station—but it was Leah and Eunice who rushed forward to help. The cameras eagerly captured the moment—and then the PAs were there to sweep an afternoon's worth of Magda's hard work into trash bins and clear the way for the next tower to be judged.

Naturally, she didn't win.

She'd thought Mac might actually be in the running for the top prize—his Empire State Building was rock solid and neatly sculpted—but then the judges had sampled his ginger snaps and flinched, declaring them salty to the point of being nearly inedible.

No one looked more shocked than Eunice when she was declared the winner over Abby, while Tim looked deeply pissed to have been in the middle.

Magda held her breath as she was scolded for her flavors and her lack of attention to detail, Mac was called out for his massive error with the salt, and they were both lectured that the judges expected better of them, like they were children being taken to task.

They were saved only by the fact that Cherise's cookie tower had never managed to get upright, and she'd only managed to get three kinds of cookie on her display. Abby's sister had been strongly in the middle of the pack until then, but today had destroyed her.

It didn't actually feel great to know Magda was only in the competition for another week because of someone else's complete collapse.

She just wanted to get back to her room and lick her wounds. Today had been a marathon. It had to be after dark already, but when the director called cut, he followed it, ominously, with "Hold positions!" Which invariably meant there was more coming.

She couldn't do another bake tonight. She just couldn't.

Then Stephen stalked into the room. He hadn't been on set all day, and all of the producers tensed as they watched him take a position where the judges usually stood.

"Attention!" he bellowed. "Effective immediately, production is shutting down."

Chapter Twenty-Three

They knew about the kiss.

That was Magda's first panicked thought when she learned the production had been shut down. But of course they knew. A PA had caught her and Mac in the act. And now, less than twenty-four hours later, the production was suddenly being shut down? Was there any way those two things weren't related?

Her fear wasn't exactly assuaged when she begged Julia to know what was going on and the producer said, "Legal has been made aware of a potential for bias in the contest, and we have to wait for them to let us know we're okay to continue."

"But we will continue," Mac said, from where he stood behind Magda in the Proving Room. The production might be shut down, but all of the bakers were still huddled in the space, pleading for answers.

"At this point, we don't know," Julia admitted.

Magda exchanged an uneasy glance with Mac. "Is this about—"

Julia cut her off before she could figure out how to even ask that question. "We can't tell you anything because this is an ongoing legal matter and you may need to be deposed. At this time, all you need to do is go back to the inn and remember the same rules apply—no outside contact, don't go anywhere."

"So we're just stuck here?" Abby asked, angrily.

"Production is still determining how to move forward."

"Are you considering disqualifying someone?" Magda asked.

Julia met her eyes. "I'm sorry. I really can't tell you anything."

Sugar. She'd been scared of being eliminated, scared of this experience ending too soon, but she'd never thought it would be this. The entire production being shut down because she and Mac had kissed.

Except it might not be that. Right? The timing could be a coincidence. Couldn't it?

They'd crammed in post-bake interviews before judging, but the usual "how do you feel about making it to another week" stuff had all been called off for the night. Perhaps because they wouldn't all be making it through?

They were bundled into a van en masse and shuttled back to the inn, where no one was ready to go to sleep. For the first time, all of the remaining bakers—Mac and Magda, Leah and Tim, Abby, Eunice and Zain—huddled together in the inn's common room.

Which meant that Magda couldn't talk to Mac about the fact that they might have broken *Cake-Off* with their ill-advised kiss. But she didn't know what she would have said even if they were free to talk.

"What do you think it is?" Leah asked as they passed around beers—and Magda resisted the urge to look guiltily at Mac.

"Someone who got voted off is bitching about it, threatening a lawsuit," Tim said with his usual absolute certainty.

"Would they shut down production for that?" Abby asked. "It probably happens twice a season at least."

Tim glowered around the table. "Was it one of you? The legal threat?"

"Why would we want to shut down the season?" Leah asked incredulously.

"You don't think they'd actually cancel the season?" Eunice asked, her voice wavering as she sat with both hands wrapped around her cold beer bottle.

"It would have to be really serious," Abby said. "They've invested a lot in us. They have, what? Six episodes in the can? That's half a season. They'll want to get us back in the kitchen if there's any legal way they can."

"They must have known this morning," Mac said. "Did you see how they were rushing all day? How the producers seemed stressed and hurried through the confessionals?"

Which would make sense if the legal problem was something that had happened last night in the hallway outside Mac's room. But would they really shut down production for a kiss? It seemed extreme. She'd much more expected them to try to exploit it than put a stop to it.

"Someone is cheating," Tim declared, again with his air of stating a fact that only he knew for certain. "They're getting ready to announce that one of us had a 'family emergency' and had to leave the competition."

Before anyone could react to Tim's announcement, producers Julia and Greg walked into the common room.

"Oh, good, we have all of you," Greg said, his expression more businesslike than Magda had ever seen it. "A decision has been made."

Leah grabbed Magda's hand, squeezing it tightly, while on her other side Eunice continued to grip her beer bottle like a lifeline.

"Production has decided to send everyone home until this matter can be resolved—" Julia was drowned out by cries of dismay and paused long enough for the room to quiet again. "This does not mean that the season has been canceled. In fact, you should act at all times as if you will be returning to filming as soon as possible."

"You will be contacted as soon as we have more information," Greg went on, picking up the thread. "But in the meantime, please remember that all details about this season are still covered by your NDAs. The initial press release announcing the new season went out yesterday afternoon, before we were made aware of the potential legal concern, so you are now all allowed to share that you are on the Archrivals Edition of the *Cake-Off*, but you may wish to hold off on doing so until this matter is resolved."

"How long?" Tim demanded. "How long are we just supposed to wait?"

"We don't know," Julia said firmly. "We'll arrange your travel home. And back again, should the season resume. If you're contacted by legal, please cooperate with the ongoing inquiry."

"You should pack tonight," Greg advised. "Flights out are being arranged for tomorrow morning."

And with that, they left.

The seven remaining bakers stared at one another in a daze.

"Shit," Leah whispered, after a long moment. "They must be expecting it to take a while, if they think flying us all home at the last minute and back again is going to be cheaper than keeping us here for the duration. This is more than one or two days."

Abby was the first one to stand up. "I'm going to go pack." She glanced around the table. "I guess I'll see you if I see you."

The group broke up shortly after that. They all had packing to do. Magda gave both Leah and Eunice long hugs, since they didn't know if they would see one another in the morning—or ever again. They promised to keep in touch—though they weren't even sure if that was allowed. Did the usual nonfraternization rules apply? How could they if they were all at home? They'd get their phones back. They'd have access to recipe books and the internet. The bubble would officially be broken.

And none of them knew what any of that meant for the future of the competition.

Magda walked upstairs with Eunice and Leah, pausing to hug each of them one more time. Eunice had been fighting tears, and finally started sniffling and darted inside her room.

"They have to bring us back, right?" Leah reassured herself as she paused with her own hand on her doorknob. "They've invested too much in us to just scrap the season, haven't they?"

"Absolutely," Magda agreed, with more confidence than she felt. Honestly, she was less worried about them tossing out the entire season than she was of being disqualified herself. For almost hitting Mac. For kissing Mac. God, it was always about Mac.

"Magda?"

And there he was. Waiting outside her room as she turned the corner after saying goodbye to Leah.

"Mac."

She didn't know what she felt when she looked at him. It wasn't the same bristling animosity that had built over the last decade, or even the tension of the last two weeks. When she looked at him she just felt overwhelmed.

There was too much going on. Too much uncertainty. Too many feelings. And she couldn't spare the brain space to figure out what was happening here.

"I just wanted to make sure you were all right," he said—and she realized she could probably invite him into her room, if she wanted to. They were about to be sent home. The production couldn't enforce rules about them not being alone together, even if they wanted to.

But she still didn't know *why* they were going home. If there was even the slightest possibility that it was related to the kiss or the not-quite-slap, if there was any chance things might be further complicated by her being alone with Mac, she couldn't risk it.

At least that was the rationale she gave herself when she said, "I'm fine, we're fine—but with everything that's going on right now, I just need some time to think. Okay?"

"Yeah." He took a step back, even though he hadn't been blocking her path to the door. "Absolutely."

She moved toward her room, resisting the urge to ask him if he thought this shutdown was about them—as if by not saying it out loud she wouldn't validate the ridiculousness of the fear.

"I guess I'll see you in Pine Hollow," he said, and she nodded jerkily.

Once he was gone and she was inside her room, she leaned against the door, wondering if she should have invited him in. She didn't have much to pack, and she knew she wouldn't be sleeping anytime soon. It would have been good to have someone to talk to—and strangely, Mac was someone she almost... well. Did she trust him? Was that what this was? Only hours ago she'd been in a panic, wondering if the kiss had been strategy on his part, but now that everything had blown up, did it matter?

She needed to act like it did. She needed to act like they were going back, but what if they didn't? What if the entire season was canceled? She hated not knowing anything.

She'd almost made up her mind to go knock on his door when a knock came at hers.

Magda rushed to open it, her heart in her throat—but it wasn't Mac standing in the narrow hallway.

A young PA held out her phone to her. "A car will take you to Pine Hollow in the morning if you can be ready by nine," he said.

"I'll be ready," Magda promised, accepting her phone like she was receiving the Holy Grail. She barely resisted the urge to kiss it. Twelve days without contact with her friends and family didn't sound like much, but it had been several lifetimes in terms of all that had happened.

As soon as the PA was gone, Magda eagerly dug her charger out of her bag and powered up her phone. She would see Mac tomorrow—they were both going back to Pine Hollow and they were both very familiar with carpooling between King Arthur and their hometown. But in the meantime, she desperately needed to talk to Kendall and Charlotte.

Chapter Twenty-Four

Pine Hollow hadn't changed, but then it rarely did, and he'd been gone less than two weeks. The historic town hall, the picturesque square with its gazebo and bandstand, the rec center where the roof had caved in and been rebuilt a few years back—everything was exactly as he'd left it.

Mac was impatient to get to the Cup and make sure it was exactly as he'd left it, too, but he had the driver take him up the hill to his place instead. The converted carriage house was also exactly as he'd left it—complete with the cat on the front step, who gave him a look of searing disdain and stalked off to punish him for his absence.

He made a mental note to pick up a rotisserie chicken to make it up to the cat, and stepped inside long enough to drop his bags before heading to his grandmother's house.

He hadn't been able to sleep last night with all the uncertainty, so he'd been packed up and in the common room at six a.m. when a van heading to the Burlington airport had been leaving. The driver had agreed to swing by Pine Hollow on his way back to King Arthur, so Mac had caught a ride.

Magda had said she wanted space to think, so it was a win-win. He got home earlier, and they didn't have to sit in awkward silence in the van together, wondering what was coming next.

He had his own thoughts to sort through.

But after ninety minutes of speculating with Tim and Abby about why the show had been shut down and another forty-five minutes chatting with the driver on the way back to Pine Hollow, he was still no closer to any answers.

Would the show go on? Were he and Magda on hold until it did? Was there anything with Magda to *be* on hold? They'd been feuding for so long, and now he didn't know what they were.

But he knew he needed to tell his grandmother about the show before she heard it somewhere else.

The historic Newton house sat on top of a hill a short walk from downtown Pine Hollow. His ancestors had been among the founding families of Pine Hollow, but they hadn't built the house until the mid-nineteenth century, when one of his great-great-grandfathers had fallen madly in love with a Newport Beach heiress and brought her back to Vermont with him.

The house—or more accurately, mansion—was three stories of architectural intimidation. The rooms were drafty and somber, with dark wood paneling and heavy velvet drapes at every window. Portraits of long-dead ancestors hung above all the fireplaces. There was a weight to the place—the weight of history and family legacy.

Mac preferred the airy and fully renovated carriage house, which gave him a sense of privacy but kept him close enough to help his grandmother whenever she needed him. It had been strange, being away these last couple of weeks, even though he'd known Connor would look in on his gran.

He crossed the gravel drive and climbed the little hill to the main house.

Eight thirty on a Friday morning. He found his grandmother on the veranda, looking out over the view of the hollow while she ate her grapefruit.

Her thinly tweezed eyebrows arched when she spotted him, but otherwise she gave no reaction. "You're back."

"I am." He dropped a kiss on the top of her head, which she tolerated with a little huffing noise. "Though maybe not for long," he added, pulling out the black metal patio chair with a scrape across the pavers. "I couldn't tell you before, but I've actually been filming a TV show—*The Great American Cake-Off*."

"I know," his grandmother said, without an ounce of surprise. "You were in the town newsletter."

Mac blinked. "What? When?"

"Yesterday. Linda Hilson put out a special edition. Hot off the presses—two of our hometown heroes in a televised baking competition."

"I'm sorry I couldn't tell you. Nondisclosure agreements."

"I figured as much," she said, utterly unperturbed as she daintily removed a section of grapefruit. "What does 'not for long' mean?"

"There's been a production delay," he explained. "That's why I'm back. But as soon as they're ready to resume filming, I'll be heading back there."

"Well. That makes more sense than four weeks in New York with a newly married woman."

Mac blinked, startled that his grandmother knew about Cleo, but then all his life she had always seemed terrifyingly omniscient.

"Can you tell me how it's going?" she asked. "Or is that against the rules?"

"It's frowned on. But I will say I like it." He hadn't always been sure about that. It was stressful, but it was a good stress. "And I think I'm good at it." And he really wanted to go back. Not just for the competition. The entire experience. Magda . . .

His gran huffed out a soft breath that was her version of a snort. "Of course you are. You can do anything." She said it as if it was fact, her confidence in him absolute, and Mac smiled.

His grandmother could be a taskmaster—she had strong opinions, and they'd butted heads constantly when he was a teenager. If not for his grandfather's intervention, they might not have both come through those difficult years alive, let alone speaking to each other. His grandfather used to say they were too similar, though Mac couldn't see it. But in the years since his grandfather's death, they'd come to know each other in a different way—and he'd never doubted her confidence in him for a second.

She'd wanted him to go back to college at one point, and they'd argued for months, but now she seemed to genuinely just want him to be happy and follow his dreams. Though he was realizing he hadn't been as honest with himself as he might have thought he was about what those dreams were.

"Do you think I avoid commitment?" he asked her abruptly.

If she was startled by the out-of-the-blue question, she didn't react with so much as an eyelash twitch. She simply reached for her tea and considered him. "Yes," she said calmly, absolutely, after a moment.

"That's it? Yes?" Julia's words had been bugging him for over a week, and his grandmother acted like they were a given.

"Did you want more of an answer?" She eyed him over her tea. "The second someone becomes an obligation, you start to pull away."

Mac grimaced—he'd known only to ask if he wanted a real answer. His gran didn't pull her punches. "That makes me sound pretty crappy."

"Not at all," his grandmother argued. "You take your

obligations very seriously. Probably too seriously. I was your first stop, wasn't I? Checking up on your doddering old gran?"

"You aren't doddering, and you aren't an obligation."

She waved his argument away with one elegant hand. "Yes, of course. Love isn't an obligation and all that. I only mean that you have a horror of letting anyone down, and therefore you're excessively careful not to commit." She picked up her fork and pointed at him with it. "I think your grandfather and I overcorrected with you. Far too much emphasis on responsibility and legacy. Scared you away from the whole thing."

"You didn't scare me away from anything," he argued. If anything, his grandparents had been a shining example. It was his parents who were the cautionary tale.

"Hm," she grumbled, noncommittally. "What brought this up?"

"Just something one of the producers said. About why I'm single."

His gran's eyebrows arched speculatively. "A female producer?"

"It's not like that." Not that Julia wasn't attractive, but his brain hadn't even registered her in that way. There was such a clear line between the contestants and the producers at the show—and the only person he'd been interested in kissing was the one he'd kissed. Though he still hadn't been able to talk to Magda about exactly what that was.

A moment of insanity brought on by the near hostage situation environment of the show bubble? Something else?

Did she still hate him? He certainly didn't hate her. But he was starting to think he never had.

"Hm," his grandmother mumbled, her sharp blue eyes missing nothing. "So. You did run away with Magda Miller after all."

His eyebrows flew up. "That's a very loose interpretation of reality."

"Hm." She studied him enigmatically for another moment, then seemed to decide to let something go, taking a breath and turning her attention toward the carriage house. "That cat of yours has been all over town in your absence. Looking for you, I imagine."

"I saw him at the carriage house. George has been feeding him, but I think I'll need to grovel for forgiveness for leaving."

She nodded once. "Good to have you back."

His grandmother wasn't effusive, and he smiled as he stood and dropped a kiss on the top of her head for the second time—which he knew would make her try to smack him with her fork. "Love you too, Gran."

He dodged the fork and started down the hill toward the Cup, to see how his other "obligations" had fared in his absence.

Mac had caught an earlier shuttle.

Magda wasn't quite sure what the significance of that fact was—could he be avoiding her? Or was he just ready early? She told herself not to overthink it as Julia escorted her to the car that was waiting to drive her to Pine Hollow—but overthinking it was pretty much her natural state. She'd been overthinking all night.

She turned to Julia when they reached the car, desperate for some scrap of information that might ease her mind. "I know you aren't allowed to tell us anything about the ongoing legal stuff, but can you maybe say what it isn't?" she asked.

Julia winced, starting to shake her head. "I'm sorry—"

Magda cut her off before she could give her an answer she didn't want to hear. "Can you just tell me if it's about Mac and me?"

Julia blinked, visibly startled by the question—and Magda's hopes lifted. "You and Mac?"

She wasn't going to mention the kiss unless she absolutely had to. "That thing at the photo shoot, I know that can be grounds for disqualification, and I wasn't sure if that...or maybe some other accusation of, um, misconduct? If that might have been leveled against...us?"

Julia's expression cleared. "I probably shouldn't say anything, but I don't see how it can hurt—no accusations have been leveled at any contestants."

Which did nothing to clear up why they were shutting down production, but it was a huge relief to know it wasn't because she'd stupidly kissed Mac.

Now she just had to figure out how she felt about stupidly kissing Mac.

She chatted with the driver some on the drive, but spent most of it texting with Kendall and Charlotte. She'd FaceTimed with both of them last night, so they'd already been through all the news about the Archrivals Edition, production shutting down, and Mac being there, too.

But she hadn't mentioned the kiss. Not to either of them.

She hadn't told them about almost slapping him or working with him, or about him helping her when her oven malfunctioned. There had been so many other things to say that it had been easy to avoid the things she still couldn't quite wrap her head around.

Charlotte and George had been trying to conceive for months, and while Magda had been away she'd had a false-alarm positive pregnancy test, and Kendall had new sonogram photos to share, so it had been easy to dance around the subject of Mac.

She was going to tell them. She just wanted to do it in person. And when she let herself into her apartment and saw them waiting for her there, along with Cupcake, her heart swelled.

The comfort of being home was acute, but it wasn't just that. It was the realization that no one was watching her. She could just be herself. She didn't have to worry about being judged—and as soon as she threw her arms around her dog, who went into paroxysms of delight, wriggling and licking and making little noises of joy, she nearly burst into tears at the magnitude of the relief.

She hugged her friends next, barely keeping it together as they helped her drag her bags across the threshold and into her apartment, talking over one another and so happy to see her.

She'd been spotted in the square. The whole town would know she was back before long. She'd already seen the latest town newsletter with the special announcement about the show. But somehow even knowing all of Pine Hollow was watching her was still a relief after the constant surveillance of the last two weeks.

"We've been dying," Charlotte said, with her usual drama, as Magda curled up on the floor with her arms around Cupcake. "I wanted to text you every single day to ask how it was going, but we knew they'd taken your phone."

"I wished I could text you. It was so stressful."

"Was it the timers?" Kendall asked.

"The timers, the cameras, the lights, the questions—knowing they're always watching you and building a story about you and you have no control over what they're going to say, but I know a bunch of it is going to be about my feud with Mac—which is the absolute last thing I want to be defined by in front of the entire country, but that's who I am now, the girl who hates

Mac—who, of course, is doing amazing. Though I'm not sure I'm supposed to tell you that."

"Cone of silence," Kendall promised. "Nothing leaves this room."

"I'm so confused," Magda admitted. "I wanted this so badly, but it's not at all how I thought it would be—"

"Because of Mac being there?"

"Maybe? Sort of? It's the whole rivals thing—pitting us against each other—and yes, I know it was always going to be a competition, but it's all different this year. It's like they care more about how much we hate each other than what we're baking. I was so thrown when he walked in—and then I told myself I wasn't going to let him ruin the experience for me—but then I nearly hit him, and he could have thrown me to the wolves, but he didn't, and he let me use his oven—which nearly cost him the cupcake round—and I just wanted to know why, but then he kissed me and the production shut down and I don't even know if we're going back—"

"Whoa whoa whoa!" Charlotte held up both hands. "Back up. He kissed you? Mac?"

"I don't know what happened. One moment I was yelling at him, and then—it was this insane moment in the hallway—"

"I love a hallway kiss," Kendall murmured fondly.

"And then a PA interrupted us—we weren't supposed to be fraternizing off camera, and I thought we were going to be kicked off the show, but the producer said the shutdown wasn't about that—or at least she sort of implied it, but I don't know what it *is* about and now I'm wondering if I just *thought* that was what she was telling me when really they're assembling their legal team to boot us both off."

Kendall and Charlotte stared at her, and then Kendall

smiled wickedly. "You guys did always have a ridiculous amount in common—"

"Bite your tongue!" Charlotte glared at her.

"What?" Kendall asked innocently. "I just wondered if it was a good kiss."

"We are *not* encouraging this! He was a dick. We're Team Magda," Charlotte reminded Kendall.

"I'm always Team Magda. But you have to admit they have insane chemistry—"

"Yeah, like nitroglycerin," Magda muttered. "But it doesn't matter. It can't happen again. I need to focus on the show." He'd already gotten in her head. She'd been so off during that cookie challenge. Her thoughts all muddled. "I *like* being single, not worrying about men and dating—and I don't need the distraction right now. Besides, how could I trust that he was kissing me for the right reasons and not because of some convoluted strategy to throw me off my game so he can beat me and steal my grandmother's recipe?"

"Exactly," Charlotte encouraged. "We don't trust him."

"What I need to be focusing on is how to find the soul in my baking when we go back to the competition. If we go back."

"Optimism!" Charlotte insisted. "You're going back. This is a blip. And your bakes have tons of soul!"

"The judges don't think so. Alexander Clay thinks you can't see me in my bakes."

Charlotte bounced. "I still can't get over you knowing Alexander Clay."

"I wouldn't say I know him. He just periodically tells me I'm basic and uninventive."

"Sounds fun," Kendall said dryly.

"It wasn't, actually. But it should have been," Magda said.

"I was so busy panicking about winning and being perfect and Mac that I forgot to actually enjoy the experience. I spent two weeks baking in front of the *Cake-Off* judges—living my freaking dream—and I feel like I missed it."

"You'll get another chance," Charlotte soothed. "It's not over."

Except it might be. She didn't know what was happening with this mysterious legal challenge. And she had no idea if they were going back. Which meant everything was on hold. Her confused feelings about the show. Her confused feelings about Mac. All of it.

"I think I was...I don't know. I didn't mean to hold myself back, but I had this feeling like I needed to be something else. Some*one* else. Like they'd only picked me because of Mac, and I only won when I was with him—except I was good at the skills stuff, but I don't want to be the baker who is technically amazing but *boring*."

"You are *not* boring," Charlotte insisted staunchly.

"And you don't have to be anyone but yourself," Kendall reminded her. "Just go wild, Mags. Stop trying to please everyone and let yourself go. You've got this."

"Maybe." Except she might not get the chance to try again.

She would just have to wait and hope.

Until they heard more.

Chapter Twenty-Five

"H eard anything yet?"

Magda looked over as Mac flopped down into the folding chair beside hers. It was Sunday afternoon, and the canine obstacle course behind the Furry Friends animal shelter was packed with people and pets attending their annual Agility Competition fundraiser, but somehow Magda had managed to find one of the comfy non-bleacher seats to watch with Cupcake—who was not agility inclined.

Charlotte and Kendall were both at the starting gate with their golden retrievers getting ready for their runs and trash-talking aggressively—even though everyone in town knew that Charlotte's sister Elinor's Australian shepherd, Dory, was unbeatable.

Magda hadn't expected to be here this weekend for the event—which was quickly becoming one of her favorite early-May traditions. And she certainly hadn't expected that Mac would sit down next to her for a cozy little tête-à-tête. But *Cake-Off* had changed things.

It wasn't even the kiss—which they were both studiously pretending hadn't happened. It was the fact that they were the only two people in town who seemed to understand the strange kind of limbo they were in.

Nine days. It had already been *nine days*.

"Nothing since the deposition on Tuesday," Magda said. It had been mostly questions about the first day of filming, though she wasn't sure what that meant. "You?"

"Same." Mac had a baby stroller with him—the kind with massive off-road tires—and she assumed he must be watching one of his friends' kids while they ran the course with their dog, until she saw a fluffy tail waft up from where the baby should be.

"Did you get a *stroller* for your *cat?*" she asked incredulously.

"Connor was getting rid of it—and it took me nearly a week to get my cat to stop using my shoes as scratching posts to punish me for my absence. I figured this was better than leaving him home alone."

They both fell silent for a moment as Connor's wife, Deenie, who taught obedience classes at Furry Friends, ran the course with their oversized Great Dane mix, Maximus—and a toddler who was shrieking with glee as she chased after the dog. Connor bolted onto the course to scoop up his daughter—which distracted Maximus, who began barking and loping in circles around his people.

A bulldog somehow got loose and ran onto the course, chased by Astrid, a teenager who worked at the shelter, and half a dozen other dogs began barking and straining to join the fun.

Glorious Pine Hollow chaos. Right on schedule.

Meanwhile, Cupcake barely looked up, lazing peacefully against Magda's feet.

"That reality blogger was saying it was something about the new format," Mac said, picking up their previous topic. "The rivals thing. Some contestant saying it was rigged."

"Are we supposed to be reading the blogs?"

Mac lifted a hand to wave to someone, his arm brushing hers

as he resettled in his chair. "The producers are the ones who sent us home. They had to know we'd be curious."

"I'm just focusing on staying ready," Magda insisted.

The first couple of days back had been nonstop—checking on the bakery and restocking all the frozen dough, going to family dinner at her parents' place and being equal parts grilled and feted by her *entire* family for several hours, and doing her best not to worry about the show—or think about Mac. But then, as the days had stretched to a full week, as there was no more room in the bakery freezer and she'd run out of places to put all her practice bakes, it had gotten harder and harder not to think about it.

Not to wonder and worry.

She caught Charlotte watching them from the starting area, frowning at Magda with Mac.

"I should probably—" Magda began at the same moment Mac said, "I've been wanting to talk to you."

She'd wanted to talk to him, too. Far too much. Though she told herself it was just because he was the only person who understood the waiting game.

She glanced at him, keeping the visual contact brief before looking back at the course where a tiny fluffy dog was now bounding through it like it was spring-loaded. "I'm pretty sure we're still not supposed to collude."

"Are you mad that I kissed you?"

"What?" she flushed, instantly flustered. "Why would you— why would I—" *Why were they talking about this in front of the entire town?*

"You've done a pretty good job of ignoring me for the last week."

"I always ignore you."

"So this is just normal ignoring and not special ignoring?"

"Strictly normal ignoring," she agreed.

"Good." There was an air of finality to the word, but he didn't move away, and after a moment he said, "So you're not mad? We never really talked about—"

"We don't need to talk about it. It doesn't have to be a thing—"

"We should at least acknowledge—"

"We talked about it. I told you I want to stay focused on the competition."

"Yeah, me too," he agreed, falling silent. After a long moment when they both watched the next run, he abruptly asked, "Do you worry about letting people down?"

"You mean on the show?"

"Yeah, I guess."

She turned her head to look at his profile, but he was still watching the dogs, so she did the same. "That's part of why I didn't want to tell my family," she admitted. "I knew they'd be *intensely* supportive, rooting for me, and I'd feel like I needed to apologize to all of them when I got voted off."

Her mother had *not* been pleased when she realized Magda had hidden her involvement in *Cake-Off*—but her family had rallied by immediately throwing a massive barbecue that had made her feel like she was the center of a very intimidating and very hot spotlight for an entire afternoon. It had been everything she'd dreaded it would be.

"And if you didn't get voted off?" Mac asked. "If you made it all the way?"

She grimaced. "I don't think I really thought I would. Even making it this far, halfway...I always dreamed about winning, but it didn't feel like something that would happen to me. Not real me. Just dream me, you know?"

He nodded. "I never expected to win—I just wanted the experience. And yeah, I wanted to win, but I didn't look ahead to the end. One step at a time. Just making the choice that's right in front of me."

"You could do it," she said, albeit a little grudgingly. "You're good at it. The show stuff. It's so easy for you to be yourself."

"Don't know how to be anybody else."

Magda made a face at that easy platitude. It had always been harder for her. "I always feel like I'm not...I don't know, impressive enough. Basic boring Magda. That's why it drove me so crazy every time it felt like you were telling me I wasn't good enough."

"When did I tell you that?" he asked incredulously. "You've always been terrifyingly good at all things baking. I was sure you were going to win the whole thing. You're a beast in the kitchen—and the least boring person I know outside of it. How do you not know that?"

She met his eyes. "You didn't want me to be your pastry chef."

"When you were eighteen?"

"No. When I came back from France."

He snorted. "I couldn't afford you. And you were yelling at me about the maple cake—"

"Which you wouldn't admit was suspiciously like the one I made for you—"

"It was a great cake. But I made my own version, based on a recipe I found in *my* gran's kitchen. Which I would have told you if you'd ever asked."

She flushed, a little embarrassed. "I might have been overly sensitive. I just felt like you thought I was a joke, and I wanted you to regret the way you'd treated me."

"Oh, believe me, I have."

"I probably cared too much what you thought," she confessed. "It made me irrational."

"You always drove me crazy, too," he admitted. Then, after a heavy pause, "I wasn't ready to move the Cup."

"What?"

"Back when you took that spot on the square. I had the deposit, but I was dragging my feet, scared to commit to the lease. If it hadn't been you, someone else would have taken it. I wasn't mad at you for that—I was mad because it felt like you were doing it to spite me. As some kind of revenge."

"I wasn't." She paused. "At least, not entirely." People were looking at them now—the infamous rivals sitting side by side. "How did it get so out of hand?"

"I don't know." He bumped her shoulder with his. "But it made me better, trying to keep up with you. I never really thought about how much the competition with you motivated me until we were at *Cake-Off.*"

"And then you really wanted to destroy me?"

"No," he said, as if the word surprised him. "Then it felt wrong that we were on opposite sides."

She looked over then, finding him watching her, and he didn't look away. She searched his dark brown eyes, trying to find the manipulation in them. Trying to see the lie. But all she saw was a sort of puzzled consideration.

"You always scared the shit out me," he said softly—and she didn't know why those words should suddenly make her mouth go dry, but they did. All at once, her breath was short and she felt a tingling along her arms.

But they were still competitors...weren't they? Was he playing the long game for when they went back to the competition?

Trying to throw her off? Or was this something else? Did this thing that felt like it was stretching across the short distance between them have nothing to do with the *Cake-Off* at all?

She didn't know why she'd been so honest with him. Why it was so easy to be real with him.

She'd always wanted him to see her. And during that first summer, it had felt like he did. And now, with him looking at her this way...could she trust it? Could she trust him?

"Mags! Come help!"

Charlotte was suddenly there, her voice a little too loud, and three degrees too cheerful. She grabbed Magda's hands, dragging her up out of her chair and flashing Mac a too-bright smile. "You don't mind if I steal her, do you?" she asked, already dragging Magda and Cupcake away.

"What was that?" Charlotte hissed, when they were halfway to the starting line.

Magda just shook her head. "I wish I knew."

"So what's going on with you and Magda?"

Mac kept his expression neutral and his eyes on his cards. He'd wondered how deep into poker night he'd make it before someone lobbed that question at him. They'd rescheduled three times, but had finally managed to make it happen Sunday night after the fundraiser—and he'd made it through greetings and gathering of snacks and drinks, and halfway through the first hand before Connor had oh-so-casually tossed the words out along with his raise.

"You did look awfully cozy today," Kendall's husband and the newest addition to their group, Brody, chimed in before Mac could.

"We were just talking," he said mildly, calling Connor's raise.

"Ten whole minutes of talking and no one had to call in a referee," Ben commented lightly. "It must be a record." Pine Hollow's mayor, and one of Mac's oldest friends, he tossed his own chip onto the pile in the center.

"Maybe we've grown." Mac took a casual sip of his beer.

Around the table, five matching expressions of surprise met that comment. Then Levi mumbled, "I didn't know that show worked miracles. Reraise."

"You gonna tell us about it?" George asked, mild as always.

"Can't," Mac said, setting down his cards as Levi started pushing the pot higher. "My lawyer advised me against it."

Connor smirked as he called Levi's reraise.

His friends didn't push for more, but he could feel their curiosity. Just as he'd been able to feel the entire town's curiosity for the last week. Everyone wanted to know what had happened on *Cake-Off.* He'd been working at the Cup every day, trying to keep busy and distract himself from the impatient itch to get back to the competition, but he'd mainly stayed in the kitchen. Hiding from that curiosity.

And thinking about things.

About Magda. About the competition. About his entire freaking life.

His life hadn't taken the path he'd expected, but he wasn't unhappy with where he'd ended up. Who he'd become. He didn't often think about it, but he didn't really have regrets because his life had sort of felt inevitable to this point. He'd made the best choice he could from moment to moment.

Dropping out of school when his grandfather was sick. Staying home and opening the Cup to be close to his grandmother—who had always thought there were bigger things in store for him and wanted him to go back to school. But Mac had stayed, for his family—maybe irrationally, maybe because his parents hadn't stayed for him—but he didn't regret it. He'd loved running the Cup. Loved growing it over the years. Bit by bit.

Yes, he'd avoided serious relationships in his twenties, keeping things casual, pulling back and letting things fade when they started to get too intense—but that was just because he was still a work in progress, still figuring out who he was. Letting life happen.

There had been a period, a few years back, when Ben, Connor, and Levi were all engaged at the same time, and Mac had thought maybe it was time for him to settle down, too—but it hadn't happened. His pattern had stayed the same, even as his friends got married and started having kids. George had recruited him to join his band—and then George had married Charlotte. And even Cleo, who had never wanted anything serious, had cut off their friends-with-benefits relationship and tied the knot with another lawyer at her firm.

Mac wasn't one of those people who thought you had to be married with kids to have a fulfilling life, but he'd always kind of thought he would go the family route eventually. But he hadn't done anything to actually make that happen. He'd just sort of waited for the future to come to him, instead of going after it. Letting the choices make themselves.

Don't want things you can't have, and you won't be disappointed.

But was his grandmother right? Was he just scared of being needed?

He'd always considered himself an emotionally evolved

guy—his grandmother had started taking him to family therapy when he was eight because she'd wanted help to ensure he never felt he was in any way responsible for his parents not being more involved in his life.

But honestly it was the Broadway musicals that she'd taken him to that had really connected him to his emotions as a kid. Given him permission to feel the big things. He'd done community theater in high school and had planned to major in that in college—until his life had gone in another direction.

He didn't regret it. But he was also realizing that for all his supposed emotional maturity, he was still dodging the big feelings. *Don't want things too much...don't try...*

"Are you guys ever scared of letting people down?" He must have had more alcohol than he'd thought, because that question came out almost without thought.

"Constantly," Ben and Levi said instantly and in unison—and then lifted their beer bottles to clink the necks together in salute.

That made sense. Ben was Mr. Mayor, Superdad, and Superhusband. And Levi was the chief of police and protector of the whole town. Mac was just a cook.

"I only care what Kendall thinks," Brody announced to the table. "Used to care about everyone else, but it was messing me up, so I stopped."

"You just stopped?" Mac asked.

"Yep," Brody declared. As if it was that easy. And Mac barely resisted the urge to glare at the golden boy. Brody was a freaking Olympian and recently retired professional athlete, so his perspective might be somewhat skewed.

"Is this about the *Cake-Off*?" Connor asked.

"No." It was like he'd told Magda—he hadn't expected to

win. No pressure to be the best. But the question still nagged at him...

"Is this about Magda?" George asked softly.

He said no again, but he hesitated too long this time. And they were all watching him. All these guys who knew him best—well, the four who knew him best and Brody.

"She drives me crazy," he said finally. But he didn't say the words the way he would have six months ago. Or even six weeks ago. There was less aggravation and more bafflement behind the familiar words now.

"Didn't look like a problem today," Ben commented.

"We were talking about the show." Because, oddly, as much as the show pitted them against each other, it had also brought them together in a way he wasn't sure any other force on earth could have.

She didn't feel like his adversary anymore. She felt like someone who had been bonded to him by this bizarre gauntlet they were both in the middle of. They were connected now. But he still had no idea what that meant. She wouldn't talk to him about the kiss—which was a pretty strong indication that she didn't want an encore performance—but he couldn't stop thinking about it. About the taste of her. The feel. The curve of her neck. The flare of heat in her eyes.

"Maybe the fear of letting people down isn't the problem," George said. "Maybe letting it stop you is."

Thankfully, Connor's two-year-old chose that moment to run into the game room buck naked and dripping wet, accompanied by a pair of barking dogs—and Mac was spared any more discussion resulting from his ill-advised question.

By the time Connor had the kid and the dogs turned back over to Deenie, everyone had forgotten Mac's moment of existential crisis about letting people down.

They went back to playing poker and shooting the breeze, and Mac switched to water so he wouldn't say anything stupid— or start belting out show tunes, as he had an unfortunate tendency to do when he got a little sloshed.

By the end of the night, he still hadn't told anyone about the kiss. Or anything else that had happened at the *Cake-Off*.

It felt like their secret. And he found a big part of why he was so eager to get back to the competition wasn't for the competition itself. It was to get back into that bubble with her and see what happened next.

It was a different world. Anything could happen.

Chapter Twenty-Six

They got the call to go back to set on Wednesday.

By Thursday morning they were all back at King Arthur, comparing notes and nervously waiting for more information. Nothing felt stable now. They all seemed to know the competition could be halted at any moment.

A van had picked up Mac and Magda that morning, but it had already been filled with other contestants on their way from the airport, so they hadn't talked to each other on the drive back to King Arthur.

"I heard it was Caroline—first out," Leah gossiped, as they all huddled together in the Proving Room.

Eunice nodded. "She did seem more angry than sad."

"She claimed it was unfair that only the blue team had known about the archrivals twist in advance—"

"Which it was," Abby grumbled.

"And that she was completely thrown by seeing the ex-friend who had slept with her husband and only lost because of that," Leah concluded. "And the lawyers had to prove that the baking competition itself was fair and that the contracts we signed had clearly indicated that they were not responsible for any stress we might feel either from being on a reality television show or interacting with the other contestants—regardless of our previous relationship or lack thereof with those contestants. Or something like that."

"So the show won?" Magda asked.

"I think they just got the legal team to sign off on the production continuing while they continue to fight it out. But yeah. The show must go on."

And this time, Magda was going to enjoy herself.

Going home and not knowing if the show was going to continue had reminded her that this was her dream, this was what she'd been working toward for the last three years, and she wanted to *enjoy* it. Her anxiety hadn't gone away completely, but it was exponentially less than it had been when they'd first arrived a few weeks ago.

She knew the rhythm of the show now, and what she needed to do. And she wasn't going to be distracted by Mac.

Though it was hard not to notice him with only seven bakers left.

She'd just gotten back from hair and makeup and taken a seat next to Eunice, Abby, and Leah, grabbing one of the sandwiches that had been left by craft services when Leah glanced past her shoulder. "Are we staying Red Team strong?"

"I guess. Why?" Magda asked, confused.

Leah nodded past her shoulder. "Because Big Red is on his way over here."

Magda looked up as Mac approached, back in his *Cake-Off* apron with a long-sleeved T-shirt pushed up to show off his forearms. Her mouth went dry as she tried not to stare. It wasn't like she hadn't seen him a million times before.

"Have you guys noticed Tim is being extra dickish since we got back?" Mac asked by way of greeting.

"You may stay." Leah magnanimously waved him to the empty chair beside Magda.

He dropped onto it, grabbing a sandwich of his own.

Eunice and Abby were speculating about what the next challenge would be when Mac leaned closer and lowered his voice for Magda's ears alone.

"Excited to be back?" he asked.

"I am, actually." She took a bite of her sandwich before admitting, "I was so stressed before that I forgot to have fun. And this time...I don't know. I'm still nervous, but it's like good nervous, you know?"

"Yeah."

She met his eyes as they ate in silence, and after a moment her awareness of him prompted her to whisper, "I still want to stay focused on the competition."

"Me, too." He nodded, instantly catching her meaning.

She felt her face heating, but a producer called them into the kitchen before she could say more.

Mac's grin flashed out. "Good luck, cupcake."

For once, the nickname didn't feel like derision. It almost felt like flirting...and far from throwing her off her game, she felt excited and more focused as they all funneled into the *Cake-Off* kitchen once again.

Nothing had changed. They were all directed toward their stations for the day and then the host and judges entered at the front of the room. The introductions continued as if nothing had happened, as if there hadn't been a mysterious break where they were all sent home for almost two weeks.

Week seven. Bread Week. Seven bakers remaining. And a Skills Challenge to start.

Magda took a deep breath, a buzz of excitement humming in her blood.

It felt right, possibly for the first time since she'd been in the *Cake-Off* kitchen. This was her dream.

Starting now.

The Skills Challenge was brioche.

Mac didn't know if it was the fact that it was bread week, or the pause in filming that had reset everything, or the fact that things with Magda felt like they might actually be on okay footing, but something was different today, and the bake... the bake was freaking excellent.

He hummed to himself, the familiar tune of "It Only Takes a Taste" from *Waitress* adding a cheerful lilt to his action as he divided his dough into loaves. At a station near the front of the room, Magda was chatting with the cameras, her tone light and breezy. He still found himself tuning into that sound, but it wasn't a distraction today. It was music.

It was good to be back. This place was chaos and pressure, but being away had made him realize he also loved it. And he wanted to do well—not so he could beat Magda or win, but just to prove something to himself. That he was actually a baker and not just here by default so they could get Magda on the show.

His brioche took first—earning him a nebulous advantage in the next challenge. Abby was second and Magda third. Tim was struggling this week—and Mac found himself silently rooting for the arrogant pastry chef to go home. But this was only the first challenge. It had taken so long—with the dough needing time to prove and chill—that they wouldn't film the second half of the episode until tomorrow.

After interviews they trickled back to the inn, where the remaining members of the Red Team gathered in the inn's common room—this time with a karaoke machine that Eunice had brought back with her.

"The Brioche King!" Leah bellowed as soon as he walked into the room—proving both that she'd already dipped into the wine, and that the archrivals dynamics had been all but abandoned. Thank goodness.

The seven of them had bonded after the show was nearly called off. Well. The six of them. Tim still seemed to think he was among peasants.

Leah appeared to be deep into the bottle of white already—her Skills Challenge today had not gone well. Judge Joanie had murmured a disappointed "Oh dear" when she'd tasted Leah's underproved brioche. Leah's only comfort was that Tim had been right there in the bottom with her.

Magda and Eunice seemed to be doing their best to comfort and distract her when Mac joined them, accepting a beer.

"Magda tells us you're a singer," Eunice announced.

Mac gave Magda an arch look. "Does she?"

"He's in a band," Magda confirmed, though she was looking at him and not at her friends. "And if you have any Broadway music on that thing, I guarantee you he knows every single word."

"Broadway, huh?" Leah asked.

"What can I say? I love when people randomly burst into song." He crouched down to pet the inn's cat, who had come over to investigate his presence.

Eunice was frowning at a list of songs in a little paper booklet. "I don't know if any of these are Broadway. Normally I'd just plug my phone into the machine and get whatever song we want, but since they take away our phones we're limited to the ones that come preprogrammed."

She handed Mac the booklet, and he drank his beer as he skimmed through the popular titles—"Don't Stop Believing," "Rolling in the Deep," "Material Girl." There didn't seem to be any Broadway—until he got to the duets section. Then his gaze caught on a title and he laughed out loud.

"What?" Eunice asked. "What did you find?"

"It's a duet," he said, turning the page toward Magda to show her.

She snorted. "We've done that one before. At Elinor's birthday party. A couple of years ago?"

"I don't have clear memories of that night." There had been a significant amount of alcohol involved before Mac and Mags had taken the stage to essentially yell at each other via song.

"Neither do I," she admitted.

"Well, now you have to do it," Leah announced.

And so Mac found himself standing in the middle of the common room beside Magda as the opening bars of "Anything You Can Do (I Can Do Better)" began to play from the karaoke machine's speakers.

There was only one microphone.

"Do you want to hold it?" Mac offered.

"No, it's fine. You can hold it."

"Are you sure? I don't mind—"

"No. You have more experience with microphones."

"I mean, I don't think singing at the bar—"

"Mac, just hold the microphone."

"Fine."

They'd missed their cue, and Eunice offered to restart the music, but Magda waved her off. "No, we're good."

Mac waited, looking to Magda as Annie Oakley's lyrics appeared on the little screen. And she looked right back at him.

"That's your line," Magda prompted.

"No, it's yours. That's the female part."

"You sang it last time."

"I'm sure I didn't." Admittedly, he didn't have clear memories of that night...

"I'm sure you did."

Okay, he probably did. "Still, if you want it this time..."

She waved to the screen. "It's all yours."

"You should really do it—"

"Your voice is better than mine."

"You have a nice voice—"

"Mac, would you just take the lead?"

By then they'd missed the entire first chorus.

"Restart?" Eunice offered again, but Leah was laughing so hard they decided to just jump in and carry on.

It was...awkward. Neither of them seemed to want to fight anymore, so the playful competition of the song—which hadn't been quite so playful the last time they'd sung it, according to Pine Hollow legend—fell flat. When they got to the line about neither one of them being able to bake a pie, Leah snorted wine out of her nose—which distracted them from finishing the song.

"That was weird," Eunice announced. And she wasn't wrong. "Try another one."

"I should probably—I think I'll head upstairs," Mac said. "Don't really want to be hungover on national television."

"Yeah, good call," Magda agreed—and Mac realized he'd inadvertently signaled the end of the impromptu party.

They all headed upstairs, drifting off toward their various rooms...and Mac lingered in the hall until it was just him and

Magda. He didn't know why he stayed—though in his defense, Magda did also.

"That was..."

"Awkward?" he finished for her.

"It's nice that we don't want to kill each other anymore," she said—though she didn't sound like she thought it was nice at all. "Is it weird that I kind of miss the edge, though?"

His eyes met hers, holding them. "You want an edge?" he asked, his voice deepening.

Magda's breath caught as it was suddenly back, that crackling tension that had always existed between them. But it was different now. It wasn't anger. It was something else. Something that had probably been there beneath the anger all along. Fueling it.

"No," she whispered, the word breathless. "Just focusing on the competition."

He nodded as the door to her room closed between them, cutting off that flash of heat.

Right. *Cake-Off.* Anything else would have to wait.

Chapter Twenty-Seven

And the winner this week, who blew us away with his brioche and stunned us with his cinnamon swirl, whose braided bread was nothing short of brilliant—as I'm sure will come as no surprise—it's Mac!"

There was a polite round of applause and a few slaps on the back—but everyone had known Mac was going to take it after finishing first in the Skills Challenge and earning a "flawless" from Alexander Clay and an "I could just eat that all day" from Judge Joanie in the elimination round.

Magda tried to be happy for him, but she stood at the other end of the row of bakers—gripping Leah's hand tightly in hers. They all knew what was coming, and she just wanted to slow time, to drag this out so it didn't happen, or go back in time to change things, to add a few more minutes in the oven.

There was no coming back from raw dough inside your bread braid.

Don't cry. Just don't cry. Magda stared straight ahead, struggling for composure.

"And this is the hard part. It really does get harder every week," Jeffrey Flanders said with fake emotion, as if he had actually gotten to know any of the contestants. "And this week is the hardest yet. We are really going to miss this baker, who was always such a bright light in the kitchen, who gave us incredible quality week after week, and we're so shocked to see leaving us..."

Dontcrydontcrydontcry.

"We will genuinely miss you...I'm so sorry." Jeffrey Flanders took a deep breath, really milking it, until Magda wanted to throw something at his face.

She'd wanted to delay the inevitable, but this felt like torture.

Flanders nodded once, pityingly. "I'm afraid it's Leah who will be leaving the kitchen."

Magda sniffed. Leah nodded, her face a mask of resignation. That raw dough. As soon as Alexander Clay had cut into her braid and *tsk*ed, they'd known the only thing that would save her would be someone else messing up even worse. And the rest of them had muddled through.

As the judges murmured their sympathies, Magda turned to hug Leah with tears in her eyes.

"Oh God, Mags, don't cry!" Leah said, her own eyes growing wet.

Eunice rushed over to join their hug, and Abby was there, patting Leah on the back, and then everyone was there, circling her with sympathy. They all wanted to win, but because they achieved baking brilliance, not because someone else fell apart. Even Tim came over and seemed vaguely sympathetic—though Magda had her doubts about his sincerity.

"You better win," Leah said to Magda and Eunice, gripping each of them by the arm as the judges walked over to add their mumbles of sympathy.

Normally they would all be funneled back to the Proving Room, where Leah would be whisked away for her final interview and the rest of them would be quickly cycled through the confessionals to talk about the results, since they'd already discussed the bakes in detail while the judges were deliberating. But today, the producers instructed Leah to head back to the proving room and asked the rest of them to resume their marks.

The cameras watched them all wave to Leah as she made her noble, slightly tearful departure—probably just another shot Stephen wanted for this episode—but then instead of releasing them, Jeffrey Flanders struck his "And now there's a twist!" pose.

"I know you all must be exhausted after the *longest* Bread Week bake in *Cake-Off* history," he intoned dramatically, "but we have a little business to take care of before you can go collapse."

Collapse sounded about right. Magda's shoulders ached from kneading, and the marathon bread challenge had completely wiped her out.

"Now, some of you may have looked around and noticed that there are only six of you left..."

Oh no.

Magda's heart suddenly started pounding harder at those words, her exhaustion swallowed by a surge of nerves. She'd forgotten. Or assumed they wouldn't be doing it this year with all the Archrival gimmicks, but she should have known better.

Six bakers...

"And that means it's time for the infamous Chocolate Shop Challenge!"

Beside her, Eunice made a sound that resembled a whimper.

"As always," Flanders powered on, "you will be divided into teams of three, and each team member will be responsible for three batches of twenty-four identical chocolates. These chocolates will be displayed in your 'shop,' and each team member must also contribute to the showpiece—which must feature three different types of chocolate, and whether it is a cake, a sculpture, or, as we saw one year, a chocolate waterfall, every bit of your showpiece must be edible. The winning team will be safe, and someone on the losing team will be going home."

Magda tried not to look terrified. Every *Cake-Off* fan knew this challenge. Almost every season it sent a frontrunner home. The temperatures in the kitchen were always too warm for chocolate work, and someone's showpiece inevitably melted.

"Now," Jeffrey Flanders announced, cheerfully oblivious to the terror he was inspiring—or, more likely, enjoying it—"since this challenge takes a bit of planning, you'll divvy up into your teams tonight and have the weekend to practice. Mac, since you won the last challenge, you'll be one team captain and you'll have first pick, and Abby, as second place during Bread Week, you will be the other. Abby and Mac, if you'd like to join me."

Before Mac and Abby could move, someone shouted for everyone to hold and Jeffrey was coached through reshooting his lines since Stephen hadn't been satisfied with the way he introduced the team captains.

The minutes stretched on as Flanders did take after take, and Magda had more and more time to worry about who her team would be.

Tim had been bragging about his chocolate work from day one, and wowing the judges whenever he added sculpted or molded pieces to his bakes. He was the obvious first choice. Zain had gone to Belgium to take a special class on chocolate, specifically in preparation for this week—but Magda wasn't sure Mac knew that. Had he heard when Zain told Leah in an obvious bid to impress her? Eunice had said she was most scared of Chocolate Week...but Mac hadn't been there, had he?

All the various combinations of teams rattled around in her head. If she ended up on a team with Abby and Eunice and they lost, would Magda still make it through? Eunice had been inconsistent, but the judges loved her, and Abby had been near the top the entire time.

Finally, it was the moment of truth. Mac and Abby were standing on either side of Jeffrey Flanders, who turned slightly toward Mac. "As the winner of Bread Week and team captain, who would you like to pick as your first teammate?"

Mac didn't hesitate. "Magda."

Her jaw fell. She was *at best* third-pick material when it came to chocolate, but Mac looked utterly calm as he announced his choice. Abby picked Tim, no surprise. And then Mac announced his next pick.

"Eunice."

Sugar. They were going to lose. Abby had the two best chocolate workers on her team, and she was a beast herself. Magda knew she should be panicking, but there was another feeling swirling in with the panic, and she wasn't sure what to make of it. Was she . . . was she *happy* he'd chosen her?

Standing next to two chocolate experts, he'd chosen her *first*. It just didn't compute.

She just hoped she didn't let him down, because if they weren't able to defeat the juggernaut of chocolate genius that was the other team, someone was going home.

"Okay, the first thing you *remember* baking. Go."

Magda looked up from the raspberry truffle she was drizzling with ruby chocolate, searching her memory at Eunice's question. It was a game they'd been playing all afternoon as they worked their way through the second of their two five-hour practice sessions in the inn kitchen. One of them would toss out a question, and the other two had to answer as quickly as possible, without thinking about it.

They'd already been through which "one" are you (Mac: "The handsome one, obviously"; Eunice: "The nervous one, also obviously"; and Magda: "Oh God, I'm the one who cries, aren't I?"), favorite thing to bake (Mac: cinnamon bread; Eunice: fruit tarts; and Magda: vanilla cakes), who would you most like to see eliminated next (everyone: Tim), and who would you most like to see win if you can't (over which Mac and Magda had both hesitated far too long before each saying "Eunice"; and Eunice had answered: "Magda. Sorry, Mac.")

"Snickerdoodle cookies with my gran," Mac said at Magda's side. He was close to Magda, so close their arms kept brushing—but it was a small kitchen. It didn't mean anything.

"Magda?"

"Angel food cake with my aunt. And yours?"

"Chocolate chip cookies. So basic."

"All right, what will you do with the money if you win?" Magda asked, starting to move her finished chocolates to the display they'd created. The first time they'd made the chocolate centerpiece it had . . . not gone well. But today it actually looked good—and like it might stay upright.

Which was a good thing, because the other team's practice time had been before theirs, and their showpiece had looked intimidatingly amazing.

"Easy. Move the Cup to a location that *isn't* too small and falling down around my ears. Eunice?"

Eunice hesitated so long that Magda glanced behind her to Eunice's station just to make sure she was okay. Her hands had stopped moving and her expression was slightly lost.

"I don't know," Eunice admitted. "When I think about winning, it's not the money . . . I just think of the look on my parents' faces. Being able to say, 'See, I am good at this. See, this is a real career. I don't need to be an accountant.'"

"You've already proven that," Magda said. "Do you know how many people apply to be on this show? And you've made it to the top six! We all have."

It was wild to think of it. To realize they'd come all this way.

But there was no time for dwelling.

Half an hour later, they all stared at their chocolate display. It looked good. It tasted good.

"Now if we can just do it half an hour faster tomorrow, we'll be in great shape," Mac said, snagging one of Eunice's chocolates and popping it into his mouth.

The producers had left them alone—they didn't film the practice sessions—but Eunice put as many of the chocolates as she could fit on a tray and carried them out to give to the crew while Mac and Magda began to clean up. Edible bribery was never a bad idea around here.

Magda tried not to be too hyperaware of his arms as they brushed past each other, gathering up all the dirty pans and bowls. It was domestic, and sort of nice, moving around each other in the inn's kitchen—even if she was disconcertingly aware of him.

Until his arm brushed hers and a bowl of chocolate mirror glaze slipped from her fingers to splatter all over the floor. "Oh, crumb!"

She glanced over to find Mac's eyes glinting at hers with entirely too much humor.

"What?"

"*Crumb?* Do you ever swear?"

She flushed. "I don't have a problem with swearing. I just—my aunt Lena, the one who taught me to bake? She would always say *crumb* and *biscuits* and *sugar* instead of swearing, and I guess it rubbed off."

"So when I call you cupcake, you think I'm swearing at you?"

She narrowed her eyes. "When you call me cupcake, I think you're doing it because you know it drives me crazy."

"Would you prefer sugar? Honey? Mon petite croquembouche?"

"*No.* Do not call me a croquembouche."

"As you wish, my little baumkuchen."

Magda groaned. "That sounds so dirty."

"Does it?" he asked, his eyes glinting wickedly.

Thankfully she was saved from answering by Eunice returning.

"Oh no! What happened?" she exclaimed, seeing the chocolate glaze all over the floor.

"It was nothing," Magda said. "I was just clumsy. You don't have to help clean up—you did more than your share yesterday."

"No, of course I'll help."

"Did the crew get enough chocolate?" Mac asked, a note in his voice that Magda couldn't quite identify.

"They did," Eunice confirmed. "But apparently there's a school group staying at the hotel down the street where the crew sleeps, and one of the PAs said they'd take anything we have left over. But I can take them after we clean up—"

"No, go ahead," Mac urged. "We've got this."

Did he want to be alone with her again? Magda held her breath, focusing on mopping up the spilled chocolate until Eunice was gone again with another tray of chocolates.

"I was sorry to hear about your aunt Lena," Mac said from the massive sink, where he was piling bowls.

"It was ages ago," Magda reminded him.

"Yeah, but I know how much she meant to you." They were both silent for a moment, but it was an easy silence. A together silence. "You never gave your answer," he said finally, when she stood from cleaning the floor and began on the counters. His hands were deep in a sink full of suds.

"What answer?"

"What you would do with the money if you won."

"I don't know. I kind of want to open another location. Like Eunice, I'm not sure I really thought about it."

"Something to prove to your parents?"

"No. Just... something to prove to myself, I guess." A few weeks ago, she would have thought she had something to prove to him, but that had never been true. In some messed-up way, it was almost as though she'd thought if she won *Cake-Off*, it would *prove* that she was lovable—even if he hadn't loved her. "I always admired that you never... You didn't care what anyone thought."

"Defense mechanism," he said without looking away from the dishes. "Don't want their approval, and you won't be disappointed if you don't get it. I'm not sure if my therapist would be incredibly proud or incredibly horrified by that."

"Your grandmother's proud of you."

"Your family is proud of you," he reminded her.

"Yeah, I guess they are. I always felt kind of invisible before, but this is definitely changing that."

He scoffed, still without looking at her. "You were never invisible."

Magda let the glow of those words seep into her, holding on to them as she made the counters shine.

After a long moment, Mac said, "My gran thinks I'm afraid of commitment because I have a horror of letting people down."

Magda snorted. "That's ridiculous. You're Mr. Commitment. You show up to every town event, and you're always there for your friends—and I should know, because I haven't been able to avoid you for the last ten years because of it."

"You calling my gran a liar?"

"No. I'm just saying she's *wrong*."

"Impossible."

She smiled and, finished with the counters, moved over to the sink area to help him dry—but she must have moved too quietly, because when she appeared at his side he jumped, dropping the bowl in his hands into the water. The splash hit him full in the chest—soaking his T-shirt, since he'd already removed his chocolate-smeared apron.

"Biscuits," he grumbled—and she smiled at his choice of words, even as she winced at his sopping appearance. And tried not to notice the way his abs were defined beneath the clinging fabric. Of *course* the man had a six-pack.

"Sorry." Magda tore her eyes away.

"You didn't do anything."

But neither of them spoke for the next few minutes as they worked side by side. Only this time, the silence didn't feel comfortable and warm and fuzzy. It felt taut. And itchy. And like she needed to say something, *anything*, to alleviate it before she went up in flames.

"Do you think we're ready?" she blurted, when she couldn't stand it any longer.

"As ready as we'll ever be." He handed her the last dish, his shirt still soaking as he bent to release the water in the sink. "Try not to worry about it. Just get a good night's sleep and do the best you can."

It was good advice. But she did worry about it. Because if they lost...one of them would be going home. Her or Mac or Eunice and right now...right now that felt like a tragedy.

"Why did you pick me?" she asked softly.

He didn't ask what she meant. "You're the best," he said back, just as quietly.

"Not at chocolate."

He met her eyes from a distance of inches, and for a moment she thought he was going to argue or tell her to believe in herself. His dark brown eyes held hers, and then a wry smile flashed out, making his dimple pop. "I'm operating on a theory."

"A theory?"

"That working with people I like will have better results than working with people who are convinced they're the best."

People I like.

He liked her. Warmth pooled low in her belly.

His dimple flashed again. "That. And I'm starting to think we bring out the best in each other."

Her heart thudded irrationally hard. He'd picked her first because he liked her. Because they brought out the best in each other. She shouldn't read more into that. She shouldn't feel this fizzy delight. This was a competition, and she needed to stay focused on winning.

But she really, *really* liked his reasoning.

She felt herself leaning toward him, just listing gently, like a slowly collapsing éclair tower—

The kitchen door swung open again, Eunice returning, and

Magda leapt away, four feet suddenly separating them. "Are you guys okay if I send the cake over to the kids, too?" Eunice called out, oblivious to whatever she might have interrupted over by the sink.

"Yeah, that's great," Magda answered, stupidly breathless and not looking at Mac.

She needed to get out of here. She'd told him she didn't want any distractions, and here she was about to throw herself at him in the practice kitchen. "I'll see you guys tomorrow," she said, looking at neither of them as she grabbed her things and hustled toward the door.

"Bright and early," Mac agreed—and if he'd felt anything in that taut, itchy moment by the sink, it didn't show in his voice.

Maybe it was just her. Maybe she was the only one slowly losing her mind. But she fled the room before she could forget why she was really here.

Cake-Off. It was all about the *Cake-Off.*

Chapter Twenty-Eight

"Five minutes! Five minutes remaining!"

"We aren't going to make it." Magda's hands were shaking.

Eunice was frantically popping her chocolates out of the molds. Mac and Magda had already finished theirs and added them to the display, but Eunice had volunteered to make the chocolate ring box portion of their centerpiece—and she'd ended up having to remake it when it shattered to pieces, so she'd been late getting her chocolates into their molds. They'd barely had time to set, and Magda would normally be helping her, but their flaming heart chocolate sculpture was refusing to stay upright.

She should be using this time to spray it with the hot-pink edible glitter, but instead she was bracing it between her hands and trying desperately to figure out something edible they could use as a prop so it wouldn't go crashing to the floor the second she was forced to step away.

"Don't worry. We've got this." Mac's voice was cool and calm—and entirely too close to her ear as he reached around her with a can of freezing spray. His chest brushed against her arm, the heat of him making her flush even in the insane heat of the kitchen. He blasted the icy spray at the joint where the vertical portions of the sculpture connected to the base. "It'll set. It just needs to cool."

"How is it supposed to cool when it's eleven million degrees in here?"

"Don't worry, sugar. Just give it the ice queen glare you've been giving me for the last decade and we'll be golden," he quipped, aiming at another joint.

"Ha."

He flashed her an impish grin that absolutely did *not* melt her knees—she refused to think about melting *anything* right now—and then moved again. Magda bent as he twisted, contorting himself to hit another melting joint with the freezing spray, and his breath stirred the hairs at the back of her neck.

She shuddered, fighting to keep her hands steady.

The chocolate. It was all about the chocolate. She was *not* attracted to this man. Even if he was a calm, competent leader who never let them get discouraged and always rallied with a quick change of plans when part of their plan fell apart. Even if they had been working in close proximity for the last few days, in a hot kitchen that had left him just sweaty enough that his auburn curls were sticking to the back of his neck—which she absolutely should *not* be noticing. Even if his hands seemed to be constantly brushing hers, his arms bumping hers, little accidental working-in-tight-quarters touches that had amped her up for three days straight until she was one giant aching nerve—

"Okay. Release."

It took her stupid, hormone-addled brain a moment to realize he meant the sculpture.

"Let go," he repeated. "It should stand now—and if it wobbles, we need to know where."

"One minute, bakers!"

Magda forced herself to take a breath and opened her hands, still gently bracing the sculpture between them for a moment without holding it before tentatively, oh-so-carefully spreading her hands wide. She heard Mac catch his breath and held her own, her gaze locked on to the sculpture even as she felt the heat of his body behind hers, his hands in the air below hers in case the chocolate started to fall.

"It's holding!" she gasped.

"Eunice." Suddenly his warmth was moving away from her, and she remembered their third teammate was still desperately trying to get the last of her chocolates onto the display area.

Magda whirled, following him to Eunice's station. "What do you need?" she asked Eunice and the girl looked at her with wide and panicked eyes as Flanders called out, "Thirty seconds!"

"The dipped chocolates haven't set!"

"Doesn't matter," Mac said, taking the tray of slightly gooey dipped chocolates and rushing them over to the display, Magda and Eunice hot on his heels. They all quickly transferred the chocolates, ignoring the chocolate smudges on their gloves.

"Five...four..."

"We've got this," Mac muttered—and Magda wasn't even sure he was aware he was speaking out loud. Their hands flew back and forth.

"Two...One...Hands in the air!"

Magda flung her hands in the air, taking a step back—and straight into Mac. When she would have bounced off him— right into the table holding their display—one of his arms closed around her stomach, yanking her back against him, and her breath whooshed out as her back connected to his chest.

They were both breathing hard—from the challenge, just from the challenge—when Eunice marveled, "I can't believe we just did that."

Magda's heart was beating out of her chest—but the cameras

were rolling, even if the challenge was over, and she held herself perfectly still as Mac's arm moved and the pressure of Mac's body shifted away from her back. His hands steadied her waist for a moment, to be sure she had her balance. And then his touch was gone, Eunice was hugging her, and she was trying to remember what the world had felt like before this moment.

"All right, bakers! Time for interviews!"

Their chocolate showpiece was dripping.

Mac's heart thundered as the judges examined it from every angle. They'd decided to do both a cake and a sculptural piece in the hopes that even if the sculpture collapsed, the deliciousness of the cake would save them. It had been Eunice's idea to make their entire "shop" Valentine's themed. Dozens of heart-shaped chocolates. A heart-on-fire sculpture perched on top of a three-tiered cake—at the base of which was a molded chocolate ring box with a sugar-diamond ring inside.

If it hadn't all been melting, it would have been amazing.

Mac stood lined up with Magda and Eunice, watching the judges eye their work, and comforted himself that at least the other team's sculpture was also melting. It was taller than theirs, but it was listing gently to the side. Would that be enough?

Judging was often an out-of-body experience, but today that feeling was exacerbated by Magda and Eunice being judged alongside him. Suddenly he wasn't so confident about the way he'd picked his team. If they were in the bottom, one of them would be going home. Which meant either him, Magda, or Magda's closest remaining friend in the competition, whom he'd become incredibly fond of over the weekend working together.

So much for strategy.

Magda squirmed at his side as the judges spoke, and he

reached out, almost without thought, and caught her hand. He squeezed gently and was rewarded with a python grip as the judges' words washed over them.

"Beautifully tempered…gorgeous mirror glaze…decadent…"

That had to be good, right? Decadent?

Magda's hand tightened on his, and he clutched her back, probably squeezing too hard. He wasn't ready for any of them to go home—but the judges had raved about the other team's chocolate. It was going to be tight.

The last few days had been brutal…but he'd never had so much fun in the *Cake-Off* kitchen. Eunice had been easy to work with, but it was Magda who had made him laugh—even when they were panicking about whether they could get chocolate to temper properly in the heat. Magda who had made him feel calm and centered and like he was exactly where he was supposed to be, doing exactly what he was supposed to be doing.

A song whispered in the back of his head, but it wasn't "I Hope I Get It" from *A Chorus Line*, which usually ran through his head on repeat during judging. It was "Bad Idea" from *Waitress*. He'd had that musical stuck in his head a lot over the last few weeks—half the songs were about baking pies—but this particular song was about irresistible attraction.

Bad idea, me and you…

He'd been trying to ignore this thing between them. She didn't want a distraction. That was smart. But this thing…it wasn't going away. The more he ignored it, the louder it got, screaming through his body.

And it felt like it had been going on for much longer than a few weeks. He'd always fixated on her, and he felt more alive on the days when he sparred with her, and yes, the feud wouldn't have lasted as long as it had if he hadn't cared—intensely—what she thought of him, but *he* was the one who'd rejected *her*. He could have said yes, all those years ago...

Except it felt like he couldn't have. She'd been so young, and she'd looked at him with that little edge of worship in her eyes, and it had felt *wrong* somehow, like he would have been taking advantage of Elinor's baby sister's little friend's adorable crush. So yes, he'd destroyed her, and it was the right thing to do. Because taking what her earnest, hopeful face had been offering would have been wrong on a visceral level.

But he'd always liked her. Even back then. Even when she was eighteen. She was smart and funny—though most people didn't notice those things about her because she was so quiet, she would disappear in the noise of her much louder friends and family—but that just made it that much more special that he'd figured it out. Like her awesomeness was a secret that only he knew.

He'd loved that summer. Driving with her. Talking with her. Baking with her. He'd liked her far more than he should—but she was a baby, and he shouldn't take advantage, so he'd tried to take them back to being just friends and ended up burning their friendship down in the process.

Then she'd come back, at a time when he'd felt off-balance and unsteady. She'd looked older—she'd *been* older, but it had been her eyes. No longer eager and hopeful, with that disconcerting edge of hero worship. They'd been confident, those eyes. Sure of who she was in a way that was *insanely* sexy. And yes, she'd probably still been too young for him. But she'd walked into the Cup like she was his equal—when in fact she had already surpassed him. She'd chased her dream. She'd seen the world. She'd been too good to work for him—and then she hadn't wanted to. Her anger about the cake recipe—which he *hadn't stolen*, damn it—had been so visceral, and when she'd stalked out of the Cup, he'd thought it was for the best. Working with her would have been a minefield.

But then she'd stolen his location, and he'd overreacted. Then she'd refused to be on a committee with him—or maybe he'd said something about how they wouldn't work well together, and it had gotten blown out of proportion? Hell, who remembered after all these years?

All he knew was that she'd become his nemesis—but also his obsession. Gorgeous. And challenging. Nothing had ever fired him to want to be more, to want to succeed, more than Magda. It had mattered so much that he always be there, toe to toe, matching her.

Shit. Had he secretly had a thing for her this entire time? A secret even from himself?

And then he'd come here—for the money, he'd told himself—and everything had changed. All the walls they'd built between themselves over the years had started to come down, and suddenly it was him and Magda again—only this time it didn't feel like such a bad idea. This time she didn't feel like an adoring teenager or a pastry academy graduate who had catapulted past him. It felt like they were equals, finally. Like they respected each other—with a respect built from competing with each other for the last decade. If one of them had won every competition, it wouldn't have been fun. They were so evenly matched...and now for the first time in years, it felt like they weren't competing against each other.

Which was insane, because they were *literally* competing against each other. But now...this...even when they weren't working together on chocolate centerpieces...they felt like a team. She felt like the perfect complement, clicking into place.

At least he felt that way.

He didn't know how Magda felt.

But he wanted to find out. Tonight.

Top five. Magda paced in her room, too agitated to sleep. She'd made it to the top five of *Cake-Off*. They'd barely edged out the other team—thanks, the judges said, to the cake they'd made, which had tipped them over the top. The cake had been Eunice's idea, but Mac had baked it and Magda had decorated it, and it really had been a group effort. They'd survived—and the naked disbelief on Tim's face when the winning team was announced had been almost as satisfying as the win itself.

Though seeing Abby eliminated as captain of the losing team had really driven home that anyone could be eliminated at any time.

Abby, who had been winning challenges since the beginning, who everyone had expected to win the whole thing, was gone.

But that wasn't what was keeping Magda awake.

It should be. She should be completely focused on the competition, getting her rest in preparation for the next challenge tomorrow. But instead she couldn't stop thinking about Mac. About his hand on her back as he brushed past her while they were working, or the glint in his eyes when he made a joke at his own expense.

Was this just insane attraction? Or was she falling for him all over again? Like she had when she was eighteen. But she'd been so wrong about him last time. She'd thought there was something building, and then he'd yanked the rug out from under her. She needed to be wary of letting her emotions run away with her. Especially with *Cake-Off* on the line.

Of course, last time he hadn't kissed her.

But they'd never really *talked* about that insane moment in the hallway. Which had been her call, absolutely her call—she wanted to focus on the competition, she *needed* to focus on the competition—but now it was driving her crazy not knowing. What that was. What he wanted.

Was this thing, this *feeling* that seemed to be building between them, this friendship and connection and sense that they just *fit*, was that real? Or all in her head like it had been last time? Or was Mac, the king of short-term flirtations, just flirting with her—not with malice or ill intent, just for the fun of it, but it still didn't mean what her stupid, desperate heart seemed to want it to mean?

He had talked to her about avoiding commitment the other day. Had he been warning her off?

Why couldn't she just be sophisticated and play it cool? Why did it have to *mean* something just because it was him? She'd been so happy when she didn't care what men thought. When all she wanted was *Cake-Off* and she stopped caring about whether or not she had someone in her life—

But the truth was she'd kind of like to have someone in her life. If it was the right someone. She didn't *need* to be alone, even if she was perfectly whole and happy that way. Even if being alone was a perfectly respectable choice. She still wanted *him*, in spite of all her better judgment arguing against it. She loved being with him. The thrill in her blood—

The knock at the door made her jump.

It was a soft knock. It was late, after all, but her light was on, and whoever was on the other side of the door must have been able to see that. She was in her pajamas—blue fleece ones with little pink cakes on them that Charlotte had given her last Christmas. They were cozy and comforting, and Charlotte had been calling them "*Cake-Off* PJs" for so long that they'd become a sort of talisman. Armor.

Magda knew who would be on the other side of the door before she opened it.

"Mac."

He stood in the hallway, still wearing his clothes from this afternoon's bake. She could see a smudge of chocolate on one sleeve, and she focused on it so she didn't get sucked in by the dark chocolate intensity of his eyes.

"This isn't working."

That brought her gaze up to his. "What?"

"Pretending there's nothing here. Putting it off. It's distracting."

Oh good heavens. Was he suggesting they give in to this? She was suddenly ridiculously aware of the fact that she wasn't wearing a bra.

"I know you want to focus on the competition, and I respect that," he said—and she blinked. So not a proposition? What was happening? "But I just—I thought maybe we could talk."

"Talk," she echoed, sounding as baffled as she felt.

"I don't know when this started. I think it's been under the surface for a long time. But it's getting harder and harder to ignore. I can't think anymore. This…"

"This?" she echoed. She seemed to be doing a lot of echoing.

"Magda…you know that I'm attracted to you…"

Do I? Had she known that? She'd wanted to believe it, but after last time…Then she heard herself whispering, "I'm attracted to you, too." But. There was always a but.

And he heard it even though she didn't say it out loud. "But?"

She looked up at him. She wanted to give in to this. She wanted to go crazy. But she heard Charlotte's voice in her head—Charlotte, who was almost *never* the voice of reason, sounding worried and disapproving.

"But why now?"

It was subtle—a slight withdrawal in his eyes, a shift of his weight back onto his heels, his chin notching up ever so slightly, making her more acutely aware of his five o'clock shadow. All the tiny signs that he'd realized she didn't fully trust him.

"It had to be now," he said, no defensiveness in the words, just fact. "We were so locked into the feud in Pine Hollow, we had to break out of it to see what was underneath it." His gaze held hers. "Doesn't it make sense, in a way? No one has ever driven me as crazy as you do. This *feeling* between us. We've always been raw with each other. Maybe because we started by being so completely honest with each other. I'd never told anyone some of the things I told you that summer—and then, yeah, everything exploded, but I still kind of felt like you were the only one in town who actually knew me, the real me, you know? I felt more alive when I was with you—I still do." He shook his head. "And I'm not saying this to throw you off or mess with your game. I know you must think that—I've certainly earned your mistrust over the years. But being in this limbo is driving me crazy, and I just want to know if it's just me. Alone in here."

Magda bit her lip, holding his gaze, and then whispered, "It isn't just you."

He started to take a step toward her, and she held up her hand. His chest slammed into it, and they both gasped as if electrified by the contact. "It isn't just you," she repeated, her hand flexing on his pectorals. "But I can't do this. Not now. I can't let this be about us, do you understand? Not during the competition."

He nodded, shifting back on his heels again, easing the pressure against her hand. "And after?"

She forced levity she didn't feel into her tone. "Are you still going to want to after, if I trounce you?"

He grinned, that dimple popping. "I've never been intimidated by your badassery in the kitchen, Mags. It's sexy as hell."

Her face heated to cupcake briquette temperatures. "Okay. Then we'll talk. Once one of us gets knocked out."

"The finale's only a week away. I can wait. Now that I know what I'm waiting for."

She felt like a candle was glowing inside her chest. A flicker of hope and possibility. "Okay."

He started to back away, and she suddenly fisted her hand in his T-shirt. The one with the chocolate stain on the arm. She used the soft fabric to yank him forward. Mac was a lot bigger than she was, if he'd wanted to, he could have easily stopped her, but he came willingly, his eyes flaring with interest and surprise a moment before she used her other hand to reach up and guide his head down toward hers, her palm curving around the back of his neck. Even on her tiptoes, he had to bend for her to reach his mouth.

She smiled a fraction of a second before their lips made contact, and whispered, "How about a preview?"

Then he was smiling, too, and their smiles were brushing for just a moment before they fell together into the kiss.

For two days *awareness* of him had sizzled over her skin as he brushed past her and worked beside her. The little touches. The little smiles. She'd been buzzing on him, attuned to him, and from one heartbeat to the next all that sensation came rushing back—and then surged right past the point it had been during the competition and into wildfire territory.

His hands were in her hair, hers still gripping his shirt and nape, as the kiss went on and on. It grew and burned, and

Magda realized dimly that without someone to interrupt them, it might just go on forever, or until one of them passed out from exhaustion or oxygen deprivation.

She pulled away with a gasp, and Mac lurched backward, breathing hard. "Shit," he mumbled, raising one hand to his lips. "Okay. Good preview."

"Right. See you tomorrow," Magda said—all in one breath, retreating back into her room and shutting the door before she could do something entirely too reckless and drag him in there with her.

They still weren't supposed to fraternize—though on the nights when they didn't have any advance notice of what they'd be doing tomorrow, she didn't know how it could be a problem. But no. She was doing this for herself. This show was *hers*. And even if the possibility of *them* bubbled in her blood like hot caramel, she didn't want that to touch this.

Even if they got together, they might break up someday, and she didn't want to look back at her *Cake-Off* experience with questions or the bitterness of a missed opportunity. So for now, a preview would just have to do.

Chapter Twenty-Nine

"You wanted to see me, boss?"

Julia stood in the doorway of Stephen's office, waiting for him to wave her in, even though she'd been summoned. Deanna hadn't been the kind of showrunner who liked being called "boss" by her subordinates, but Stephen had proven he enjoyed those little reminders of his power. He smiled slightly as he lifted a hand to gesture her toward the chair opposite his desk.

"I've been thinking about the finale problem," Julia said as she moved toward the chair he'd indicated.

The "finale problem" was something all of the producers had been brainstorming nonstop for the last few days. Since they'd had to stop filming for a week thanks to the Sanderson lawsuit, and since the original contract for use of the King Arthur facilities had been tightly scheduled, if they continued on the current schedule, they were going to lose their filming venue on the day before the finale was supposed to shoot. All options were being considered—shortening the season with double eliminations or shorter challenges than had been originally planned—and Julia was hoping her current suggestion was good enough to divert attention away from whatever Stephen had called her here to take her to task about.

It probably had to do with Mac and Magda. They very clearly didn't hate each other anymore, and that was probably antithetical to all of Stephen's archrival plans.

"You have a solution?" he asked, half of his attention still on his tablet.

"What if we used Pine Hollow?"

He frowned, still only half listening. "What's that?"

"It's the town not far from here where Mac and Magda both grew up. Apparently it has a cute little town square where they do festivals and whatnot. We could book it—and if Mac and Magda are both in the final—"

"And if they aren't?"

"It's still a cute town. Built-in audience for the filming. People cheering them on as they bake live in the square."

"Hm," Stephen said noncommittally. Then he tapped something on his tablet, still not looking at her, and said with icy calm, "I'm considering firing you."

Her mouth went dry. "Why?"

"I'm assuming you have a very good reason for not telling me that Mac and Magda are now engaged in a romantic relationship. A PA caught them kissing?"

Julia's face heated. Shit. She should have said something, but she'd hoped they could just focus on the baking. That Stephen would never have to know. "It was the night we heard about the lawsuit. I came here to tell you about it, but we had so much going on, and at that point I wasn't even sure there would be a show—"

"And when we came back?" Now he was looking at her, his pale eyes steady on her, and Julia wished he would look back at the tablet.

"There was so much good material without it—"

She fell silent as Stephen suddenly leaned forward, steepling his hands on his desk. "Julia. I know you're one of Deanna's. I know you're used to being part of a team, and making warm, fuzzy, *boring* television. But this isn't Deanna's show anymore. It's mine. I'm building a narrative. I'm making America love these people and loathe them. I want every bake to be dramatic not just because a freaking chocolate whatever might collapse, but because we desperately want one particular asshole's chocolate whatever to collapse. I'm a storyteller—you understand that, right?"

"Yes, sir."

"Then why would you try to hide some of my story from me?"

"I didn't mean to hide it—"

"That's even worse. If you're going to sabotage my show, at least be bold about it. Own it."

Her stomach curdled. She was absolutely being fired. And beneath the anxiety and panic that thought inspired, there was also the tiniest whisper of relief.

Stephen stood. "I've decided to give you one more chance. And I need you to do something for me."

Her stomach knotted queasily. "What is it?"

He rounded his desk, extending his tablet toward her. "I need you to play this for Magda. Tomorrow. On camera."

She looked down. It was an audio file. No video. "What is this?"

"Go ahead." He waved toward the tablet, and she pushed Play.

Mac's voice came through, clear as a bell. *"... needy. Desperate."*

Then she heard her own voice, *"And you don't like needy."*

"Needy is too much responsibility." A brief pause. *"I can't stand people like that. Just pathetic."*

Julia frowned, tapping the Stop button. "You edited this. He only used the word *pathetic* when he was talking about how badly he'd done at the cupcake challenge—how he was nearly eliminated."

"Does it matter? We're building a story."

"You want me to tell Magda he said these things about her— but we don't need this. People are going to love them together. They're going to want them both to go forward because of the showmance—"

"Maybe. But we don't have any usable footage that really sells that story. So you either get me that—them confirming their feelings for each other in the confessionals, really adorable shit—or we have this. Either way, I want you to show it to her on camera. We might need that reaction footage if the lovebirds angle doesn't pan out. Better to cover our bases."

"You don't need this," Julia pleaded. "People tune in for the bakes and the wholesomeness."

"Julia. The show was stagnating. Same old format, same old ratings. And in this business, if we aren't growing, we're failing. This is harder, I get it. But the rewards are worth it. You'll see. This is where the good shit is."

"You'll be lying to them."

"No. You will. If you want to keep your job." He took his tablet back from her. "I've emailed you the file. Make sure you show her tomorrow."

"Stephen..."

"If they're really together, they'll clear it up. Don't worry. When you've been in this business as long as I have, you won't even blink at something like this."

Julia rose and walked numbly out of the room with a single thought ringing loudly in her mind.

I certainly hope not.

"Have you seen Magda?"

Mac frowned at the note of panic in Julia's voice. Their usually calm producer looked almost frantic as she continued to scan the Proving Room. "Greg just grabbed her," Mac answered. "He said he had to show her something."

Julia swore under her breath, and then her eyes focused on Mac. "Stephen figured out you two don't hate each other anymore, and he wants to poke the bear. He made this edit of you saying all sorts of crap about Magda—things taken out of context—and he must have told Greg to show it to her if I didn't."

"Shit." A hard knot of dread tightened in his chest. Magda already didn't fully trust him. Last night, after the "preview" she'd given him, he'd felt pretty good about where they'd left things. He'd gone back to his room restless, but it was an eager restlessness, looking forward to two weeks from now, when they could just be together and figure this out. Though part of him had worried that when they got back to Pine Hollow things wouldn't be the same as they had been inside the show bubble.

And now this. She was already primed not to trust him, and now they'd taken his own words and twisted them to trick her?

"Where are they?" he demanded, standing up. "Where does Greg film his confessionals?"

Julia hesitated for only a moment before nodding. "Come on." She started toward the rear door—but it opened before they'd made it two steps. Magda entered, with Greg at her side. She was frowning, and Mac tried to read every nuance of that frown.

He took a step toward her, hearing Julia's soft curse a fraction of a second before one of the other producers called out, "All right! It's time! Into the kitchen!"

Mac tried to fall into step next to Magda on their way into the kitchen—it wasn't hard. There were only five of them now. Zain and Eunice moved behind them while Tim strolled confidently ahead.

"Hey," he murmured, acutely aware that cameras were watching them walk into the room and they were both miked.

"Hey," she mumbled back, with a quick not-quite-genuine smile. Did that mean she'd seen the video thing? He didn't know what he'd supposedly said, so how was he supposed to defend himself?

"Julia said Stephen took a bunch of stuff out of—"

"Quiet, please! Time is tight today, kids. Let's get to our marks!"

"Mags—" Mac tried, but a producer was suddenly there, redirecting him toward his station.

"You're in the back today, Mac. Magda, you're up front."

It was almost like Stephen was actively preventing him from being able to talk to Magda before or during the challenge—which, given the impression he had of Stephen, didn't sound all that far-fetched.

"Good luck," she said over her shoulder as she moved toward her station.

That was a good sign, right? If she hated him, she wouldn't wish him luck. Maybe Julia had been wrong, and Magda hadn't seen it. Though if she had, she'd probably play it cool while they were on camera, wouldn't she?

He was distracted as Flanders and the judges took their

positions at the front of the room to announce this week's challenge. Agitated music buzzed in his head, refusing to resolve into any one song.

"Welcome to Sugar Week, bakers!" Flanders began, and Mac nearly groaned. They'd just made it through Chocolate Week, and now they had *another* week of fiddly sculptures and fancy decorations. He was good at flavors, good at the actual *bakes*, but this fancy stuff was a whole different animal.

"Since we're getting closer to the semifinal, the judges really wanted to test you with today's Skills Challenge—which, as you know, is always judged blind, so we have to shoo them off." The judges filed out—as if they hadn't just been marched in to stand around silently for five minutes. "Now that we're alone"— Flanders waggled his eyebrows—"the judges have assigned for you this week the classic cream puff and caramel magnificence of the croquembouche! And they are looking for *perfection* for those who want to make it to the next stage of the competition."

Mac nearly groaned. He'd barely survived pastry week, after his éclairs had been rock hard and his crème pâtissière had been runny. Now he had to repeat the pâte à choux and crème pât misery, while adding caramel to the mix and making all the little cream puffs stick together in a caramel-glued tower.

"You have two hours."

He just had to focus. He could do this. Sort of. But his thoughts scattered in every direction with the words "Your time starts . . . now!"

Mac forced himself to yank the cloth off the covered ingredients and stared at them blankly. They'd been given a tiny laminated card with the "recipe"—though the first instruction was simply "Make choux pastry."

Right.

How did one make choux pastry again? It was heated, right? But not as heated as Magda could be.

Did she hate him again? What had they told her? What could he possibly have said that could have been taken out of context? He'd talked so much in that confessional—words on top of words on top of words—often when he was tired and not really thinking after five hours of baking and judging and waiting. What was the worst thing he could have said?

A clatter at the front of the kitchen made him look in that direction—and then suddenly his view was blocked by a camera—as if they'd homed in on his paralysis.

"How are you feeling about the croquembouche?" a junior producer asked from beside the cameraman.

"Like I have no idea what I'm doing." The producer winced, and Mac instantly went again, without having to be prompted. "I've never made a croquembouche before, and I have no idea what I'm doing." He paused for a moment, staring blankly at the ingredients. "I've seen them." In the window of Magda's shop, from time to time. "And I know I start with choux pastry."

So he'd better start making that. Two hours. He just needed to focus.

He reached for the butter. Trying to ignore the impending sense of disaster.

Someone's caramel was burning.

Magda was all the way at the front, and she resisted the urge to look behind her and see who had smoke rising from their station.

"Ten minutes remaining!"

The acrid scent of burnt caramel hung in the air, but she focused instead on carefully constructing her cream puff cone. Not enough caramel, and the little filled puffs wouldn't stay in place; too much, and it would look sloppy. She wanted to win this one.

Over the last few hours, her hands had never stopped moving—which had allowed her agitated brain to slow down and settle into calm.

She'd felt sick when Greg had first played the audio file for her. It had sounded like Mac was giving voice to all her fears—that she was pathetic and desperate and unimportant—but even as she'd listened, even as her stomach had roiled with each new word, she'd reminded herself that this audio could have been from weeks ago. A time when she'd doubtless said worse about him. A time when she'd sabotaged him and nearly smacked him in the face. Of course he'd said some awful things.

It had to have been from before the kiss. Before everything changed. Perhaps that was why it was just audio—because the video would give away the fact that it had been filmed weeks ago. That was just the kind of bullshit Stephen liked to pull. Pitting them against each other. Always trying to get a dramatic response. And the only way to win was to not give him the satisfaction.

He'd probably played a similar file for Mac. She'd felt a queasy anxiety, reentering the Proving Room after Greg had given up on getting anything other than "Well, we did come here as rivals," out of her. They'd been instantly ushered into the kitchen—such an obvious tactic from Stephen to make her cook when she was off-balance. But then Mac had fallen into step beside her, and his low "Hey" had instantly reassured her.

He'd said something about Stephen taking things out of the show, and she hadn't had time to ask what he meant—just to offer good luck as she was rushed to the front of the kitchen.

As she'd made her pâte à choux, her brain had cleared even more and she thought of another reason why it had only been a sound recording—for all she knew they'd hacked together a Frankenstein's monster of patched-together clips, and he hadn't even been sitting there ranting about how pathetic she was. But even if he had, they were different now. And she trusted him.

Trust.

It was a funny way to realize she trusted him, but even listening to the tape, even hearing his voice saying those words, she'd still found herself remembering all the things he hadn't had to do. Covering for her with the almost-slap. Letting her use his oven. And other things, little things—like telling her he thought she could win. He didn't have to do that. If he were really playing the game, he'd be undermining her. There was just no advantage to bolstering her confidence when they were alone and talking trash behind her back to the cameras. If it had been the other way around, she might have thought it was about protecting his image, but he was sweetest to her when there were no cameras, no audio, when it was just them. Sitting at the Furry Friends fundraiser, hearing him call her a beast in the kitchen, telling her she could win the whole thing…

They might drive each other crazy, but Mac would never hurt her, or let anyone else hurt her if there was anything he could do to stop it.

"One minute! One minute left, bakers!"

Her croquembouche was complete. She even had time for a few finishing touches—decorative strings of caramel swirling around the tower of cream puffs. When there were only fifteen seconds remaining and she had literally nothing left to do, Magda let herself glance over her shoulder, let herself consider the competition for the first time.

Tim was directly behind her, and dang it, his croquem-bouche looked amazing. Eunice behind him was a little mess-ier, her caramel a shade too dark, but it still looked respectable. Zain's cream puffs looked too pale—perhaps not cooked fully? But Magda looked past him to the rear station, and her heart sank as she realized where all the smoke had come from.

Mac was scrambling as Jeffrey Flanders counted down from five in his usual dramatic fashion. His tower wasn't complete—a full third of it was missing. His caramel was much too dark—clearly burned and globbed heavily on some puffs while being virtually nonexistent on others.

Flanders called time. Mac backed away, shaking his head. And then he looked up, his eyes locking on hers across the length of the kitchen, and she realized with absolute certainty that she didn't want him to go home.

And unless a miracle happened in the next bake, he absolutely was.

Chapter Thirty

Things just went downhill after the croquembouche fiasco. "And now, for the tough part of the week..."

Mac stood in the line-up of bakers, waiting to accept his—extremely obvious—fate.

He'd come in dead last in the croquembouche Skills Challenge—to absolutely no one's surprise. And not by a close margin. He'd been so ridiculously outclassed that even Tim had seemed sympathetic over how completely screwed he was, going into the Sugar Spectacular on Wednesday.

It would have been hard enough for him to make up that ground, but then he'd struggled to get his isomalt to set, and his Sugar Spectacular had shattered five minutes before the timer went off.

There was no coming back from that.

Magda had rushed over to help him, her own Sugar Spectacular complete, but there was nothing to be done. He'd presented the pieces, but he'd been mentally steeling himself for this moment all through judging and the interviews. They all knew it was over.

Tim had just been announced the week's winner, shocking absolutely no one. And now...

"This just keeps getting harder, and this week is no exception," Jeffrey Flanders intoned dramatically. "This baker has always been a smiling presence in the kitchen, and we're so, so sorry to have to say goodbye...to Mac."

It didn't feel like Jeffrey Flanders had dragged that out as much as he sometimes did, but maybe that was just what it felt like when it was you.

Bad news came at you fast.

At least he knew he and Magda were on good terms. He'd caught up with her in the Proving Room yesterday to clear the air as soon as the Skills Challenge was over, and she'd immediately assured him that while Greg *had* played an awful audio recording for her, she'd shrugged it off as being part of their earlier animosity and didn't blame him at all—especially since she'd given as good as she'd gotten back then.

His relief had been potent—but it hadn't made him magically any better at working with melted sugar. All of his weak areas had been exposed this week.

So he was out.

Magda and Eunice both tried not to cry. Zain shook his head in commiseration, mumbling, "It could have happened to any of us." And even Tim shook his hand, as the judges clapped him on the shoulder and said what a pleasure it had been.

He'd gotten so close. Top five. It had been a good run. Better than he had expected when he'd been recruited. He said as much when he was ushered out of the kitchen and into an interview room.

"Do you want to talk about what went wrong today?" Julia asked gently.

"Besides everything?" he joked. "I was outclassed. There are some amazing bakers in this competition, and today I just couldn't keep up."

Julia smiled sympathetically. "Do you have any predictions on who you think might win this year?"

"Magda." He didn't hesitate.

"So no hard feelings for your old rival?"

He smiled. "No. No hard feelings. Magda and I...we're on good terms now, I think. This contest has actually been really good for us. When we worked together...I think we really brought out the best in each other. And when we were competing, she made me want to try harder, be better. I learned a lot while I was here, and not just about baking. I just, um..." He paused, trying to find the words to express himself, something that usually came so easily to him, and finally settled on "I'm really, really glad I came."

Julia smiled. "That was great. Anything else you want to say? On the record, before we wrap your final confessional?"

Mac glanced around the room, small and crowded with equipment. He remembered his early days of toying with Julia, refusing to tell her anything beyond the name of his cat. Now it felt so natural, just talking about his hopes and fears on camera. Cooking to a timer with Jeffrey Flanders yelling out countdowns that always made Mac want to throw something at him—if that wouldn't have taken precious time to do. Standing stock still while the judges *hmm*ed and *oh dear*ed over every tiny flaw. Trying not to smile too hugely under their praise. Singing karaoke in the common room at the Inn. Kissing Magda...

Mac smiled. "I'm gonna miss this place."

Guilt *sucked*.

Magda paced in the common room at the inn, watching the front door for Mac's van to arrive. She knew the routine when a contestant was voted off. They were brought back to the inn, packed, and then, depending on what time their flight had been arranged for, they either left right away or early the following morning. They were never still around by breakfast—and Magda didn't want to miss Mac.

It was her fault.

She knew that thought was irrational. She knew she hadn't actually done anything to sabotage Mac—this time. But part of her had been looking forward to them not competing against each other anymore so they could be together without any of the competition stuff getting in the way—and now he'd been knocked out, and she felt like that little subtle wish had somehow tipped the scales.

Which was ridiculous. She knew it was ridiculous. But she still needed to see him.

She hadn't realized how much he had become tangled up in this experience with her. How *wrong* it would feel to walk into the Proving Room tomorrow morning and not have him there, cracking jokes or humming a song or just generally making everything a little brighter.

She wanted this for him. When just a few weeks ago she had wanted nothing more than for him to be kicked off the show.

He still made her crazy, but when he won, it felt like she was winning, too, and when he'd lost, when they'd announced that he would be the one going home, it had been like a kick in the gut, even though she'd known it was coming. She'd still been hoping, irrationally, pointlessly, desperately.

"Magda? What are you doing still awake? Do you need something?"

Magda turned, surprised to find Aubrey, one of the production assistants, approaching from the back of the inn. "I'm just waiting for Mac to come in," she said, waving vaguely toward the front entrance, as if that explained everything. "I wanted the chance to say goodbye—"

Aubrey shook her head, frowning. "But Mac came back hours ago. His van got here a few minutes before yours did."

Magda's heart began to pound out a blistering rhythm. "He's here?"

"Upstairs, I think. Do you know your call time—"

Magda missed the rest, already hurrying toward the stairs and calling a thank-you over her shoulder.

She didn't run—but it was a near thing. Taking the stairs quickly and then fast-walking down the corridor to the room Mac had been assigned. Her fist cracked against the door, the knock probably too loud, he could be asleep, she should have thought this through—

But then the door opened, and he was there—his red hair, his ridiculous arms—and the words spilled out of her mouth. "I'm sorry you got kicked off—"

"I'm not."

The words were a growl.

Then his hands were on her shoulders, pulling her into his room, and his lips landed on hers. She caught herself against his chest, her head tipped back all the way for optimum kissage since he was a million inches taller than she was, kissing him back for all she was worth as his gorgeous shoulders curved over her, blocking out the world.

Okay, maybe there were *some* perks to him no longer being on the show. The antifraternization rules clearly no longer applied.

He kicked the door shut, and crowded her against it, never breaking the kiss—or maybe she dragged him by her death grip on his shirt. Who could say?

"You weren't in your room." His voice was all growly as he released her lips and kissed his way down her neck.

She tilted her chin to give him better access. "I thought you weren't back yet—" Her words broke off on a gasp as his hands closed on the backs of her thighs and lifted her—those bread kneading muscles put to *very* good use. His arms flexed as he effortlessly lifted her off her feet and up to his level, then higher—her back braced against the door, her thighs bracketing his abs, her face a couple of inches above his now. It was a position that felt somehow both powerful and vulnerable, and she was a little breathless as she finished her sentence. "I was waiting for you downstairs."

He kissed her again, devouring her mouth like his favorite dessert—then his hands slid up her sides, underneath the hem of her shirt, touching skin, and she made a little squeak of surprise in her throat at the shock of sensation.

Mac lifted his head instantly. "Is this okay?"

From a distance of inches, his eyes searched hers. They were nearly black with want, the pupils blown, but it was the intensity in them that sent a shiver streaking down her spine, even as she nodded jerkily. "Very okay."

"I kind of attacked you," he rumbled.

"Mutual attacking," she assured him. *Please don't stop.*

His mouth quirked, that wry smile that she adored, and a strange sort of relief flashed through her. This was *Mac*. All this wildness, but also the fun of him. The playfulness and the need.

They'd been building up to this for weeks—hell, possibly for years. All the crackling energy between them finally had somewhere to go.

She wrapped her arms around his shoulders and locked her ankles at the small of his back to hold herself in place—though she knew he would never let her fall, his hands now bracketing her rib cage to hold her steady.

"You have the semifinals tomorrow," he reminded her, kissing her softly now—and the softness devastated her. The rush, the heat, the frantic insanity, that was one thing. But this... this was sweetness and longing, and she freaking *melted*.

"I know," she whispered against his mouth. "Don't stop."

She didn't care about tomorrow when *tonight* was one of the brightest, hottest, most vivid moments of her life.

Kendall had been telling her for years that she needed to go wild, and Magda had always had a million reasons why it wasn't a good idea. No one wanted to go wild on a schedule that allowed her to get a decent night's sleep and open the bakery on time. Everyone in town would know, because the gossip was insane, and she didn't really want her grandparents hearing about her sexcapades. There were so few eligible men in Pine Hollow.

Excuses on top of excuses on top of excuses.

But the truth was she'd never *wanted* to go wild. Not with anyone but him.

And no one had ever seemed to want to go wild with her. She was the good girl. The boring one. The invisible one. She followed every rule—and no one seemed to look at her and think wicked thoughts. If they saw her at all. Nice Magda. Pleasant Magda.

But Mac saw her. And she drove him wild, if the way he groaned "*Jesus*, sugar" in her ear when she ground against him was any indication.

She hadn't always made him crazy in the way she'd wanted to, but now it was like all their anger and passion and frustration of the last fourteen years had finally clicked into alignment, and it wasn't anger at all. It was this thing they'd been fighting. Him, at first because she was too young, and then her because she was too hurt, and both of them because they had fallen into a pattern of hate that was easier than admitting that this scary massive thing between them might be *this*. That it might be the wildness inside her that had never wanted to get out until him.

"Is this a bad idea?" he asked, his lips on her neck again.

"Absolutely." Her breath caught on a sigh, and he started to stiffen, started to pull away, but she sank her hands into his hair to keep him from going far, and made him meet her eyes. "Let's make *all* the bad decisions."

His answering smile was pure, wicked heaven.

Chapter Thirty-One

"D o you really not care that you were eliminated?"

It was two a.m. and they were baking muffins in the inn's kitchen—which was a terrible idea on multiple levels. Mac was being picked up in six hours, Magda had a nine a.m. call time, and both of them should be sleeping, but instead they'd thrown on his pajamas and snuck down to the kitchen.

Magda wore Mac's button-down flannel pajama top and a pair of his boxer briefs, while Mac wore the matching pajama bottoms and a white undershirt that had been worn to threadbare softness. Magda had never really been comfortable lolling about naked—even after sex. But there was something about sharing his PJs that somehow felt more intimate than if they'd been naked in bed together.

They'd both been wide awake and starving. So an impromptu private muffin competition had been irresistible. They'd each made one tray of six muffins—Magda's blueberry crumble and his maple bacon jalapeño—and were now waiting for them to finish baking.

Anyone could walk in on them—and Magda wouldn't put it past the producers to try to make this part of the show—but she was having a night of *very* satisfying bad decisions. And she was tired of playing by the rules. Their rules sucked.

"I mean I *care*," Mac answered, peeking through the oven

door to check on the muffins. "I would have loved that quarter of a million dollars—can you imagine the kind of space I could have gotten for the Cup with that? But I was always going to need an act of God to get past Sugar Week, and I guess She was busy elsewhere."

"I was terrified of Bread Week," Magda admitted. "I think I trained for that week more than any other. That and Sugar Week. I can't count the burn scars on my hands anymore."

He removed his muffin tray from the oven and set them aside to cool, then handed Magda the oven mitt so she could take her own muffins out.

When she set down her muffins, she turned to face him, leaning back against the counter. "It isn't going to be the same without you."

Something fierce kindled in his eyes. "You better not stop fighting for it just because I'm gone. If you let Tim win, I'll never forgive you."

She laughed. "As if it's my choice? I just decide who wins?"

"Why not? You've always had the skill. You were the only one who thought you couldn't take the whole thing."

"I only won when you and I were partnered together. The closest I ever got by myself was second or third—good baking, good technique, but nothing special. No X factor."

"You won that Skills Challenge," he reminded her. "The one where you sabotaged me and Tim."

"A *Skills* Challenge. Where they want us to replicate something they gave us. No creativity needed. But no one ever wins *Cake-Off* by being a perfect technique robot."

He caught her hands, pulling her toward him. Her monogrammed inn slippers skidded across the tiles. "You aren't a robot," he insisted. Their fingers tangled together as he bent to kiss her. "You're holding yourself back." His head still bent close to hers, he murmured, "I've never understood how someone as brave as you are doesn't want to take risks with her bakes."

"Brave?" she asked incredulously. "Me?"

"You don't think going to France when you didn't know anyone and barely spoke the language was brave? Or starting your own business all by yourself? Or coming on a baking show and signing up to have everything you do criticized on national television?"

"I started my business with my aunt, so it never really felt like I was doing it alone—and I was mad at you. Which I guess makes me brave, because I was mad at you when I decided to go to France, too."

"And the show? Was that also part of your quest for vengeance against me?"

It was so strange to have him talk about her hating him with that little quirk of his lips, as if their feud for the last fourteen years was now an inside joke they shared. "That wasn't about you."

"So why? What first made Magda Miller want to compete on the *Cake-Off*?"

"It scared me," she admitted, meeting his eyes. "Charlotte had just broken up with her awful ex and wanted us all to get dogs and swear off men."

"I remember that."

"Right. George." Mac and George had become friends while Charlotte had been mid–Puppy Pact. "Obviously that didn't quite work out. But for me...I'd never really dated all that much—but I always felt like I *should*, you know? Like everyone was just waiting for me to get married and settle down and bake birthday cakes for my kids. I don't know how much of that was people actually expecting that and how much of it was me thinking that was what I was supposed to do, but when we made that ridiculous pact, it was like suddenly there was this other choice. My 'little bakery' didn't have to be what I did until I got married and had kids. It could be my thing. My *main* thing."

He nodded, but didn't interrupt, and Magda went on. "I started thinking about what I would do if I didn't care what I was supposed to do—I loved going to that pastry academy. It was terrifying, and it was not at all what I was supposed to do, but I *loved* it. So I asked myself what I would do if I wasn't scared. If I wasn't trying to follow the rules. If I just *went for it*."

"*Cake-Off,*" he said, and she nodded.

"I'd wanted to be on the show since the second I first saw it, watching with Aunt Lena, but that was when I knew I had to go for it. I knew I had to try, or I would always wonder what if. Even if it scared me senseless."

"See?" His lips quirked in that smile. "Brave."

She met his eyes—and tonight? Tonight she did feel brave. And she couldn't believe how much she'd held herself back.

Her stomach chose that moment to growl, and they both grinned. "Come on," he said. "The muffins should be cool enough by now."

They sampled the muffins right there in the kitchen, imitating Joanie and Alexander Clay and mock-judging each other. But when Magda tasted his maple bacon jalapeño muffin, she groaned.

"Damn it. You win. This is so much better than mine."

"Nonsense," he immediately countered. "Have you even *tried* this?" He pinched off a piece of her blueberry crumble and held it up to her lips.

She took the bite, and she had to admit that it was

delicious—though the feeling of his thumb grazing her lower lip after she took the morsel into her mouth might have impacted the experience somewhat.

"They actually complement each other," Magda commented, taking a bite of each.

"See? Bringing out the best in each other since..." He trailed off.

"Approximately ten days ago?" she finished for him.

"It's weird. It feels like a lot longer."

"*Cake-Off* Standard Time." She eyed him, taking another bite of his muffin.

Time moved differently here. They were still in the *Cake-Off* bubble. Everything was heightened and more immediate, and they were with each other 24/7. Would it be different when they got back to the real world?

Well, obviously it would be *different*, but how?

They'd vaguely mentioned "after," but she didn't want that outside world to intrude here, didn't want to come right out and ask if this had been a show fling. Even if this felt like the beginning of something. Or, if she was being precise, like it was the evolution of something that had been building between them for years.

She didn't want to think about it too hard. He was leaving in a few hours, and she just wanted to stay inside this moment, the light and easy and slightly against-the-rules moment of baking in the middle of the night with him.

His gaze was intent on her mouth. "You have a little something..."

He reached out a thumb, and she ran her tongue out to meet it. Mac's eyes did that going-black thing that made her toes curl and he bent his head. "Here, let me." Then he was kissing her, his own tongue stroking her lip and into her mouth, and he tasted of blueberry and maple and salt, and she pressed her thighs together on a rush of heat until he grabbed her waist, boosting her up onto the counter, and she was very glad there was nothing hot or sharp in range because a kitchen was a *terrible* place to make out, even when it wasn't a *public* kitchen—

She broke away with a gasp. "The PAs," she panted.

Mac swore, jerking back with his hands in the air like Jeffrey Flanders had just called time on a Skills Challenge. "Upstairs?" he asked, still breathing raggedly.

Magda jumped down from the counter and scooped the remaining muffins into a bag, quickly tossing the muffin tins into the dishwasher alongside the rest of the dishes they'd used. Mac tossed in the soap and hit the button to run it, grabbing her hand as they raced out of the kitchen and up the stairs, laughing and shushing each other the entire way.

"I should let you sleep," he said as soon as the door closed behind them. But he was still prowling toward her.

And Magda had never been less tired. She didn't know what tomorrow would bring, but she *knew* she didn't want tonight to end. She tossed the bag of muffins aside. "Don't you dare," she said, pulling his head down to hers for a long, lingering kiss.

When they finally came up for air, Mac was grinning. "You're the boss, sugar."

"And don't you forget it."

Chapter Thirty-Two

The phone in Mac's room rang entirely too early the next morning. Light was piercing through the drapes, but he groaned, and groped for the phone, certain he hadn't had more than two hours of sleep.

Not that he was complaining. It had been the best damn sleepless night of his life.

He grabbed the receiver before it could ring again, listening with half an ear as someone at the front desk told him his car would be ready in twenty minutes. Shit. So not a lot of time to grab a shower and throw his things into his bag.

But still he didn't launch out of bed as soon as he hung up. Instead he curled back around Magda, who sighed sleepily and settled against him. Somehow the ringing hadn't woken her. He looped one of her curls around his finger, studying her sleeping face. She looked even more like an angel than usual.

He wasn't sure what time it had been when they'd finally fallen asleep. One of them had knocked the bedside clock to the floor, accidentally unplugging it, and since he still hadn't gotten his phone back from the production people, they'd had no other way to tell time.

Though if he had gotten his phone back it probably would have been against the rules for Magda to spend the night. Hell, it might still be against the rules, but Magda's Good Girl Rule-Follower façade had firmly cracked last night.

He hadn't planned this. He hadn't even been sure he'd see her last night after he was voted off. Sometimes it seemed like the former contestants just vanished into smoke, never to be heard from again. He'd gone to her room when he got back to the inn—more than once—but she hadn't answered when he knocked, so he'd figured she was already asleep.

He'd been considering writing a letter, slipping it under her door before he left in the morning, but there was no stationery in the room, and he wasn't sure she would have been able to read his writing anyway.

And he didn't know what he would have said. That the worst part of being voted out was that he wasn't going to be seeing her every day anymore? That he wanted to see her every day and bake with her and tease her and call her cupcake just to watch her eyes light with that fire? That he, Mac Newton, who had always waited for life's choices to come to him and pulled away when things got too serious, *wanted* serious? That he didn't want her to drift out of his life? That he wanted to hold on—even if part of that scared the shit out of him?

And then she'd shown up at his door.

He hadn't planned on kissing her. But some things were inevitable.

He'd been so *relieved* to see her, and his agitation had melted seamlessly into need, and something he'd been denying for years had surged past all his pointless barricades and swallowed them whole. They hadn't thought about tomorrow, but now tomorrow was here.

"Mags." He kissed that spot on her neck that always made her shiver, and even in her sleep her breath caught, but then she burrowed down deeper into the covers, and he couldn't bring himself to wake her. She had more time than he did before her first call, anyway, and she was baking today. She would need as much rest as she could get. If he'd been any less selfish last night, he would have insisted that she get more sleep, but that night had felt like stolen time, and when she'd insisted she didn't want to waste it sleeping, he hadn't been able to tell her no.

Mac slipped out of bed without waking her and took a quick shower, humming "As Long As You're Mine" from *Wicked* the entire time. After shaving and brushing his teeth, he dressed quickly, without really paying attention to what he was wearing, and threw the rest of his stuff haphazardly into his duffel. He was just being driven back to Pine Hollow, after all. He'd probably sleep in the van.

Then it was only five minutes before his ride was due, and he couldn't put it off any longer. He'd already discovered there was no paper in the room, so he couldn't leave her a note, and he definitely didn't want her to have to answer questions about why she'd missed her call time because she was sleeping in his room and no one could find her.

"Mags. You've gotta wake up, sugar."

He shook her gently, and this time her eyelids cracked open on a groan. "You're leaving already?" she asked blearily, sitting up and shoving her hair out of her face with one hand while using the other to hold the sheet to her chest, even though she was still wearing his pajama top. It had been buttoned up wrong, and he smiled at the oddly endearing sight.

"My car's here," he explained. "I thought we should smuggle you back to your room so you don't miss your call."

"Right," she mumbled, rubbing her face. Her bare legs slipped out from beneath the covers and she stood, still looking half-asleep, and something in Mac's chest tugged.

He couldn't resist. He crossed the short distance between them and cupped her face, tipping it up to him and sinking his hands into her thick curls as he lingered in a kiss. When he lifted his head, she was definitely more awake, even if her eyes were still a little dazed.

"Good morning," he murmured.

"Good morning," she whispered back. Her hands had come up to hold his wrists, but she released him as he groaned and forced himself to let his hands drop.

"I wish I didn't have to go." He grinned. "Mostly because I wanna watch you kick some ass."

She blushed, ducking her head as she smiled—always too humble.

"Do me a favor?" he asked, and she lifted her eyes to meet his.

"What?"

"Enjoy yourself, okay? And win the whole damn thing."

"You really think I can?"

"I've always thought so. But that doesn't matter if you don't believe it. So believe it."

She smiled as he kissed her again—until the landline started ringing again.

Time to go.

Magda dressed quickly in yesterday's clothes. They snuck quickly down the hall, saying a quick, silent goodbye at her door—a rushed kiss, a squeeze of her hand—and then he was jogging down the stairs.

It was really over.

Strange that this was the moment it hit him, trotting down the stairs at the inn for the last time. He hadn't really processed it last night, that he was going home, even though he'd known intellectually that his time here was over.

He really was going to miss this. His fellow bakers. The ever-present PAs. The makeup artists who talked about their kids when they were muttering about his bone structure. The sound guys with their never-ending supply of truly awful dad jokes. Even some of the producers—the ones that weren't trying to screw with his life.

No more bakes. No more postmortems with Julia. No more unlocking his knees to keep from passing out as they stood in a row to be judged for what felt like hours. No more Skills Challenges where he had no idea what he was doing. No more sneaking a look at Magda's station. Or hearing her voice across the kitchen. Or brushing against her as they worked together...

Though maybe that part didn't have to be over.

Maybe this fragile thing that had built between them during the show could survive the trip back to Pine Hollow. Maybe they were different now.

He certainly felt different.

He'd always been good at laughing off his mistakes—because he'd never pushed himself. He'd never let himself want something so much that it would crush him if he didn't get it. His easygoing demeanor had become a shield. If he failed, no big deal, he hadn't wanted success that badly anyway. He rolled with the punches. And so he was never disappointed.

No regrets.

But this felt like a regret.

Like he'd missed an opportunity because he hadn't wanted to admit to himself that he wanted this. What Magda had said last night about training for bread week lingered in his thoughts as he said his goodbyes to the crew members around the inn and climbed into the van that would take him back to Pine Hollow.

He could have done more to prep than watch a few episodes.

He could have practiced. He could have learned. But instead he'd planned on improvisation and adaptation to carry him through.

And they'd carried him pretty far. He was *good* at improvising and adapting. But maybe sometimes you had to want something enough to try—and to care when you failed.

His grandfather had always told him to bet on himself. And Mac had taken that to mean he could rally from any failure, but what if he'd meant something more? What if he'd wanted Mac to take the big swings? To *try*?

He cared about the Cup, but he'd shied away from the big changes, slowly evolving over the years. Letting things happen. It wasn't Magda's fault he hadn't taken that space on the square. She was just an excuse for not growing faster. Not taking that risk.

He took what life handed him—the good and the bad—and he rolled with it. If he didn't let himself want more, he was never disappointed.

But Magda…Magda wanted things so sharply, even when she was afraid she wasn't good enough for them. She was so freaking brave, even if it drove him crazy how she didn't believe in herself. There was humble, and then there was deluded. He wanted to savage anyone who'd ever made her feel like she wasn't good enough—even if he himself was on that list.

She couldn't seem to see how amazing she was—

"Here we are."

Mac blinked, startled as the van pulled to a stop. That had *not* been long enough to get them to Pine Hollow.

He looked out the window and frowned. He was back at King Arthur, and Julia was standing out front with her tablet, waiting for him to climb out of the van.

What the hell?

He opened the door, warily stepping out. "What is this? What's going on?"

Julia approached him, calm and smiling. "Sorry. Just a few more things. Stephen wants some promo shots. We have these black aprons, and we never got footage of you wearing one in the kitchen." She fell into step beside him, heading toward the familiar entrance. "As soon as we finish this up, we can give you your phone back and get you on your way."

Right. He still hadn't gotten his phone. He should have known. "Sure. No problem."

Apparently his time at *Cake-Off* wasn't quite over yet, but it felt odd being here and out of the competition. The energetic makeup crew was subdued as they quickly did his face. The sound guy's usual dad joke was deeply unfunny as he wired Mac up with a microphone. He didn't know why that was necessary for promo footage where he'd probably just be pretending to bake, but Mac had learned not to question the show.

Once he was made-up, miked, and wearing the black apron, Julia escorted him through the Proving Room and then pointed him toward the kitchen doors. "Okay. Go on in," she said. "Stephen wants footage of you walking into the kitchen. Just go on up to station one."

The finale.

That was when Mac realized what they were doing. They were close to the end. The bakers would probably wear the black aprons in the finale. And in the finale, each baker walked into the kitchen by themself, one by one, rather than in a group. They were trying to get footage of him doing the finale walk so they could drop it into promo footage and fake people out. Throw them off the scent of the real finalists.

Always with the mind games.

Mac schooled his features into something he hoped looked suitably neutral and stepped into the kitchen, one last time.

The stations had already been set for today's competition—three, just like in the finale. The judges were there, alongside Jeffrey Flanders—which seemed like overkill for a fake shoot, but Mac just played his part, walking up to the first station and stopping.

The door opened behind him, and he glanced back—as Abby walked into the room, also wearing a black apron.

Mac wasn't sure whether to frown or smile. Abby had been eliminated days ago—going out as team captain in the chocolate challenge. Had they really brought her back just for this? Or kept her here? She'd been so eager to get back to her family, but she didn't look pissed. She looked determined. Fierce.

Mac's face decided on a confused frown as she took the spot at station two and the Proving Room door opened again.

Leah stepped out, also with her game face and a black apron on. Leah, who had been kicked off last Friday.

What the hell?

Were they bringing back *all* the eliminated contestants? Making them all go through this ridiculous song and dance?

Leah took her place at station three, and Mac turned back to the front, just in time for Jeffrey Flanders to begin speaking, using his most over-the-top host voice.

"Welcome…" he intoned dramatically. "To the Redemption Round. At the end of today, *one* of you will be rejoining the competition."

He kept speaking, but Mac couldn't make out the words over the sudden rushing in his ears.

Holy shit. He still had a shot.

Chapter Thirty-Three

Magda was dragging. She didn't know if it was the lack of sleep—*bad idea, such a bad idea*—or the fact that Mac was gone—*should not matter, but absolutely did*—but she was barely able to focus as she went through the motions of getting ready for today's bake.

The set felt empty with only four of them left, and maybe the producers sensed that, because they didn't have them gather in the Proving Room until immediately before it was time to go into the kitchen.

Eunice gave her a double thumbs-up of encouragement, and Magda smiled back, attempting to look like she wasn't about to try to bake her way into the final on only two hours of sleep.

Then they stepped into the kitchen, and Magda wondered if she was hallucinating.

The stations were already occupied—bakers in black aprons standing at each one. Leah. Abby. And Mac.

Magda's heart began to race. *What was happening?*

"What's going on?" Eunice asked quietly.

"I hope you're ready for a twist, bakers," Jeffrey Flanders called out dramatically as they approached the front of the kitchen.

The final four were directed to the front of the room, to stand next to the judges and Flanders facing the three black-aproned bakers.

"There will be four bakers in the finale this year...but you may not be the final four. Today, you aren't here to bake... you're here to watch. Welcome to the finale of the Redemption Round," Jeffrey Flanders announced when they were in their places.

Redemption.

"For weeks your eliminated compatriots have been competing for a chance to get back into the competition. Leah has been a force, defeating those who came before her, and now she will face off against the two most recently eliminated bakers in the final bake—after which one baker will earn redemption, a spot back in the competition, and a chance to fight their way into the finale."

Magda met Mac's eyes, her heart thundering in her ears. They did this on other cooking shows—she'd seen it on *Top Chef*, and she was pretty sure *MasterChef* had done it once or twice, but *Cake-Off* didn't bring bakers back. Ever. They hadn't even done an all-star season, though Magda had frequented the fan sites that constantly called for them to bring back the most beloved bakers.

Finally there was something *good* in all the awful changes Stephen had brought to the show.

Mac had a chance.

The judges began laying out the parameters, and Magda was as nervous as if she was cooking.

"This won't be easy, my dears," Joanie said—one of her most terrifying catchphrases. "Today's challenge is a classic, and we are looking for bright, fresh flavors—but we will be *exacting* when it comes to technique."

"We are looking for nothing short of perfection," Alexander Clay announced—issuing *his* most famous catchphrase.

"But this one will be judged blind, so our judges will now excuse themselves..."

Jeffrey Flanders waited until the judges had filed out before turning to the black-aproned bakers with an ominous air. "Today we'd like you to bake for us...a lemon meringue pie."

The bakers all looked relieved—at least it was something they'd all heard of, something they must have all made before.

"You have one hour—"

The smiles fell off their faces.

"And your time starts... *now*."

All three bakers bolted for the pantry, and Magda reminded herself to breathe. It was somehow a million times more stressful to be standing here watching, knowing there was nothing she could do.

Mac raced back, his arms full of ingredients—and a camera was suddenly blocking her view.

"Anyone you're particularly rooting for to get back into the competition?"

"Is *no one* an option?" Tim said dryly.

"They're all such good bakers," Eunice gushed, "but I'm pulling for my girl Leah."

"Magda?"

She knew she should be rooting for all her friends equally— Leah had gotten such a bad break, but Magda's heart was fixated on one station. She shifted to the side so she could see him.

"They're all so talented," she murmured, never taking her eyes off Mac.

"I didn't know." Mac said the words as soon as they were back in the Proving Room after the challenge, his hand on Magda's wrist and his voice pitched for her ears alone—though they were both still wired for sound. "I had no idea about the redemption round last night—"

"I didn't think you would intentionally short yourself sleep if you knew you had to bake today," Magda assured him.

"*You* did."

Her lips quirked. "Well, yeah, but I'm wild and unpredictable. A rebel."

His smile was like a secret they shared—until Julia interrupted them.

"Mac, let's get you into the chair to talk about your pie."

He gave a little duty-calls grimace and followed the producer through the door, leaving Magda with only the after-warmth of his fingers on her wrist.

Leah and Abby had been whisked away as well, leaving Eunice, Tim, Magda, and Zain waiting around with no bake of their own to discuss.

Magda grabbed a protein bar and sat next to Eunice on one of the couches to wait out this next section. They might still be baking today, and she needed to fuel if she was going to be functional, since she somehow doubted taking a nap on the Proving Room couch was an option.

"How do you feel about this latest twist?" one of the junior producers asked, clearly trying to stoke a discussion and hovering out of the roving camera's sightlines.

"It's bullshit," Tim instantly obliged—though they'd probably have to bleep that if they included it. "They got voted out, fair and square, and now, what? The usual rules don't apply?"

"I like it," Eunice dared to argue, though her high voice wavered a little. "I'm glad they're getting a second chance."

"You realize this is a one-shot thing," Tim snapped. "They aren't going to do it again when you get voted out."

God, he was such a dick. So much the opposite of the normal *Cake-Off* contestants, who were always people you wanted to root for in varying degrees. Even the most arrogant contestants were never assholes. And yet, there was Tim.

Magda stared at him, frowning, until he snapped at her. *"What?"*

"I'm just wondering how the show is going to make people root for you if you win. Do you suppose you'll ever speak in the final edit?"

His glower darkened even more, but they were all distracted by a rush of movement. The black-aproned bakers returned, much sooner than usual, and were ushered through the Proving Room and back into the kitchen. Magda stood, ready to follow, but a PA told them to "sit tight right here during judging" and she sank back onto the couch.

She glanced around nervously, but there were no clocks in the Proving Room—like in casinos, it often felt impossible to gauge the passage of time on set—so there was no way to know how long they sat there, waiting.

Eunice reached out, catching her hand, and Magda squeezed it—though she was pretty sure they weren't silently rooting for the same person.

The single cameraman who had stayed behind to get their reactions got bored of the silence and asked Tim who he wanted back in the competition. He launched into a pompous monologue about who would be easiest for him to beat (Leah), who would be most likely to fold under the pressure of the final (Leah), and who he thought was most likely to have won the lemon meringue pie challenge (anyone but Leah)—and Magda did her best to tune him out.

She knew this didn't *really* matter. In the grand scheme of things, whether Mac got back into the competition or not wasn't going to change the course of her life dramatically. Tim was actually (as much as she hated to admit it) probably right about Leah being easier to beat. But she still wanted Mac to win. She wanted it for him, with an intensity she didn't want to look at too closely.

And it was killing her not knowing what was going on in the kitchen.

It felt like three lifetimes passed, and then the cameraman suddenly moved, getting in position in front of the door moments before it opened.

Leah came through first, grimacing slightly, shaking her head. Then Abby, whose tight expression gave nothing away.

And then Mac—the only one of the bakers who was no longer wearing a black apron. His was a bright sunshine yellow, and he grinned, spreading his arms. "I'm in."

Magda squealed. She didn't think about the cameras, she didn't think about the others watching, she just leapt up and threw her arms around him. "You did it!"

Mac's arms closed around her, and he laughed. For a moment it felt like they were the only two people in the world. Then the others were there, congratulating him, even Tim, who seemed to have realized he might not be giving the producers enough non-dickish footage.

Magda fell back, her face flushed, suddenly embarrassed by the fierceness of her reaction. She bumped into Leah, and her happiness diminished by several dozen notches. "Oh, Leah..."

"It's okay," Leah said, and Magda wanted to cry all over again.

She hugged her friend, squeezing her tight. "I wish you could have both come back."

"It really is okay," Leah said. "I'm glad I got the chance to fight my way back in, even if that bastard had a freaking unbeatable pie." Magda tried to ignore the flush of irrational pride that Mac had produced an unbeatable pie. Leah must have seen something on her face, because a knowing light sparked in her eyes. "He isn't so bad." She gripped Magda's arms and stared into her eyes. "But you better win this thing, you hear me?"

Magda almost asked if Leah was going to tell Eunice the same thing, but there was something about the ferocity of the words that stopped her. And instead, for the first time, she heard herself saying "I will."

Leah grinned—and then Eunice was there, and they were all talking and laughing and trying to hold on to these last few minutes with Leah before the producers broke up the party and made them all go sit in the confessional chairs.

Magda sat in her chair—sleep-deprived and buzzing with contact adrenaline. Her defenses were down, which was why Julia's first statement caught her off-guard.

"That was some hug…"

Magda flushed, feeling like everything they'd done last night must show on her face. Julia must know—though she couldn't know, could she? They hadn't been spotted. That they knew of.

"So you and Mac…?" Julia coaxed.

She had to give them something. Magda searched her brain for the right words, honest words, but ones that wouldn't give *too* much away. "I really wish Leah could've come back too—and Abby. But I was happy to see Mac back in the competition," she said. "I know we started out as rivals, but this experience… We're actually… I don't know, we're good now. I never expected it, but yeah, maybe we're not rivals anymore."

"And what are you?"

"I think we're friends." More than friends, but the friends part was there, too—which might be even more surprising than the incendiary chemistry. There had always been heat underneath their arguments, but the friendship was the thing that made her feel a strange sort of wonder. "It's a *Cake-Off* miracle."

The interview didn't last long. Julia asked her a few more questions and then released her back into the Proving Room. Several of the other bakers were still being debriefed, but Mac was there. Craft services had put out sandwiches, and she approached the table where he'd just picked one up, grabbing one of her own.

"Good to have you back," she said, unwrapping the sandwich, and fighting the urge to grin at him.

"Yeah?"

"Yeah." Then she looked up at him innocently. "You're going to be so easy to beat in the final."

A laugh burst out of him. "Oh yeah?"

"*Oh* yeah," she confirmed.

They'd been trash-talking for years, but this time it felt different. Playful and wicked and *fun*. His dark eyes were glittering with equal parts heat and humor as they held hers. They still had to get to the final—but it was so close, and somehow that felt more possible than ever.

"Bring it on, cupcake."

Chapter Thirty-Four

The Skills Challenge that afternoon was mille-feuille. It was French Patisserie Week, and Magda was in her wheelhouse—thank goodness, because she was still operating on only a few hours' sleep. Even sleep-deprived, she was second only to Tim for the top spot. Eunice was in the middle. Mac's cream split, but he still fared better than Zain, who hadn't gotten all the elements on the plate.

There were no practice bakes that night, and by unspoken agreement, all the bakers—Mac and Magda included—separated to their respective rooms as soon as they got back to the inn. Tomorrow's challenge would determine who got into the final, and they all needed their sleep.

The final challenge was deceptively simple. A frangipane fruit tart. Three hours. Exquisitely decorated.

It was actually, much to Magda's surprise, plenty of time for the challenge. Which would have normally had her second-guessing and worrying that she hadn't done enough, but today she was met with an eerie sense of calm. Her ginger apricot tart was elegant. It was classic. It wasn't wild or risk-taking, but it was *her.* And if she was going to go out, she wanted to go out making something that she was deeply proud of.

She stood during judging, squeezing Mac's hand on one side and Eunice's on the other—and then they were in. She barely registered Tim winning. She knew she should feel bad for Zain—being eliminated so close to the final—but all she could think, over and over again, was *We did it.*

Then the producers were lining them up again, and Jeffrey Flanders was announcing yet *another* twist and Magda nearly groaned aloud. They'd been so close to the final—but the day was still young. Was there another bake today? Another elimination?

"This year, for the first time ever, we're going to be having our final competition in front of a *live* audience. Yes, there will be people applauding your apple fritters and cheering for your churros. And the setting of our thrilling finale will be quite familiar to a couple of our bakers, as the special *Vermont* edition of *The Great American Cake-Off* will hold its finale in none other than Pine Hollow, Vermont! The hometown of two of our finalists!"

Magda's jaw dropped. "Oh..."

Mac finished for her. *"Sugar."*

Pine Hollow was somehow both the best and worst possible place for the finale to be filmed. Magda was delighted they would be baking on her home turf, in front of a cheering section filled with all her friends and family.

And horrified because they would be *filming in front of all her friends and family.*

"Isn't that unfair?" Magda asked Julia, as the producer escorted her through the halls of King Arthur, where the crew members were rapidly packing up equipment. The set had already started to look less like a set and more like the tourist attraction and baking school that it usually was. And for once there weren't cameras lurking around to catch her reactions. "Home field advantage for me and Mac?"

"We'd already spoken to the others before the semifinal, and they all signed off on it. Eunice actually loved the idea. We're flying out some of their supporters, and bringing back the rest of the eliminated contestants. It'll be just like our traditional finales, only with four of you instead of three and outdoors rather than here."

It was only May, but Magda's brain immediately went to the unpredictable weather conditions—*no chocolate work*—but what she said was "There are ovens outdoors?"

"We're running power from some kind of pavilion."

The bandstand. Which powered the massive Christmas tree and all the town lights every year.

"It was either this or find a warehouse to set up in. Because of the shutdown, we ran out of time here." Julia frowned. "Are you really not excited? I thought you'd be happy."

"No, I am, I just..." It was hard to put into words. She'd been able to break out of her shell on *Cake-Off.* To be herself without worrying about what anyone thought of her—which was a little insane considering she was on a reality television show and the entire world was going to be able to watch this, but there'd been a freedom in being here, in this bubble.

But now...going back to Pine Hollow, where everyone knew her and *expected* things of her...

That was it. The expectation. She'd always found it so hard not to worry about those expectations, not to frame her life around living up to them. And now they were all going to be watching her, expecting things of her. No more safe little bubble. No more playing mind games with herself to pretend that what happened on the show would stay on the show. She'd always known the outside world would intrude at some point, but she'd been very good at pretending it wouldn't—and now she couldn't pretend anymore.

"Since we won't have an official *Cake-Off* house in Pine Hollow, I got Stephen to sign off on you and Mac being allowed to stay at your own places. Sleep in your own beds."

Magda immediately thought of Cupcake—and Charlotte and Kendall. "Aren't we still sequestered?"

"You're still under NDAs, so you can't talk about the happenings on the show, but we aren't going to stop you from seeing your family. You'll even get your cellphones back—though we'll confiscate them again on the morning of the finale."

Contact with the outside world. It had been all she'd wanted when she first came to the show, but now she was almost hesitant about going home. About leaving King Arthur and the show bubble. She'd found herself here. Now she just needed to hang on to that feeling as she made her way home.

Julia guided her around a stack of crates waiting to be loaded onto trucks, and through the outer doors.

It was surreal to think that it was almost over—and that somehow Mac and Magda were both in the finale. The Pine Hollow finale. She couldn't wrap her head around it all.

Magda didn't know where the other contestants were. After the results, they'd been split up for confessionals, and now everyone seemed to be in a hurry to break things down and clear the premises. The contestants were just in the way.

It was Friday afternoon, and the finale would be filmed all day Sunday. There was virtually no time to mentally prepare—but that seemed like standard operating procedure for this season. Always keeping them off-balance.

Julia quickly briefed her on the finale protocols as they walked.

The contestants would all be driven to Pine Hollow tonight, where Tim and Eunice would stay at one of the inns—though not the one Mac's grandmother owned. And thirty-six hours later, they would be taking their positions in the town square for the final competition to determine the winner of the whole shebang. And $250,000.

No pressure.

They exited the building, and Magda headed on autopilot toward the contestant van, but Julia caught her arm, drawing her to a stop in the no-man's-land halfway across the parking lot. "Before you go..." Julia's voice was pitched low, barely reaching Magda's ears, and she noticed that the producer had removed her ever-present headset.

"I was reviewing some footage the other morning—new stuff that had logged overnight. We don't have enough cameras to cover the entire inn, but Greg thought it might be good to have footage of bakers sneaking in practice bakes, so there's a motion-activated camera in the kitchen."

Oh no. Magda's breath stilled, vivid memories of Mac boosting her up on the counter replaying in her mind. "The kitchen at the inn?"

"Mm-hmm. I figured with the time stamp, it must have been an error—the inn cat wandering through the room, so it started randomly recording in the middle of the night." Julia met her eyes meaningfully. "And that was probably what it was, but the footage was corrupted anyway. Totally useless. I just deleted it. Before anyone else saw it. No way to recover it, so..."

Magda's face felt like it was burning, and she met Julia's gaze with unbridled gratitude in hers. "Thank you," she whispered.

"Who knows where else that cat might have wandered that night..."

"I think I, um, saw it that night in the upstairs hallway—right by Mac's room. And then maybe the following morning, wandering between his room and my room."

"Oh, well, that shouldn't mess up any footage," Julia assured her. "No cameras up there. That hallway is way too dark and twisty to get any useful shots."

"Right," Magda said, nearly melting with relief. "Of course."

Julia nodded and seemed to gaze absently back toward the building, but Magda had the strong impression that she still had something more to say. After a moment, she spoke, almost as if she was musing to herself.

"I used to love this part of the season. When it's down to the final few, and you start to see what the story of the season is going to be. At the beginning, you just try to get everything, because you never know what's going to develop, who's going to rise and who's going to be a shocking early departure. But this is when it all comes together and you know who's the fan favorite and who's the underdog—and which bakers really grew and came into their own."

She looked back toward Magda then, meeting her eyes. "I'm really glad I was finally able to get you on the show, Magda. I always thought you'd go far."

"Finally?"

"You were the first baker I picked out of the pile, two years ago, back when Deanna was training me on how to put together a season. 'This one,' I said. 'She's gonna be special.' And I love it when you prove me right."

"Two years...but I didn't get on." She *hadn't* been special enough.

Julia shrugged. "A lot of things go into putting together a cast. Our scouts raved about your bakes, but the cast for that season already included two other pretty French-trained bakers in their late twenties. Helene had barely missed making the top thirteen twice already, and Yvonne was from Chicago—and you know how much they like to have locals. I think that's part of why Deanna wanted to film at King Arthur so badly this year. She already had her eye on you."

"Me?" Was that possible?

"Yeah. That, and she loved Vermont." Julia sighed. "I wish she'd gotten to film here. It would've been a very different season."

Magda still couldn't wrap her head around the fact that they'd filmed at King Arthur *for her*. At least in part. She'd been so sure that she wasn't special enough for *Cake-Off*, that there was something lacking in her. She'd felt like she needed to be someone else—and all along the fact that she hadn't been cast her first time out of the gate had been chance. Timing. Putting together a cast from different cities and different backgrounds.

She'd been so completely *wrong*. About so many things.

"I'm not supposed to tell you this," Julia said, her voice barely audible, but the words instantly snared Magda's full attention. "But Stephen's really determined to find something on you and Mac. I figure it's your choice when you make your relationship public. If you say 'just friends' in the confessional, I'm giving Stephen friends. He doesn't actually have any footage proving otherwise, so if he wants to sell a more salacious storyline, it will just be rumors and hearsay." Her lips twitched up in a side smile. "Maybe if he doesn't have anything else to use, he'll actually make the show about baking."

"We can only hope," Magda said lightly—but her brain was still snagged on a single word Julia had said.

Relationship.

Was that what this was? She'd managed to avoid thinking past the finale—much—but the idea of going public about their relationship, about all of America knowing they were dating, let alone all of Pine Hollow, felt very intimidating.

"When did you know?" she whispered. "That we were..."

"I didn't *know* until I heard about the kiss, but I suspected as soon as I had you both in the chair talking about each other. There was always something about the way you said each other's names. All of the rivals seemed to hate one another. But with some it was cold. And with you two? Can't stand the heat, get out of the kitchen, right? And then you made that maple cake." She shrugged. "I hope you don't mind. I might have pushed you at each other a little bit. Hopeless romantic."

"Pushed us...?"

"Who do you think scheduled your practice bakes back-to-back?"

"I assumed it was Stephen. Trying to drive us crazy."

"Well. He suggested it. But I could have ignored him. I'm getting pretty good at that." She glanced back over her shoulder. "I should probably get back."

"Right. Thanks, Julia. Truly."

Julia squeezed her arm and wished her luck, promising to see her in Pine Hollow, and sent her off to the waiting van.

Relationship. The word echoed again, but Magda pushed all thoughts of a nebulous future with Mac out of her head.

She could worry about all that on Monday. She only had a few days left before her *Cake-Off* experience was over, and she needed to focus.

She could actually win. She, Magda, could actually be the *Cake-Off* champion. It would all be over in just a few days—and she could worry then about what came next. Mac, her bakery...

She already felt new. Like the last few weeks had changed her. Looking forward felt different now—*she* felt different. Confident and sure. She could think about what she wanted because now she believed she could get it. Whatever it was.

But that was Monday.

Today was *Cake-Off*, and giving herself the best possible chance to win.

Chapter Thirty-Five

His cat was in her apartment again.

Magda's lips twitched into a smile when she saw the tabby sprawled out arrogantly on Cupcake's dog bed. The pit bull whined piteously, and she knelt, cuddling her sweet baby. "Don't you worry about that mean ol' cat," she soothed, stroking Cupcake's silky head. "You're a good girl, and he has no manners."

It was Saturday morning. The four finalists had ridden to Pine Hollow last night, after quickly packing up their things at the inn. They hadn't spoken much on the drive—Magda and Mac had answered Eunice's questions about what the town square was like and what they might be able to expect, venue-wise, on Sunday, but other than that the ride had been quiet. Everyone was focused on the finale—and Magda had fallen asleep with her head on Mac's shoulder, still catching up on sleep.

She couldn't believe they'd been so reckless in the kitchen—well, she could believe it; they had always forgotten the rest of the world existed, whether they were fighting or doing... other things.

Magda had been dropped off first, before even Tim and Eunice, so she hadn't had a chance to subtly mention to Mac that they'd been caught on camera and Julia had saved their asses. She'd gotten so out of the habit of having her phone on her that it didn't even occur to her until this morning that she could have texted him the information.

As it was, she had stumbled up to her apartment, said hello to Cupcake, whom Charlotte had dropped off as soon as she knew Magda was coming home, and immediately fallen asleep for ten straight hours.

It wasn't just the short night with Mac. It was like everything that had happened over the last month had all landed on top of her all at once and she'd flopped face-first onto her mattress and not moved until Cupcake woke her up with the urgent need to pee at five in the morning.

Once she was up, she was up, and she'd gone down to the bakery and checked on the inventory. The frozen stock had held up reasonably well, but a few favorites were running low. She should be taking this time to practice for the final—but instead she found herself taking comfort in the habit of baking old favorites, humming to herself with Cupcake curled around her ankles.

She baked until her niece came in to open up the shop at eight—and then kept baking, hiding in the kitchen through the familiar sounds of the Saturday morning rush. It sounded busier than usual, and she heard several patrons ask if she was back. She'd found out from Charlotte last night that the people of Pine Hollow had known about the finale being filmed there for nearly a week, and several of them had already been interviewed, issuing their opinions on who was most likely to win, Mac or Magda.

Magda knew the TV crew would be roaming town all day, getting more footage. She heard dozens of locals telling her niece to wish her luck, and she knew she'd be mobbed with good wishes if she made an appearance, but she'd snuck upstairs at lunchtime, not wanting to see anyone.

Except Mac.

He probably had even more catch-up to do at the Cup than she did at the bakery, and she hadn't wanted to disturb his own prep for the finale. But if his cat was here...

Well.

Magda tracked down her cellphone and dialed.

"Miss me?" he asked, instead of saying hello.

She grinned, though she tried to make her voice fierce. "Your cat is in my apartment again."

"You keep leaving those windows open." His voice was rich with laughter.

"Come get your cat, Mackenzie."

She hung up the phone, and didn't even have time to toss it on the counter before a knock came at her door. She opened the door, and there he was.

"Did you teleport?" she asked incredulously.

Cupcake rushed over to sniff him, and he knelt to greet her, his large hands gently stroking her soft head. Still crouching, he glanced up at Magda with a crooked grin. "I'm not saying I brought the cat over and released him beneath your open window just because I wanted to see you, but if I had done that, it would be charming, not creepy, right?"

She laughed. "Reasonably charming. Your cat is still Satan, so..."

He stood, his gaze dropping to her lips. "I missed you."

"Likewise," she murmured, already going up on her toes to meet him as he lowered his head.

"Are we allowed to be fraternizing?" she asked, once he'd kicked the door shut and greeted her properly.

"If they didn't want us to conspire about the finale, they shouldn't have given us our phones back."

"Is that why you're here?" she asked. "To conspire?"

"Of course," he said—but given the fact that he was already carrying her toward the couch, his lips finding that spot he liked on her neck, she didn't think they'd be doing much conspiring for a while.

Cupcake heaved a sigh and went to curl up on the rug, gazing longingly at the dog bed where the tabby still reigned.

"Your cat is bullying my dog," Magda said, but given that Mac was still kissing his way down her neck, the words were more breathless than heated.

"Your dog has no spine," he said, distractedly.

He wasn't wrong. And he was incredibly good with his mouth, so she sank her hands into his curls and forgot about the world—until a thought crashed into her head that had her stiffening abruptly. "Oh!"

He froze immediately. "You okay? What happened? Did I hurt you?"

"No! No, you're amazing. I just keep forgetting to tell you—there were cameras in the inn's kitchen."

Mac's eyes flared wide. "Oh shit."

"But Julia killed the video! Sorry, buried the lead. She told me yesterday as things were breaking up at King Arthur. I meant to say something, but—"

"The show," he finished for her. They both knew how rare it was to have a private moment to talk in the *Cake-Off* bubble. "Thank God for Julia."

"Thank God she's the one who found the footage," Magda agreed. "She said Stephen's trying to craft some salacious narrative."

"I'm not surprised. Connor said the guy who interviewed him and Deenie was asking all kinds of personal questions about us—like if we'd ever had a secret affair or something. He thought it was just going to be 'Who do you want to win?' but I guess it got pretty weird pretty fast."

"Oh, God, my parents. They're going ask my parents that stuff."

"And my grandmother."

Magda groaned. "The entire town already thinks—"

"Do we care what they think?" he interrupted her spiraling.

"Do I want to care, or do I actually care?" she asked rhetorically. "Won't people think it's fast?"

Mac arched a brow. "I'm pretty sure Connor thinks we've been flirting for the last decade."

"Kendall, too," she agreed. "Though Charlotte will *not* be pleased. She's protective."

"And I was a dick."

"I had my dickish moments, too. She'll get over it." At least Magda hoped she would. Because she was hoping that they would be together long enough for Charlotte to have time to get over it.

"Look, I know you're Magda Miller of the Miller Dairy dynasty, and I'm Mackenzie Newton, scion of two Pine Hollow founding families, and we are therefore automatically gossip, but does it matter if people think we're dating?"

"So we're dating?"

Mac indicated their position—sprawled on the couch with her on his lap and his hand on her lower back beneath her shirt. "Are you trying to tell me you're just using me for my body?"

"No, I just...We hadn't talked about after the show, and I know it was this weird sort of world unto itself, and now we're back and it's Pine Hollow and people are going to talk and it's going to get back to your family and my family and all of our friends—"

"Magda."

"Which is going to be incredibly awkward if we ever break up, because I'm not sure if you've noticed, but all of my friends keep marrying all of your friends—"

He cut off her diatribe with a kiss. Then held her gaze when he lifted his head. "Do you want to date me? Maybe go steady? See where this goes?"

She blinked, and the answer was so stupidly obvious. "Yes."

He grinned. "Good. Then that's that."

"So none of the rest of it bothers you?"

He arched his eyebrows. "You honestly think it's going to be *more* uncomfortable if we're exes than it has been for the last fourteen years, when we were plotting each other's demise?"

"I'm not saying I ever *actively* plotted your demise..."

He growled, and his hand found a ticklish spot on her side that he'd discovered the other night. Magda squeaked and tried to wriggle away, but the wriggling just wound up with her underneath him on the couch and his lovely shoulders above her and... okay, she wasn't complaining.

"I've been so stressed," she murmured, sometime later. She was lying with her head pillowed on his chest, stretched out on the couch, listening to the steady thud of his heart. "But it was good stress. The show was the best possible reason to be stressed, so I can't complain. But you just make it..." Better. So much better.

"Always at your service to help you de-stress," he rumbled.

"Are you nervous about the final?"

"A little," he admitted. Cupcake had moved closer and now leaned against the edge of the couch, gazing at Mac adoringly as he petted her with one hand, his other idly tracing patterns on Magda's back. "I realized something the other night, when I thought I was out of the competition for good. I hadn't really let myself want it. I hadn't let myself *try*, because then I couldn't be disappointed if I failed. You did all this prep work and threw everything you had into it, and—"

"I know. Always trying too hard."

"No," he said, the word startling in its force. "It's amazing. You inspire me." His hand hesitated for a moment on her back, and the next words came like a confession. "I was practicing this morning. I know it's last-minute and probably too late to really make a difference, but I don't want to feel like I didn't put my all into this, you know?"

She propped herself up so she could see his face. "Yeah?"

"I guess I decided some things are worth caring about—even if it might hurt like a bitch if you fail." His eyes held hers. "And then I came to see you."

"You still have a chance to win it all."

"One of us better. We can't let Tim take home the prize. I wouldn't mind if it was Eunice, but she's always struggled with the time limits, and the finale is always *massive*—"

Magda pushed herself up to a sitting position. "Wanna rewatch the finale of every season and see if we can figure out what they're going to make us do?"

"Hell yes."

They both knew that Stephen would undoubtedly try to shake things up, adding his own sadistic twist to the usual format, but they still cuddled up on her couch and watched, identifying winning and losing tactics, groaning and cheering. After the second finale, they put the show on her tablet and went down to the bakery, baking as they watched.

It was almost like being back in the *Cake-Off* kitchen, working together on a challenge—moving around each other, his light touches on her hip or the small of her back to let her know where he was so they didn't bump into each other. As if she ever would have been unaware of his presence in her space. The heat of him, the sweet tension of this man she could never ignore. But it was also comfortable now. And so welcome.

They still didn't know what to expect the next day, but her nerves had receded. Whatever it was, they would face it. And one of them would win.

They agreed not to spend the night together—they both wanted their sleep and knew they wouldn't get much of that if they were together. He kissed her in her kitchen until the timer went off to take the last batch of cupcakes out of the oven, then they went upstairs together so he could collect his cat.

The tabby was an excellent chaperone, because Magda didn't want to get anywhere near Mac once he'd picked him up. The last thing she wanted was to go into the final tomorrow with her face and arms scratched and bleeding.

It was already dark out when they said goodbye at the door, but Magda knew it would be a while before she slept, her nerves running too high. She put on her cake pajamas and curled up in her bed with Cupcake and her phone, reading recipes in the dark—until Mac started texting her "You Can Do It" gifs.

They stayed up too long, texting in the dark, and she fell asleep smiling.

Chapter Thirty-Six

"A rgh!"

At the shriek of surprise, Mac jerked awake at his grandmother's kitchen table, his whole body flinching away from the door where his gran stood with a hand pressed over her heart.

"Mackenzie! You scared me. What are you doing in here?"

"Last-minute recipe cramming." A loose recipe he had been reading stuck to his face, and he swiped it off. Restless when he'd gotten back from Magda's last night, he'd come in here because his grandmother had more cookbooks than he did. "I must have fallen asleep," he mumbled, stating the obvious.

The cat walked across the books on the table as morning sunlight streaked in through the kitchen windows—

Shit. *Morning* sunlight. Mac searched frantically amid the recipe book debris on the table until he found his cellphone and saw 6:12 a.m. on the screen.

Thank God. He hadn't missed it. He wasn't late. Yet.

His gran came deeper into the room and picked up one of the recipe cards that cluttered the surface of the kitchen table. "You're studying?"

"Yeah, well…" He shrugged, a little embarrassed by the effort. "Better late than never, right?"

She pressed her lips together and nodded. "Have I told you how proud I am of you?" she asked, her gaze still focused on the recipe card in her hands. "Not just for the show, but for everything you've accomplished. Of the man you've become."

He flushed, fighting the urge to squirm. "Thanks. You're pretty great, too."

She smiled gently at his discomfort, looking at him instead of the card in her hands. "I wish your grandfather could see you now. He'd be so proud."

"You sure about that?" Mac asked, forcing his tone to lightness. "He always thought I was 'squandering my potential.' He hated the baking. He *hated* the Cup."

"He only hated the Cup because he thought it was you giving up your dreams for him," his gran corrected. "Studying theater. Going off to be a Broadway star."

"I was never going to be a Broadway star."

"But you were on the path. You were *so happy* doing those campus productions. Being away at school."

And then his grandfather had gotten sick. The cancer was already advanced when they caught it. Advanced enough that no one was talking cures. The discussions were all about life-extending measures and the best quality of life for the time remaining.

Six months. Tops.

His grandfather had gotten the diagnosis at the end of Mac's sophomore year. He'd come home for the summer, and the idea of going back in the fall had been unfathomable. His grandfather had raised him. Mac had loved him more than any other human on the planet besides his gran, and he couldn't imagine a world in which he didn't take a deferment on his education so he could grab as much time as possible with his grandfather before it was over.

They'd said six months, but it had been over a year before

he passed—and during that year, Mac had needed *something* to do besides watch his grandfather slowly die. The Cup had started out as a distraction. A project. He hadn't wanted to work at the family's inn, where everything would remind him of his grandfather—and where they didn't really need his help, the staff more than capable.

He'd wanted something that needed his focus and his time.

And the town really did need a decent cup of coffee.

He'd become a coffee snob during his time away, and he complained about the lack until his grandfather told him to do something about it. So he did.

He'd grabbed the cheapest commercial rental space he could find—a janky old building with a cramped kitchen and not enough seating—and thrown together an espresso bar. Whenever his brain needed an escape from the slow slide toward the end at home, he would focus on the Cup. On how he could make it better.

When his grandfather had died, he could have gone back to school. He could have closed up shop and left. But his gran was alone, and he couldn't leave her. He couldn't be that person. So he'd deferred another year. He'd channeled his grief into growing the business more, and then he'd come up with more reasons not to go back. All his classmates would have graduated. Did he really need a degree? Wasn't he happy right where he was, keeping an eye on his gran and becoming a member of the community, focusing on the Cup?

"He never wanted you to hold yourself back," his grandmother said softly. "Especially not for him."

Mac had told himself that his dreams had just changed—though he did sometimes wonder what path his life would have taken if he hadn't stayed. Still. He was happy with who he was.

The friendships he had. The way he was part of this community, embedded in it.

He'd been telling himself he was happy for years, but now he felt that contentment in his soul. It was different now. Was that Magda? Or something else?

He'd taught himself at a young age not to want things that were out of his control. Like for his parents to want to be actual parents. He'd learned to let the disappointments roll off of him by not trying too hard. Enjoy the things that came easily. There were plenty of those. If you didn't really *try* for something, then you couldn't be disappointed.

But the best things in life were things you couldn't control.

He'd had a crush on Elinor when they were teens—back when she only had eyes for Levi—and he used to wonder what would have happened if he'd told her how he felt during one of the offs of their on-again-off-again relationship. But he'd been firmly in the friend zone, and her feelings were something he couldn't control—so he didn't take the risk.

When he auditioned for shows, he never auditioned for the lead: *Take any part they give you, just be part of the experience—and don't rehearse your audition too much, because then if you don't get in, it just wasn't meant to be; it doesn't mean you aren't actually good enough.*

All those defense mechanisms. All those layers of bubble wrap around his heart.

He'd had a lot of therapy. He knew all his baggage, but it was still there. It didn't go away. He just learned how to carry it better. So it didn't get in his way.

He couldn't control the outcome of the *Cake-Off.* And he couldn't control how Magda felt about him. But he *wanted* both. He wanted to win—though he also wanted Magda to win, and it was complicated and he wasn't sure which outcome he wanted more—but he really wanted her.

And he wanted, for the first time, to *try*.

"My Shot" from *Hamilton* had been playing in his head all night. He wasn't throwing away this shot. Not this time.

"I'm not holding back anymore," he promised his grandmother, and her smile filled with pride.

"Good." Then her smile shifted to something almost sly. "I like this girl. She's a good influence."

"What girl?" He hadn't mentioned Magda to his grandmother.

"Boy, I'm old, but I'm not blind. The girl all of Pine Hollow is talking about. The one you went to see yesterday when you thought nobody was looking. Don't worry. I won't ask what you were doing."

He was a grown man in his thirties—and his grandmother could still make him blush. "It's complicated."

"I imagine it is when you're competing against each other for a big old pot of money and you've been quietly at war for the last decade. But I look forward to hearing all about it on a morning when you *don't* have to go be on national television. And I'll just say this: it's really good to see you in love."

The words clogged his brain like a wrench thrown in the works, grinding all the gears to a halt. "I . . ." Was he in love with Magda? Was that what this was? This feeling that made everything feel worth it—all the risks he hadn't let himself take in the past. They seemed easy now.

Because he finally wanted something enough to care? And that something was her?

"What time do you need to be down there?"

Mac glanced at the clock, anxiety spiking. "Right, yeah. I should go."

Go compete against the woman he loved for a quarter million dollars. As one does.

"Here we are, with the soon-to-be winner of *Cake-Off* Archrivals Edition and her two amazing very best friends in the whole wide world—on the morning of the finale, watching the last-minute prep that goes into the *making of a champion.*"

Magda glanced over at Charlotte, grinning even as she scolded, "You know you can't post that anywhere."

Charlotte shrugged, never lowering the cellphone she'd been recording on since the second she walked through the door. "I'm capturing the moment. You can post it after the show airs. Trust me. You're gonna want this."

Magda wasn't so sure. Right now she was just trying not to lose her breakfast.

Fifteen minutes. She was due at the square—which was literally right across the street—in fifteen minutes.

"Nervous?" Kendall asked.

"Petrified."

Cupcake leaned against her leg, and Magda reached down to pet her as her phone buzzed on the counter—she almost jumped, but that wasn't the timer she'd set so she wouldn't be late. It was a text notification. She picked up the phone and saw a message from Mac.

Good luck today. Own your awesomeness, my little baumkuchen.

She giggled and typed out a quick response wishing him luck as well—then looked up to find both of her friends staring at her. Charlotte had even lowered the phone.

"What?"

The words burst out of Charlotte in a rush. "Okay, I promised

Kendall I wouldn't ask you until after the finale, because we're not supposed to distract you, but literally the entire town is talking about it and you're giggling at your phone—and if you don't want to talk about it that is totally fine because today is about you and I want you in the best possible headspace, all baking, all the time, but is it okay for me to ask what the heck is going on with Mac?"

Magda blushed. "We're dating?"

"Oh my God!" Charlotte exclaimed as Kendall frowned and asked, "Was that a question?"

"No," Magda said, more firmly. "We're dating. And it's fine to talk about. It's not going to derail me."

She had been a little nervous. Thinking about people's reactions, feeling like the eyes of the entire town were on her. Needing to be her *Cake-Off* self here, in front of everyone. With everyone knowing about Mac as well. All her inner pieces had been exposed, but maybe that wasn't such a bad thing. Maybe it wasn't about being perfect Magda who always obeyed the rules and avoided getting herself in the gossip column. Maybe it was about being herself and going a little wild sometimes.

Because she didn't regret going wild with Mac. She wasn't ashamed or nervous about people seeing them together. She was excited. She was proud.

And she was ready to own her freaking awesomeness.

"Are you sure about this?" Charlotte asked, her face wreathed in worry. "He hurt you. And now you want me to just forgive him?"

"It was a long, *long* time ago," Magda said. "And I love that you're protective of me and you've always taken my side even though Mac is friends with your sister and your husband, and you've never made me feel ridiculous for my extremely ridiculous vendetta—but now the best way for you to be on my side is to be on his too. I really, *really* like him."

She wasn't willing to say *love* yet. She'd jumped to that conclusion way too fast when they were younger, but this...this felt completely different. And yet somehow perfectly the same. The connection was still there—all the times he made her laugh, all the things they had in common—but it was deeper now. Stronger.

"And you're not worried this is about the show? About letting him win?"

"If he wants to win, he's going to have to beat me at my best. I'm not letting him do anything—and no. I'm not worried it's about the show. We didn't even..." She flushed. "We waited until he was eliminated, and neither of us had any idea he was going to have a chance to get back in—which you absolutely cannot talk about. It's covered by the NDA."

Charlotte looked at Kendall. "Aren't you going to say anything?"

"What do you want me to say? I've thought they should hook up for years."

Charlotte gaped at her—

And the alarm on Magda's phone went off.

Her heart immediately began to pound. "Time to go wild."

Magda wore her bedazzled "Not Here to Make Friends" apron as she walked between Kendall and Charlotte toward the square. The bakery was closed for the occasion, along with all the other businesses that lined the square. A giant tent had been set up in front of the bandstand, and the backs of the bleachers from the annual tree lighting ceremony blocked her view of the inside.

It wasn't even eight o'clock in the morning, and the competition would likely take most of the day, but the square was already swarming with people—crew members and townspeople and former contestants. The bakers would be performing in front of an audience for the finale, but that wasn't what had Magda the most nervous.

This was it. What everything had been building up to.

A production assistant spotted her and whisked her away to the contestant area. She heard Charlotte behind her, grumbling about her phone being confiscated, as Magda was ushered into a much smaller tent and her own phone was taken away.

Eunice spotted the "Not Here to Make Friends" apron and burst out laughing, rushing over to give her a hug, before they were separated to go through hair and makeup, and Magda had to trade her apron for an official *Cake-Off* apron.

Across the little tent, she spotted Mac and smiled. He grinned, too, making an exaggeratedly fierce face to make her laugh.

The hairstylist gave her a little extra hairspray, making a comment about the long day ahead, and complimenting her on her curls—which for once weren't frizzy. Charlotte had suggested hot-pink streaks in her hair for the occasion, but that was such a Charlotte thing, and she just wanted to feel like herself today.

Tim was focused. Eunice was fidgeting. Mac seemed relaxed. But Magda just felt...right. Like she was in exactly the moment she was meant to be in, and she had every intention of enjoying it.

There were cameras in the tent, swirling around, asking them how they felt, but she didn't see Julia, and it was Greg who sat across from her at the confessional, asking her what being in the finals meant to her and showing her videos of support from her friends and family.

Magda would never know how she managed not to cry.

When they were done with the interviews, time moved quickly. She felt like she blinked and they were being ushered into the big tent, one by one, with Magda last of all. As soon as she stepped into the tent, a massive cheer went up, and Magda jumped a bit at the wall of sound.

She saw her parents. Her entire massive family. Her friends. Mac's friends. His grandmother. Her third-grade teacher. Her customers. All the former contestants. The mayor and his family. There were Team Mac shirts and Team Magda shirts—and even a few Team Mac-da shirts that made her laugh and look over at Mac, who had entered before her. Handmade posters for Eunice and one for Tim, held by a stern older man.

Magda lifted her hand and waved, drinking in the moment. The buzz of it. The sparkle of anticipation.

She even saw Julia, up in the bleachers, though she didn't know what her producer was doing up there. Filling a seat? Coaching the audience?

A production assistant directed her toward her station—and Magda looked at the baking stations for the first time. They actually looked remarkably like the *Cake-Off* kitchen—if you didn't notice that the floor gave slightly beneath your feet, giant checkerboard flooring placed down over the grass. Ingredients were tucked beneath a box with a *Cake-Off* logo on it—as they were before a Skills Challenge—and Magda's heart began to drum in her chest as she took her place and the judges entered with Jeffrey Flanders to a roar of cheers.

It was really happening. She was here. In this moment.

"Welcome," Jeffrey Flanders intoned dramatically, "to the finale of the first ever Archrivals Edition of *The Great American Cake-Off*!"

Magda smiled. *Okay, Mags. Just be yourself.*

Chapter Thirty-Seven

Mac's hands were shaking.

They started out with a Skills Challenge, as was traditional—but it felt like a freaking race. Sixty minutes and they had to make a soufflé. A freaking *soufflé*. Outside. On a May morning that hadn't started to warm up yet—which was a little like trying to bake in the middle of a walk-in refrigerator with no time to redo anything that went wrong.

There were heat lamps around the tent to try to compensate for the chill, but there seemed to be a gap in the tent flaps immediately to his left that kept letting in a frigid breeze.

And there was an audience.

Mac had always loved cooking—but it had never been a spectator sport before, and there was something incredibly distracting about the gasps and murmurs and rustles of several hundred observers. He had to fight to keep his attention on his task, struggling to remember which steps he'd already done.

His only saving grace was that he'd practiced soufflés yesterday with Magda. He knew what to do.

It was just the doing it that was the trick.

He was aware of Magda at the station next to his—Tim to his left and Eunice on the other side of Magda to the right—but he tried to keep his focus on his hands. Cameras popped up in his face periodically—sometimes with producers and sometimes without—asking him how he was feeling, if he'd ever made soufflé before, and what it would mean to him to win a quarter million dollars. Just in case he was likely to forget what was at stake here. When the cameras weren't on him, he tried to hum show tunes—which usually calmed him down—but he couldn't even remember the lyrics to his favorite songs. All knowledge of *Hamilton* had been wiped from his brain.

This actually caring and trying thing *sucked*.

It was so much easier to be Fun Mac. Easygoing Mac. Devil-May-Care Mac.

But he *did* care. It wasn't even about the winning. It was about knowing he'd put his all into this moment. That he'd let himself want it. That he'd been as brave as Magda was.

He let himself glance over at her then. Her soufflé was in the oven and she was crouched down in front of it, staring at it like she could *will* it to perfection, and his heart lurched.

It's really good to see you in love.

Ever since his grandmother had said it this morning, the words had been floating around in the back of his thoughts. And the funny thing was…they didn't feel wrong. They felt right. Ridiculously, perfectly right.

He was in love with her. And it felt like he had been for a while. He hadn't come for the money. He'd come for her. And now that he knew, he wanted to tell her.

Magda looked up, catching him watching her, and flashed him a smile—before a timer went off at his station.

He had a soufflé to finish. Telling her he was madly in love with her would have to wait.

"And…*time!*"

Magda already had her hands in the air, staring down at her

chocolate soufflé. It was good. She knew it was good. It was one of the things she and Mac had practiced yesterday—though there hadn't been a timer and cold breezes and a crowd of spectators then.

The crowd cheered, and Magda looked up at her friends and family, half-laughing with relief and residual adrenaline.

Eunice was at her side seconds later, and the final four were being herded back to the little tent. "How'd yours go?" Magda asked Eunice as Mac fell in beside them.

"Okay?" Eunice said, the word more question than answer. "I might have overwhipped my eggs, but it didn't collapse, so yay?" She made a wincing face. "And yours?"

"Decent?" Magda responded with the same degree of certainty. "It looks right, but we won't know until they take a bite. Mac?"

Usually he would make a joke at his own expense, at ease with his mistakes, but now he just shook his head. "I don't know if it's better to know what you're doing or not know what you're doing. Knowing involves a lot more panic."

Magda laughed, taking his arm automatically—though they were out of view of the audience now, ducking into the little tent.

They were immediately split up and siphoned off toward the row of director's chairs that had been set up as confessionals while they were baking. Tim was already sitting in one, talking about his years of experience making soufflés in the best kitchens. Magda squeezed Mac's arm and headed to her own chair— but instead of Julia, Greg sat down across from her.

"Where's Julia?" she asked, looking over to see that Mac wasn't being interviewed by her either. "Is she busy?"

Greg smiled, but something about the gesture seemed off. Fake. "Julia isn't here."

Magda shook her head. "But I saw her. She's in the stands."

"What I mean is she isn't here as a producer. Just a fan." He gave her another fake grimace. "I'm afraid she was let go."

The kitchen footage. Magda felt the blood drain from her face. "Why?"

"Sometimes people just aren't a good fit. Now, we don't have much time before judging, so let's talk soufflé!"

"No."

Greg blinked. "I'm sorry?"

"I need to talk to Julia—"

"As I said, she isn't with the production any longer—"

Magda dug in her heels. "I'm not talking about the bake until I talk to her. I saw her in the stands. Go get her."

"Look, I know you two bonded and all, but we're almost to the finish line. How did you feel when you heard that the final Skills Challenge was going to be soufflé?"

"This will go a lot faster if you just go get Julia."

Greg forced another smile. "Tell you what. I'll send a PA for her, and we'll talk until she gets here."

Which meant he had no intention of sending the PA, and she was going to be conveniently rushed back to be judged before Julia arrived. "I'll wait."

Greg glowered. And called over a PA.

Five minutes later, Julia appeared beside that same PA.

"Hey," Julia said, when she got to Magda's side. "Are you okay?"

"Are you?" Magda demanded. "You got fired?"

"Don't worry about that," Julia insisted. "It had nothing to do with you."

Which Magda didn't believe for a second. "When?"

"Friday night. About ten minutes after I talked to you. And

honestly? I was relieved. I am not cut out for this new version of *Cake-Off*. But I couldn't miss this." She grinned. "I had to cheer you guys on."

She didn't seem heartbroken. If anything she seemed lighter. Less stressed than she'd been for the last several weeks. But Magda still felt like it was all her fault. That she'd been reckless, and Julia had been punished for protecting her privacy.

"What are you going to do next?"

"Honestly?" Julia said, "I'm trying not to think about that. Maybe I'll pitch a cooking show with one of my new favorite bakers." She bumped Magda's arm with a smile. "But in the meantime, I just want to see one of my favorites win this thing. You can do this, Magda."

Magda glanced back at the chair where Greg was waiting with zero patience whatsoever. "I should probably..."

"Go talk soufflé. And good luck."

They hugged quickly, and then Magda rushed back to her chair. She barely had time to talk through the Skills Challenge before they were called back for judging—now that there were fewer stations to clean, the space between baking and judging had gotten shorter.

They reentered the main tent to another roar from the crowd, and Magda smiled nervously, waving. She lined up to face the judging, holding Mac's hand on one side and Eunice's on the other. "We've got this," she whispered to them. And the judging began.

For the first time all season, they weren't told who had ranked where in the Skills Challenge. The judges marked their scorecards, but no results were read aloud, and the comments were so vague it was impossible to tell who had come out on top.

And before they could react they were ushered back to their stations.

The final bake of the season was always a marathon, and this year was no exception. Six hours. An edible illusion that had to be at least two feet tall.

Mac had decided to go with bread, because, well, he was good at bread. He could make a picnic basket out of braided breads—which would have an actual baguette, quiche, and tiny little tea cakes inside it. He wasn't going to be able to compete when it came to airbrushing fiddly little decorations onto an illusion cake, so he was going his own way.

And he didn't have time to think about anything else. He had kneading and proving and mixing to do—and it was going to take every second of the time allotted, so there was no point thinking about Magda. Or the fact that playing on repeat in his head was "If I Could Tell Her" from *Dear Evan Hansen*. That particular song... it was all about wishing you could tell someone that you loved them. Which felt glaringly on the nose.

He hummed as he kneaded, listening to the sound of Magda's voice as she described her illusion. "It's going to be a dog, with a cupcake on its nose—I adopted my dog, Cupcake, around the same time I decided I wanted to try to come on *Cake-Off*, so it felt wrong that I hadn't done any bakes dedicated to her. This dog is going to be a little smaller than she is, but not by much. Four tiers of raspberry white chocolate sponge with lemon buttercream icing."

Eunice was making a dragon out of chocolate cake, and Tim had decided on a ginger-lemon Parthenon.

Mac chatted up the cameras when they came by, but then all of his focus landed on his hands, and the rest of the world faded away. It felt like he blinked and suddenly Jeffrey Flanders was calling out, "Fifteen minutes!" as he assembled his basket.

Hamilton had been playing on repeat in his head for the last hour, and Mac focused on his hands as he carefully decorated his basket. He thought the basket was firmly on the table, but he was so focused on the part right in front of him that he hadn't noticed the back edge creeping off the edge of the counter.

Until it started to tip.

The audience gasped.

"No-no-no-no!" His instinct was to reach for the basket handle—but it was just a cinnamon twist, delicately attached to the rest of the basket with a caramel glaze. If he grabbed that it would just break off, and if he grabbed it anywhere else, the basket would probably break in half under the pressure—it was already filled with goodies that were weighing it down—

A pair of hands was suddenly there, catching it and sliding it back onto the counter.

"Oh, thank God." He met Magda's eyes across his station and blurted, "I love you."

She laughed. "You're welcome," she called, already moving back to her station to put the finishing touches on her masterpiece.

"I meant that!" he called after her.

She glanced over her shoulder, her brow wrinkling for just a second before she threw back "Save it for the judges, Romeo! Now stop distracting me."

He'd have to tell her again, to make her believe it, but for now he grinned, turning his attention back to his basket as Jeffrey Flanders began counting down—this time joined by the entire audience.

When the time was up, Mac raised his hands—and felt all the tension drain out of his body. It was over. They'd done it. There was nothing left to do but wait for the judging.

He turned toward Magda—and she was already moving toward him.

It wasn't thought. It wasn't premeditated or planned. He just sank his hands into her luscious curls, bent his head, and kissed her for all he was worth. And Magda fisted her hand in his apron and dragged him closer to kiss him right back.

Mac was only aware of the hoots and cheers from the crowd when Eunice jokingly shoved at his arm. "Get a room, you two!"

And then Magda was hugging her friend and they were all laughing and Magda was shouting, "We did it!" And he couldn't help picking both Magda and Eunice up and swinging them around.

Confessionals. Clean-up. Final judging.

It was almost over.

The producers started herding them back to the tent, and one of Mac's hands took Magda's, waving to the crowd with the other. In the small tent, the producers pointed them toward the confessionals—but Mac stopped her with his hand tightening on hers.

"I wasn't joking. When I said I love you."

"Mac..." Her eyes were wide, and he rushed on.

"I think I've been in love with you for fourteen years—even when I didn't want to be. Or maybe it was just the potential for love, and it wasn't until *Cake-Off* that I fell. Head over heels. I don't know. You make me crazy, but we go together like maple bacon jalapeño and blueberry crumble muffins. Two things that really shouldn't work, but absolutely do, and now that I've had them together, I don't want to have them apart."

She stared up at him, speechless, but he had enough words for both of them.

"I'm not brave like you," he went on. "You were right. I wasn't afraid of letting people down—I was afraid of them letting me down. Don't want things you can't have. If you don't try, you won't be disappointed, right? So I told myself I didn't want you. I adapt, I take life as it comes, but I don't chase dreams. Not like you do. You put your heart on the line when you were eighteen years old and you didn't let the fact that I was an ass stop you. I just took what life handed me. But I don't want to do that anymore. And I'm not saying you'll never let me down, or that I won't let you down. I'm saying I love you enough to want to *try*." He met her eyes, holding them. "When I think of my future, when I let myself dream, all I want is to bake muffins with you."

Magda's baby-blue eyes were swimming with tears, but her smile was magnificent. "You, Mackenzie Newton, are so cheesy," she said as she draped her arms around his neck. "And salty. And sweet. All my favorite flavors." He laughed, but she wasn't done. "You are such a good man. And everyone in this town knows it—including me. Which has made it really hard to keep hating you all these years. These last five weeks have been a whirlwind. A month ago, I thought I hated you. Fourteen years ago, I thought I loved you. But that was just a crush. What I feel for you now is bigger and wilder and more real than anything I dreamed up back then. I was scared to want this, because whenever I've wanted things in the past, it's never worked out. But that's the thing about baking and love. It's all about the timing."

He grinned, bending his head to kiss her, and she said the words he was never going to get tired of hearing against his lips. "I love you, Mackenzie Newton."

He was smiling when he lifted his head. "I'm glad you told

me now. Because after I win this thing, I would think you were only after me for my money."

Though the truth was he was convinced she was the one who was going to win. He'd always thought she would.

She smacked him on the bicep, and he laughed.

It didn't even bother him when he heard Stephen asking a cameraman, "Did you get all that?"

He kind of liked the idea of the whole entire world knowing Magda was the love of his life.

The producers split them up then to talk about their final bakes—and their feelings for each other. Then it was back into the tent for judging, another wait as the judges deliberated, and finally—racing the light to get the results announced before it got dark—they were hustled back into the tent for the announcement of the winner.

Stephen told them to line up in a row, but Mac stood behind Magda, hugging her shoulders from behind as she held on to his arm with one hand and Eunice's hand with the other. The producers must have liked how it looked because they didn't make them move.

The judges and Jeffrey Flanders took their marks.

"Ladies and gentlemen, this was, without a doubt, the closest finale in *Cake-Off* history," Alexander Clay began—and to hear those words from a judge who was not given to Flanders's level of hyperbole was almost jarring. "The competition has never been so fierce. We went back and forth, parsing the tiniest little details to make our decision. And we'd like you all to know that on any other season, any one of you could have won."

"As Alexander says, it came down to the smallest things," Joanie agreed. "An incredible flavor..." Mac's breath caught. They'd always talked about his flavor. "An impressive technique..." That had to be Magda, right? Or maybe Tim..."But in the end, the baker who won today was the one who just elevated to the next level, stretching themself and really taking us all by surprise."

Mac tightened his arm around Magda's shoulders. It had to be her. She deserved this. She'd worked so hard. And her winning would feel like him winning. He stared at the judges, willing Jeffrey Flanders to say her name as he opened his mouth.

"The winner of the Archrivals Edition of *The Great American Cake-Off* is..."

Chapter Thirty-Eight

Four months later...

"Have I mentioned how much I love knowing who won?" Charlotte asked. "It makes me feel so smug and omniscient."

"You have mentioned it. Repeatedly," Kendall replied irritably—though she could be forgiven for being a little extra irritable these days since little Oskar was not yet a good sleeper, and she was still operating on about four hours of sleep a night. Brody currently held the tiny baby, cradled against his chest on the opposite side of the massive theater room at Mac's grandmother's house, where they were having the week three watch party.

Magda had wondered if after the first week some of the enthusiasm for the watch parties would dim, seeing as everyone in town knew exactly how the show had ended, but if anything, the excitement had only grown with each successive week.

The mayor, Ben, and his wife, Ally, were there with their kids. Deenie and Connor had gotten a babysitter and shown up with Charlotte's sisters, Elinor and Anne, and their spouses. Two of Magda's sisters had joined her watch party—though most of her family had elected to watch at her parents' house—where Magda usually made an appearance after the show was over. Watching herself on television was weird enough without her parents watching her watch herself on television. It was slightly less uncomfortable with all of Mac's poker buddies and her friends and their spouses all talking over one another and calling out bets about whose cookie was going to quite literally crumble.

And Mac's grandmother had become one of her favorite people over the last few months. Mac groaned constantly about how much they'd bonded and how often they ganged up on him, but it was obvious he loved every second of it.

She and Mac split their time between the carriage house and her apartment over the bakery. Cupcake and the cat were even learning to cohabitate. Last week, Magda had caught them curled up together on Cupcake's dog bed.

She and Mac hadn't actually committed to the whole living together thing yet—but that was mostly because they couldn't decide between the convenience of her spot on the square and the perks of having more space and being closer to his gran.

Some of that might depend on where the Cup ended up.

The Cup was officially moving. Mac had decided to go for it and move to a bigger, better location, finally letting go of his cramped little espresso shop roots and transitioning to a fully functional restaurant. He had a bid in on a location that used to be an old train depot—which would take some renovating, but neither of them was afraid of the challenge.

Business had been booming ever since they'd been announced as *Cake-Off* contestants, and things had only gotten more insane these last few weeks as the show had started to air. Rumors were already flying online about the two of them and their "showmance." The show people had clearly done some creative editing—taking things out of context to set the stage for their rival reversal. Magda did her best to ignore the gossip sites, but Mac seemed to find it all deeply entertaining—especially when they got things wrong.

But it was certainly good for business.

Magda had hired more help at the bakery and was still barely keeping up. Mac had pitched the idea of her taking over the space he currently used for the Cup as a secondary location for the bakery, and she was giving it some serious thought.

She was a little worried that the business would drop off after the finale. Mac kept telling her to bet on herself, but she didn't want to bank on anything. Especially since it was Eunice who had taken home the top prize.

Magda hadn't even been sad for a second. She'd squealed and hugged her friend, and it had felt almost fitting that it hadn't been her or Mac. It meant so much to Eunice. And when it came right down to it, Magda hadn't needed it. She'd needed to learn to own her awesomeness—as Mac liked to tell her. She'd always had it in her, but she couldn't see it before. And now...

She'd performed well in the finale. Her feedback had been amazing. She hadn't defeated herself—she'd *excelled*. And so had Mac. They had no regrets. And considering how competitive they still were with each other, it was probably a good thing neither of them had won.

The opening credits began to roll, and everyone cheered the familiar theme.

This was the maple cake episode—when they were literally tied together, and as it began, Magda was tempted—as she always was—to hide in the back of the room.

But then arms closed around her, a chin rested on her shoulder, and a deep voice murmured in her ear. "I think we've created a monster. Ben is talking about making *Cake-Off* Day an annual event. He thinks people would come from all over the country to watch Pine Hollow's two star bakers compete against each other in the town square. He wants to sell tickets."

Magda grinned and leaned back into his arms. "It isn't a terrible idea. We could bring in impartial judges—and whoever wins could take ownership of the maple cake recipe for the year."

He groan-laughed. "I've stopped making that cake."

"I know. But it doesn't really seem fair, since we made it exactly the same distance in the competition, and we'll never know which one of us was closer to beating Eunice."

For a moment, they both fell silent, watching as Terrible Tim beat Magda in the Skills Challenge. "I'm really glad he lost," Mac mumbled, and Magda silently agreed.

"Leah heard one of his former assistants is suing him for sexual harassment. She was positively gleeful."

Mac rumbled a laugh. They'd kept in touch with about half of the *Cake-Off* crowd…which was a small number relative to the other seasons, where they were all still on group chats, but the Archrivals season had been *weird*.

It was getting mixed reviews. Many of the *Cake-Off* faithful *hated* the negativity of the new format. Stephen had already been replaced as showrunner for the next season—after a scheduling conflict with his previous show—but Julia was still out. Magda and Mac kept in touch with her, and they knew she was still looking for her next show, but she'd stopped pitching them on the idea of their own baking show when they'd told her they were planning to stay away from television for a while.

Though that might change. Mac really was amazing at chatting with the viewers while he baked, and Magda had heard a rumor that the next season of *Cake-Off* might be an all-stars edition. She didn't know if she would be invited, but if there was a chance to take another swing at the trophy…she might not be able to resist.

Their season had been difficult and incredibly stressful—but it had also been one of the best experiences of her life.

And it had brought her Mac.

Even if he did try to make her listen to Broadway playlists in the kitchen and insisted on bringing his demon cat along in a baby stroller whenever she walked Cupcake, she still loved the man.

The show came back from commercial, and Magda gripped Mac's arms where they wrapped around her waist. Tim was about to announce the teams. She and Mac were about to have a massive fight on national television during the prep time—and she had no idea how much of that had been left in the final edit.

"It's okay," his voice rumbled against her ear. "I've got you, my little baumkuchen."

She snorted. Trust Mac to know exactly what she needed. "You are the worst," she grumbled, snuggling even more deeply into his arms.

On screen, the fight started. Magda groaned, closing her eyes.

Until a sharp voice rang through the room.

"*What? That's* what you were fighting over?"

Magda opened her eyes to see Mac's grandmother standing in the middle of the room, no longer facing the television, where Mac and Magda continued to bicker.

"All these years over a *cake*?" she demanded incredulously.

"There was a little more to it than a cake," Mac said. "Though that was, admittedly, part of it."

"And you still haven't admitted that you stole it," Magda said, without any heat.

"Because I didn't," Mac insisted.

"Of course he didn't," his grandmother declared stridently. "*I* did."

Magda's attention snapped back to Mac's grandmother, still

standing in the middle of the room—and now with everyone's attention as someone had thought to pause the show.

"*You* did?" Mac asked, his arms dropping from Magda as he came around her to approach his grandmother.

"Of course I did. I was eighteen and madly in love with your grandfather, who simply *would not* propose to me, because he thought I was too young for him—and there was Maryann Miller, bragging to anyone who would listen about how she had this magical man-catching maple cake."

Mac arched his eyebrows at Magda. "*Man-catching?*"

She shrugged, but Mac's gran was already going on. "I caught myself the love of my life. And I don't regret it for a second."

"So it was stolen." Mac marveled. "I can't believe you."

"What? I only made it the one time. Only needed to catch one man. It's not my fault you dug it up out of my recipe box and got yourself into trouble."

Mac turned to Magda. "I officially apologize for my family stealing from your family fifty years ago."

Magda laughed. "And I officially apologize for accusing you of stealing from me for a decade. I'm pretty sure what I did was worse."

"It's not a competition," Mac reminded her.

"Can we get back to the real competition?" Connor shouted. "I want to see if they kill each other or make this cake!"

The watch party resumed, with Mac and Magda leaning against the back wall, shoulder to shoulder. "Man-catching?" he asked under his breath, once everyone else was engrossed in the show again.

"I did think I was in love with you," she reminded him.

"And you did eventually catch me."

She looked up at him, and he bent his head, leaning sideways for a kiss.

Her nemesis. The man who drove her crazy. Whom she couldn't imagine her life without.

"Are you bummed we didn't win?" she asked softly as, on screen, they began to bake together, working in perfect harmony.

He looked down at her, his brown eyes warm, one auburn curl falling over his brow, and a little crooked grin on his face. "Who says I didn't win?"

Acknowledgments

This book has been a long time coming. The feud started all the way back in *The Twelve Dogs of Christmas*, and I always knew I wanted to bring Pine Hollow to a close with Mac and Magda. I love a good enemies-to-lovers story, and I hope that it lived up to expectations for all the Team Mac and Team Magda readers who have been patiently waiting for this one.

The baking show in the book is very fictional, but you can probably guess I'm mildly obsessed with *The Great British Baking Show*, *Top Chef*, and *MasterChef Junior*. Many thanks to my friends (who shall remain nameless) in unscripted television who answered my questions. I intended *Cake-Off* to be a mishmash of several of my favorites, but I took quite a few artistic liberties, and any similarity to any people who have competed on or worked on those shows is unintended and accidental. I was also fortunate to be able to draw on my experiences appearing on *Jeopardy!* and visiting the set of my Hallmark Channel movie, *Sweeter Than Chocolate*—though mostly in relating to Magda's nerves and excitement.

Thanks to Kim Law and Addison Fox, who joined me on one of my many research trips to Vermont, and went with me to the King Arthur Baking Company. It is a very real (and very cool) place, and I highly recommend visiting—though again, I took significant artistic license and hope they will forgive me for setting my imaginary baking show in my imaginary version of their kitchen.

As always, I must thank my friends and family who tolerated all of my "it's so much better if she knows that he knew, right?" yammering as I was working through plot holes. I could not be more grateful for your unwavering support—Kris, Kali, Leigh, and my parents (including my mother, who really does say "oh, crumb!" when she's frustrated).

I have also been incredibly fortunate, on this Pine Hollow journey, to have a wonderful team at Forever Publishing championing the books. Thanks to my agent, Michelle, for introducing me to my first editor at Hachette, who wanted a Christmas book about dogs finding forever homes. And thank you to Leah, Sabrina, and Junessa—editors extraordinaire who helped me make the books better. Also to Lori, Stacey, the cover designers, and the rest of the production team for catching my typos and errors and making the books beautiful. To Dana and Estelle and the rest of the publicity team for all your enthusiasm, cheerleading, and support getting the books into readers' hands. And to Francesca and Joelle, thanks to whom we now have Pine Hollow books in languages around the world. I know there are even more unsung heroes behind the scenes whom I've failed to mention here, but know I'm incredibly grateful.

And finally, I need to thank the readers, librarians, and booksellers who have fallen in love with Pine Hollow. This series has been a delight to write. I got into romance because I wanted to put a little more love into the world, and seeing readers connecting with these books has been a dream come true. Thank you for coming along on this journey with my imaginary friends—and their adorable dogs (and cat).

About the Author

As a lifelong dog-lover and book nerd, **Lizzie Shane** is a sucker for stories about pups dragging their humans into love. Born in Alaska to a pair of Hawaii transplants, she graduated from Northwestern University and began writing romance in an attempt to put a little more love into the world. Lizzie is currently based in Alaska, but she's an avid traveler who has written her way through all fifty states and over fifty countries. Her books have been translated into seven languages, her novel *Sweeter Than Chocolate* was adapted into a Hallmark Channel Original movie, and she also writes for film and television, but her favorite claim to fame is that she lost on *Jeopardy!*

Learn more at:
    LizzieShane.com
    Facebook.com/LizzieShaneAuthor
    Instagram @LizzieShaneAK